BOOK THREE: PART TWO
HEROBRINE'S MESSAGE

by SEAN FAY WOLFE

To my mentor,
Kyoshi Chick Gavitt
(1967–2015)
With great respect
どもありがとうございました

First published in the USA by HarperCollins *Publishers* Inc in 2016 as part of THE ELEMENTIA
CHRONICLES: BOOK THREE: HEROBRINE'S MESSAGE
First published in Great Britain by HarperCollins *Children's Books* 2016
HarperCollins *Children's Books* is a division of HarperCollins*Publishers* Ltd

HarperCollins Publishers,
1 London Bridge Street,
London SE1 9GF
The HarperCollins *Children's Books* website address is
www.harpercollins.co.uk

1

Copyright © 2016 Sean Fay Wolfe

ISBN 978-0-00-817358-6

Printed and bound in England by
Clays Ltd, St Ives plc

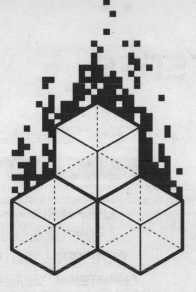

"Everyone sees what you appear to be. Few
experience what you really are."
—Niccolò Machiavelli

CONTENTS

PART I: THE ULTIMATUM

CHAPTER 1: The Free Ones   8

CHAPTER 2: Underground   34

CHAPTER 3: The New Plans   57

CHAPTER 4: The Last Chance   81

CHAPTER 5: The Battle of the Adorian Village   110

CHAPTER 6: Return to Nocturia   136

CHAPTER 7: Prelude to War   164

CHAPTER 8: The Battle of Element City   196

CHAPTER 9: Fighting a Myth   218

PART II: HEROBRINE'S MESSAGE

CHAPTER 10: Endgame   250

CHAPTER 11: The Message   279

CHAPTER 12: Return of the Heroes   313

CHAPTER 13: The Last Battlefield   339

CHAPTER 14: The Duel of the Gods   372

CHAPTER 15: The Two Cities   409

EPILOGUE: A Promise Fulfilled   440

12
THE ULTIMATUM

There was silence in the Capitol rotunda, save the sound of hundreds of pairs of feet marching. Row by row, the black-clad troops filed into lines. Jayden and G glanced around the room nervously at the dozens of dark figures positioned in the upper balcony, all of whom had loaded bows aiming down into the giant mass of soldiers.

G took a deep breath and let it out. He knew what was going on. Four days had passed since he had left Sirus alone in that obsidian chamber with a diamond pickaxe in his hand, and now Tess had ordered that all soldiers meet in the rotunda for an emergency.

Sure enough, Tess emerged on the highest, most ornate and most pronounced balcony of the rotunda, made from chiselled quartz blocks. There was no hint of joy on her face. There was only a scowl as she looked down on all the soldiers. Gazing back up at her and cowering under her intimidating leer, they were all silent. Finally, Tess spoke.

"Last night," Tess announced, "our hostages from the Adorian Village escaped captivity."

A collective gasp rolled across the soldiers as they realized what that meant.

"To escape, the hostages tunnelled through a five-block-thick wall of solid obsidian," continued Tess.

"This is a feat that would take at least two full days to complete if done by anything other than a diamond pickaxe. And seeing as no guards saw any sign of an escape in progress during their check-ups, this can only mean that somebody in this room managed to sneak a diamond pickaxe to the hostages."

A collective burst of panic rose off the crowd, and though nobody dared to speak, the tension in the room could be cut with a sword.

"I know that someone among us is the traitor," Tess said slowly as her eyes swept over the soldiers below her. "If you step forwards and reveal yourself to me now, then you shall simply be executed by firing squad, quickly and painlessly. However, if you don't, then I shall be forced to begin interrogations, and when I discover who it is, you will be tortured without mercy before you become food for the Zombie villagers. If anybody would like to speak out, you may do so now."

G, who was struggling to keep his own heart from exploding with panic, heard Jayden beside him take a deep breath, let it out, and then raise his hand.

"I confess," Jayden said, a slight warble in his voice. "I did it."

G's mind went blank, refusing to comprehend what was happening. He turned to stare at Jayden in utter shock, totally blindsided and utterly bewildered by what his best friend had just said.

"Is that so?" asked Tess, a hint of surprise in her voice as all the soldiers around Jayden backed away from him in abhorrence. G followed suit, convinced that he had gone totally insane. "How did you do it, Drayden? And what was your motivation?"

"My name is *Jayden*!" he exclaimed, pulling off his black leather cap, throwing it to the ground, and stomping on it. "I am a member of the governing council of Element City and a friend of President Stan2012. I have been living undercover among you for these past weeks, working to free the hostages you have taken from us. Now, my work here is done." A manic smile crossed Jayden's face as he pumped his fist into the air and, with patriotic fervour, he bellowed, "LONG LIVE THE REPUBLIC! LONG LIVE PRESIDENT STAN!"

G's mind was still reeling from what was going on. He was hardly able to comprehend that Jayden had just revealed himself for no good reason, and that soldiers were drawing their bows and taking aim at him. Suddenly, a lightbulb clicked on in G's head. There was at least one good thing that could come from this turn of insanity. G leaped forwards and into the ring, letting the overwhelming despair that was boiling inside him burst from his mouth.

"How could you do this?" G shouted, tears streaming

down his face as he let all the white shock he was feeling burst through his voice. "You were my friend! I trusted you! How could you work for that evil president?"

Jayden glanced back at G, and caught his eye. For an instant, he looked miserable, as if all he wanted was to be able to say "sorry." However, the look soon vanished, to be replaced by nothing but zeal.

"I'd never lower myself to the level of calling myself the friend of a Noctem!" Jayden spat in disgust.

There were so many things that G longed to say but knew he couldn't. He was forced to simply stand still, quiet and motionless. It was all the same, though. Words could not describe the agony that wrenched his heart as two soldiers pinned Jayden to the ground, and a third raised a bow to his head. G looked away, preparing for the arrow to fly.

"Hold your fire!" Tess's voice rang out from the balcony above.

G looked up, hardly daring to believe his ears. The collective group of soldiers, including those who were restraining Jayden, seemed to follow suit as their eyes locked on Tess. She was staring back and forth between Jayden and G, an intrigued look on her face. G's heart skipped a beat. Did she suspect something?

"Executioner, stop," Tess said again, holding up her hand. "I have a better idea. All troops, move out. Leave this rotunda.

Guard and MasterBronze, stay put."

G was petrified as the troops began to move out around him, giving him uncomfortable glances as they flooded through the doors. The executioner put his bow away and drew a glowing diamond sword, jabbing it up against Jayden's back and grunting, "Hands in the air, dirtbag." Jayden complied, and his eyes darted to the side and met G's. He could tell they were both thinking the same thing.

Tess knows, G thought in a panic. *She's got to know. Why else would she have singled me out? All the recruits probably realize that Jayden and I have been talking this entire time. And why did Jayden reveal himself anyway? She might not have ever guessed it was me. He didn't need to sacrifice himself!*

The sounds of footsteps on the stone-brick floor echoed throughout the cavernous rotunda as Tess made her way to the centre. G and the executioner snapped to full attention as Jayden scowled at her.

"General Tess," the guard asked in disbelief, "why did you tell me not to execute this spy?"

"Trust me," Tess replied, a devious grin creeping across her face, "I know what I'm doing. Guard, you are dismissed now."

The guard stared at Tess with a total lack of comprehension, and then turned round and made his way to the door, grumbling the whole way. Jayden watched as he went, hands still raised, and Tess drew a glowing diamond sword from her own inventory, pointing it at Jayden.

"MasterBronze," Tess said slowly, turning to face G, "I understand that you are friends with this traitor. Is this correct?"

"I thought I was," G grunted, trying to sound hurt and betrayed, and not let his true dread be too obvious. "He always seemed like such a nice guy, I can't believe that he's been working for President Stan this entire time."

"Well, I hope that you can bring yourself to believe it," Tess chuckled, "because you're going to be the one who kills him."

G heard, but he didn't understand. "I'm . . . sorry . . . ?" he finally croaked.

"For the past few weeks, I have been training you as my apprentice, MasterBronze," Tess continued matter-of-factly. "I must say that, so far, I am quite impressed by your progress in combat and skills training. However, if you are truly going to become a great leader of the Noctem Alliance, you must learn to make sacrifices for the sake of our cause . . . even if it means stabbing your best friend in the back. And besides, if your loyalties are in the right place, then you should be able to get over it quickly."

G stared blankly at Tess, still not understanding what he was being asked. Then, out of the corner of his eye, G saw

Jayden staring at him with wide, fearful eyes, and finally snapped back to his senses.

"Um, well . . . ," G sputtered, trying to think fast. "I mean . . . General Tess, ma'am . . . can I at least kill him in private? It's . . . going to be difficult enough without you watching."

Tess sighed and rolled her eyes. "Whatever. We'll go to the holding chamber. Move it, you worthless piece of trash!"

Tess poked the diamond sword into Jayden's back and he began to walk forward, hands still raised above him. G followed Tess down the hallway. He realized that they were headed towards the room where Sirus and the others had been imprisoned. G glared with contempt at the back of the general who was walking in front of him, and his hand started to crawl towards his pickaxe before he stopped himself. As easy and satisfying as it would have been to strike Tess down right then and there, he knew that he couldn't do that. They were the only ones in the room, and Jayden was unarmed, so the rest of the Alliance would know that he had done it. And regardless of what happened, he still had to cure Mella and Stull, something that would be much easier if the Noctem Alliance trusted him.

It wasn't long before they reached the obsidian room. At Tess's command, G pressed the button to open the iron door. Once it had swung all the way round, Tess gave Jayden a kick in the back, sending him tumbling. He face-planted on the floor of the now vacant obsidian chamber. G glared at Tess with burning hatred but forced himself to curb his anger as she turned to face him.

"I'm coming back shortly," Tess decreed sternly. "And I will expect you to bring me his weapon."

And with that, she stepped back into the hallway and pressed the stone button again, swinging the iron door shut.

"What were you thinking?" bellowed G, spinning round to face Jayden the second the door closed.

"Don't yell at me!" Jayden retorted, crossing his arms over his chest. "Do you have any idea what I just did for you?"

"You almost left me without a best friend?" spat G. "You made Tess expect me to kill you? You put me into an incredibly difficult position? Take your pick, they're all true!"

"Oh, open your eyes, man!" cried Jayden. "It was only a matter of time before Tess realized that *you* let those prisoners go. Since I took the fall for you, you can stay in Nocturia for as long as you want! You can free the villagers, you can find out so much information, do so much damage to the Alliance. For the first time since we started fighting this war, Element City has eyes on the inside of the Noctem Alliance, and that's not something worth giving up, even if it means I have to die. Actually, the fact that Tess ordered you to kill me makes all of this so much better!"

"How do you figure that?" exclaimed G incredulously.

"Because now she's going to have total faith in you!" Jayden said, sounding as if this should be incredibly obvious. "She's already rearing you up to be her little lackey. If you do this, then she's going to trust you with anything and think that you're totally devoted to the Noctem Alliance, and to her."

"Oh, my apologies. You're right, Jayden!" G replied, a mock cheerful tone in his voice. "I mean, gee whiz, why didn't we do this in the first place? Oh, yeah, that's right! Because in order for this plan to work, it still required *me killing you!*"

"Oh, don't be so sure," Jayden replied with a smile. And with that, he reached into his inventory and pulled out a bottle. The potion within it was transparent, almost clear, but it had a definite grey tint to it. G gasped.

"Jayden. Where did you get that?"

"I swiped it," he replied, taking the bottle and tipping it down his throat in one giant gulp. "Yesterday, we went to the Brewing Plant in the Nether while you were surveying the grounds with Tess. Here, catch!"

Jayden's hand plunged into his inventory for a second time and out came his diamond axe, which he tossed through the air towards G, who caught it. "Just wait until the potion takes effect, then show the axe to Tess, and I'll slip out through the door, invisible, and make my way back to Element City!"

"Wha . . . wait," G said, as he put together what Jayden was saying. "You're . . . you're leaving me?"

"Well, the alternative is that you kill me, and I think that option is considerably less appealing to everyone," Jayden replied, sounding a little annoyed.

"But . . . you can't leave!" cried G. "I need you here! Tess has been working me into the ground, never leaving me alone, making me be with her all the time, taking me away from everyone else so she can train me. The fact that she's so nice to me isn't even cool any more – it's just uncomfortable! I can't lose the only person that I can still talk to!"

Jayden simply stared at him for a moment in disbelief. Finally, he managed to get out, "Dude . . . do you . . . realize what you're saying? Do you see *any* hint of irony at all in *anything* you just said?"

G stared back, looking confused. Then, without warning, Jayden began to fade away, becoming dimmer and dimmer by the second.

"The potion's taking effect!" exclaimed Jayden, pulling off his armour and frantically reaching into his inventory and tossing random items to the ground, making it look like a player had died. "G, go open the door now, and hurry! I don't have much time before the potion wears off, and I have to get all the way into the tundra. I'll say hi to Kat and the others for you when I see them . . . bye!"

And with that, Jayden disappeared.

G stared at the place where his best friend now stood, invisible, and then down at the diamond axe in his hand. He knew that Jayden was right. He forced himself to walk to the iron door. He gave three sharp knocks on the iron face, and seconds later the door swung open. G stepped out and felt a rush of wind behind him, indicating that Jayden had silently taken off down the hallway.

"Did you finish the job?" Tess asked.

G took a deep breath, reached into his inventory, and pulled out Jayden's diamond axe. He handed it to Tess, who took it, looking thrilled.

"Well done, MasterBronze!" Tess exclaimed, patting him on the shoulder, which made his skin crawl. "In honour of your loyalty to the Noctem Alliance and to me, I am promoting you to the rank of Corporal. You will, from now on, have the duty of being my assistant commander in the training programme."

"Thank you, ma'am," G replied. He knew he ought to be thrilled at this promotion, which would allow him access to even more high-level secrets, but he still couldn't shake the feeling of total isolation now that Jayden was gone, and he was stuck with this Tess, this player who had total control over his life.

"Now, come with me, Corporal MasterBronze," Tess continued, a grin crossing her face. "It's time to go and see your fellow trainees, and present their new second-in-command to them."

G's stomach churned as he followed Tess down the hallway. She was talking to him so affectionately, like he were her prized show dog instead of another person. It made him feel powerless, degraded and humiliated. G shuddered and wished that somehow, he still had Jayden to talk to.

"Charlie, please . . . let me take a turn, I can see how bad you're hurtin' . . ."

"Leonidas, for the last time, I am *fine*!" Charlie bellowed, whipping around to face him. "Stop interrupting me or we're never gonna get to Element City!"

"OK, fine, calm down, man!" Leonidas cried out, raising his blocky hands defensively.

Charlie shot one last steely glare at him before turning back around, and continuing to hack away at the solid cave wall with his stone pickaxe. Leonidas stared at Charlie's back, illuminated by torchlight. He had been baffled by the hostility Charlie had been showing towards him. Since they had joined up with him and Stan, Leonidas had been pleasantly surprised by how quickly everybody had warmed up to him. Everybody, that was, except Charlie. And even as

Leonidas watched Charlie mining, it was clear that he was hurting. Every swing of the pickaxe brought another grunt of discomfort, and every step he took through the newly mined cave saw another limp.

Leonidas was the only one who even noticed Charlie's outburst, however. Commander Crunch was busy tunnelling forwards alongside Charlie, while Stan, Kat, and Cassandrix walked behind, talking among themselves. Stan put torches on the wall as they walked, and Rex trailed lazily behind Kat.

"I still can't believe that we're being forced to sneak into our own city," Kat spat in disgust.

"Oh, I'm sorry, dear. Allow me to play you a sad song on the world's smallest violin," Cassandrix replied, sticking her bloated lip out in mock sadness before reverting back to a scowl. "Kat, we're all down here together. There's no need to whine about what we're all feeling!"

"Shut up!" cried Kat, so loudly, that Stan cringed and raised his hands to his ears. "There's no need to be so obnoxious about it!"

"I'm sorry, what's that, Commander?" Cassandrix said loudly, looking over at Crunch, who was still firmly fixated on his digging. "I'm sorry, I can't hear you. There appears to be an infant who's crying because her feelings are hurt. I do wish the parents would take care of her."

Kat turned red as a beet, and was about to retort when Stan forced his way between the two of them.

"Enough, you two!" he cried, indignantly glancing back and forth between them. "We're all stressed enough as it is in this stupid tunnel. We don't need your bickering making things worse!"

"She started it," Kat mumbled, causing Cassandrix to roll her eyes and shrug with an arrogant sigh.

"I don't care *who* started it, I'm finishing it," said Stan firmly, as he continued to walk forwards between Kat and Cassandrix. *Man, I'm so glad to be back with everyone,* Stan thought to himself, trying to think as optimistically as possible. *I missed talking with everybody so much . . .*

"Hey, Charlie!" Kat hollered right next to Stan's ear, causing him to cringe again. "Are we past the wall yet?"

"If my calculations are correct," Charlie replied, trying to keep his breathing steady as he winced with the effort of mining, "we passed underneath the wall a little while ago, and we should be underneath the Merchants District of Element City by now."

"Hey, did you hear that, everybody?" Stan asked, looking around the mine at all his friends. "We're back in Element City! Welcome home, guys!"

There were lacklustre murmurs of assent around the mine as Charlie and Commander Crunch tunnelled into a sizable natural cave. Stan sighed. He knew that they had to get to Element City as quickly as possible, and the fate of all of Minecraft might lie in their hands. But that didn't change the fact that they had been walking for three straight days with no sleep, and everybody was worn out.

"OK," he said, finally letting his inner exhaustion come forwards. "Maybe we should take a break for a little while and rest."

As soon as Stan said this, the entire group collapsed onto the ground, letting the fatigue of weeks of trekking with almost no rest finally hit them. Stan lay down as well, not even caring that the stone-block floor below him was uncomfortable. Rex curled up at his feet, and Stan was just about to doze off when he suddenly had a startling realization.

"Hey, guys, we can't all go to sleep yet," he mumbled, forcing himself to sit up. "Somebody has to stand guard."

"I'll take care of it," Leonidas said, grabbing a ledge on the cave wall and pulling himself to his feet.

"NO!" Charlie cried, causing everybody to snap up right as Charlie jumped, wincing as his bad leg hit the ground. "Get back to sleep, Leonidas. I'm standing guard."

"Come on, Charlie!" exclaimed Leonidas, looking concerned. "You've been mining all day. You really ought to take a rest!'

"What's that supposed to mean, huh?" Charlie demanded

accusatorily. "Are you saying you don't think I can do it?"

"No, I . . ."

"Then shut up and sit back down!" Charlie spat out bitterly. "I don't recall asking for your help!"

Leonidas stared at Charlie, amazed at the harshness in his voice. After a moment, Leonidas lay back down and, with an uncomfortable glance at Charlie, rolled over to face the wall. Stan was outraged, and was about to chastise Charlie for his harshness when, without warning, an explosion erupted in the wall beside them, showering the entire group with dust.

Within seconds, all six players and the wolf were on their feet again, weapons drawn, glancing into the misshapen hole in the cave wall. A shadowy form appeared in the smoke, and as the dust settled, a row of figures came into view. The form of Creeper Khan, with Arachnia, Enderchick, Lord Marrow and Zomboy standing directly behind him.

There was a moment of silence. Stan and his friends stared at the mobhunters, transfixed in horror that they had been discovered. Meanwhile, the members of ELM stared back, their eyes alight with joyous amazement.

"Fancy seeing you here, Stan," Arachnia hissed with a grin, stepping forward to the front of the group.

"How did you find us?" Stan demanded as he uncomfortably forced himself to look into Arachnia's eight red eyes.

"Lucky break, I guess," she replied with a grin. "We were just about to set some traps for you guys down here. We didn't expect you to get back here so quickly."

"We've been walking nonstop," Stan replied slowly, trying to buy time as he wildly thought of how they could escape from these bounty hunters. "We wanted to make it back to Element City as fast as possible."

"Aw, poor tragic you," Arachnia sneered. "You tried so hard, and got so far . . . but in the end, it doesn't even matter."

"Haha! I ged id!" Zomboy shouted. "Because dose are da words to a song! And you used dem in . . ."

"Shut up, Zomboy," Arachnia said offhandedly.

"OK," he replied meekly, looking to the ground.

"Well, congrats to you," Stan said, still desperate for more time. "You finally managed to catch up to us. Now what?"

"Well, you're going to come with us, Stan," Arachnia replied in a disturbingly sweet-sounding voice that made Stan's skin crawl. "Lord Tenebris is most anxious to see you. And as for your friends, well, they're of no use to anybody any more, so they will be disposed of."

"Well, I'm sorry, Arachnia," Stan retorted, keeping his voice pleasant and conversational as he realized that there was no escape, and they would have to fight. "But I'm afraid that I can't let you do that."

And before the mobhunter could respond, Stan leaped

forwards and locked his axe against the glowing diamond sword that Arachnia had pulled out, and the two of them began to duel. Immediately, the players who had been standing behind the two leaders leaped into action. Kat lunged toward Enderchick with Rex at her heels, Cassandrix and Creeper Khan struck at each other simultaneously, and Commander Crunch rushed in to help Cassandrix. Lord Marrow and Leonidas both released a barrage of arrows at each other, while Zomboy lunged at the nearest target, Charlie.

Charlie feinted backward to avoid the giant stone axe that the oversized player slammed into the ground, leaving cracks in the stone blocks of the cave floor. As he moved, Charlie felt a sharp pain in his foot, and it nearly gave out, but he managed to stay on his feet, cringing in pain. Charlie glanced up at Zomboy, who was raising his axe and preparing for another attack. *He's not very fast,* Charlie noted to himself, and *he's taking way too long between attacks. He must be a heavy fighter.*

Charlie became aware of explosions going off behind Zomboy as Creeper Khan started to use his pyrokinetic powers and Lord Marrow fired off explosive arrows, but Charlie forced himself to focus on his own fight. Zomboy continued to walk towards Charlie, swinging his giant stone axe from side to side, forcing Charlie back down the cave towards the way they had come. Charlie saw multiple openings in the attack that would allow him to counter, but each time he was about to strike, the pain in his leg flared up again, and he was forced to fall back to avoid another attack.

Finally, after a frustrating minute of dodging, Zomboy launched a particularly powerful downward axe strike, which Charlie sidestepped. The axe blade shattered the stone block beneath it in a shower of sparks and became lodged in the ground, forcing Zomboy to struggle to pull it out. Seeing his chance, Charlie launched himself forwards off his good leg, and sunk his stone pickaxe directly into Zomboy's chest. The giant mobhunter winced and staggered backwards, axe still in hand, before collapsing to the ground with a massive thud.

Charlie took a deep breath, and let it out as he looked down at the massive body of his defeated adversary. He was infuriated with himself. That giant thug was so unskilled that it should have been an effortless kill, but his leg had made it much more difficult than it had to be. A dark thought crossed Charlie's mind. What if he came face to face with a skilled opponent? Not somebody like Leonidas in their fight in the forest . . . someone who actually wanted to hurt him? Charlie shuddered as his mind clouded with these thoughts, and he began to walk back towards the fight, past the body of Zomboy, determined to prove himself.

What Charlie hadn't expected was for Zomboy's axe to fly up off the ground and directly at him.

Charlie managed to pull his backup pickaxe out of his inventory to block the attack, but the impact of the oversized stone axe on his weapon still sent him flying across the cave. He hit the wall with a smack, landing hard on the stone-block floor, right on his bad leg. Charlie let out a holler of pain and clutched his damaged limb in agony, glancing up through his teary eyes to figure out what had just happened.

Zomboy was back on his feet. His stone axe was held firmly in his right hand, Charlie's pickaxe was still lodged in his chest, and he was staring at Charlie with a grin, no sign of pain on his face at all.

Charlie was perplexed, not sure how it was that Zomboy was still alive, until it hit him. Zomboy was part of the assassin team, and, according to what Stan had told him, each member of their team seemed to be modded to have some sort of special ability. Charlie realized that this player must be modded to have extra HP, and be able to take a ton of punishment before he died.

As the giant beast of a player lumbered towards Charlie, he prepared to kick off the wall, and get out of the way of the incoming attack. Zomboy began to raise his axe over his head as Charlie kicked off the wall, only to have his knee buckle under the pressure. Charlie hardly noticed, though; he was too focussed on the axe raised over Zomboy's head.

Just as the blow was about to fall, an arrow flew from

deep in the cave and lodged itself into Zomboy's skull, right between his eyes. The giant player gave a yelp of pain, and then proceeded to look down the tunnel towards the source of the arrow, not dead from the blow (somehow) but most certainly angry.

"Hey!" he bellowed down the mine, his eyebrows, with an arrow sticking out between them, knitted in fury. "Wads da big idea?"

Charlie glanced down the cave, and his face lit up in amazement and relief. There, standing in the mouth of the cave, was Sirus, bow raised, and an army of twenty players, all armed with stone weapons, standing behind him.

"Charge!" the crazed redstone mechanic bellowed.

The entire mass of players barrelled through the cave, sending arrows and flying weapons at Zomboy. Sensing that he was overwhelmed, the massive mobhunter turned, the attacks simply sinking into his back to no effect. With his axe in hand, he dashed down the cave and back towards his comrades.

As the wave of freed hostages continued to rush past Charlie, Sirus stopped to help him to his feet. "Hey, Charlie, man, long time no see, how're you doing?"

"I'm . . . fine," Charlie replied. He couldn't believe his eyes. From what he had heard, Sirus had perished in the Battle for Elementia. "I . . . I'm *really* glad to see you. But . . . I thought you . . ."

"Oh, I get it, you thought I died," Sirus replied with a short laugh. "Yeah, I thought that, too, but I respawned, and I saw somebody duck into the woods and I figured that the hill probably wasn't safe, so I decided that I wanted to go out into the middle of the Ender Desert because I thought that could be fun, but then I got hungry and tried to eat part of a cactus, and it kind of caused me to hallucinate to the point where I imagined that I was at a wedding between a cantaloupe and "

"I'm sorry, but do we have to talk about this now?" Charlie cut in urgently, jerking his head towards the blasts and shouts of the ongoing fight down the cave.

"Seriously though, dude," Sirus continued, as he got into position to help Charlie up, "you must have done something pretty bad to that leg of yours, 'cause it's totally busted, gone south, practically useless, comparable to the poop of—"

"OK, I get it, Sirus," Charlie cut in, irritated. "I'm already frustrated enough without your commentary."

Sirus merely shrugged and pulled Charlie to his feet. Charlie attempted to take a step forwards, but his bad foot couldn't take the slightest bit of pressure without him screaming in agony. Sirus noticed his suffering and placed Charlie's arm around his shoulder, slowly helping him follow the horde of Adorian Villagers that had surged down the cave and towards the ongoing fights.

Look at me, Charlie thought to himself bitterly. *I can't even walk by myself. I'm nothing but a cripple now.*

As they reached the end of the cave, Charlie saw that, to his confusion, there was no fighting. Stan, Kat, Charlie, Cassandrix and Commander Crunch were all standing around, looking exhausted and in various states of injury, but the assassins had vanished.

"Where'd they go?" Charlie inquired to Commander Crunch as Sirus helped him sit down on a loose stone block.

"They warped away, lad," the Commander replied as he nursed a blast wound on his arm. "As soon as Sirus 'n' his scallywags arrived, the other scallywags realized that they were outnumbered, 'n' couldn't win. Th' poppet that goes by th' name o' Enderchick grabbed her mates, 'n' they all warped away. T' where, we can only venture guesses, but I doubt they'll be comin' back anytime soon."

Charlie nodded in understanding and looked around at the scene around them. Sirus and Stan were in deep conversation, Stan's eyes wide, as if he were talking to a ghost. The hostages were wandering around the cave, some of them tending the wounds that had been inflicted during the fight. Suddenly, there was a commotion in the back of the cave, and two of Sirus's followers came forwards, holding Leonidas with his arms behind his back.

"Hey, what do ya think you're doin'?" Leonidas demanded,

clearly too tired from the fight to resist them.

"We found another one of them, Sirus," one of the two players said, and Sirus turned to face them. Immediately, his jaw dropped.

"Leonidas of RAT1! Force him down, men!"

And with that, the two players delivered sharp kicks to the back of Leonidas's knees, forcing Leonidas to fall to the ground, a grunt of agony escaping his mouth as Sirus loaded an arrow into his bow.

"I'll take care of this," he announced heroically, and he was about to let the arrow fly when Stan realized what was happening. He knocked the bow out of Sirus's hand, sending the arrow flying down the mine.

"President Stan, what're you doing? This is a dangerous criminal who needs to be executed!" Sirus cried out.

"Sirus, calm down, it's OK! Leonidas is on our side now. He's realized the errors of his ways and he's fighting for Element City."

Sirus looked at Stan incredulously for a moment, and then raised an eyebrow in scepticism.

"President Stan, with all due respect, this player is responsible for tons of terrible things that happened during the rebellion against King Kev, and he's killed more people than you'll ever realize as a part of RAT1, so are you sure you don't want me to kill him?"

"I am positive!" Stan barked in fury. "I'm granting Leonidas a complete presidential pardon for his past actions. He's been traveling with me for weeks, and has proved to me time and time again that he's sorry for what he did under King Kev and the Noctem Alliance. Now, he's willing to give everything that he has to make up for what he did in the past! So I'll thank you for not being rude to him!"

Sirus opened his mouth, and then closed it again. He gave a sideways glance at Leonidas, who had pulled himself to his feet and was shooting a dirty look at Sirus. Finally, Sirus spoke again, his voice still sounding suspicious.

"If you say so, President Stan," Sirus replied slowly, and with that he turned to work on Charlie's bad leg.

"Thanks, man," Leonidas said, smiling at Stan for a moment before going to tend to a burn wound left on him by one of Lord Marrow's attacks.

"Don't mention it," Stan replied offhandedly, barely paying attention as he came to a startling realization.

Within the next day, Stan would be at the underground bunker of Element City, which held his friends and all his citizens. They would surely be overjoyed to see him, along with Charlie, Kat, Cassandrix and Commander Crunch. However, he had never considered how the citizens of Element City would react to Leonidas.

As clear as it was that Leonidas had had a change of heart

now, Stan still couldn't change the terrible things that Leonidas had done in the past. And as he led his citizens forwards in the greatest challenge that Element City had ever faced, Stan wondered just how they would take it when they found out that he had granted a full presidential pardon to one of King Kev's most powerful soldiers.

As the frigid winds of the eternal blizzard tore through the streets of the Nocturia complex, the Noctem Capitol Building stood tall and looming. Throughout the war, the Elementia forces hadn't come close to scratching the capital city of the Nation of the Noctem Alliance, and the Capitol was proof of that. The building was totally untouched, and still the crowning jewel of the Noctem Empire with its gothic stone-brick block design, gold and lapis lazuli block accents and beacon blocks that shot radiant pillars of light into the sky. The building was also by far the largest and tallest in Nocturia – the highest spire of the building extended out of the base castle and far into the sky.

Atop this spire, a single light could be seen. Torchlight shone from an open window, the only pinpoint of luminescence in the midst of the raging snowstorm. And it was within this one window atop the highest tower of the Noctem Capitol Building that Lord Tenebris sat on his throne of obsidian and quartz, deep in thought.

Lord Tenebris had his eyes closed, yet he could quite clearly see through the eyes of one of the Withers, patrolling the skies over Element City. Lord Tenebris had been experimenting in private, drawing energy from the server itself to bolster his power and discovering more and more new skills by the day. However, this particular new ability that he had discovered had proven to be the most useful by far. On a whim, Lord Tenebris could borrow the eyes of any player or mob, provided, of course, that he knew where they were, and see all that they could see.

In the past few weeks, during the Noctem Alliance's drive to take Element City, this power had been especially helpful. Between clairvoyance and his ability to speak using telepathy, Lord Tenebris had been able to have direct control over the troops on the battlefield through the eyes of General Drake, while still staying hidden away in Nocturia and Fungarus. And he knew that it was for the best that he remain hidden. After all, though the Noctem Alliance now had the upper hand in the war, fear was still by far their greatest asset.

To be honest, Lord Tenebris quite enjoyed the feeling of commanding the troops from far off and tactically manoeuvering them to ensure total domination over a region. Furthermore, he was also well aware of how necessary this step was if he truly wanted control over the server. Lord Tenebris knew that, if he wanted to, he could destroy all the Elementia forces in a matter of minutes using just his own abilities. However, he fancied himself a wise leader, and he was well aware of the vast difference between destroying all the enemy forces and winning the war.

Lord Tenebris saw through the eyes of the Wither that soldiers, clad in black, with bows, weapons and potions at the ready, patrolled the streets of Element City, securing them in the name of the Noctem Alliance. He gave a sigh of satisfaction. Finally, after all these months, Element City was back in the hands of the players who had earned it, those who had toiled and struggled to raise the city after starting from nothing but a meadow.

At long last, they had done it. The Noctem Alliance had conquered Elementia.

One thing still tainted Lord Tenebris's perfect victory, however. Although the Noctem Alliance now had military control over the entire server, they had yet to capture Stan2012. Lord Tenebris actually found it rather surprising. Drake knew exactly what Lord Tenebris was going to do to him should Stan return to Element City. If there was one thing that was certain, it was that Drake would go to any lengths to save his own neck. When added to the fact that Drake had hired a group of trained assassins to track Stan down, Lord Tenebris found it difficult to believe that Drake hadn't delivered Stan to him yet.

Lord Tenebris stood up from his throne and stopped using his clairvoyance, looking once again into the plain stone brick–block room, flickering in the light of the torch.

The time had come, he decided. The military offensive was now over, and the Noctem Alliance had a strong foothold in Element City. There was no purpose in his staying in Nocturia any longer. It was time for him to return to the city that he had worked so long and hard to conquer.

Lord Tenebris took a deep breath, focussed intently on the Council Room of Element Castle, and vanished in a puff of purple smoke.

G felt disgusted with himself as he dragged himself up the quartz stairs towards Tess's office. He still couldn't get the image out of his mind of the wounded recruit in a blue and green jumpsuit, lying on the ground and clutching the cut on his side. He had stepped in and declared the round of the sparring tournament over, and ordered that the fallen recruit be given medical attention, but the two soldiers overseeing him had cut him off. He could vividly remember the Noctem captain in the metallic Creeper costume staring him in the eye and growling those hateful words.

"If you're a true Noctem corporal, you'll tell him to finish the job right now."

Despite the fact that every fibre of his body was telling him to stand up for the fallen recruit, G found himself unable to speak. Before he could, though, a messenger arrived and told G that Tess was looking for him. As G had left to make his way to the stairs, the two corporals had turned back to the sparring recruits, and right before G turned a corner, he heard one of them say, "All right . . . finish him!"

G still couldn't get the sound of that last shout out of his head. He could only imagine what they were doing to the wounded player now . . . and here he was just walking away. Even if that player was in training for the Noctem Alliance, he didn't deserve the abuse and harassment that G was sure was coming his way. In fact, he had half a mind to turn around and go help that player, but he knew that he couldn't. Jayden had been willing to sacrifice his life to keep G in Nocturia, and there was no way that he was going to risk anything until he cured Mella and Stull, regardless of what the cost may be.

Finally, G reached the top of the staircase, and was standing at the threshold of General Tess's room. The room was beautifully designed. The walls were made out of quartz blocks fashioned into different patterns, the floor was carpeted with blue-wool blocks, and the ceiling was covered in glowstone blocks. A fire burning eternally in a Netherrack fireplace projected a warm glow into the room, and picture frames, showing pixel-art paintings, hung on the walls. There were glass windows that revealed the howling storm outside, and behind a cedarwood plank desk sat General Tess, her diamond sword hanging in an item frame behind her.

"Greetings, ma'am," G said automatically, suppressing

his self-loathing for the time being.

"You took a long time," Tess retorted, not bothering to return the greeting. "Please try to be quicker next time, Corporal."

"Yes, ma'am," G replied, his disgust with himself now replaced with irritation at Tess.

"I have a task for you," Tess continued. "I need you to patrol the grounds again."

"Yes, ma'am," G replied, glad that it was only a mundane task that was being asked of him, and he turned back down the stairs to go carry it out.

"Oh, and one more thing, Corporal," Tess continued, sounding almost lazy. G turned around and watched as she reached into a chest next to her desk and pulled out a Potion of Slowness. "Tell Captain Zingster to execute those twenty Elementia prisoners today instead of tomorrow. Now that we've taken Element City, there's really no point in keeping hostages any more."

G's eyes widened, and he did all that he could to hold back a gasp of horror. Regardless, Tess still raised an eyebrow, setting her glass back down on the table and glaring at him.

"Do you have a problem with that, Corporal?"

"No, ma'am," G replied quickly, the gears in his mind spinning as he tried to work out how he could possibly save these prisoners without arousing Tess's suspicion.

"Well then, get to it," Tess ordered, taking another sip of potion as she reached into her desk a second time. G was about to go down the stairs when he paused for a moment.

All throughout his stay in Nocturia, G had spent hours upon hours with Tess. Because of her constant presence, incredibly high expectations of him and casual talk as if they were the best of friends, G had felt incredibly awkward and hated every minute of it, but he had forced himself to do it for the sake of Element City. And he had done his job quite well, never letting on to his aversion to Tess, and always letting her feel like they were becoming close friends. And perhaps now would be the perfect time to try to get some payoff for all his hard work for the sake of rescuing those trapped players from Element City.

"Um . . . excuse me, ma'am?"

"Why are you still here, Corporal?" Tess asked in irritation as she glanced up. She had been searching for food in the chest, and hadn't realized that G hadn't left yet.

"Well, because I have a suggestion for you."

"I don't want to hear it, Corporal. You have duties to attend to."

"Please, ma'am, I think that it may be important."

"Fine!" Tess shouted in frustration. "What do you want, Corporal? And make it fast. I have a lot of work to do, and so do you!"

G took a deep breath, and let it out before continuing.

"Well, it occurred to me that the war in Elementia is going to be over soon and it seems like we're on the verge of winning. I think that, if we're going to rule over the citizens in Element City again, perhaps we might be able to get more support from them if we were to be a bit lenient."

"Oh?" Tess asked, her eyebrow raised suspiciously as she eyed G. "And how do you propose we do that, exactly?"

"My suggestion," G replied tentatively, aware of how Tess was probably going to react to his proposal, "is that we don't execute the soldiers just yet. We hold them captive here until—"

"That is a preposterous idea."

There was a moment of silence as Tess glared at G, and G struggled to hold his feelings in. He knew what he had to do, and even though he was aware that he was pushing his luck, he tried to press on.

"Well, the reason I think that is—"

"What are you trying to say, Corporal? That the atrocities that the soldiers of Elementia have committed during the war deserve to go unpunished?"

"No, of course not, but—"

"Then I see no reason why this conversation should continue."

"Please, listen to me!" G exclaimed, something snapping in his head as he felt a surge of anger toward Tess for all the wrong reasons. "I've been following you faithfully since the day I arrived here, and I've devoted my life to you. The least you could do is hear me out!"

Tess's face took on a dangerous look. "You're treading on thin ice, Corporal."

"Please, General," G said again, trying to curb the acid boiling in his stomach. "It would mean a lot to me if you would just allow me to—"

"I am your commanding officer, Corporal MasterBronze," Tess shot back, standing up at her desk and giving him the evil eye, "and I am *this close* to having you executed for insubordination! Stand down right now!"

G stood still, his mouth still slightly open, and found himself unable to speak. As Tess had yelled at him, a startling realization had hit G like a train. He merely stood still for a moment as he flashed back to over a month ago, when he was standing in the hallway of Element Castle, enraged and hurt, and he had yelled . . .

"Get a move on!" Tess barked at him. "Are you just going to stand there all day? You have no idea how lucky you are that I haven't already ordered you out in front of the firing squad!"

G barely heard her. He was making his way down the quartz block stairs, back towards the group of recruits, his mind swimming in a vortex of realizations and guilt.

Since G had entered Nocturia, he had given barely any thought at all to Kat. The two of them were clearly done and over with, and with far more important things going on, the issue had been dormant in G's mind for quite some time. However, the last time he *had* thought about her, he was still under the impression that she was being unreasonable in not getting over their fight, and that she had been stupid to want to break it off in the first place, given how much attention he was lavishing on her.

Now, though, G found it amazing that, given everything General Tess had put him through since he had joined Nocturia, Kat hadn't come to his mind sooner. It hadn't occurred to him for a second, all this time, that the way that he had treated Kat, his former girlfriend and fellow council member, was disturbingly similar to the way that General Tess, the commanding officer of the organization that he had sworn to destroy, had treated him as an underling.

It felt like a void had opened in G's chest as memories came flooding back to him. All that time, he had thought that he had been an amazing boyfriend to Kat, and he was frustrated because he didn't feel like she was putting in as much effort as he was. But now, G could see quite clearly that he had been far too demanding of her, and incredibly disrespectful. She had agreed to go out with him, and continued to make an effort even when things got difficult while still keeping sight of her responsibilities. But he had neglected his duties to the council, only wanting to spend time with her, and was infuriated when she hadn't done the same.

And to top it all off, he had only put up with Tess because he had to. Why Kat had put up with him at all, G could only guess . . .

G sat down on the stairs for a moment, overwhelmed. He had just snapped at Tess for something that he himself had done before. Because he had done that, Tess was now suspicious of him, and his cover would surely be blown soon. And if he was executed as a spy, not only would Mella and Stull never be saved, but G would never get a chance to return to Element City and let Kat know how sorry he was for what he had done to her.

G stood up, his stomach blazing with resolve. He knew what he had to do. It was do-or-die time now, and drastic actions were called for. All at once, an insane plan formulated in G's head, and he knew that he'd have to go through with it. If it worked, then not only would he spare the hostages' lives but free them as well, along with curing the NPC villagers and escaping the nightmarish Noctem Capitol. If the plan failed, then they would all die.

G took a deep breath, let it out, and set off down the stairs to put his plan into motion.

CHAPTER 2: UNDERGROUND

A roar of furious shouting erupted from the base of the cave as Ben walked off the stone brick–block balcony. Even as he walked back inside the command post that had been carved into the cave wall, he could still hear the threats and boos that followed his most recent announcement. He gritted his teeth in frustration. He still couldn't stand the fact that he'd had to cut the food rations *again,* but unfortunately there was nothing else that could be done.

Ben shut the wooden door behind him, yet he could still hear the jeers. Sighing, he walked into the room, which was nothing more than a small cave that had been cleaned up and turned into the head office of the military as long as they were stuck down in the bunker. A few chests sat pressed up against the stone-block wall, and some maps and papers sat on a wood plank–block table, but other than that, the room was barren. Bob was sitting on Ivanhoe, and upon his entry, they both looked up.

"Sounds like it went well," Bob muttered bitterly, glancing at the door, which was doing nothing to block out the noise.

"Well, how did you expect them to react?" asked Ben, a resigned look on his face as he pulled another wood-plank block from his inventory, set it on the ground, and plopped down on it. "I'd be pretty upset, too, if somebody told me that I'd only be getting two slices of bread a day, every day, for the foreseeable future."

Bob gave a grim nod. The two brothers sat in silence for a moment. Both of them knew that they had the same thing on their minds. It had been the only thing on their minds since the incident.

"It's eerie," Bob finally said, his voice sounding almost disconnected as he stared off into space, "to think that it's already been four days."

"Yeah," Ben replied, glancing at the ground. "It's even more eerie that the two of us are still here and talking to each other, like normal, while . . . while Bill is . . ."

Ben couldn't bring himself to finish the sentence. He had finally managed to stop the waves of nauseating depression over the past few days, and he wasn't going to allow them to return. They were still fighting a war, and grief had no place in a war. Ben choked back his sob, letting it out as a raspy sigh. Bob was about to open his mouth to respond when, all of a sudden, there was an earsplitting crash.

Both brothers leaped to their feet, bow and sword drawn, ready to defend themselves as they whipped around to face the source of the sound. What they saw was the door they had just exited through knocked down, window broken and a brick lying on the ground not too far inside the room. With no door, there was no barrier to protect the two brothers from the raging, hateful taunts from the basin of the cave below them.

Ben let out a growl of fury, which was drowned out by the jumbled chants of protest from outside the door. "This is ridiculous!" he yelled to his brother. "What are they complaining about? Yeah, sure their food supply got cut. Well, you know what? At least they're safe from the Noctem Alliance for now! At least they're not dead!"

Bob sighed in disgust. "And I suppose you want to go out there and tell them that?"

Ben was about to respond when, without warning, the Mechanist hurdled into the room through an entrance in the back wall, pickaxe drawn.

"What's going on?" he demanded. "I thought I heard a . . ."

Suddenly, the Mechanist realized that Ben and Bob were in the room, and he stopped in midsentence. He hadn't spoken to the brothers, except through messengers, since Bill's death.

"Well," the Mechanist said, recovering and attempting to regain his composure. "Is everything all right out here? I thought that I heard a crash."

"Yeah, someone threw a brick through our door," replied Ben forebodingly, gesturing to the wooden door and brick lying in the empty doorframe, through which the boisterous anger of the crowd was still raging. The Mechanist's eyes widened at the sight.

"It would seem," Bob continued for his brother, giving a look to the Mechanist, "that the citizens aren't very happy with us right now. Since we've been holed up in this bunker, they haven't gotten any good news at all. The only thing that we've done for them is cut off their food supply."

"Well, what do they expect?" the Mechanist asked, baffled. "We're doing everything that we can for the cītizens. What else do they want us to—"

"Oh, open your eyes!" Ben yelled, the anger that he had barely been holding back since the Mechanist's arrival surging forward. "These people have had their entire lives uprooted! The Noctem Alliance has taken over their city, stolen their homes, and forced them to lock themselves down in this stupid mine! Some of them have friends who are still up there, and the Noctem Alliance is probably abusing them, or worse! They need to hear good news!"

"But . . . I . . . ," the Mechanist sputtered. "What do you expect . . . We don't have anything good to tell them . . ."

"Well, that's your job!" bellowed Ben, marching up to the Mechanist and now yelling directly into his face. "Like it or not, when you volunteered to take over Stan's job, you took on the responsibility of keeping your people happy! And since the beginning, you've stayed holed up in the castle, drinking yourself into a stupor, and running the country without caring what your people think of you.

"Even now, when we're all trapped down here, do you have the nerve to talk to your citizens face to face? *No!* You just locked yourself in your room, feeling sorry for yourself, and had me and Bob take the fall for you! We've been trying as hard as we can to keep the people of Element City from hating us. What have you done to make the situation better? *Nothing!*"

There was a moment of silence, broken only by the ongoing, enraged roar of the crowd, during which the Mechanist stared into Ben's furious eyes, unable to speak. Ben glared back, his anger slowly fading, and grief starting to well up in his face.

"My brother died to save you," Ben spat bitterly. "And so far, I don't think that you're worth it. You'd better prove me wrong."

And with that, Ben shoved the Mechanist away from him and, with tears streaming down his face, he marched out of the room.

For a moment, Bob and the Mechanist just stood there. The Mechanist stared blankly at where Ben had just stood. After a moment, Bob turned around and had Ivanhoe run out the back door and down the hall after Ben, leaving the Mechanist standing alone in the midst of the barren stone room.

Ever since he had woken up and realized that Bill had sacrificed his life so that he could live, the Mechanist had been totally distraught. After he had joined Stan's militia all those months ago, the Mechanist had sworn off SloPo. Yet, in the stresses of running the entire country, the Mechanist hadn't been able to resist the relaxing allure of the potion. If he had had the power to resist, to keep off the potion, Bill would still be alive.

And the more he thought about it, the Mechanist realized, in horror, that Ben was totally right. He hadn't done anything since they had entered the mines, too wrapped up in his own self-loathing, only ordering cuts to the food rations when supplies began to run low. He had abandoned his police chiefs and he had abandoned his country. And now the Mechanist knew what had to be done.

Taking a deep breath, the Mechanist walked out the doorway and onto the stone-block balcony, overlooking the basin of the giant cave, which was swamped with players. The mob of players, which was beginning to become slightly calmer, erupted yet again at the sight of the Mechanist. Now, however, the anger emanating from the crowd was far more potent. This was the first appearance the Mechanist had made before his people since before the construction of the bunker. All the hatred at the overwork and ruthless discipline that the Mechanist had ordered came surging forward.

"Excuse me!" the Mechanist yelled, raising his hand,

struggling to be heard over the tumult of the masses. "I have something I would like to say to you all."

The noise did not die down. Rather, another brick flew up out of the crowd, straight towards the Mechanist. Acting out of instinct, the Mechanist whipped his pickaxe from his inventory and shattered the brick in midair. Shocked and appalled, he looked down into the crowd and saw soldiers surging into the throng to apprehend the one who had thrown the brick. He forced himself to take another deep breath.

"Anyway," the Mechanist continued, trying as hard as he could to ignore the struggle between the attacking player and the soldiers going on below him, "I would like to personally thank all of you for your continuing cooperation. Being holed up in this cave is difficult for everybody, but it is necessary to—"

"It's not hard for you!" a single voice rang out above the noise. "I bet you've been on SloPo every minute of every day since the war started!"

A fresh round of fury burst forth from the crowd at this accusation. The words stung the Mechanist, and he gave a shudder of disappointment in himself before responding.

"I fully admit that since the departure of my fellow councilmen, I have not always acted as I ought to. I have made many mistakes, and for that, I offer you my sincerest apologies. However, in the present situation—"

"You're nothing but a dictator!" the voice cut back in, from a player somewhere in the centre of the crowd who the Mechanist couldn't see. "You've done nothing but lay around and drink while us normal people have been doing all the hard work!"

"OK, guards, apprehend that player. I can't get a word out!" the Mechanist spat out without really thinking. Had he given it any thought, he would have realized just how big a mistake it was.

"He's trying to silence me!" the player screamed, sounding disturbed and terrified. "He's gone crazy with power!"

The soldiers, who had just finished detaining the brick thrower, now surged towards the shouting player, who was in the centre of the crowd. However, the rest of the citizens began to fight back. They were punching the soldiers, slamming into them, doing all they could to keep them from reaching the centre of the crowd where the one player was. The Mechanist watched in total shock as the soldiers drew out their weapons and began to fight against the hundreds of players now pressing into them.

What the Mechanist was witnessing was a revolt.

"Please, calm down!" the Mechanist cried out in desperation. "Guards, I order you to stand down. Return to your positions immediately!"

The guards couldn't hear him. They were too busy

fighting against the citizens, who had drawn their own weapons and were starting to attack the soldiers. As he stared down into the crowd, awestruck, the Mechanist suddenly realized that something else was flying directly at him. He ducked down under the cobblestone-wall railing of the balcony, and watched the arrow fly directly through where his head had been seconds before and stick into the stone-block wall above him.

The Mechanist's heart was pounding out of his chest as the gravity of the situation dawned on him. One of his people had just tried to assassinate him. He would never be able to find out who. The entire population had turned on him. A full-on battle was breaking out among the people of Elementia.

All of a sudden, the Mechanist knew that he wasn't safe any more. Nobody was. The Noctem Alliance hadn't even found their cave yet.

The Mechanist realized that he had to find Bob and Ben. They, of all people, might be able to fix this dangerous mess. He crawled across the cobblestone balcony and was about to enter the room again when an explosion echoed throughout the cavern.

All concerns for safety flying out the window, the Mechanist leaped to his feet, terrified at the thought that somebody in the crowd below had detonated a TNT block. However, looking down into the throng, he saw no sign of the blast. Rather, all fighting had ceased in an instant, and all eyes were now turned to a giant hole that had been ripped in the upper wall of the cave.

Everyone watched with bated breath. What was this? Was it some sort of military operation? Was it an accidental TNT detonation? Had the Noctem Alliance finally found them?

Then, one by one, players emerged from the opening, standing on the ledge, and the Mechanist's heart lifted.

He recognized the tattered army uniform and scraggly beard of the navy officer Commander Crunch and the dirty white robes and full red lips of Cassandrix. Kat's orange shirt, pink shorts and blonde hair were still radiantly bright despite their heavy wear and tear, and Rex's head poked out joyfully beside her. Charlie hobbled up next to her, his leg clearly damaged but still in one piece.

And then, from amid a group of people that the Mechanist could see standing behind the four players, another stepped to the front of the pack. His turquoise shirt was stained, his navy trousers were torn, there were scratches and bruises pock-marking his face, but it was still completely undeniable as to who this player was.

"People of Elementia!" Stan2012 announced to the stunned mass of hundreds of players. "We . . . are . . . back!"

And with that, Stan pumped his fist into the air in a triumphant gesture as, all at once, the entire population of the cave burst into applause. The Mechanist could only stare, tears of joy in his eyes, as he took in the wonderful, wonderful truth that his friends were home alive.

Ben and Bob rushed out of the door and stood beside the Mechanist.

"What's going on out here?" Ben demanded, astonished by the aura of amazing joy that was now echoing throughout the cave.

The Mechanist said nothing. He simply turned back around and pointed up at the hole in the wall. As soon as the two brothers realized who they were looking at, they erupted into hoots and cheers, hugging each other and jumping around, totally elated.

And there, far up on the ledge, as his friends broke down in tears at the fact that they were finally home, and they hugged each other, and danced, and shouted their love down into the crowd, Stan didn't move. He simply stood still, his fist still raised into the air like a beacon of victory, and looked down into the faces of his people, his heart filled with joy such as he had never known before.

Within minutes, he knew that he would have to meet up with the Mechanist and the three police chiefs. He knew that he would have to reveal the tragic news of DZ's death. He knew that he would have to lead his people. He knew that he would have to plan an attack. He knew that time was of the essence. He knew that the fate of the game of Minecraft may very well be resting on his shoulders.

But Stan still allowed himself, just for a minute, to live in the moment. He had worked so long and hard to return, and he had sacrificed and lost so much, that never, in a million years, could this moment be ruined.

The holding room was nothing but a giant cube, constructed of cobblestone blocks and taking up a sizable space within the Noctem Capitol Building. Torches lit the perimeter of the room, making it light enough to see and prevent other mobs from spawning. Cutting through the solid wall of cobblestone on the upper half of one wall was a row of glass, through which any curious onlookers could see what the two Zombies were doing.

These two Zombies did not resemble typical Zombies. Rather than the square head reminiscent of a player, they had elongated heads, with bloodshot red eyes and giant, droopy green noses hanging down off their faces. These Zombies, one fully grown and the other half the size of the first, had once been two villagers.

They were once mother and son, named Mella and Stull, and they had lived happily together in their village, which was now long gone. Not that they knew it, though. Besides their names, Mella and Stull had no memory of their previous lives. Oh, it was there, hidden somewhere deep within the layers of instinct and bloodlust that had overtaken their already primitive reasoning upon being bitten by a Zombie.

The two of them lumbered around aimlessly. For the past month, this had been their life. They had spent the majority of their time ambling around this room. Occasionally, they had been pulled out by the players who had put them there to serve as a communication bridge between the players and the mobs, and they had soon after been rewarded by unconscious players, who they would devour with pleasure.

It had been quite some time since they had been utilized, however. The Noctem Alliance's mobs had been of great use on the battlefield, but now that the fighting was all but over, they served little to no purpose besides controlling the Withers. In fact, Lord Tenebris had made it clear that no tamed mobs were to be allowed into Element City. Only players who had been members of the Noctem Alliance would be allowed to live freely within the walls. Not that the villagers knew this, though. The only thing they knew was that at some point, the iron door on the ground would open again, and it would be time to feast.

Sure enough, the door did eventually scrape open, and Mella and Stull glanced at it. Through the frame marched a player, a bronze skin showing under his black armour, followed by another black-clad player with a thunderbolt across his red face, and around twenty players in soldier uniforms. The Zombies were beside themselves in anticipation. They had never seen so many players in one place before.

"Are you sure about this?" the lightning-faced player asked, turning to face G.

"Hey, don't look at me," said G, sounding annoyed as he gave a noncommittal shrug. "I'm just following what General Tess told me."

"Yeah, but I heard something totally different," the player replied, sounding confused. "She told me to bring these players to the firing squad, not the Zombie chamber. And it makes more sense to do it that way. I mean, there are way too many players here for the Zombies to eat all of them at once."

"Look, Zingster," G retorted, looking Corporal Zingster directly in the face. "I *just* came down from talking to Tess, and she told me that she wants *me* to knock out these players and let the Zombies have them."

"But—"

"But nothing!" G spat at him. "As of today, I outrank you, Corporal, so you'll do what I say!"

Corporal Zingster stared at G for a moment.

"Yes, sir, Captain MasterBronze," the Corporal replied, giving a respectful salute before backing out of the room, the door closing behind him.

Wasting no time, G started rummaging through his inventory. He knew that it would only be a little while before Corporal Zingster discovered that he wasn't really a captain like he had said. G hated that he'd had to lie to Zingster like that; it was just another complication to be thrown into the plan, but he knew that it was the only way to ensure that Zingster obeyed him without question. In any case, it didn't matter now. If this plan worked out, he would most likely never see Zingster or Tess again until they met on the battle-field.

"Take these!" G said, as the horde of captive soldiers, who had been looking on in terrified silence, now stared at him in surprise. From his inventory, he threw dozens of pick-axes into the crowd, which he had looted from the supply room.

One of the soldiers caught the pickaxe, and looked it over uncomprehendingly before returning his gaze back to G.

"Who are you?" he asked in awe.

"My name is Goldman2," G replied hastily. "I'm a spy for Elementia and a member of the Element City Council of Eight, and we're busting out of here."

Instantly, a ripple of excitement spread throughout the crowd, though, with the discipline of the soldiers they were, they remained quiet. G continued to look through the sup-plies he had stolen until he found what he was looking for. He held a liquid Potion of Weakness in his right hand, and had a golden apple on standby. G turned to face the two zombies, who had been looking at him expectantly since his arrival.

"Come here, Mella and Stull," G called out to them like dogs. "It's time to eat."

Their eyes flashed red with excitement as they lumbered towards G. Then, when they were a few blocks away, G launched the Potion of Weakness in their direction. The glass bottle shattered on the ground, enveloping the two villagers in a cloud of fumes. The two forms of the villagers stumbled around in confusion within the cloud for a few seconds before falling to the ground. Without hesitation, G took a deep breath and sprinted into the cloud. He shoved the golden apple down the throat of Mella, and then drew a second golden apple and did the same to Stull. The mother and son sputtered for a minute, before falling unconscious to the ground, golden wisps of smoke curling up off their bodies.

G barrelled out of the smoke, and finally allowed himself to breathe in the fresh, nontoxic air. After he had regained his breath, he turned to face the soldiers, who were all looking at him.

"Start digging," G commanded. He pulled a compass from his inventory, glanced at it, and then pointed toward the left wall of the room. "Aim that way. And hurry up, we don't have much time before the Noctems discover that we're gone."

The soldiers nodded and immediately began to tunnel into the ground, creating a sizable staircase down into the underground in a matter of seconds. G called over to a few soldiers to help him carry the shuddering Zombie villagers, who were slowly but surely becoming less and less green.

Two of them hoisted Mella up over their shoulders, while the other scooped up Stull in her arms.

As the last of the soldiers disappeared down into the tunnel, G gave a sigh of relief. He couldn't believe how well his plan had worked, and allowed himself a moment of self-congratulation. Then, he picked up a handful of loose cobblestones on the ground, descended into the tunnel and placed the blocks back into the floor. The room was now identical to how it had looked just minutes before, save the absence of the two Zombie villagers who were nearly cured and en route back to Element City.

Lord Tenebris looked around the Element Castle council room, upon the stone-brick table of the Council of Operators. He found it odd that when Stan2012 had taken control of Element City, he had not destroyed the throne, which Lord Tenebris now sat on. Perhaps he had kept it as a reminder of King Kev's rule, so that the decisions that they made should never allow a monarch to rule Elementia ever again. In any case, Lord Tenebris couldn't help but feel an innate sense of contentedness sitting on the throne. He had waited so long, and worked so hard for this throne, that, no matter who sat on it, he knew that it would always truly be his.

The feeling of satisfaction only lasted for a moment, however, before Lord Tenebris's dormant rage swelled back up. As relieved as he was that the Noctem Alliance had now conquered the entire server of Elementia, it was still inexcusable that Stan2012 had not been located yet. Furthermore, although the citizen population within the city was locked in their houses under quarantine, it was obvious that not all of them were there. A good number of the Element City citizens had clearly escaped to somewhere.

The five-note doorbell, ringing out through the unseen note blocks, signalled that somebody was at the door. Lord Tenebris reached down to a button on the side of his throne and clicked it. Within seconds the redstone circuit executed its job, and the iron door swung open.

Through the open door frame marched eight figures. The five players dressed as hostile mobs, who Lord Tenebris knew to be called ELM, dropped their jaws in awe. Lord Tenebris was familiar with this reaction. It was typical for players to respond this way upon first laying eyes on him. He hardly cared about them, however. Lord Tenebris was far more focused on his generals, Drake, Tess and Spyro, as they proceeded past the council table and knelt before him.

"Greetings, my generals," Lord Tenebris said unemotionally as he looked down upon them.

"Greetings, my lord," all three generals responded in unison, still looking down at the ground.

"First and foremost, I would like to congratulate you on

the work you have done," Lord Tenebris continued. "At long last, after months of planning, of struggling and of toiling, we have done it. The Noctem Alliance has conquered Elementia. The dreams of King Kev have now been realized, and we are on the threshold of creating a perfect server, where those who have earned their place reign supreme, and the weak are in their equally rightful place. I could not have accomplished this vision without your undying loyalty."

"Thank you, my lord," all three generals replied again, their voices full of elation. To be directly praised and thanked by Lord Tenebris himself – it was more wonderful than they could have ever imagined.

"However," Lord Tenebris continued, his voice suddenly full of anger, causing all in the vicinity to look up in alarm, "the fact that we have accomplished so much is irrelevant next to the fact that Stan2012, his military leaders and his council members are still at large! I will have you know that I blame each of you for this failure."

"My lord," Drake replied submissively, terror in his voice, "I assure you, I have been doing all that I—"

"Silence, Drake," Lord Tenebris hissed, and instantly Drake stared back at the ground in shame, shaking in horror. "I shall get to you in a moment." First, he turned to face Tess. She had been looking up at him in respect, but now she looked to the side, finding it impossible to meet his empty, white eyes.

"I admit, Tess, that out of the three of you," Lord Tenebris spoke on, "it is you with whom I take the least umbrage. You have done a perfectly respectable job in your rearing of the new recruits, and during your time as a commander on the front lines, you were properly able to keep Element City under lockdown while I prepared the Withers for the final strike."

"Thank you, my lord," Tess replied, trying to sound as humble as possible.

"That does not excuse the fact," Lord Tenebris continued, "that the highway through the Nether has yet to be completed. I'm sure I don't need to reiterate how much easier it would be to find Stan if our soldiers could easily fast-travel all throughout the server."

"I apologize, my lord," Tess replied, sinking into a deep bow, "but it's been very difficult. The more troops that leave Nocturia to join the occupation of Element City, the longer work will be delayed. I've even forced the new recruits to mine for Nether quartz, rather than training them, so that I would have more soldiers available for construction of the highway."

"Do not expect any lenience from me, Tess. It's been over a month now!" Lord Tenebris said, not raising his voice, but still commanding enough power to echo throughout the council room. "Either force your people to work faster or I will make an example of you to inspire their work ethic."

Tess gulped in fear, but still managed to get out, "I understand, my lord. Thank you for your mercy."

"You, Spyro," Lord Tenebris continued, glaring down at Spyro, who shuddered as he forced himself to look up.

"I am extremely disappointed in you. The fact that four prisoners escaped from Fungarus and you were not able to stop them is unforgivable. I would think that after I gave Drake what he deserved for allowing the escape, you would do all in your power to ensure that they were captured."

Drake's face returned to a grotesque wince as he remembered the sheer agony that Lord Tenebris had put him through as punishment for his mistake.

"My lord . . . I apologize most dearly. I did send many of my forces out into the ocean to search for them . . . I would have sent all that I could, if I weren't preoccupied with the revolution on the Lesser Mushroom Island—"

"That is no excuse!" Lord Tenebris replied, glaring down at Spyro. "Your army should have no difficulty in subduing the ruffians of that island, especially after the Great Purge."

"Well, there was no trouble at first!" Spyro replied, his eyes wide with fear. "We kept the republic citizens as hostages, as you requested, while we hunted through the remains of the city for those Lesser Tribesmen who had escaped the Purge. But now, the republic citizens and the surviving Tribesmen have begun to fight back! They've rallied around a leader who calls herself Goddess Olea, and even though we've done all we—"

Spyro cut off in midsentence, and his hands flew to his throat. A small choking sound escaped his mouth, and Drake and Tess, who were watching him in horror, whipped around to face Lord Tenebris, who was leaning forwards and glaring intently at Spyro. The white-eyed demon surveyed his prey with emotionless eyes as Spyro began to levitate into the air, his eyes bulging and his legs flailing.

"Perhaps you don't understand me," Lord Tenebris said in a deadpan as Spyro continued to struggle. "The rebellion in the Mushroom Islands *will* be eradicated in a timely manner. Do you understand, General?"

There was a moment of tense silence, broken only by the continued coughing and sputtering of Spyro. Then, a raspy "yes" managed to escape his throat, and Lord Tenebris relaxed his gaze, leaning back in his throne. The Noctem general crashed to the ground, lying still for a moment before finally raising himself onto shaking hands and knees, coughing and taking in deep breaths.

"Thank you . . . my lord . . . ," Spyro croaked, "for your . . . forgiveness . . ."

"Enough of your grovelling, Spyro," Lord Tenebris replied lazily. Then, Lord Tenebris turned his head very slowly, until finally, his vacant white eyes landed on Drake, who cowered in dread.

"General Drake," Lord Tenebris said slowly. "I'm sure that you remember what I said, regarding what I would do to you if Stan2012 was not in my custody by the next time we met."

"My lord," Drake stammered, "I can explain—"

"Tread carefully, Drake," Lord Tenebris said, in a voice that was nearly a whisper, which was somehow ten times more terrifying than if he were yelling. "You're one wrong step away from feeling the full extent of my wrath."

"My lord, I beg you to hear me out," Drake pleaded, looking up at Lord Tenebris, forcing himself to look into his eyes, only to glance away a moment later before continuing. "I've been leading your invasion force during the entire campaign against Element City. I've graciously accepted the task of being your eyes and ears on the battlefield, and as a result, the entirety of Elementia is now under your command."

"That does not change the fact that Stan2012 is still at large," Lord Tenebris replied, a slight taunting sound in his voice.

"Please, my lord," Drake simpered on. "I've hired the most renowned assassin team in Elementia to hunt Stan2012 for me. If they've been unable to apprehend him . . . well, then I'm not sure what we're to do."

Lord Tenebris gave a slow nod and looked down at the floor, as if he were debating something in his mind. The entire room, especially Drake, waited with bated breath for him to speak. Finally, Lord Tenebris raised his head.

"You five, back there . . . come forward, please."

The three generals spun around to face the back of the room, and their eyes fell on the five mobhunters of ELM. The jaws of Arachnia, Enderchick and Creeper Khan dropped to the floor. Lord Marrow's eyebrows raised slightly, while Zomboy's face lit up, like a teacher's pet who had just been called on in school. However, none of them hesitated in walking forwards, around the council table, and standing in a line behind the three Noctem generals.

"You are the assassins that General Drake has hired to capture Stan2012?"

"Yes, sir," Arachnia replied, stepping forwards and keeping remarkably well poised given how terrified she was to be speaking to this monster. "My name is Arachnia, leader of the Elite Legion of Mobhunters, the most renowned bounty hunters in Elementia."

"Indeed," Lord Tenebris replied, nodding slowly. "And you have encountered Stan2012 multiple times since you have started hunting him, yes?"

"This . . . is true, sir," Arachnia replied, recovering from her horror that Lord Tenebris knew this. "We have encountered Stan2012 twice since we started hunting him. Both times, he was joined by accomplices, and he managed to evade our grasp. As I'm sure you are well aware, sir, Stan and his friends are the highest-calibre fighters in all of Minecraft . . . regardless, we are still hot on the trail of—"

BOOOOM!

The massive explosion knocked Arachnia to the side and into Enderchick, while Creeper Khan tumbled to the ground. Lord Tenebris's hand was still pointed towards the spot where, just seconds before, Zomboy had stood next to Arachnia; there was nothing but a cloud of black smoke there now. Slowly, the smoke wafted away, allowing the seven players on the floor to stare in blank shock at the body of Zomboy lying dead on the stone brick floor, his items in a ring around him.

There was a moment of silence as nobody moved a muscle. The four remaining were unable to process the fact that their team-mate, who had been modded to be twenty times as hardy as a normal player, had just been taken out in one shot. Lord Tenebris lowered his hand.

"Your services will no longer be required," Lord Tenebris said coldly. "Leave my presence now if you know what's good for you."

There was no hesitation. Within seconds the room was cleared of the four mobhunters, all of whom glanced down in disbelief at Zomboy's body before exiting through the door. Not a second after Creeper Khan left and closed the door behind him, the body of Zomboy vanished, leaving only his various items on the ground. However, even when the mobhunters were completely gone, the three generals still couldn't help but stare at the ring of items, jaws dropped and traumatized looks on their faces. In front of them, Lord Tenebris gave a satisfied smile.

Perhaps now they will take their work a little bit more seriously, he thought to himself.

"We are changing our tactics," Lord Tenebris announced, causing Tess, Drake and Spyro to turn back towards him. "It's about time that we ended this war once and for all. Drake!"

"Yes, Your Glory?" Drake replied, bowing to the floor and looking up at him.

"I believe that it's about time that we reunite the people of Element City. You know where Mecha11, the police chiefs and the rest of the population of Element City are hiding, correct?"

"Yes, indeed, my lord," Drake replied hastily, as if Lord Tenebris would be more impressed the faster he delivered the information. "They're located in a cave they dug below the city, and I know where the entrance is. It's in the side of a hill right outside this castle, as a matter of fact. I've known ever since—"

"Silence," Lord Tenebris ordered, to which Drake looked to the ground in shame. "It's time for action. Drake, prepare the troops in the city to lead an attack on the underground bunker. Spyro, return to the Mushroom Islands, and put down the resistance there within the next week. Tess, return to Nocturia, and order half your troops to march to Element City. Send the two villagers with them, and I'll send the third one your way, with whom I will expect you to start to create a massive army of mobs. You will have the troops here by tomorrow."

"But . . . my lord!" cried out Tess in surprise, as Spyro stared at Lord Tenebris in confusion. "I won't be able to transport all my troops to Nocturia in one day. Even if the highway through the Nether was completed, I couldn't do that! And it will take General Spyro at least three days to make his way to the Mushroom Islands . . ."

Lord Tenebris smiled. "Don't fret, my generals . . . Lord Tenebris would never ask something impossible of his underlings."

And with that, Lord Tenebris stood up from his throne and stretched out his hands: one towards Tess and the other towards Spyro. He closed his eyes, took a deep breath, and tightened his focus. Then, in one instant, his eyes flew open, and he released all the tension in his body. Tess and Spyro's bodies flashed for a moment, and then, in the blink of an eye, they were gone.

Drake glanced around wildly, trying to figure out what had happened. The thought that Lord Tenebris may have just killed his two comrades flashed across his mind, but just as he was about to let out a shout of horror, the sound of Lord Tenebris's voice echoed throughout the room.

"Do not concern yourself with them, Drake. I have merely used my abilities to transfer your two fellow generals to exactly where they needed to be. Tess is now in her office in Nocturia, while Spyro is in the Capitol Building of the Lesser Mushroom Island."

Drake's mind took a moment to comprehend what Lord Tenebris had just said, but as soon as he did, he stared up at him, awed by this incredible display of power. Lord Tenebris allowed Drake a moment of marvelling before glaring down at him. The second his piercing white eyes met Drake's, the general cringed yet again.

"Now, go, Drake, and prepare the armies of Elementia for the invasion of the bunker. The end of the war is near."

Drake gave a zealous nod of agreement, and with that, he stood up and was out the door of the council room within seconds, the iron door slamming shut behind him.

The stone-block command room was silent as the players filed in. Stan took a seat at the head of the makeshift cobblestone table as Kat, the Mechanist and Commander Crunch sat down around the other sides. Ben, Leonidas, Cassandrix and Sirus stood against the stone wall behind them, while

Bob sat beside his brother on Ivanhoe, Rex sitting obediently beside them. Only Charlie, who was getting his leg checked out by a medical team, was missing.

"First off," Stan said, as he looked around the room, meeting the eyes of each individual player, "I would like to say how happy I am to finally be back here with you guys. You're all like family to me, and there's nobody else that I'd rather be defending my home with than you. And even though . . . we've lost . . ."

Stan took a deep breath, and fought to retain his composure. Although this was the first time that he had spoken to this entire group since he returned to the mines, the knowledge of which of their comrades had fallen since they last met had spread through the group rather quickly. The memories of DZ, Bill and so many more whose fates were unsure still lingered in his memory as he continued his speech.

" . . . and even though we've lost many brave players along the way, it is our duty to ensure that their deaths weren't in vain. Though it's true that during the course of this war, the Noctem Alliance has pushed us to the brink of extinction, one crucial fact remains true: *we're still here.*

"The republic – the *true* government of Elementia, which is willing to fight to the death to defend the principles of equality for all – is still alive and well. My friends, we are that government. And it's our mission to take back our city and once again turn Elementia into the place that its founders intended it to be. We have been hiding, defending and running from the Noctem Alliance for far too long. The time has come, my friends, to fight back."

There were nods and murmurs of assent around the table, as looks of grim determination took to the faces of all in the vicinity. Everybody knew that what Stan was suggesting wouldn't be easy . . . or perhaps even possible. But they also knew that he was right. They couldn't hide forever, and sooner or later, they would have to retaliate.

"Ben, Bob," Stan said inquisitively, looking at the two police chiefs. "Do you have a prediction on how long it will be before the Noctem Alliance discovers this cave?"

"Well, I doubt that they'll find us anytime soon," Bob replied reasonably. "This bunker is pretty far underground, and it's far away from Element City's active mines. When we closed the bunker, the pistons shifted the dirt blocks to make the hill look totally natural, so they'd never recognize it as a mine entrance. You can thank the Mechanist's redstone designs for that."

Several players gave a nod of congratulations to the Mechanist, who glanced down at the table, as if he were embarrassed. Stan found this odd; the Mechanist had never had any false modesty regarding his redstone creations before (although he had never been excessively braggy either). In any case, it didn't matter. They had a game plan to assemble.

"OK, I trust your judgment," Stan said to Bob, nodding in approval. "If that's the case, then we've probably got a little bit of time to get a plan together. Now, here's the question: what do we do?"

"Well, where's the best place in the city to strike?" Kat asked. "We have enough manpower down here to take at least part of the city back by force, and then at least we'll be above ground and have access to resources again."

"I don't think that will work," Ben replied gravely. "We've been sending spies out into the city to monitor the Noctem occupation, and it seems like they've formed some sort of impenetrable web across the city. Their military operations run like clockwork; if we try to invade part of the city at dusk, we'll have the entire force of the Noctem Army bearing down on us by morning."

"I have an idea," a voice came from behind the players. They turned around and saw Charlie. He hobbled across the room into his chair.

"What did TrumpetBlaster say about your leg?" Bob asked anxiously, as Ivanhoe gave a grunt from beneath him.

"I didn't go," he replied, a dark look on his face. "I heard that you guys were having a meeting to discuss what to do next, and I figured that I should be there. I'll go see him afterwards. Anyway, did I hear you say that you're looking for an idea of how to take back Element City?"

Stan nodded. "What's your idea?"

"Well, what if we at least tried to sneak into the city under the radar?" Charlie asked, his face lighting up. "If we somehow managed to get a bunch of footholds all across the city – you know, like, take over houses in a bunch of different parts of the city – then we could launch an attack from all over the city at once."

"Negatory, sir," Bob said, shaking his head. "The Noctem Alliance would never let an operation like that go undetected. Their surveillance is incredible, and they have invisible troops stationed all over the city, on the lookout for anything suspicious. We can only send out one spy at a time because their security is so tight. We'd never be able to carry out an operation that big without them noticing."

"Now hold on a sec, I think Charlie's idea could still work!" Leonidas replied thoughtfully. "I mean, maybe if we were extra careful, and only let a few of our guys into the city at . . ."

"He said it wouldn't work, Leonidas, so drop it!" Charlie spat, glaring at Leonidas. All eyes in the room turned to Charlie, caught totally off guard by this alarming display of hostility. However, when Charlie looked up, his face showed nothing but crestfallen depression, and there was a collective, unspoken decision around the room to forget that it had happened.

Nonetheless, though the conversation continued, Leonidas found himself staring at Charlie. He had tried to be polite to Charlie, to try to get around whatever it was that he was holding against Leonidas. Clearly it wasn't working, leaving Leonidas to wonder if his efforts to befriend Charlie would ever pan out.

"So what should we do?" Charlie demanded, an urgent tone in his voice. "We need to get out of this stupid cave, and we have to do it fast! The Noctem Alliance is going to bust in here any—"

"Hold on a moment," Cassandrix cut in, her eyes lighting up and a smile crossing her face.

"What is it?" Stan asked, as the entire room turned to look at her.

"Charlie, you seem to be experienced in underground navigation," she said slowly, and Stan could see the gears whirring in her head. "How long do you think it would take to dig a tunnel to the Adorian Village from here?"

"I don't know," Charlie sighed, still looking crestfallen. "A couple of days, maybe . . ."

"Then that's what we ought to do!" Cassandrix exclaimed. "We should dig a tunnel and invade the Adorian Village! They'll never be expecting that!"

There was a moment of silence as the idea sank in. Then, Ben spoke up.

"Cassandrix . . . that's brilliant! All of the Noctem Alliance's attention is focused on securing Element City. They'll never be prepared for an attack on the Adorian Village. And once we take control of the village, we can use the resources stored there to launch an assault on Element City!"

"Hold your horses, Ben," Bob cut in, turning to face his brother. "I think that this is a good plan, except for one thing. The citizens that we have down here in the mine aren't all soldiers. Not only that, but being down here for so long has done a number on them. Before we reveal ourselves, we have to be sure that those who aren't able to fight have somewhere safe to go. The second we invade the Adorian Village, it's going to turn into a combat zone."

"Well, why don't we just have them stay in the cave for now?" Kat suggested. "You just got through saying that the cave is probably gonna be safe for a while, Bob."

"Uh . . . guys?" Charlie said slowly, sounding mortified, as if he were on the verge of divulging classified information. "I . . . um . . . *really* don't think that this cave is safe. I think that we should leave . . . like . . . as soon as physically possible."

"What are you trying to say, Charlie?" Leonidas asked, not sure that he wanted to hear the answer.

He was cut off by an ear-splitting explosion.

The blast shook the walls. Seconds later, the sounds of terrified screams started to ring through the air, followed by a second explosion. Stan leaped to his feet and dashed onto the balcony, his friends hot on his tail.

He looked wildly around the basin of the cave and saw people running around panicking but no visible signs of damage. A third explosion rattled the cave, but yet again, Stan could see no damage.

"What's going on?" he yelled to his police chiefs, struggling to make himself heard over the sound of yet another explosion.

The two brothers sputtered in confusion, trying to piece together what was happening. Suddenly, a soldier burst onto the balcony through the door. Ben whipped around to face him.

"Private! What's going on here? What's the meaning of the explosions?"

The private gulped, took a deep breath, and spoke.

"It's the Noctem Alliance, sir. They've found us, and the Wither is blasting its way in."

Although the Wither's assault on the outer walls of Element City was nearly a week in the past, the fires continued to blaze on. There were still piles of loose stone-block rubble scattered around the perimeter of where the proud wall used to stand. The remnants of pistons and mechanisms scattered the ground, forming a barrier of rubble that served as a border to the city in its own right. Although the buildings adjacent to the wall within the city had taken some damage through the invasion and the subsequent fighting between the two armies, the outside of the wall had fared far worse.

A plain of stone and dirt blocks extended around what had once been the outer wall, expanding far out of sight until it finally connected to the untouched forest. This battlefield, blasted far below ground level by TNT cannons, still bore the scars of the fights that had raged at the wall for so long, and the four players who were now trekking through the silent plain had to avoid craters, blazing fires and arrows stuck in the ground as they continued to hike hastily away from Element City.

The four members of ELM did not speak. Since they had watched Lord Tenebris strike down their comrade and then threaten to do the same to them, they hadn't stopped moving, running through the streets of Element

City until their legs ached. They continued to walk until, at last, they reached the outer wall. Crossing the threshold of the city into the war-torn biome beyond, the four mobhunters saw no reason to stop walking. After all, they had nowhere to go. It wasn't like they were aiming for anywhere in particular.

After trekking across hundreds of blocks of stone, the mobhunters finally reached a steep incline of dirt blocks, atop which sat the forest. Upon reaching the hill, they didn't break stride, opting instead to make their way up the hill using the path of least resistance, occasionally punching dirt blocks out of the way.

Arachnia reached the top first, and she turned around to watch her team scale the incline behind her. One look at their faces and Arachnia knew that it was time to take a rest. She jerked her head over to a clearing a way into the forest, and without speaking, they walked over and proceeded to pull an assortment of spare blocks from their inventories to set up camp for the night. Creeper Khan placed a Netherrack block in the centre of the clearing and stretched his hand out over it. A tiny explosion erupted in midair, just grazing the block enough that it caught fire.

The four players huddled around the makeshift campfire, and Arachnia reached into her inventory, a sombre expression on her face that was reflected by the other members of ELM. She extracted four bottles, which were filled with liquid.

She was a bit disappointed that water was all they had, but it was better than nothing. The bottles were distributed around the fire in silence. As soon as everybody had one, Arachnia raised her bottle into the air. The others followed, and she took a deep breath, and let it out.

"To Zomboy," she whispered.

"To Zomboy," Creeper Khan and Enderchick mumbled in response, and Lord Marrow gave a grave nod of the head. The four glass bottles tilted back, and within a moment, all the water had drained. With nothing left in the capsules, the four remaining members of ELM bowed their heads in respect and pitched their bottles into the fire. The items burst into flames and disappeared an instant later, sending a shower of sparks into the sky.

"I still can't believe that he's, like, actually gone," Enderchick sighed, staring into the fire.

"Yeah," Creeper Khan grunted. "I mean, the guy got under my skin like nothing else, but it's hard to think that he's dead."

"Well, it's true," Arachnia replied, and the three other mobhunters looked up at her. "Zomboy *is* dead, and we've officially failed our biggest job ever."

There was a moment of silence as the four mobhunters let those facts sink in, the fire crackling and blazing in the background. Finally, Creeper Khan spoke.

"So . . . what're we gonna do now? We can't stick around here. You couldn't pay me to mess around with someone that powerful. Do we go back out into the desert?"

"Oh please, you can't be serious," Enderchick laughed darkly. "After losing a job that was, like, *this* big? We'd be total losers. There's no way I'm going back to that dump."

"Then there's only one thing to do," Arachnia replied.

"What?"

"We're gonna capture Stan2012 ourselves."

Enderchick and Creeper Khan stared at her, eyes wide, as if she'd gone insane. Even Lord Marrow, who was leaning against a nearby tree and examining his bow, looked up in surprise.

"Uh . . . *scusi*?" Enderchick asked softly.

"Did I stutter?" Arachnia scoffed, standing up and looking down at her accomplices.

"Oh come on, Arachnia. You can't really—"

"Shut up!" she spat, causing Creeper Khan to growl in anger as she began to rant.

"We have put so much time and effort into finding this player. We've travelled all across the server. We've slept in caves and swamps, we've had to fight against some of the most skilled players in Elementia, and now we've lost Zomboy. Enderchick is right, there's no way that we can show our faces in the desert with any dignity without completing this mission, but it's become more than that. Drake sent us out on a mission, guys . . . and with everything that we've put into it, there's no way that I'm gonna back out now."

Arachnia's eyes were blazing with a fiery passion, and she spoke with such earnest fervour that the other three mobhunters couldn't help but realize that what she was saying was true.

"Now that you mention it . . . I was forced to sleep for, like, an entire week in a disgusting, icky, slimy suh-*wamp*," Enderchick groaned, shuddering in disgust at the memory before standing up alongside her leader. "It would be, like, a total shame if all of that was for, like, nothing. I'm with ya, girl – we've gotta find Stan."

"All right!" bellowed Creeper Khan, leaping onto his feet and pumping his blocky fist. "Let's show Drake who's in charge!"

As the three other mobhunters converged to develop a strategy for finding and capturing Stan, Lord Marrow looked towards them. He surveyed them for a moment, as they schemed away with zealous enthusiasm, bloodlust and vengeance in their voices. Then, he looked at the ground, shook his head in sadness, and went back to inspecting his bow.

"Take *this*!" Stan screamed, launching his fist in Sally's direction.

Quick as a whip, she feinted to the side, causing the

energy blast to hit the dirt blocks below in a massive explosion. Unfazed, Stan started throwing a blitz of rapid jabs, as Sally gracefully dodged the energy shots blasting the ground to rubble below her and started to fly directly towards Stan, weaving between his blows as she did so. Stan realized what she was doing, and summoned an axe to his hand. Sally somersaulted forwards through the air, her sword slices turning the space around her into a globe of death as she rammed into Stan. With expert skill, he manoeuvered his axe with incredible speed, blocking every sword attack she threw at him. However, he was totally unprepared when she delivered two final uppercuts, which left his stomach exposed and allowed her to combo into a kick.

The force of her foot on his stomach sent Stan tumbling backwards, causing him to hit the ground so hard that he loosened the dirt blocks around him. Aware that he was in massive pain, Stan focussed all his energy on feeling better. In an instant, he was healed, just in time to see Sally rocketing down towards him, sword outstretched and ready to deliver the final blow.

A split second before Sally's sword could impale him, Stan teleported to the side, causing Sally's diamond sword to plunge deep into the ground. Stan reappeared beside her, and used the brief moment of disorientation to launch a punch into her side. She flew through the air but landed safely on all fours, sliding across the dirt blocks in a trail of dust. Stan took a moment to catch his breath, and watched as her eyes, burning with determination, locked on to him for just a moment before she disappeared in midair.

The back of Stan's neck quivered in anticipation, and he spun around to counter the sword strike that Sally had launched from behind. As the two blades ground together, sparks flying from the point of contact, Stan and Sally both teleported at the same time. The duo warped through the air again and again, each desperately trying to outdo the other, but equally matched and continuously locked together. Before long, both realized that their efforts were futile and, in one motion, they pressed into the other's weapon, sending them flying apart. Stan and Sally teleported backwards and simply hovered in midair.

Both players were staring each other down and breathing heavily. They each had a smile on their face that was one part exhilaration, one part frustration and one part admiration.

"I gotta say, Stan, I'm impressed," Sally panted, giving a quick laugh as she tried to catch her breath. "I've taught you well."

"Well, every good student will one day surpass their master, Sal," Stan said with a devious grin. "And you're about to realize that right . . . *now*!"

And with that, Stan stretched out his hand and sent a

volley of fireballs from his palm towards Sally. *This is his grand finale?* She snickered to herself as she lazily raised her hand, conjuring a wall of bedrock to block the fireballs, which proceeded to hit the blocks and dissipate. However, without warning, Sally found that more and more bedrock blocks were appearing all around her, and before she could react, she found herself totally covered, unable to breathe and nearly unable to move.

Stan lowered his hand, looked at the cube of bedrock floating in the air away from him and laughed out loud. *Ha.* He smirked. *She can't survive in there for long . . . I'll be seeing her respawn on the ground any second now . . .*

"I must admit, Stan," a voice rang out inside Stan's head, "that you managed to catch me off guard. You truly have become an operator worthy of the title. However . . . if I were you . . . I wouldn't count your chickens before they're . . . *hatched*!"

As she shouted, a roar rang out through the server as the sky turned black, an evil, terrifying roar that resembled the cries of the Enderman, elephant and T-Rex all rolled into one. Stan recognized the roar, and gave an involuntary shudder as he realized what was about to happen. Then, the bedrock cube exploded, blocks flying everywhere as a giant pair of black wings opened wide, propelling a giant dragon, with a black hide and a silver exoskeleton, into the air. As the

Ender Dragon rose higher and higher into the sky with each beat of its mighty wings, Stan could only watch in stunned silence.

Aw, he thought to himself bitterly. *Why didn't I think of that?*

Underneath the rising dragon, Sally floated in midair, her hand pointed up towards the dragon and a wide grin on her face. She turned to face Stan, and their eyes locked for a moment. Then, Sally swung her hand forwards, and the dragon took off like a jet plane, rocketing at top speed towards Stan.

Stan warped to the side, only to have the dragon make a tight U-turn and be on him again in seconds. Shocked, Stan warped again, axe raised and ready to assault the dragon, but the great black beast whipped its head to the side quicker than Stan could react, and he just barely managed to avoid a snap of its powerful jaw.

Stan was floored. This Ender Dragon was, for whatever reason, much more aggressive than the one he had fought in The End all those months ago. Stan continued to warp backwards and out of range of the dragon's claws and teeth, sending dozens of fireballs from his hands, which peppered the dragon's face with miniature explosions. Nonetheless, the dragon didn't slow down, and Stan knew that it was only a matter of time before the monster landed a hit on him.

Suddenly, Stan had an idea. He warped away from the dragon (seeing Sally enjoying the show from a distance out of the corner of his eye) and, as it proceeded to speed towards him, he focussed with all his might until a giant white mob appeared in midair in front of him. Stan warped to the side as the dragon collided with the Ghast in a flurry of shrieks, wails, roars and explosions. Wasting no time, he proceeded to turn and face Sally, and reach his hand out towards her.

All at once, Sally felt herself unable to move. She focussed as hard as she could on warping away, but she couldn't. She looked down in shock as Stan drew his hand slowly towards himself and, without warning, Sally rocketed towards him. A scream of surprise escaped her mouth as Stan dropped his axe to the ground below him and summoned a diamond sword, glowing red with enchanted heat, outstretched in his hand. Sally flew towards him, unable to do a thing about it as she collided with his sword, the blade impaling her through the chest and her body disappearing the instant the blade stuck through her back.

With his sparring match now over, Stan turned to face the dragon. The great monster was still recovering from its run-in with the Ghast, and it seemed out of sorts. Formulating a plan instantly, Stan proceeded to fly at top speed towards the dragon, sword outstretched beside him. As he flew past the dragon, the sword grazed the black hide, leaving a flaming cut on the monster's side, causing it to cry in agony. Not checking his speed at all, Stan proceeded to warp again, right next to the dragon, and landed another blow.

Stan rocketed around the dragon like a bug, repeatedly warping around it and dragging his sword across until the Ender Dragon was completely covered in trails of flame. Sensing that the Dragon was weak enough to finish, Stan proceeded to teleport directly under the monster and, aiming skywards, he stretched his sword out in front of him and burst through the dragon's neck swordfirst, leaving a large, gaping hole.

He took a deep breath and looked down at the dragon. The monster was frozen in midair. Stan watched as rays of light erupted from within the Ender Dragon until, finally, the monster exploded in a beautiful burst of light.

"Well done, noob," Sally smirked, applauding Stan as he levitated downwards and landed next to Sally with the crunch of dirt block underfoot. "I admit it, I got too cocky. You fully deserve that victory."

"Well, you're not wrong," Stan replied smugly, a self-indulgent smile wide on his face. "That was a good warm-up. What've you got to show me today?"

Sally smiled and shook her head. "There's nothing else to show you, noob. Your training is complete."

Stan did a double take, and then stared at Sally, mouth

hanging slightly open. "Are you . . . are you serious?"

"Come on, noob, when am I not?" Sally replied again, conjuring a wool block beneath her and plopping down on it. "We've been working at it for weeks now, and I've finally shown you everything that I know. Ha . . . You know, I remember back when you really were just a noob . . . walking into the Adorian Village, training with me and the guys, and heading off to Element City for the first time. And look at you now. You're an *operator*, Stan."

An overwhelming feeling crashed over Stan. He didn't know how to describe it – it wasn't sad, but it certainly wasn't happy, either. It was as if, in that moment, the entire weight of how far he'd come crashed down on him like an avalanche. He remembered all that he'd learned . . . all the people he'd come to know . . . all those he'd lost . . . and all that he had left to do.

"Sally," Stan said, turning around to look at his teacher. "Do you . . . do you really think that I'm going to be able to beat Lord Tenebris?"

"You know, Stan, that's something that's really bothered me," Sally spat out in annoyance. "You know *who* Lord Tenebris really is. And you know what he's doing to Elementia, and thousands of other Minecraft servers, as we speak. He's the most evil and destructive force that Minecraft has ever faced, so the least you can do is call him by his real name."

Stan shuddered. It was true. He, along with the rest of his friends, had avoided calling Lord Tenebris by his true name. It just seemed that if they didn't say it, they wouldn't have to face it. They wouldn't have to face the reality of what they were going up against, what they had to destroy. Stan took a deep breath and spoke again.

"Fine. Sally, do you think that I'm going to be able to defeat Herobrine?"

Sally looked at the grass-block ground for a moment, and then looked up at him, an earnest look in her eyes.

"Stan, do you want my one-hundred-percent honest answer?"

"Yes."

"I don't know. I have no idea whether or not you're going to be able to beat Herobrine. I mean . . . something that has the ability to steal energy from the game of Minecraft itself . . . to put thousands of servers at risk . . . just to make itself stronger? If he can do *that*, then I can only guess what he's fully capable of, and I'm not sure if you're going to be able to defeat him, even if I do somehow manage to hack operating powers onto you in Elementia."

Stan felt like the air was being drained from his lungs, and he was forced to conjure a block below himself and sit. It hadn't even occurred to him that he probably wouldn't be able to get operating powers in Elementia at all . . . and that he was more than likely going to have to fight Herobrine without any aid, armed with only an axe. The Elementia Army had no plan to defeat Herobrine – in all their strategy talks, they had treated Herobrine like the elephant in the room. Nobody was willing to bring him up, terrified by the prospect of what he might be able to do. If Stan didn't get operating powers . . . they were all doomed. And even if he did . . .

"But I'll tell you one more thing, noob." Stan turned to face Sally, who was giving him an encouraging smile.

"If I had to pick anybody in Elementia to fight Herobrine, then I'd choose you in a heartbeat."

Stan smiled. For a while, they simply looked at each other. Nothing was said. Nothing was done. They just stared into each other's eyes, taking in the immense respect that they shared. Before long, though, Stan stood up.

"Well, I'd better go now. The tunnellers are probably under the Adorian Village by now, and they'll be getting ready for the attack."

Sally nodded. "Good luck, noob. I may not be sure if you can take down Herobrine, but I have no doubt at all that you'll be able to take back my hometown."

Stan gave a laugh as he nodded in agreement, but then, his face hardened. Stan focussed, and once again, the words flashed in his mind.

DISCONNECT FROM SERVER?

"Yes."

"The preparations for the attack are all ready, sir," Sirus reported, standing in full salute and sounding official. "We're directly underneath the main street of the Adorian Village, and we're all ready to, you know, totally blow our way in and take out all the Noctem soldiers by surprise. Haha, they won't know what hit them!"

"Thank you, Sirus," Bob replied, nodding his thanks. "Please go and prepare the troops for the assault. I'll be there in a minute."

Sirus nodded and took off as Bob turned to his brother, who was sitting next to him alongside all the other Elementia leaders in the base of the cave. "Come on, Ben," he said, commanding Ivanhoe to walk away from the circle. "Let's inspect the troops. And get ready, guys, we're gonna launch the assault as soon as Stan gets back."

Bob and Ivanhoe walked away from the circle of players and towards a mass of troops further down the tunnel. Ben followed them. Leonidas watched them go and looked around.

This cave wasn't a natural mine that had been expanded, like the bunker beneath Element City had been. This was a square-shaped tunnel, carved through the stone block underground by hundreds of miners, desperately digging as fast as possible to avoid the encroaching Wither that was blasting its way in, with Noctem troops not far behind. About twenty troops had stayed behind in the bunker to man the redstone traps that had been set up, and although the Noctems hadn't followed them into the tunnel they had dug out of the cave, they hadn't heard back from the troops either.

Leonidas, lost in his train of thought, suddenly realized that everybody was looking at something. He followed their line of vision and saw that everybody was staring at Sirus, who was conversing with the two police chiefs in his jittery fashion.

"I still can't believe that he's alive," Kat said.

"I still don't completely understand that," Cassandrix said, turning to face Kat. "Could you please explain to me what happened to him? And why everybody finds this so amazing?"

Kat was quite pleased to find that Cassandrix was talking to her in a civil manner. Although Kat tried to be pleasant towards her, Cassandrix only returned the attitude half the time, while reverting to her snappy, unbearable personality the rest of the time. Kat was glad to see that, today at least, she was being agreeable, and answered her question.

"You see, Cassandrix, Sirus was our redstone engineer

during the Battle for Elementia, when we first took down King Kev. That was back before the Mechanist joined us."

Hearing his name, the Mechanist looked up, revealing his tired and stressed face for a moment before returning to the book he was reading.

"Anyway, a lot of players died in that battle, and he was one of them. And even though none of us saw it, one of our friends named Archie said that he saw Sirus get killed in battle. Apparently, it happened right as the battle was ending, right before the castle tower blew up, in fact. We all thought that he was dead, and according to him, he was. Yet somehow, he managed to come back."

"I see," Cassandrix replied, looking mystified. "But . . . do you have any idea how? I mean . . . the server's difficulty is locked on Hardcore, and there's no way to change it unless King Kev himself did it. And even then, he gave up his operating powers! So there's no possible way that Sirus could have gotten back onto the server through simply respawning!"

"Yer guess be as good as any o' ours, lass," Commander Crunch responded solemnly, "but fer now, thar's no way t' know fer certain. More than likely, it had t' do wit' some sort o' glitch, but fer now, we 'ave more important thin's t' worry about."

There was a dark silence around the circle of leaders. They all knew that that was the understatement of the century. Nobody knew what to say. They all knew exactly what they were about to go into, and yet at the same time had no idea.

"I still can't believe that the Noctems managed to find us," muttered Kat.

"Why is that so surprising?" Charlie demanded defensively. "They've been inspecting every block of the city nonstop since they've broken through the wall. It's not *that* surprising that they've managed to find us!"

"Calm down!" exclaimed Kat, shocked by Charlie's aggressive tone. She had no idea what had come over him since they had rescued him from the prison on the Mushroom Islands, but Kat didn't like it one bit. She had expected that by now he would be back to his normal, friendly, soft-spoken self, but if anything he had only gotten worse.

"What I meant," Kat continued cautiously, "was that Ben and Bob have been sending spies out into the city, to see how close the Noctems were to finding us. According to the intelligence they gathered, the Noctems were doing most of their searching in the Merchant's District, on the total opposite end of the city. If that's true, then it makes no sense that they managed to discover us here so quickly."

"Well, however it came about, th' attack couldn't 'ave come at a worse time," Commander Crunch replied darkly. "We 'ave t' act fast, now that th' Noctems know where we be, 'n' we 'ave no time t' put together an actual invasion plan. We be forced t' jus' rush willy-nilly into th' Adorian Village, 'n' hope that this cockamamie assault wit' no thought put into it somehow works."

"You're right," growled Leonidas in disgust. "Why couldn't the Noctems have broken in, like, just two or three days later? That would have made everythin' *so* much easier!"

Suddenly, Charlie leaped to his feet, prompting all to turn towards him. He looked distressed and mortified, and it seemed as if he were on the verge of tears. For a moment, nobody moved as Charlie looked like a deer in the headlights of his friends' concerned looks. Then Charlie turned around and marched away from the circle without a word, a sob escaping his mouth as he limped down the tunnel.

"Wha' be his problem?" Commander Crunch asked incredulously as he turned to look at his comrades, and saw that nobody had the slightest idea what was wrong with him.

"I'll be right back," Leonidas said determinedly and, before anybody could stop him, he stood up and took off down the tunnel after Charlie.

"What do you want?" demanded Charlie as Leonidas caught up to him, weaving around a group of soldiers pulling on diamond armour as he went.

"I wanna know why you're so upset, man," Leonidas said straightly. "You've been totally out of it ever since we met up, and you seem like you're upset with me. Listen, dude, I know I haven't really known you for long, but it's pretty obvious to me that you've got somethin' going on."

"Oh it is, is it?" Charlie spat, looking beyond outraged. "Well, thank you for noticing!"

"Charlie, listen . . . I know that your injury has been bothering you—"

"Shut up!" Charlie bellowed at the top of his lungs, causing all in the vicinity to turn and stare at him. "Just shut up and go away! I don't want you to be here! Just . . . *leave!*"

And Charlie took off, hobbling down the mine as fast as he could, crawling under the nearest outcrop of rock that he could find.

Leonidas took a deep breath. Although he could feel his frustration at Charlie's attitude boiling in his stomach, he knew that in this case, he had to be the bigger man. From what Stan had told him, Charlie was usually calm, collected and even timid. In other words, miles from what he had just witnessed. Something was very wrong, and Leonidas was going to find out what.

Slowly, he crept over to the edge of the cave, to the outside of the stone-block dimple in the wall. As he peeked into the crack, he was surprised to see that Charlie was actually crawling awkwardly out of the hole. Leonidas stepped back as Charlie grabbed on to the cave wall and pulled himself to his feet, bearing his full body weight on his good leg. He looked up at Leonidas, eyes still slightly red, but a tired, apologetic look on his face.

"Sorry," Charlie mumbled, unable to meet Leonidas's eyes. "Look at me, what I've become . . . screaming, throwing a fit, running away and hiding in a cave . . . pathetic . . ."

"Charlie, I know that ya don't think highly of me," Leonidas said hastily, unwilling to acknowledge that what Charlie had just said was true. "Maybe you're having a hard time forgivin' me for the things I did in the past . . . maybe it's something else I did, I dunno. But trust me, man . . . I'm not just some idiot who's only good for a fight, I've got a brain, too, and I've seen a lotta crap since I've joined Elementia. If you're willing to talk, I wanna do what I can to help ya. So please, Charlie . . . can ya tell me what's wrong?"

Charlie sighed. "I don't have a problem with *you*, Leonidas. . . . Well, I mean, I do, but it's not a real problem. It's totally unfair to you, and I know that. . . ."

"Tell me."

"It's just . . . ever since you joined us, you've been nothing but amazing. You've helped us fight, you've talked with us, you've become a part of our group. Everybody loves you, and I was just really jealous of that – the fact that you've done terrible things in the past, but you're one of our greatest assets now. For me, it's exactly the opposite. I mean, look at me. I can barely walk, let alone fight, and . . . since I was imprisoned, I've really hurt our cause. And now there's nothing I can do to fix it."

"What're you talking about?" exclaimed Leonidas, taken aback. "I mean . . . OK, man, I'm gonna level with you. Since we've met, ya haven't been very helpful to us in the fightin' department, but you've done other stuff! I mean, it was your idea to tunnel under the wall to get into Element City! Where's this idea that you've done more bad for us than good comin' from?"

Charlie looked Leonidas in the face. "Leonidas, can I tell you something? And if I do, do you swear you won't tell anybody else?"

"Sure, man," Leonidas replied, genuinely concerned now. "What is it?"

Charlie took a deep breath. There were tears streaming down his face, and his features expressed more pain and disappointment in himself than Leonidas had ever seen. There was a moment of silence, only broken by the scuffle of troops down the cave preparing for battle, as Charlie prepared to reveal his darkest secret.

"I'm the reason that the Noctem Alliance found this cave. I told Drake where the entrance was when he was torturing me on the Mushroom Islands."

Leonidas's jaw dropped. He looked at Charlie, hardly able

to believe what he had just heard, as Charlie rambled on, sobs interspersed with his choked-up speech now.

"I didn't want to. . . I held out for as long as I could, trying to endure the pain that those savages put me through in that prison. The last thing I wanted was to give them what they wanted, our secret war plans . . . but then they started on my legs . . . it was unbearable, Leonidas. They forced my legs into a pit full of silverfish and told me that the only way out was to tell them where the secret bunker was . . . the little monsters started to chew at my legs, gnawing away . . . it was too much, I had to make it stop. . . so I told them.

"I should've held out. I should've died, rather than tell them where the bunker was. I mean, Crunch held out fine. He just shook it off, the way I couldn't. . . And now, because of me, we're all in danger. They forced us to move before we were ready, and throw together this half-baked assault that'll cause who knows how many of our fighters to die. And I can't even fight on the battlefield alongside my friends to make up for my mistake."

As Charlie finished, Leonidas stared at him. He was utterly speechless. There was no anger in the stare, no exasperation, not even shock. Only sympathy shone on Leonidas's face as he absorbed everything that Charlie had just told him.

Charlie said nothing. He looked down at the ground

again, gave a heavy sigh, and proceeded to limp away from the crack in the cave wall towards Ben and Bob, leaving Leonidas standing alone.

"Look at them all."

"I'm sorry?" Cassandrix replied, looking up from the iron boots she was pulling on to look over at Kat, who was already armoured up with Rex sitting beside her, watching a large group of players load up their own gear. Judging by their mostly leather armor, they were lower-level players. Despite the fact that the army had distributed the armour for the battle, it had somehow occurred that the lower-level players had gotten the weaker armour (not that Kat or anyone else had time to fix this inequity).

"I can't believe that those players are being forced into combat," Kat replied sadly.

"They haven't been forced!" Cassandrix replied vehemently. "Bob and Ben have made it very clear that only the soldiers are required to take part in the invasion. All others are volunteers. Those players wouldn't be part of the invasion if they didn't want to be."

"Yeah, well, they might as well have been forced into it," Kat spat in disgust. "I mean, sure, we didn't outright say that they had to, but what would happen if we lose? What would happen to the lower-level players? What would they have to come back to? Face it, Cassandrix, those players aren't fighting because they want to. They're fighting because they're afraid of what will happen if they don't."

"Honestly, darling," Cassandrix laughed, rolling her eyes. Kat's ears perked up in alarm, as they did whenever Cassandrix used the word *darling*. "You're acting like putting lower-level players into combat is the worst thing in the world . . . as if the little brats shouldn't have to fight, just because they're new and inexperienced. Well, Kat, darling, I have a question for you: if they don't fight, then however are they going to *gain* experience?"

There was a moment of silence as Kat stared at Cassandrix.

"Exactly," Cassandrix continued. "You need to stop holding the hands of the lower-level players, Kat, or they'll never learn anything for themselves. Why, I never had a group of upper-level players looking after me when I first joined Elementia – there *were* no upper-level players! But did that stop me from taking part in the Terramist War? No, of course not! I fought that war, and in doing so, not only did I help to establish the original Kingdom of Elementia, but I also learned the skills of Minecraft by myself!"

Cassandrix looked smugly at Kat, as if positive that there would be nothing that Kat could say that would pass over her insurmountable wall of logic. However, Kat merely returned a knowing smile.

"So, let me get this straight, Cassandrix: You took part in a war when you were a new player, and that's how you learned to fight so well?"

"That is correct, dear."

"OK, OK. And Cassandrix . . . during that war . . . how many times did you die, and spawn back in your warm, comfortable bed?"

"Well . . . to be honest, there was more than one time that I found myself dead, and respawned."

"And if you were in that same scenario today – if you were a new player, and you took part in a war with no combat experience – what would happen to you if you died?"

There was no reply. They both knew what happened if a player was killed in Elementia today.

"Cassandrix, I have no problem with the way that you learned how to play Minecraft, and I even see where you're coming from," Kat said pointedly, "but the world has changed. The rules of the server are different from when you were a new player. If new players today make one wrong move, they'll be kicked out of Elementia with no second chance, so I don't see the harm in helping them out a bit. Just keep that in mind."

And with that, Kat stood up and walked down the tunnel towards the makeshift armoury, Rex following behind her, leaving a speechless Cassandrix in their wake.

All throughout the night, preparations went on for the invasion of the Adorian Village. By morning, everyone was ready. All leaders, soldiers and volunteers were brimming with armour and weaponry. Charlie was staying behind in the cave, to watch over those players who didn't have enough armour, or were too weak from hunger to fight. At the break of dawn (according to the single golden clock that somebody had managed to take into the underground with them), the fighting forces of Elementia congregated around a section of cave wall. This particular wall was covered with ladders leading up to the roof of the cave. The group of players was clustered around one specific ladder that had been designated the night before.

Before long, a cheer erupted from the crowd. President Stan was climbing the selected ladder, and when he reached the halfway point, he jumped off and onto a nearby ledge of coal ore blocks that was jutting out from the wall. He was wearing a smile ear to ear. In the night, a wonderful, unexpected surprise had befallen them, which he was happy to share with his citizens who were as of yet unaware.

"My citizens, at long last, the day that we've been awaiting for weeks is finally here. In a few minutes, we will burst into the Adorian Village, swarm the streets and drive the forces of the Noctem Alliance out, taking a giant leap towards returning control of Elementia to its rightful, elected rulers!"

Another round of applause and shouts of admiration erupted from the crowd.

"I cannot thank you enough for your patience, endurance and valour, my citizens. I am fully aware of how difficult your lives have been since the Noctem Alliance declared war on Elementia months ago. However, by the end of today, all our pain and toil will finally come to fruition when we raise the colours of Elementia over the Town Hall of the Adorian Village!

"Now, my citizens," Stan continued, the roar of the crowd dying instantly as they realized he had more to say, "I have a very exciting announcement. In the middle of the night, a very special player came to us. He arrived in our cave after trekking for days across the server, avoiding Noctem forces, and taking another few days to find the entrance to our cave. He is a good friend of mine, and a loyal leader of yours. Ladies and gentlemen, please welcome back Councilman Jayden!"

The applause rumbled through the cave as Jayden climbed up the ladder and took his place on the ledge next to Stan. It was amazing, he thought, that so many of the people were happy to see him. Most of them hardly knew who he was, yet they were as excited to see him as Stan, Kat, Charlie and the others had been the previous night. He supposed that

that was simply an added benefit of being friends with Stan.

"OK now, everybody be quiet!" Stan commanded, and the crowd immediately complied. "Councilman Jayden has agreed to join our assault as a general, even after his long journey. As such, you are to do what he says and follow his commands the same as you would myself or any of my comrades. Now, prepare to mobilize, troops. When I give the signal, swarm up the ladders, through the ground, and into the streets!"

And with that, Stan climbed up the ladder, Jayden directly below him, ascending higher and higher towards the roof of the cave and leaving the electric energy of the troops below him as he vanished into the dark belfry of the cave.

After Stan had been totally enveloped by the darkness in the upper dome of the cave, it wasn't long until he reached the ceiling above him. He looked upwards and aimed a punch at the block directly overhead. The sound of his fist on the wooden block reverberated through the spacious cave, sending the scattered bats that had been nesting in the darkness flying down to where he had just come from.

Stan looked down at Jayden, who was still clinging to the ladder beneath his feet. "Give me the potion," he ordered.

Jayden complied, reaching into his inventory and handing it up to Stan, who pocketed it carefully. Aside from the joy that Jayden's return had brought to Stan and his friends, they were also elated that he had managed to sneak a few potions out of Nocturia. The Potions of Slowness, in particular, were of vital importance to the first part of their plan.

Stan drew out a diamond axe, and for a moment, he allowed himself to relish in the feeling of completion that washed over him as he held his choice weapon once again. DZ's diamond sword (now sitting in a chest in the mine; he had plans for it later) had served him well on his odyssey to return to Elementia, but there was no feeling in the world like having an axe clutched in his hand. Wasting no more time, Stan drew back the axe and shattered the wood block above him in two strokes.

He pulled himself up and through the opening and found himself in the main room of a house. Stan grinned. Charlie's aim had been spot on when he had calculated where to dig the hole. Stan turned around and pulled Jayden out of the hole, and they surveyed the house. It was plain, with hardly any outstanding features, just a cobblestone counter with a dispenser on it, some potted plants and wood plank–block walls with glass window panes. Outside the windows, Stan could see the streets of the Adorian Village.

This was Stan's first time in the village since it was reopened, and very little had changed in that time. After the Battle for Elementia, Stan had immediately delegated a team to rebuild the burned-down village. It looked largely the same now as it did then – houses similar to those in an NPC village, gravel roadways and a brick Town Hall in the centre. However, there were two major differences that struck Stan as he surveyed the village in the early light of dawn.

The first was the wall. Thinking that it was wise to defend the village against any more attackers, Stan had ordered a cobblestone wall to be built around the village, fortified with the Mechanist's redstone defences (though not nearly as impenetrable as the Element City wall had been). Stan could see the top of the wall over the houses of the village. Several Noctem troopers were patrolling the top of the barricade, their black armour silhouetted against the sunrise. That was the second change. Even at this early hour, Stan could see Noctem soldiers standing guard at the corners of the stone-block side-walks, and platoons of troops marching through the streets.

Suddenly, Stan became acutely aware of footsteps over his head. He turned around just as a player burst into the room from up a flight of wooden stairs that he hadn't noticed before. This player was skinned as if she was planning on attending a disco party, with a tie-dye shirt, pink shorts and rainbow tights. The bright colours bore a sharp contrast to the black tunic on her head.

"Who do you think you—" she started to demand, but was cut off when the bottle of potion Stan had thrown shat-tered on her face. Slowly, her eyes slid out of focus, and a slurred "intruders" slid out of her mouth before she slumped to the ground, unconscious. Stan was relieved that the potions Jayden had snagged were so strong; they had plenty of time to take her back down into the mine and imprison her until the battle was over.

Stan gestured to Jayden, who hoisted the limp body of the unconscious player over his shoulder and descended back into the mine. Moments later, he re-emerged, and a line of other players followed him up the ladder and into the house.

"Charlie's got her in a holding prison, along with all the others we had to knock out," Jayden said to Stan. "Phase one went off without a hitch. We now have troops in houses all over the village, and when you give the signal, we attack."

Stan was beside himself. He couldn't believe that the plan was progressing so flawlessly. He reminded himself to thank Charlie the next time they met up; without his amazing mining prowess, they never would've been able to calculate so precisely where to make the tunnels. Stan's only regret was that they hadn't been able to dig under the Town Hall, which was their primary target – the floor was made of obsidian. However, that was a minor concern. With an ambush this size, Stan was confident that they would be able to overpower the Noctem forces; after all, most of them were still in Element City, according to their spies.

He realized, with a start, that he was being watched; the eyes of all soldiers in the room were fixated on Stan, awaiting his command. Stan took a deep breath and drew his axe. The time had come to take back the Adorian Village.

"Give the word to start the assault!" Stan bellowed down into the hole they had just climbed out of.

"Roger that!" Charlie's voice echoed up out of the mines.

Within seconds, Stan could hear yells and shouts outside, immediately followed by the clash of blades and a series of explosions. With a war cry, the soldiers in his house rushed out the door, Jayden at the helm. With one last deep breath, Stan let out his own battle cry as he charged out into the streets.

It was pandemonium. The Noctem soldiers in the city were totally blindsided, completely unprepared to deal with a wave of over a hundred republic fighters at once. Many drew their weapons to fight, only to instantly be killed by the republic soldiers, whose adrenaline levels had been inflated to the maximum in anticipation of the attack. Most of the Noctems realized that there was no sense in fighting, and instead fell back towards the centre of the city, as if the Town Hall was a huge magnet that was drawing them in.

"Don't follow them!" Stan cried out, as his soldiers sprinted back and forth around him as if he were standing in the centre of a highway during rush hour. "Spread out and occupy the streets! We need to establish a presence across the entire village if we're going to secure it!"

Stan looked around, and his eyes landed on Kat, who was busy telling her troops where they were to go. He jogged over to meet her.

"Hey!" he panted as he reached her. "So far so good, I'd say."

"Yeah," she agreed as she looked around, surveying the distribution of the republic troops through the streets. "We're lucky this village isn't very big. There aren't that many streets to occupy."

"True," Stan said hastily. "Come on, we've got to hurry. They're all falling back to the Town Hall. That's probably where they're going to mount most of their defences. We've got to get over there fast, before they dig in their heels too deep."

"Right," Kat nodded. "You grab a group of players and get to the Town Hall. I'll grab everyone else to help you."

"Sounds good!" yelled Stan, already taking off to a mass of troops. They were standing in the middle of the road, weapons drawn, on standby and waiting for orders from the commanders.

"Come on!" Stan cried, and all the fighters turned to look at him. "Follow me to the Town Hall!"

The giant mass of players proceeded to run behind Stan as he hustled down the main road of the Adorian Village. All the houses now appeared to be empty, and the streets were deserted except for Stan and his men as they rushed into battle. Before long, they burst into the town square and laid eyes on the Town Hall.

The brick-block structure stood proudly in the centre of the Adorian Village; while not a particularly tall building, it still towered over the other structures in the humble town. Stan watched as the last of the Noctem troops rushed through the iron double doors of the building. When the last of them had entered, the doors slammed shut, and the whir of redstone mechanics began to hum in Stan's ears. An instant later, the gravel around the base of the brick building sunk down, revealing a moat of lava ten blocks thick that stretched around the entirety of the Town Hall.

Stan was simultaneously impressed and infuriated. The Noctems had clearly been well trained in what to do in case of a surprise attack, and it wouldn't surprise him if the interior of the Town Hall was laced with booby traps, making it extremely difficult to break into.

Suddenly, alarm bells went off in his head as Stan realized that the Noctems were now standing on top of the Town Hall. Bows were drawn, fire charges and potions were held in their hands, and TNT cannons were being aimed down at Stan and his men, loaded and prepared to fire. However, Stan's eye was immediately drawn to the men who were standing with buckets of molten lava. All together, they tipped over their lava buckets, attaching source blocks of lava to the outside of the building. An infinite flow of lava began to rush out of the source blocks, pouring down the side of the Town Hall and eventually into the lava moat below.

The Town Hall now stood surrounded in lava, the molten liquid covering the base in an impenetrable wall of liquid fire. Stan had to give credit where credit was due; this was a superb plan. He certainly wouldn't be able to get in there without the fight of his life.

"Stan! What happened here?"

Stan turned around and saw Kat, Rex, Leonidas, Commander Crunch, Cassandrix, the Mechanist, Ben and Sirus, with the entire invasion force behind them. All were staring in awe at the giant cube of molten liquid that was the Town Hall.

"I'll tell you what happened," Stan replied gravely. "They've just set up one of the best defenses I've ever seen. I have no idea how we're going to get in there now."

"Aye, leave it t' me, laddies," Commander Crunch growled, a grin on his face and a manic glint in his eye. "I've seen this before. I know how we be gettin' past that wall o' lava."

"You've seen this before?" Ben demanded incredulously.

"Eleven times, as a matter o' fact. Now *charge!*"

And with that, Commander Crunch drew his sword and rushed forwards, directly towards the lava moat. A large chunk of the mass of troops broke off and followed after him, charging directly towards the bastille of fire. It wasn't long before arrows and fire charges started to rain down from the roof into the mass of oncoming troops, and the blasts of the TNT cannons started to follow.

"Come on, let's cover him!" Cassandrix cried, and with that, all the remaining troops drew their bows, and started to rain arrows onto the roof of the Town Hall. As they did, the fire from above spread out, now reaching them as well as Commander Crunch's troops. Stan's soldiers found that they had to spread out and encircle the Town Hall, so they could continue with their suppressive fire and not be a massive target.

"This would be so much easier if we could just blow our way in there," the Mechanist said, as he let loose another arrow. He turned to Ben, who was fighting next to him. "I don't suppose anybody has any TNT or redstone on hand?"

"No," Ben said back, harsher than the Mechanist was expecting. "We used it all up while we were making the bunker." He drew another arrow, targeting the operator of one of the TNT cannons on the roof. He fired his bow, only to miss.

"Not that you would know," he grumbled under his breath as he loaded another arrow. Though it was soft, the Mechanist heard this, and gave a great sigh as he loaded another arrow.

Commander Crunch's men were nearly at the wall of the Town Hall now. They had pulled cobblestone blocks out of their inventories and were building a narrow bridge across the lava moat. Each time one of the soldiers was hit by an arrow and knocked into the lava, another would step forwards to take his place. Commander Crunch stood at the front, sword drawn, spinning it around like an expert as he deflected the arrows that were flying out of the lava flow and directly at them. Although these arrows made building the bridge very difficult, Commander Crunch was glad that the Noctem Troops were firing at them from within the building.

If they weren't, he would never be able to figure out where the doors were, as they were hidden behind the flow of lava.

Finally, the bridge reached the wall. Commander Crunch spun his sword around like a helicopter, deflecting all the arrows that he could, and even then allowing some to glance off his iron chestplate or fly back into the horde of soldiers. This created an opportunity for a soldier behind him to reach up and place two cobblestone blocks on the wall above Commander Crunch's head. Instantly, the lava parted over the two blocks and was diverted to the sides, opening up a gap in the lavafall. Behind the gap were two open iron doors through which the arrows were flying.

The second the doors were no longer covered by lava, a flow of Noctem troops started to flow out to attack Commander Crunch and his men. Sensing that now was the time to help, Stan shouted an order back to his men and sprinted towards the cobblestone bridge. As he ran across the open gravel road, the firestorm of arrows, fire charges and TNT blocks intensified, but Stan pressed onwards, knowing that all they had to do was get inside the building to escape the onslaught from above.

Finally, they reached the bridge, and didn't break pace as they dashed down the two-block-wide cobblestone passage. As they approached the Town Hall, Stan could see the fighting going on inside, but he could also see something that made his heart stop. There, at the end of the bridge alongside the inventories of those who had been killed, lay Commander Crunch, his hand clenched to his stomach and his shattered iron chestplate beside him. Stan gestured for the rest of his men to sprint inside and join the fight, but he knelt down beside Commander Crunch.

"Are you OK?" Stan asked desperately.

"Aye, lad, I'll be fine," Commander Crunch grunted with a grimace. "'Tis jus' a flesh wound . . ."

"Here, let me see it . . ."

Commander Crunch winced as he moved his hands away from his stomach, revealing a gash that appeared to be from a sword slash. Stan's heart started to race; they had no medical supplies on hand to heal him with.

"Stan, go on 'n' fight," Commander Crunch said in a surprisingly hearty voice. "I promise ye, I'll live. I've survived worse than this. I'll jus' stay here till ye can find me some medicine."

Still worried, yet also reassured by Crunch's insanely upbeat demeanour, Stan nodded and took off into the Town Hall, leaving the wounded commander in his wake.

The fighting in the main hallway of the Town Hall was intense. While the Noctem troops were vastly outnumbered, they were also far better equipped. Stan's eyes locked on to one Noctem soldier who let loose a Splash Potion of

Weakness, causing all five republic soldiers he was fighting to wince and fall to their knees.

Right as the soldier was about to finish them off, Stan intervened, catching the soldier off guard and knocking his diamond pickaxe out of his hand, and sinking his diamond axe into his chest in the next swing. Stan's soldiers, still dazed by the potion, looked up at him gratefully. Stan called another soldier from down the hall to defend them until the potion wore off.

Stan looked around, and before long, his eyes caught sight of Kat. She was just making her way into the Town Hall, fighting off an attacking Noctem soldier as she did so. It wasn't long before she stuck her diamond sword in the player's chest and burst into the hall, Jayden right behind her. Stan dodged and weaved through the fights going on around him to meet up with them.

"We're gonna need more soldiers in here if we're gonna overpower them!" Stan cried out.

"We can't get any more in right now!" Kat cried out over an explosion from somewhere above them, as Rex tackled a Noctem soldier who jumped out at her. "They're laying down too much suppressive fire for us to get any more troops into the building!"

"Then we've gotta take out those archers and TNT cannons!" Stan replied, turning around and setting his eyes on a stairway at the end of the main hall. "Come with me! You, too, Jayden!"

Kat and Jayden nodded and followed Stan down the hall. A few Noctem troops tried to attack the three councilmen, but the trio made short work of them. As they reached the staircase, Stan turned around and saw that more and more Noctem troops were pouring out of the side doors in the hallways and joining the battle; the republic troops were getting slaughtered. Stan took a deep breath and, telling himself that shutting down the Noctems on the roof was the only way to save his people, he sprinted up the staircase, Kat, Rex and Jayden following behind him. He turned a few corners, ignoring the doors that were next to the stairs on the way up, and before long he burst onto the roof. What he saw made his jaw drop in shock as Rex started to whimper.

The roof of the Town Hall was covered with dead players. Fallen bodies were despawning all around, leaving piles of items in their wakes. Bows, arrows, potions and fire charges were scattered haphazardly around the outside edges of the brick-block floor, and the brick TNT cannons sat unmanned. There were no Noctem troops at all remaining on the roof. Instead, standing in the midst of the carnage were the members of ELM. Arachnia stood staring at Stan with a wild grin on her face, while Creeper Khan and Lord Marrow stood menacingly behind her.

Stan panicked; he hadn't been expecting them to be here, and he knew that the three of them couldn't take down these assassins alone. He turned around, ready to sprint back down the stairs. Just as he took his first step, there was a burst of purple smoke between him and the stairs as Enderchick appeared, an amused look on her face and a diamond sword raised. The three players and the wolf were trapped on the roof.

Instinctively, Stan, Kat and Jayden all drew their weapons, and stood back to back, Rex in between them, snarling. Stan was looking at Arachnia.

"What's going on here?" Stan demanded, glaring at Arachnia and trying not to let on how terrified he was of a four-on-three fight against these modded players. "Why are all the Noctem troops dead?"

"Why, we killed them, of course," Arachnia replied with a chuckle, drawing her diamond sword and examining her reflection in it nonchalantly.

"What? Why would you—"

"Because, Stan, we are no longer under the employment of the Noctem Alliance. You've managed to slip out of our grasp enough times that Lord Tenebris dismissed us."

She gave a sly chuckle. "Just think how foolish he's going to feel when we capture you before he does."

"If you want him, you're gonna have to go through us

first!" Kat shouted, brandishing her sword, as Jayden gave a hearty nod of agreement and Rex gave an aggressive bark.

"Well, if you insist!" Creeper Khan exclaimed as he aimed a punch in midair directly at Stan. He recognized this motion from his training with Sally, and he instantly knew what was coming.

"Get down!" he bellowed, tackling Kat and Jayden out of the way as the ground beneath them exploded, leaving a gaping hole in the brick-block roof of the Town Hall, through which people could be seen battling below.

"Stop that!" Arachnia yelled, whipping around to face Creeper Khan. "Stan has to be alive. You've got to be more careful! Leave him to me and Lord Marrow . . . Enderchick, help him take out the other two."

And with that, Enderchick raised her diamond sword and charged at Jayden, the closest target, while Lord Marrow drew an arrow in his bow and fired it at Stan's heart.

Stan leaped forwards and deflected the arrow, just as Jayden locked his axe with Enderchick's sword, while Kat and Rex turned to face Creeper Khan. The arrow fell to the ground, and Stan could see that it was smoking. His eyes widened as he realized that the arrow must have been hacked to have the effect of a Potion of Weakness; if one hit him, he would fall unconscious. He knocked another arrow to the side with his axe, then raised it yet again to counter the diamond sword that Arachnia had jabbed at him.

Two blades clashed over and over, but Stan was surprised to see that Arachnia was hardly trying to attack him at all. Rather, she seemed to launch a quick strike, and when Stan blocked it, she would dodge his counterattack and move around until she saw another opening, not even trying to follow up. On one such strike, Stan saw that her sword, too, was trailing grey smoke. Stan was shocked, and suddenly realized that if either Lord Marrow or Arachnia landed one hit on him, he would be knocked unconscious.

And Lord Marrow was continuing to fire at him. It was nearly impossible to block his arrows while fighting Arachnia at the same time, and even with Stan's legendary fighting skills, there were still too many close misses for comfort. Stan knew that it was only a matter of time before one of them got lucky, and he had to find a way to stop it.

A risky idea popped into his head, and, not seeing any alternatives, Stan decided to go for it. The next time Arachnia emerged for a sword strike, Stan countered, but didn't let her go. Instead, he pressed into her blade, trying to overpower her. Arachnia pressed back, clearly having the superior leverage; her blade started to slide slowly down the wood of Stan's axe, toward his hand. From the corner of his eye, Stan saw Lord Marrow about to fire. Right as Arachnia's blade was about to cut into his hand, Stan dropped his weapon, catching the mobhunter off guard as he slammed into her, sending her careening to the side and directly into Lord Marrow's oncoming arrow. His projectile sunk into her shoulder blade, and she instantly slumped to the ground, unconscious.

Stan raised his axe, preparing to finish the job, but suddenly had to hop away from more of Lord Marrow's arrows. He had been trying to shoot Stan while avoiding Arachnia, aiming carefully, but now that Arachnia was down for the count, there was nothing to stop him from firing an almost machine-gun-like stream of arrows at Stan. He raised his axe to defend himself, but still found he had to dash around in unpredictable patterns to avoid getting hit.

Realizing that he was getting nowhere, Lord Marrow went for a different approach. He began to fire different types of arrows, which erupted into fire the moment they touched the ground. Stan found himself cut off by the flames, and with limited space to manoeuvre, it was only a matter of seconds before a fiery arrow collided with his chestplate. A miniature explosion erupted directly in front of him and knocked him to the edge of the roof, his head slamming into the ground.

In a daze, Stan could barely make out what was around him. He was only aware that his chestplate was still on fire. He could barely make out the form of Lord Marrow walking up to him, notching an arrow that was leaking grey smoke, and taking aim at a kink in his armour. Stan was in too much pain to move or do anything to stop him from firing.

But Lord Marrow didn't fire. Without warning, his eyes slid out of focus, and he fell forwards onto the ground, unconscious with a sizable mark on the back of his head. His amazement overpowering his pain, Stan looked up to see who it was who had saved him.

There, silhouetted against the now-rising sun, dirty and torn up, a diamond pickaxe in his hand and a giant smile on his face, stood G. He reached down to help Stan to his feet.

"G . . ." Stan managed to get out, slurring his words from his pain, "What're . . . you doing here?"

"Oh, I was just in the neighborhood, and I figured I'd help you guys out," G replied, his grin widening. "Well, I mean, I wasn't just passing through . . . I kind of travelled half-way across the server to get to this particular neighborhood. Dude, you're hurt pretty badly. Drink this, I stole it from Nocturia."

G produced a Potion of Healing from his inventory, which Stan graciously drank. Immediately, his head cleared, and he was able to think complete thoughts again. Aware that his chestplate was still on fire, Stan ripped it off, tossing it over the edge of the roof and into the lava moat below.

"G, it's awesome to see you again," Stan said hastily, "but we can catch up in a minute. We've gotta take out those two over there!" He pointed over to Creeper Khan and Enderchick, who appeared to be getting the upper hand on Kat, Rex and Jayden.

G merely smiled even wider. "Don't worry about it, man . . . my friends'll take care of it." And with that, G put his hand to his mouth and gave a loud whistle.

Within a few seconds, the air above them was filled with Ender Pearls, tossed from the ground below. As they landed, the rooftop was flooded with players, all dressed in tattered Elementia Army uniforms and carrying stone weapons. Stan's heart leaped, but he saved the question of where these soldiers had come from for later. He stepped forwards to the centre of the mass of players that was now converging around the members of ELM.

Enderchick and Creeper Khan stood in defensive stances, looking wildly at the horde of players, as Arachnia and Lord Marrow lay unconscious behind them. Enderchick looked desperate and panicked, but Creeper Khan's eyes were closed, a pensive look on his face. Then, he opened them, and stepped forwards.

"Stand down!" Stan yelled at them, stepping forwards and raising his axe. "You're outnumbered, and I know that all of you can't teleport away at the same time!"

"You're right, **President** Stan," replied Creeper Khan with no emotion whatsoever, and suddenly, he started to glow. A dim red light radiated from his skin, casting a red filter over his Creeper-like face. Enderchick stared at him for a moment, as if trying to figure out what was going on, until suddenly, her mouth fell open in horror.

"What?" Enderchick cried. "Khan . . . you . . . you, like, *can't* be serious!"

"My mind's made up," he replied, not even bothering turning around to face her. "Get the others out of here, Enderchick."

Enderchick gave a sniffle, a tear running down her cheeks, as she grabbed the unconscious forms of Lord Marrow and Arachnia. Realizing what they were about to do, Stan yelled, "Shoot her!" and pointed at Enderchick, but it was too late. The trio disappeared in a puff of purple smoke, as the arrows cut through the violet haze and bounced off the brick blocks below.

"What're you doing?" Stan demanded, terrified to see that the red light now radiating from Creeper Khan was growing stronger and stronger. "Stand down right now, and we'll spare your life."

"It doesn't matter now," Creeper Khan said, looking Stan directly in the eye. "I've decided that it's time for us both to die, Stan. There's nothing either of us can do about it now."

"What . . . what does that mean?" Stan demanded.

"I've decided to use my Final Nova," Creeper Khan replied in a monotone. "In twenty seconds, my body is going to explode into the biggest blast that Minecraft has ever seen.

Nothing will be left of this village except a crater. The Elite Legion of Mobhunters may have been unable to take you prisoner and become rich beyond our wildest dreams, Stan, but that won't stop me from destroying you and everything you hold most dear."

"Kill him!" Stan shouted in horror. A barrage of arrows flew from the crowd of people only to bounce off Creeper Khan as if he were wearing armour with Projectile Protection.

"Nice try!" Creeper Khan said loudly, a deranged smile on his face. "Now that I've used my Final Nova, I can't be killed until I explode! There's nothing you can do to stop me!" And with that, he laughed maniacally.

Stan stood in place, totally stunned and unsure what to do. If Khan was telling the truth, then the explosion was less than ten seconds away. The entire Adorian Village would be destroyed. There was nothing that could be done. Stan's mind was frozen. He stood as still as a statue, completely at a loss as he tried to comprehend what was happening.

Suddenly, Stan heard a commotion in the crowd. G stepped forward from amid the throng of people and stood opposite Creeper Khan. He had a determined look on his face, and a tear running down his cheek.

"G!" a cry erupted from the mass of stupefied Elementia soldiers, as Jayden burst into the clearing, Kat right behind him. "What're you doing?"

G closed his eyes, took a deep breath, and opened them again, before saying, "I'm doing what has to be done."

He turned around to face his fellow councilmen, a sad smile on his face opposite the stunned confusion on theirs.

"Jayden," he said, turning to face his best friend, "thank you. For everything."

He turned his head slightly to the left, and his eyes met Kat's. There was a moment of silence, broken only by Creeper Khan's ongoing laughter and the sounds of battle from below them, as the two players held each other's gaze.

"Kat . . . I'm sorry. I hope that you can forgive me for everything I've done."

And then, without waiting for a response, before either Jayden or Kat could ask what G meant, G turned around and drew out his diamond pickaxe. With no hesitation, he took off, sprinting at top speed toward Creeper Khan, who was still laughing like a lunatic. By the time he realized what was about to hit him, it was too late.

G slammed into the mobhunter like a truck, his pickaxe sinking deep into Creeper Khan's chest. The two players tumbled backwards, across the roof. G was holding Creeper Khan in a bear hug to prevent his escape, and he made no attempt to stop as the pair of players plunged off the roof and over the waterfall of lava.

"*Nooooooo!*" Jayden cried, finally freed from his trance as he rushed over the edge of the bridge as quickly as he could, horror etched into every square inch of his face. He reached the edge just in time to see his best friend vanish into the moat of lava below, still clutching Creeper Khan as if his life depended on it.

Jayden found himself staring without comprehension into the lava pit for a few seconds before the explosion went off. Stan managed to grab Jayden by the back of the neck and pull him away from the edge just before he would have been burned to a crisp by the massive spray of lava that rose up out of the moat.

The noise was deafening, and all the players on the roof found themselves knocked to the ground by the massive magnitude of Creeper Khan's suicide attack. The ground below them shook like an earthquake, and the sounds of screaming could be heard as the supernova explosion rocked the Adorian Village to its core.

Then, just as quickly as it had started, the tumult stopped. Stan was lying on the ground, terrified to move, and only aware of one sound – the sound of sobbing beside him. Stan dared to move his head, only to see Jayden, sprawled out on the ground, crying his eyes out. Slowly, Stan pulled himself to his knees, and then to his feet. He felt shaky, and had to work to keep his balance, but it seemed like there had been no permanent damage to him from the blast.

Stan looked around, still feeling slightly dazed from the explosion and saw, to his amazement, other players getting up around him. Miraculously, it seemed that Creeper Khan's final attack hadn't killed a single player on the rooftop. Stan made his way to the edge of the roof and looked over the side. It wasn't what he saw that made Stan question what appeared before his eyes – it was what he didn't see.

The explosion, which, based on the shockwaves that it had sent through the ground, was the biggest explosion that Stan had ever witnessed in Minecraft, had hardly done any damage at all. The moat of lava was still intact, as was the flow of lava cascading down the side of the Town Hall. The only indication of the blast that he could see was a few dis-lodged dirt blocks next to the lava moat, into which the lava moat was now spilling over. Slowly but surely, Stan realized that the lava must have cushioned the explosion, and by sending Creeper Khan into the moat, G had just saved all of their lives.

As this thought crossed Stan's mind, it suddenly dawned on him what had happened to G. G was dead.

Stan suddenly felt like a fist of ice was clenching his heart. He hadn't seen G in so long . . . not since he had left for Nocturia all those weeks ago. And now, in a blink of an eye, before Stan had even had a chance to ask him how he'd been . . . G was gone, banished from Elementia. As this fact washed over Stan, it dawned on him that of all the players who had taught him the ins and outs of Minecraft, right here in this village back when his level was in the single digits, Jayden was the only one remaining.

Stan looked over at Jayden. He was still on the ground, beside himself with grief. Stan's heart swelled with sympathy – this player had lost his three closest friends in Minecraft, and was now all alone in the world. Stan couldn't imagine how he felt. It would be like if he lost Kat, or Charlie.

As much as he longed to go over to Jayden and comfort him, he hardened his heart as he realized what had to be done. They were still in the midst of a battle. They had a job to finish. And so, Stan commanded his troops to follow him back down the stairway and into the Town Hall.

Jayden didn't even notice that they were gone. He didn't notice the smoke from the explosion dying down and blowing away. He didn't hear the gasps of disbelief from below him as Stan's troops found that most of the Noctems had been taken out by the explosion. He didn't acknowledge the hoots and cheers going on below them, in celebration of the fact that the Adorian Village now belonged to Stan and the Elementia soldiers. And he didn't notice as Kat climbed back up the staircase and joined him on the roof.

Rex immediately turned his focus to Jayden, offering himself to be pet. Kat didn't comfort Jayden, though; there would be time for that later. Instead, she made her way over to the edge of the Town Hall. For the first time, she looked down at the moat, the damage on the gravel shoreline and the lava waterfall that she knew was hiding massive internal damage to the Town Hall.

She had come within an inch of death today. They all had. Creeper Khan might have destroyed the entire Adorian Village in the blink of an eye if it weren't for the player who had gone down with him.

As G had turned to Kat, and spoken the last words that he would ever say on the Minecraft server Elementia, she had recognized something in his voice. It was something that she hadn't been ready for, something unexpected and something amazing. What she had heard was sincerity.

G was sorry for what he had done to her. She had heard it in his voice, had seen it in his eyes. And he had sacrificed himself for the sake of all of them. Kat looked into the settling cloud of smoke that still hung in the air, and a single tear rolled down her cheek, falling from her face and landing silently in the lava moat far below her.

"Thank you," she whispered.

And with that, Kat turned around, took a deep breath, and walked over to Jayden, prepared to comfort him.

I t was an hour before the Adorian Village was under the full control of the citizens of Elementia. The wall around the village perimeter was occupied by Stan's troops, and the few Noctem soldiers that hadn't been killed in the battle were now imprisoned under strict supervision in the hotel. The lava flowing off the Town Hall had been removed, revealing the war-torn skeleton of a brick-block building beneath. Stan didn't really care about the Town Hall, though; he was much more interested in the storehouses.

Since he had last been to the Adorian Village ages ago, several storehouses had been constructed of brick blocks. They stretched across one side of the Adorian Village, stuffed to the brim with food, materials, medicine, weaponry and everything in between. Materials had been distributed to all the republic fighters within a day of breaking into these warehouses. The soldiers graciously healed their battle wounds with Potions of Healing, and got their first square meal in ages, before passing the food on to the citizens. These starving victims, who had stayed in the mine and were too sickly to fight, were elated to finally eat real food and have real medicine. With the essentials distributed, the warriors finally started to loot the warehouses for high-grade weaponry.

"Sweet!" exclaimed Stan, as he reached into a chest and pulled out a diamond axe, glimmering with the lustre of enchantment. Suddenly, he did a double take, not sure that he had recognized the enchantment correctly.

"Sharpness?" he asked in awe. He turned around to face Sirus, who was brandishing a new diamond pickaxe. "How did they make this?" he asked. "Only swords are supposed to have offensive enchantments on them. Did they use hacks?"

"Oh man, you're so behind the times," Sirus said in his jittery fashion. "You've been able to mix up enchantments on stuff for a while now, but you don't do it on an enchanting table now, no no, you've gotta do it on an anvil, you know, one of those things that always falls on people's heads in a comedic fashion in cartoons but would probably squash your entire body into a fleshy puddle of goop if it were to happen to you in real life—"

"He's right, Stan! Check this out!" a call came from across the room.

Stan jogged over to the end of the warehouse, where Kat was standing over a large grey block that Stan knew to be an anvil. On the top of the hunk of iron, side by side, were Kat's diamond sword, already glowing brightly with enchantments, and a book, bound with a red leather strap. For some odd reason, Kat was smashing the cover of the book in with a cast-iron hammer, a bead of sweat trickling down her blocky forehead from the effort as Rex looked up at her quizzically.

Stan was about to ask Kat what she was trying to do (he knew that she didn't like reading, but this was taking it a bit too far), but then, on a particularly hard strike, the book vanished into thin air. A cloud of glimmering dust hung in its place for a moment, before drifting through the air, as if carried by an undetectable wind, and wrapping itself around Kat's sword. The dust hung there for a moment yet again, before being drawn onto the sword by some mysterious force, causing the sword to glow even brighter.

"Look at this," Kat breathed, in utter awe of what she was holding in her hands. The sword was shining brighter than any piece of weaponry that Stan had ever seen, and the lustre was shifting in hues between red, purple and blue. "This sword is now enchanted with the highest levels of Knockback, Fire and Sharpness . . . all at the same time! From now on, I hereby name this diamond sword, 'Gas-Powered Stick.' *Eeeeek*, I'm so excited!"

Kat raised her clenched fists to her mouth and did a little dance, smile wide, like a kid whose parent had just caved in and let her buy the toy that she really wanted. Stan smiled and shook his head as Kat bathed in her own mirth, and then he became aware of Ben walking over to him and, for the first time since the death of his brother, a smile was on his face, too.

"Hello, Ben," Stan said politely, as Kat walked over to join the two of them, returning her newly enchanted diamond sword to her inventory. "How's the occupation holding up?"

"Pretty well, actually," Ben said. "We've got troops on the full perimeter of the wall, and we're ready to go totally underground in a minute in case the Withers attack. Not only that, but thanks to all the extra gear in these warehouses, we have enough to give everyone here diamond armour. Commander Crunch is actually teaching a class of new players in combat as we speak, so we'll have more soldiers on standby."

"Excellent!" Stan replied, as Kat grinned even wider.

"Anyway, that's not the reason that I've come to talk to you, Stan," continued Ben. Stan expected his tone to shift to a more serious note, but to his surprise, Ben continued to be rather cheery as he kept talking. "We've got some news, both good and bad. Which one do you want to hear first?"

"Surprise me," Stan replied with a shrug.

"Well," continued Ben, now struggling to contain a huge smile, "when G came back from Nocturia and had those rescued prisoners with him . . . well, that wasn't all that he brought back."

"Wait, what? What do you mean? Did he bring back more fighters?"

"Well, no, not exactly . . . but I still think you're gonna be pretty happy. Come on in, guys!" Ben yelled.

He turned to face the entrance to the warehouse, and Stan and Kat turned to follow his gaze. Slowly, two forms, one as tall as a player and one half the size, stumbled awkwardly into the warehouse. As Stan realized who they were, his heart lifted.

"Greetings, President Stan!" Mella exclaimed as she made her way towards Stan. Little Stull smiled up at him as he walked next to her.

"Mella! Stull!" Stan cried out in joy as he rushed over to see them, Kat not far behind him, as Ben smiled on. "I'm so glad to see you guys!"

"It is very good to see you as well," she replied, slowly yet kindly, "now we are not Zombies, and therefore we are not going to try to eat you."

Kat laughed. "Yeah, that's probably for the best. So what happened to you guys? How did you get back here?"

"I do not remember very much of what happened," Mella said, clearly thinking hard about it. "I know that I was in the village, when a large explosion took away most of my house. I went to the church, along with Stull and Blerge, and waited with the rest of my people until the sun came up. The Zombies broke through our door, and one of them attacked me. The next thing that I remember is being carried through a tunnel, with a group of kind players, led by a player who called himself Goldman.

"He told us that we were turned into Zombies by bad players, and that he freed us from the bad players and he was taking us to the village with the good players. When we got here, Goldman told us to wait in a hole that he dug near the village until a player would come to get us. We waited there for two days, and today a player returned to us and brought us here.

"And here we are!" Mella exclaimed, raising her arms in the air. It seemed that she was one step away from yelling out "Ta-da!" as Stull tried to imitate her, struggling to raise his stubby little arms into the air.

Stan gave a warm-hearted smile. He would never tire of the innocuous simplicity of the NPC villagers. As he let Mella bask in her own glory for a moment (from the look on her face, she was quite proud that she had remembered every-thing that had happened so she could recount it to him), Kat stepped forward.

"Mella, we're very happy to see you two, and we can't tell you how relieved we are that you're OK," Kat said, managing a smile for a moment, before bearing a pained expression. "But there's something that we have to tell you."

She took a deep breath, and closed her eyes before continuing. "Do you . . . know what happened to the NPC village?"

She opened her eyes, prepared to see a horrified, scared

expression on Mella's face . . . but she didn't. Rather, the villager had begun to wander around the warehouse, weaving in between the players, as if totally unaware that anybody was talking to her. Kat rolled her eyes, grabbed Mella, and pulled her back over to the group, her eyes sliding back into focus.

"We were told what happened to our village," little Stull suddenly piped up, tilting his head backwards to see. "Me, my mother and my brother were the only ones who escaped from the village alive. My father and my future wife are both dead now. This is very sad."

Stan wasn't sure what to say. Obviously, he felt terrible for Mella and Stull; their entire life had been ripped away from them by the Noctem Alliance, and they were, as of now, the only survivors of their village. On the other hand, neither Stull nor Mella, who had refocussed and was now re-entering the conversation, seemed particularly distraught about it.

"You are surprised that we are not upset," Mella said. Kat and Stan turned to her in surprise. "Do not worry about us. We used to be very sad that many of our friends and family are dead, and we were very sad that we do not have a home. However, there is nothing that we can do about it now. We cannot focus on the fact that our village has been destroyed, or that our family is dead, or that the one who brought us here named Goldman is now dead. We must simply move on."

The mention of G's name hit Stan like a sucker punch to the gut. To be honest, of all his friends, he was probably the least torn up that G was gone. The two of them hadn't been particularly close, and during the rise of the Noctem Alliance they had gone through a period of open hostility, especially when he was acting out towards Kat. However, now that he had died – and he had sacrificed himself for the sake of the entire army – Stan felt like there was a black hole in his chest where G used to be. Although G was flawed, he was still a good guy at heart, and he only ever did what he truly believed was best, even when things got hard.

Despite this, Stan had forced himself not to think about G. Right now, they had to devote all their focus to destroying the Noctem Alliance, and ensuring that nobody would ever be struck down by their tyranny again. Mella was right. They simply had to move on. He knew that it would be easier said than done, however. Kat had seemed slightly more solemn then usual since G's death, although she was slowly becoming more upbeat. Jayden, on the other hand . . . Stan hadn't seen him since his best friend's death. It occurred to him that maybe he should go in search of Jayden. . . .

Stan suddenly realized that he had become lost in his own train of thought. He looked up and saw that Mella and Stull were playing together, carefree and happy, as Ben was in serious discussion with Kat. Realizing that they must be talking about the state of the war, he rushed over to join them.

". . . and the Noctems don't appear to be preparing for any attacks," Ben said, with Kat nodding her head as Stan arrived. "In fact, from what we can see, they appear to be shifting all their efforts to defence. They're drawing in their troops from all across the server, and concentrating them in Element City."

"What do you think that means?" Kat asked.

"It means that Lord Tenebris is ready to end the war, and end it on his terms. He wants to have a battle, all our forces versus all of his, and he wants it to happen in Element City."

Stan nodded solemnly, trying to think through the implications of this. "Do you think that our armies are prepared for an attack on Element City?"

"I think we're as ready as we'll ever be," Ben replied. "Now that we have food and medicine, we've got tons more volunteers. I'd say that, as of now, we have around three hundred fighters in total, and the Noctem Alliance has probably close to four hundred in the city. I know that those odds aren't great, but they're the best that we're going to get."

"I agree," Kat said, nodding with a pensive look on her face. "So are you saying that we should march on Element City as soon as possible and confront them full on?"

"Not quite," Ben answered. "You see, according to the

spies my brother and I have sent out, the Noctems are drawing troops from all over the server – from their outposts, from the Nether, from the Mushroom Islands, you name it. And yet, for some reason, they haven't done anything with their troops in Nocturia. Their capital has about another hundred troops in it, and the Noctem Alliance hasn't moved any of them – which is kind of odd, when you consider that they seem to be preparing for a final battle. You'd think that they'd move at least a *few* of those troops."

"So . . . what are you saying?" Stan asked, confused. "Are you saying that we should invade Nocturia instead?"

Ben looked up, and Stan was surprised to see a grin on his face.

"Even better," he replied. "Do you remember back when we first declared war on the Noctem Alliance, and you had to leave the meeting because Sally was contacting you?"

"Yeah . . ." Stan replied, not sure where he was going with this.

"Well, I seem to recall that she told you something rather interesting – something about how the Noctem Alliance was planning to lure you into the Capitol Building in Nocturia, and then detonate it, because they had turned the Capitol Building into a giant bomb."

"Yeah, she did say that . . ." Stan answered slowly, still unclear as to what he was getting at.

"Well, when you told that to me, I started thinking to myself, *Gee, if they turned that entire building into a bomb, then that seems awfully risky.* I mean, wouldn't it be unfortunate if some unforeseen incident caused said bomb to go off?"

Stan's jaw dropped as he realized what Ben was suggesting. "You don't mean . . ."

"Oh, I *do*, Stan," he continued, his eyes blazing with wild energy. "We're gonna blow up Nocturia."

There was a moment of silence as Stan and Kat tried to comprehend what he had just said. Kat was the first one to speak.

"OK, Ben . . . As awesomely awesome as that sounds, I'm not sure that it's gonna work. I mean, how do we know that the place is still in danger of blowing up? That seems like a feature that they would've gotten rid of by this point."

"Because our spies heard them talking about it," Ben replied. "Thanks to the Potions of Invisibility that were stored in the warehouse, it's been a lot easier for us to get close to the Noctem leaders and spy on them. Earlier today, Drake ordered that the TNT built into the walls of the castle no longer served a purpose now that the war is almost over, and that it should be disarmed within the next three days. We need to get to the Capitol Building before they're done, and use a redstone charge to detonate a block of TNT in the building. That should start a chain reaction that will destroy the entire Nocturia complex, including everybody inside."

A chill of excitement ran down Stan's spine. He imagined that, in one fell swoop, he could take out a hundred Noctem soldiers, crippling the Alliance beyond anything they could imagine. He could hardly believe his ears.

"So what're we waiting for?" Kat demanded. "We have three days to take out a fifth of the Noctem Army all at once. Why haven't we mobilized yet?"

"Because . . . there's a complication," Ben said, looking tired. "While we were listening to the soldiers, Drake let something else slide. Apparently, they're working on building an army of mobs to help with the defence of Element City, and the base of operations is in Nocturia. Which means . . . that Oob is there."

Stan felt like all the air was being sucked out of his lungs. Here, in front of him, was the chance to launch the biggest attack on the Noctem Alliance since the war began. It would no doubt be an invaluable move if they wished to win the war. And yet . . . to blow up Nocturia would also mean to kill Oob.

"Many of my soldiers," said Ben, slowly and carefully, "have told me that they believe it is worth it to lose the life of one Zombie villager in order to take out the second-largest city the Noctem Alliance controls. I'm leaving the decision to you, President Stan."

"Hey!" exclaimed Kat in fury, butting her way in between them. "What about the other council members? Shouldn't we get a say in what to do?"

Ben shook his head. "I'm sorry, Kat, but we don't have time to debate this. It's an incredibly important matter and, given that we only have three days, we can't waste time organizing a vote."

Something clicked in Stan's head. He remembered a long time ago, as Blackraven had stood up at the council table in Element City, and yelled out at them all . . . *I only want what is best for Elementia, and I would like to see action taken against our enemies quickly, without wandering through the political swamp of your bureaucratic elections.*

Blackraven had made the exact same argument for appointing himself to the council that Ben was making now. And yet, now, everybody was agreeing with Ben, whereas half of them had jumped down Blackraven's throat at the idea.

"Stan, you can't do it!"

Stan snapped out of his thoughts and realized that Kat was appealing to him, a look of desperation in her eyes.

"You can't kill Oob, you . . . you just *can't*! I mean, we've known him for so long now . . . he's our friend! His life is no less valuable than any of ours just because he's an NPC villager! There's got to be another way to destroy Nocturia without killing him!"

Stan knew that what she was saying was true. Oob was their friend. They could never just leave him to die. That would be like abandoning Kat or Charlie! He knew that he could never do that. On the other hand, the idea of a hundred Noctem troops sitting out in the tundra suddenly made him far more uneasy than it ever had before as they prepared for the closing phases of the war. And here was an opportunity to take them out forever. Stan thought that . . . just maybe . . .

"What was that?" a voice came from behind Stan. He turned around and saw Mella walking up to him, with little Stull asleep in her arms. "I heard you say the name of Oob, who is my son. Did you say the name of Oob, who is my son?"

As Stan looked back into Mella's quizzical, trusting eyes, all hints of doubt vanished from Stan's mind in an instant.

"Yes, you did, Mella," he replied confidently. "We're breaking into the Noctem Capitol to free your son."

It had taken far too much time to put together the plan for the infiltration of Nocturia, but now that Stan had entered the subzero snowstorm yet again, he was confident that their plan was solid. He looked ahead of him, past Ben, who was shielding his eyes from the snow. Stan's eyes locked on to Jayden, who was at the front of the trio. Even though he couldn't see Jayden's face, Stan knew that he bore a look of grim determination and vengeance.

In the Adorian Village, Stan had found Jayden alone in an abandoned house. He had clearly been crying for the entire day, and Stan totally understood. When Jayden had first met him, he had gotten to know Stan, played practical jokes on him, and taught him, all alongside G, Archie and Sally. And now, months later, all three of those friends were gone. Jayden was the only one remaining, and all of them had been taken out by the Noctem Alliance (or, in Sally's case, the regime of King Kev, which had led to the Alliance's creation).

When Stan had told Jayden that they were going on a mission to blow the capitol of the Noctem Alliance off the face of the server, he hadn't hesitated to volunteer. Stan was relieved that Jayden was feeling up to coming with them; out of all of them, he had by far the most inside knowledge of the Noctem Capitol Building, having stayed there for weeks on end.

Stan only hoped that they were almost there. They had been travelling for two days through the countryside of Elementia, speckled with abandoned Noctem outposts, and were just now in the midst of the trek through the tundra. Time was running out.

Suddenly, Stan's heart leaped. A few shimmering lights shone out of the darkness of the eternal blizzard and, slowly but surely, the silhouette of the Nocturia complex faded into view. Stan took a deep breath as he realized that, if their mission went according to plan, it would be the last time that they would ever see the magnificent complex from the outside. Jayden raised his hand to indicate a halt, and he turned to face Stan and Ben.

"We're close enough," Jayden said, his voice still gruff and gravelly from his days of woeful mourning and silence. "Use the potions now."

Stan pulled the Potion of Invisibility out of his inventory and drank it along with his two friends. As Stan let the tingling feeling spread from his mouth through the rest of his body, he sincerely hoped that the last of the potion wouldn't go to waste. The Potions of Invisibility in the warehouse had proved invaluable for spying on Element City since they had taken over the Adorian Village, and the three of them had taken some of the last remaining bottles for use on this mission. Stan resolved to make it count.

It wasn't long before the potions had taken effect. All three players stood invisible, without armour on their bodies or weapons in their hands. The only indication of where Stan's comrades stood was a faint shimmering, as if the air was irradiated, that Stan could only sense if he focussed as hard as he could. After fumbling about for a moment, Stan found what he was looking for, and grasped Ben's hand, as Ben did the same to Jayden in front of him. As soon as the chain of the three invisible players was completed, they took off running.

Stan's heart, already racing from the effort, was thumping faster than he was aware was possible as they entered through the stone brick–block wall surrounding the Nocturia complex. It didn't slow as they sprinted straight past the four guards watching over the door framed with quartz blocks. The Potion of Invisibility only lasted for a short time. He could only pray that Jayden managed to locate a safe place in the capitol for them to reappear before that time came.

They were dashing past houses now, dozens and dozens of plain, tiny houses, constructed of cobblestone and wood-plank blocks, the windows on the wood doors revealing darkness inside. Stan supposed that these were the abandoned houses of the players who had made their way to Element City. For a moment, he considered questioning Jayden as to whether one of these houses would be a good place to reappear, but he decided not to. Whatever Jayden was planning, Stan trusted him. Fortunately, they reached the front doors of the Noctem Capitol Building just as a Noctem trooper was walking out, and they managed the slip through the iron doors just before they swung shut.

As the trio entered the main hall and dropped their hands, Stan allowed himself to take a deep breath, finally breathing in air that wasn't below freezing (although the air in the capitol certainly wasn't warm). There was no time to stop, though. Stan saw the other shimmers pressing onwards, and he followed.

Stan's anxiety levels were through the roof as he crossed the floor of the Capitol Building rotunda. Guards were stationed around every corner, and there were several lone soldiers passing through the centre of the rotunda. Once or twice, as Stan sprinted past a soldier, he did a double take, and Stan's heart stopped. Luckily, nobody pursued them, but Stan still felt like he was about to have a panic attack. The potion was surely close to running out.

Stan ducked behind one of his two friends into a side hallway, not illuminated by the light of glowstone as the rotunda had been. The hallway was made entirely out of stone-brick blocks. Stan followed the shimmering figure around a corner and into another hallway, just as it grew much more substantial. In a matter of seconds, it had finally turned back into the form of Ben. Jayden materialized right beside him, and Stan looked down at himself to see that he had reappeared, too.

"Don't worry," Jayden said quickly, before Stan could voice his alarm, "they won't look down here. This part of the building isn't finished. They just built it so that the capitol would be symmetrical, and they haven't actually done anything with the space yet. And best of all, this" – Jayden grinned as he gave three sharp raps on the stone-brick wall across from him – "is the outside wall of the castle."

There was a moment of silence as they all realized what this meant. Then, slowly, Ben drew out a diamond pickaxe. He walked over to the wall and struck a piece of stone brick. As he chipped away at the block, Stan held his breath. Now was the moment of truth. If the TNT had already been removed from this wall, then the first part of their mission would be a total failure. Ben raised the pickaxe and, with all his might, he delivered one final strike to the stone-brick block. It broke, collapsing onto the floor, revealing a block of red sticks, with a white label bearing the black letters TNT.

Ben pumped his fist in excitement, while Jayden smiled a wild smile and Stan sighed in relief.

"OK, Stan, you know the plan," said Ben as he handed the diamond pickaxe to Stan. "And please – I cannot stress this enough – *do not* blow up the building until we're outside."

"I promise." Stan nodded as he took the tool and started to carve out more of the stone-brick blocks, being careful to leave the TNT blocks in place. "Good luck, you guys. Be out as soon as possible, and don't do anything too reckless."

Jayden and Ben nodded as they pulled black leather armour out of their inventories, slipped it on over their heads, and proceeded to make their way back out into the main part of the building, Jayden leading the way. Stan, meanwhile, turned his attention back to his job.

Stan reached into his inventory to double-check that he had everything that he needed to complete his job. To his relief, it was all there: several stacks of redstone dust, a stack of redstone repeaters, a map and a lever. He raised the diamond pickaxe and struck the nearest TNT block. It immediately broke off, falling to the ground, and Stan pocketed it. Hastily, he continued to dig into the wall, mining through blocks of stone brick and TNT until eventually he was inside the wall. Wasting no time, Stan picked up some of the stone-brick blocks from the ground and fastened them on to the section of the wall that he had just tunnelled through. Now, if anybody were to come across this section of the wall from inside the building, it would appear untouched.

Stan knew that, even though he was concealed, he couldn't slow down. It wouldn't be long before Jayden and Ben had gotten Oob, and he would be shocked if they managed to smuggle the villager out without being discovered by the Noctem troops. If they were to get out safely, Stan would have to be ready well before they left the Nocturia complex. With that knowledge in mind, Stan dug a downward stairway through the furrowed dirt-block ground, stopping when the stone-brick wall was directly above him.

Pulling the redstone dust from his inventory, Stan

reached back up through the terraced dirt blocks and laid a trail of redstone down the steps and towards him, starting at the base of one of the TNT blocks and ending at his feet. Stan pulled the map from his inventory and oriented himself so that he was facing towards the front gates of the Nocturia complex. Pulling out his pickaxe again, Stan then proceeded to dig forwards, tunnelling through dirt and stone blocks alike, and sprinkling redstone dust behind him on the ground.

After Stan had been digging and laying down dust for what he counted as ten steps, he pulled a redstone repeater from his inventory and put it on the ground at the end of the redstone dust. The stone plate of the mechanism had a few buttons and switches on it, but Stan was most interested in the arrow inscribed on the smooth stone base of the contraption, which was pointing in the direction he had just come from. Stan knew that he had to be vigilant in making sure that each and every one of the repeaters was facing towards Nocturia, or else the entire redstone circuit would malfunction.

On and on Stan went, in a pattern: dig further down the tunnel, lay redstone dust behind him, lay a repeater every ten steps. Every once in a while he would check the map to see how close he was to being outside the boundaries of the Nocturia complex.

Finally, after what seemed like an eternity of constant

digging, Stan checked the map and saw that he was a good distance outside the outer walls of the Noctem Capitol. He aimed his pickaxe upwards, and before long, he broke the frozen topsoil and stumbled into the darkness of the eternal blizzard. Determined to finish the job properly, Stan laid the redstone dust up the hole he had just climbed, and when he got to the top, he placed the lever in his inventory on the ground, careful to ensure that it was connected to the rest of the trail of redstone.

Stan was relieved that his mission had been a success. Nocturia was now one lever pull away from becoming a massive crater in the middle of the tundra. All he had to do was wait for Ben and Jayden to emerge carrying Oob, and then activate the redstone circuit. Stan's mind was racing, and his heart was pounding with excitement as he used the pickaxe to carve a trench in the snowy ground (they had to take shelter from the blast behind something). As he worked, Stan imagined how large the explosion would be. If what Ben had said was true, and all the outer walls were laced with TNT, then Stan couldn't comprehend the size of the blast. More than likely, it would be larger than Creeper Khan's dying attack.

Suddenly, Stan stopped as this thought struck him. The memories of being on the roof of the Town Hall came flooding back to him, as he once again stood before Creeper

Khan, sure that the entire Adorian Village was about to be destroyed. The feeling of dread that had washed over him was unlike anything he had felt before, to think that all of his people were about to be wiped out . . . even those who hadn't wanted to fight to begin with. . . .

Stan knew that not everybody in the Noctem Alliance was a terrible person. Obviously, they were all terribly misguided in their beliefs, but not all of them were purely evil minds like King Kev or Caesar. In fact, Stan had trouble believing, based on what he had heard about them, that Tess and Spyro were terrible people by nature. They were just doing what they thought was right, like almost every other player who had followed the path of the Noctem Alliance. Stan realized that there was a possibility, however slim, that any member of the Noctem Alliance might one day repent, and see the error of their ways.

If Stan pulled the lever, then none of the one hundred players in the Nocturia complex would ever get that chance.

As Stan sat in the snow, frozen in conflict, his mind torn two ways, he became aware that he was being watched. Stan whipped his head up, his newly enchanted diamond axe flying into his hand as his eyes fell on a figure standing slightly below him on the hill. The player was standing perfectly still, his cloak billowing in the raging gale. As Stan squinted to make him out more clearly, he realized that the figure was wearing dark pants and shoes, with a black cape and hood that obscured his eyes, revealing only a pale mouth locked into a frown.

Stan's heart skipped a beat. Since he had met up with his friends, they had all told him stories . . . tales of a mysterious player who had appeared to each of them and saved their lives. In fact, Stan had heard that it was because of this mystery player that his friends had accepted Leonidas into their group. While he had largely ignored his friends' stories, being too occupied with the war effort to give them much thought, he remembered them saying that the player never spoke . . . and yet, somehow, they all knew his name.

As Stan looked at this player, he knew the name, too.

The Black Hood stared at Stan, still not moving, still not smiling. Stan miraculously felt no surprise that this mystery player existed. Rather, he only felt a sense of desperation, like a pupil begging a teacher for help. Somehow, he knew that the Black Hood held the answer to his dilemma, although he had no idea how.

"I can't kill them," Stan said aloud, the anxiety evident in his voice as he spoke to this spectral player. "We aren't on a battlefield. Those players are probably lying safe and happy in their beds. They think that the war is nearly over, and that soon they'll get to go home to their families. How am I supposed to take them all out?"

The Black Hood didn't answer. He simply continued to

stare at Stan, not a muscle of his body making even the slightest motion as he stood, stoic, his billowing cape forming a magnificent silhouette against the light of the building that Stan was supposed to destroy. Stan stared back, desperately hoping that, if he stared hard enough, the answer would reveal itself.

"You've always had the answer for all my friends!" Stan cried out over the blizzard, as a tear formed in the corner of his eyes. "You've always done everything you can for them! Is there anything you can do for me?"

Still, there was no response. Instead, a particularly strong gust of wind kicked a spray of snow in front of the Black Hood, obscuring him from view. By the time the snow had blown away, the Black Hood had vanished.

And yet, Stan didn't have time to acknowledge the disappearance of the mysterious player. Rather, his focus shifted to the blast of sound that was echoing up the slopes of the hills. Stan scrambled to the edge of the hill to where the Black Hood had been standing and looked down. There, racing across the tundra towards him, were two players, one of whom appeared to have a third form slung over his back. And far behind them, a giant mass of forms seemed to be swarming around the Nocturia complex like ants, turning into waves that surged towards the exit gate.

"We've got him!" Jayden's voice came out, as his face

came into view next to the form of Ben, who had an unconscious, shaking Oob over his shoulder. "Pull the lever, Stan!"

Stan glanced down at the lever, then out at the massive outpouring of troops that had reached the gates of the outer wall. He wondered how many of those players were only fighting because they felt they couldn't live in Element City under him . . . just like his soldiers back in the Adorian Village were doing now.

"What are you waiting for?" Jayden bellowed. "They'll be out of range soon. Activate the bomb!"

Stan gave his head a blunt shake. He had to do it – he knew that he had to. Without thinking, Stan reached down to the lever, but the second he grabbed it, he halted in his tracks. It was so simple. All he had to do was push the lever forwards, and it would all be over. But still, he would never be able to cleanse his hands of those hundred lives.

"Do it! NOW!" Ben bellowed.

Stan acted on instinct. He thrust the lever downwards, activating the mechanism with a distinctive click. Instantly, a surge of electric power rushed down the line of redstone dust, pausing for a split second as it hit the first redstone repeater before the revitalized charge continued down the line. For a moment, Stan couldn't hear anything as he rushed back into the trench he had just dug, alongside Jayden, Ben, and the unconscious Oob.

BOOOOOOOOOOM!

The explosion was so loud, so powerful, and so forceful that Stan felt himself slammed backwards against the back of the trench, unable to move. He squinted his eyes open against the blinding light to see a giant fireball rupturing the walls of the Capitol Building of Nocturia, reducing the entire building into rubble in a split second. The wave of fire continued from the building, spreading at the speed of sound across the countless shacks, and eventually sending the outer wall flying into the air in a million pieces. The soldiers on the ground turned around in a frenzy to see what had happened, only to be consumed by the blast. Stan forced himself to duck low into the trench to avoid being struck by the massive force. He felt it billow over his head like a train, still supremely powerful even after travelling so far.

The blasts didn't cease there. A series of smaller, yet still massive explosions continued to erupt within the giant fireball, sending loose blocks and items flying through the air like a volcano spewing out magma and stones. Single lit blocks of TNT went sailing through the air, glowing white like shooting stars through the still-raging blizzard. Some burst in midair like fireworks, while others struck the ground in blasts, peppering the snowy ground around what had once been the Nocturia complex with miniature craters the size of Creeper holes. Stan ducked his head down into the trench again for fear of being struck by a stray explosion.

For a long time, Stan didn't move. He couldn't move; his brain wouldn't let him. It wasn't until long after the last remnants of explosions had died that Stan finally dared to peek his head over the top of the bank and look over the field before him.

The Nocturia complex, which had once stood as one of the most ornate, intricate and well-crafted cities in all of Elementia, now ceased to exist. The crater from the supernova was so large that Stan couldn't make out the bottom. Thousands of blocks wide, the hole stretched down so deep that it simply appeared to be black. Not a single structure remained even partially intact, and there was no sign of life whatsoever.

Stan continued to stare, feeling a hole in his chest that felt as large as the hole that was now the gravesite of hundreds of players before him, all because he had pulled the lever. Then Stan's mind refused to take any more, and he passed out before he hit the snow.

As he stood on the bridge of Element Castle and looked down over the city, General Drake tried to remember an older time, when Element City had been a much more colourful place. After all, he had lived here once, long ago, before he had chosen to leave and join the Noctem Alliance, being fed up with his then-stagnant, dead-end life. The city looked much different now, though – darker, and more foreboding. The eternal grey cloud still hung over the towering buildings of the city, dimming the sunlight as the two Withers patrolled the skies, under the telepathic grip of the one who, at this very moment, was torturing Drake's comrade for his failure.

From such a height, Drake could see every street of Element City, all lined with troops. There were over four hundred Noctem soldiers in all, armed to the teeth with potions and enchanted weapons, prepared for the imminent attack on the city. Stan2012 had taken control of the Adorian Village, and since the admittedly unexpected destruction of Nocturia two days ago, there was only one place for Stan's army to go now.

Drake heard uneven footsteps behind him, and he turned around to see General Spyro limping towards him. His entire body was covered in burns from fire and potions, and from the agonized expression on his face, he was just barely managing to stay upright.

"I'm glad to see that he went easy on you," Drake said coolly.

"Trust me . . . so am I," grunted Spyro as he reached Drake, extracted a wood-plank block from his inventory, placed it on the ground, and wasted no time in sitting down, a sigh heaving from his mouth. "I know that I deserve . . . much, much worse than what I got. I suppose I'm lucky that Lord Tenebris is so . . . merciful . . ."

"Yes, you are. . . . We both are," replied Drake wistfully, remembering the agony that Lord Tenebris had put him through for his failures. "It will all be over soon, though. As soon as we can destroy President Stan's army, life will be easy – and we'll be heroes."

"Yeah, I know. . . . *Augh!*" The shout escaped Spyro's mouth as he moved slightly, causing the pain in a particularly burned part of his arm to flare up. Drake handed a Potion of Healing from his own inventory to Spyro, which he graciously drank.

"Thanks," Spyro said softly as he sighed in relief.

"Don't mention it."

"So, is there any news on the war front?" Spyro asked, his voice slightly stronger now.

Drake took a deep breath and let it out. *So he doesn't know,* he thought. "Actually, there is a rather big development,

Spyro . . . not a good one. Apparently, President Stan knew about the TNT hidden in the walls of Nocturia, and he activated it. The entire city is gone, and they took out over a hundred of our guys . . . including Tess."

There was a moment of silence as Spyro stood there, looking at the ground, trying to absorb what Drake had just said. Finally, he looked up, disbelief in his face.

"You're saying . . . that . . . Tess is dead?"

"Yes."

"And . . . they took out a hundred of our soldiers?"

"Yes, Spyro. President Stan destroyed just over a hundred players in the blink of an eye. That's almost twice as many as we took out in our biggest attack. And from what I heard, it wasn't just any random soldier that did it . . . it was President Stan himself."

"You're kidding."

"No, I'm not," Drake spat in disgust. "I can't believe that he would do something like that. I mean, it wasn't like when we attacked the Spleef Arena, where we had a solid reason to do it. A lot of the players in Nocturia were trainees, not even ready to go into combat. And a lot more weren't even there for combat at all. They were there for construction and mining and such. Even Tess was just there to oversee training. It's not like she was ordering out military operations from Nocturia or anything. But now, it doesn't even matter. They're all gone."

Spyro didn't respond; he didn't have anything to say. Neither did Drake, for that matter. The two remaining generals of the Noctem Alliance stood silently on the bridge, overlooking their troops and reflecting on just how senseless the loss of all those players, including General Tess, truly was.

"I don't believe you," Kat said incredulously, staring at Commander Crunch, eyes wide. "Don't you dare lie to me about something like that!"

"I assure ye, lass, I ain't lyin'," Commander Crunch replied with a proud, toothy grin. "Th' trainin' programme really has been goin' that well. All hundred o' th' new players I've been trainin' 'ave been advancin' remarkable smartly, 'n' they'll be able t' march into Element City in battle alongside th' rest o' us when the time comes."

"So . . ." Cassandrix said, the gears whirring in her head. "If I'm counting correctly . . . then that means that . . ."

"Right ye be, poppet . . . now we 'ave jus' as many fighters as th' Noctems do: four hundred apiece."

"Excellent!" Kat exclaimed, so loudly that Rex looked up at her in concern, and several people nearby glanced at her, but she didn't care. She had been worried sick ever since Ben had told her that they may potentially be going into a fight of three hundred versus five hundred, but now it seemed like they would be much more evenly matched.

"So we're up a hundred fighters . . ." Cassandrix murmured to herself before looking up at Kat. "And you're certain that Nocturia has been destroyed, correct?"

"Hey, the spies haven't led us wrong yet," replied Kat. "They say they heard the Noctem generals say that Nocturia had been destroyed. If that's the case, then I'd expect Stan, Ben and Jayden to be back any minute now."

"Aye aye-o, ma'am," Commander Crunch replied with a hearty laugh. "Now, I be gonna brin' me newly graduated students t' th' storehouses 'n' get them suited up fer battle. Could ye two do me a favour 'n' tell Bob th' good news?"

Kat and Cassandrix nodded and immediately began to make their way towards the hotel, Rex on their heels, as Commander Crunch headed towards the Town Hall.

"I'm totally speechless," Cassandrix breathed. "A hundred players, turned into military-grade fighters in just a manner of days . . . I'd never have believed it . . ."

"Well, if anybody can do it, Commander Crunch can. I mean, he may be totally insane, but he knows what he's doing. Not to mention that those players really believe in our cause," Kat answered wisely as they passed the guarded hotel rooms where the Noctem prisoners were being stored. "And they know how desperate the situation is."

"I suppose you're right," Cassandrix sighed. "I suppose

that given the circumstances, just about anybody can rise to the occasion . . . even if they're lower-level players."

Kat stopped in her tracks and whipped around to face Cassandrix, a look of sheer disbelief on her face. There was a moment where neither of them moved before Cassandrix spoke again.

"Relax, darling . . . I was only joking . . ."

Cassandrix continued walking, but Kat still didn't move. Instead, a look of understanding crossed her face as she looked at the player standing beside her. Cassandrix turned around and looked at Kat expectantly, waiting for her to say something.

"Cassandrix," Kat finally said, "have I ever thanked you for everything you've done for us?"

"Well, I hardly see occasion for that, dear. After all, I've done just as much or, to be totally frank, slightly less than you and the other leaders."

"I know that," Kat replied, "but it's just . . . what you said to me, back when we were in prison together on the Mushroom Islands . . . it was really eye opening."

"Oh come on, darling, you're not still on about that, are you? Look, I already told you—"

"What I'm trying to say is that what you said struck me as something somebody in the Noctem Alliance would say."

Suddenly, it was as if the air around them had dropped

twenty degrees. Cassandrix glared back at Kat, making it very obvious that she had entered dangerous waters.

"Yes," Cassandrix said coldly. "You said that as I was talking."

"But . . . you're not a member of the Noctem Alliance. It would have been so easy for you to leave and join them but . . . you didn't. You stayed here with us, and you've risked everything for the sake of the lower-level players."

Cassandrix said nothing. Instead, she opened her mouth, only to close it again, and then looked down at the ground. She then repeated the same motion again, clearly searching for the correct response. Then, she finally talked, and Kat was taken aback by how sincere she sounded.

"Well . . . to be totally frank with you, Kat, I initially refused to join the Noctem Alliance because I didn't approve of their methods, even if I agreed with their ideals. And I only joined the army because I was one of the only high-level players left in the city, and I hadn't been drafted yet because of my role in the Spleef tournament."

"Oh," Kat replied, sounding crestfallen. "Well, in that case—"

"That being said," Cassandrix cut in, causing Kat to look back up at her. "That may have been the reason that I joined the army in the first place, but it's not the reason that I'm fighting now. Spending all this time fighting the Noctem

Alliance, seeing all the trouble that our people of all levels have gone through to take them down, and . . . well, even talking to you . . . It's opened my eyes to quite a few things. I suppose what I'm trying to say is . . . I would fight alongside you in this army if I were to do everything over again."

Cassandrix gave a warm smile, which Kat returned. She found it hard to believe that the big-lipped, pale-faced player standing across from her was the same person who she had hated the most out of everyone in Element City just weeks ago. Kat realized that Cassandrix hadn't said that she agreed with Kat's views on how lower-level players ought to be treated, and to be honest, Kat doubted that she would ever truly feel that way. However, Kat knew in her gut that, from now on, Cassandrix would look at things in more than one light . . . as would she.

The two girls broke eye contact simultaneously, and walked the short distance to the hotel room where Bob was holed up. Kat told Rex to sit, and pushed the wooden door open. She had to do a double take to ensure that she was seeing correctly.

Bob was sitting on Ivanhoe in the middle of the room, as they had expected, but they were not alone. In front of them, sitting on another saddled pig and looking incredibly frustrated, was Charlie. He was holding a fishing rod, on the end of which was a carrot, which his pig was looking at with marked longing. Both players looked up as Kat and Cassandrix entered the room.

"Um . . . are we interrupting something?" Kat asked awkwardly.

"No, of course not!" exclaimed Bob with a grin. Unlike Charlie, he looked quite enthusiastic about whatever it was that was going on. "I've been teaching Charlie how to ride a pig, and I think that we've got this one fully trained. Go on Charlie, demonstrate."

Charlie looked miserable; he took a deep breath, let it out, and then grunted, "Forward, Dr Pigglesworth."

The pig gave a complacent grunt and began to trot forwards. With the humiliated-sounding commands of "Stop, Dr Pigglesworth" and "Turn, Dr Pigglesworth" and "Backward, Dr Pigglesworth," Charlie manoeuvered his pig all around the room.

"Um," Kat said slowly, not sure what to say as Charlie and the pig stopped in front of them. "That was . . . very impressive, Charlie."

"Wasn't it?" beamed Bob. He was clearly very proud of all that Charlie had accomplished.

"Honestly," Charlie grunted, looking as though he felt degraded, "it's bad enough that I'm forced to ride this stupid thing, but why did you have to give it a nickname like that?"

"Hey, it's not my decision!" Bob replied defensively. "All

the war pigs are given their names when they're born. And for the record, Dr Pigglesworth has always been one of my favourites."

"Well, great then!" spat Charlie in disgust. "If that's the case, then why don't we trade? If you're forcing me to act like I'm as crippled as you are, the least you can do is give me a pig that has a cool name like Ivanhoe!"

Bob's jaw dropped and he stared at Charlie, clearly stung deeply by this. Charlie continued to glare back in anger for a moment, before his infuriated look cracked and then broke altogether, revealing embarrassment and shame. Kat and Cassandrix looked on, not wanting to be there, but not positive how to walk away. After a full minute of tense silence, Cassandrix cleared her throat and spoke.

"Eh, hem. Well, Bob, em . . . we thought that it would be pertinent for you to know that Commander Crunch has trained all his lower-level players much faster than we had anticipated. They should all be prepared to fight when we invade Element City, which means that we'll have four hundred fighters in total, the same number of troops as the Noctem Alliance has."

Bob didn't look at them. He gave an absent-minded "Thank you for telling me" without moving his gaze away from Charlie. Their job done, Kat and Cassandrix scurried out of the room, slamming the door behind them. Charlie heard Cassandrix let out a muffled "Well that was fun," from behind the closed door in a higher-than-normal voice, and finally, he spoke.

"I'm sorry," Charlie said, his head drooping in shame as Dr Pigglesworth started curiously sniffing the ground, apparently oblivious to the emotions of the one riding him. "That wasn't fair."

"Thank you for apologizing," Bob replied, stroking Ivanhoe absent-mindedly between the ears, which caused the pig's nose to crinkle in pleasure. "You've got to realize, Charlie . . . I know what you're going through."

"Don't say that," Charlie grunted, a note of anger returning to his voice. "You have no idea what I'm going through."

"What are you talking about?" Bob asked incredulously. "How do you think I felt when Caesar cut my leg off? Do you think that I just hopped on Ivanhoe and carried on like nothing happened? Of course not! I was just as depressed as you are now for weeks before I accepted what had happened to me!"

"It's different for you!" cried Charlie. "I mean, look at you! Even without your legs, you're still one of the best archers we've got! You're probably better now than you were before because Ivanhoe's so fast and has so much stamina! You can still be a great archer while riding on a pig. How am I supposed to fight in hand-to-hand combat using a pickaxe if I can't use my legs?"

"Charlie, I know that it's going to be hard to adjust," Bob replied, "and . . . well, I'm gonna level with you, you're probably not going to be as good in a fight as you were before. But if you focus on what you can't do, you're gonna put yourself in a really bad place. You need to focus on what you can do, and how lucky you are."

"Lucky?" laughed Charlie bitterly. "How, in any sense of the word, am I supposed to be lucky?"

"Because you didn't end up like my brother! You're still alive!" shouted Bob.

Charlie felt the response that was about to leave his mouth hit an invisible wall. There was nothing that he could say in response to that. There was another long moment of silence as Bob stared at him, tears welling in his eyes. Finally, a sigh escaped the police chief's mouth, and he spoke.

"Charlie, I'm sorry that you have to ride into the battle for our freedom on the back of a pig, I truly am. But I'll say it again: don't think about the limitations that your condition is causing you. Instead, focus on everything that you can still do! Charlie, do you realize just how useful you've been in helping us plan this attack?"

"Well . . . I mean, I guess . . ."

"Charlie, you've been amazing!" Bob exclaimed. "You've been the driving force behind all our battle plans since we got back to the village! I mean, you've pretty much mapped out everything while Ben and I were getting the troops organized and the people safe. This attack that we're about to pull off wouldn't be half as solid without you, and thanks to your plans, Nocturia is gone! When I was reading your notes for the first time, I was totally blown away. You suggested things that Ben and I never would have thought of!"

"Well," Charlie replied, "I suppose that you're right . . . I guess I have always been better at planning than doing the actual fighting . . ."

"Exactly," Bob replied. "Charlie, your shining moment of glory isn't going to be on the battlefield, like the rest of us. Your moment of glory is going to come when we stand on the bridge of Element Castle, and look over the city that we've won back, and you know that you were the grandmaster who moved all the chess pieces around the board and made it possible."

"That's right," a voice from behind them replied.

Bob and Charlie turned around to see Leonidas standing in the doorway, a smile on his face.

"How long have you been standing there?" Charlie asked.

"Long enough to know that everything that Bob said is true," Leonidas replied, walking into the room and sitting on a wood block to look at the two pig-backed players at eye level. "Your ideas 'n' strategies have already done more for us than ya know."

Charlie smiled. "Thanks, guys. That was just what I needed to hear. I think I'm gonna be OK."

"Good," Bob said kindly. "And if you ever feel down and need to talk, come to me, OK? I've been stuck with this little guy a lot longer than you have, man," he added wearily, patting Ivanhoe on the head, "and I'm pretty used to it by this point. I'm sure I can help you out."

"Will do," Charlie replied. "Thanks for everything, guys. I haven't gotten my gear together yet, so I'm gonna go do that. I'll talk to you later. Let's go, Dr Pigglesworth."

Charlie nudged forward on his pig's head, and proceeded to exit through the door. Leonidas and Bob watched him go, smiles on their faces, as Leonidas closed the door behind him.

"Charlie's a good guy," Leonidas sighed contentedly. "I'm sure glad that he's finally managin' to shake off the demons that got into his head when the Noctem Alliance tortured him."

"Yeah," agreed Bob. "He's got a good heart, and I know that he'll do anything for our cause. It honestly didn't surprise me that he blamed himself so much when he gave the location of the bunker to the Noctem Alliance."

"How do ya know about that?" Leonidas asked in alarm.

"Our spies have brought quite a lot of information to us, Leonidas," Bob replied wisely. "And honestly, it wasn't too hard to guess. It made a lot of other stuff make sense. I didn't want to tell Charlie I knew because I knew he'd have a hard time facing me. And I don't blame him. People aren't themselves when they go through what the Noctem Alliance put Charlie through."

Leonidas nodded pensively as, without warning, the door slowly creaked open. Both players in the room looked up to see the Mechanist stepping meekly into the room. Instantly, the entire atmosphere changed; Bob glared at the Mechanist with a harsh glint in his eye, causing the Mechanist to recoil as Leonidas looked between the two of them with concern.

"What do you want?" Bob asked coldly. The Mechanist cringed yet again at the harsh tone, and his voice was meek as he responded in his quivery Texas drawl.

"I'm sorry if I'm interrupting anything . . . but I'm a little bit confused, Bob. I was looking over the plans for the invasion that you made with Ben and Charlie, and I saw instructions for all the commanders except for me. What should I be doing during the battle?"

"Well, I thought the plans made it clear," Bob replied. "The instructions for all the commanders are listed. Everyone not listed is going to be serving under the commanders."

"Wait, hold up," the Mechanist replied, as he realized what Bob was saying. "Are you implying that . . . you want me to just be a normal foot soldier during the attack?"

"It wasn't an implication, Mechanist," Bob spat. "It's written on the page, plain as day."

"But . . . but . . . ," the Mechanist sputtered, sounding incredibly hurt. "You don't need me to . . . I don't know . . . set up some redstone booby traps? Or take down their automatic defence grids? Or *anything*?"

"I think that I've made myself very clear!" Bob shouted. Everyone in the room looked on in shock as Bob dismounted Ivanhoe, clutching the wall and pulling himself upright on his good foot so he could look the Mechanist in the eye.

"All players whom my brother and I have dubbed the most experienced – *and the most reliable* – are the commanders. All others are going to serve as ground troops for the invasion. And I suggest that you stop talking back to your superior, soldier! Stand down now, or you're going to be kicked out of this—"

"Enough!" Leonidas bellowed, pushing his way in between the cowering Mechanist and the raging Bob. The Mechanist stumbled backwards in a panic, as Bob was shoved off balance and tumbled to the wood plank–block floor with a crash.

"What do you think you're doing?" Bob demanded, glaring at Leonidas as he attempted to get up off the floor.

"I'm puttin' an end to this nonsense!" grunted Leonidas as he grabbed Bob's arm, jerking him to his feet. Bob looked at Leonidas incredulously as he remounted his pig, and his look was mirrored by the Mechanist.

"We're at war," Leonidas said in the manner of a drill sergeant, looking back and forth between the two players with an authoritative expression on his face. "At some point within the next two days, we are gonna march into Element City and fight for our lives to take it back from the Noctem Alliance. It's going to be the hardest thing that any of us've ever done. And if we stand even a tiny chance of winnin', we've all gotta trust each other and work together! That means that both of y'all are gonna have to finally confront the issues you have, and resolve 'em!"

The two players looked at Leonidas, then at each other. They held their gaze for a moment before the Mechanist finally looked away in disgrace as Bob continued to glower at him. Leonidas took a deep breath and addressed the elephant in the room.

"I know that both of y'all think that the Mechanist is responsible for Bill's death."

"I'm sorry!" the Mechanist burst out; Bob's glare did not ease up. "I never should have started drinking that stupid potion again. I knew it was a mistake! Stan was gone, and I felt like I had to fill his shoes. . . I just got so stressed out, and I cracked!"

"And because you couldn't take the pressure, my brother

is gone," Bob spat bitterly. "He worked hard every minute of every day, even after the Noctem Alliance surrounded the city. He gave his life to save you, and how do you repay him? By moping in a cave, stewing in your own guilt while the people of his city were on the brink of despair and revolution!"

"I know that there's nothing that I can say that will change anything that's happened," the Mechanist whimpered, "but you need to know, Bob . . . I'm never going to forgive myself for what I did to you, and both of your brothers."

"Stop this!" Leonidas cut in before Bob, who was apoplectic with rage, could respond.

"Shut up, Leonidas, this doesn't concern you!" Bob yelled, jabbing his blocky finger at the Mechanist. "I've been holding back my anger towards this useless piece of trash for way too long now. It's about time that I give him a piece of my mind!"

"And what will that prove?" demanded Leonidas. "That you're never gonna forgive him for forcing Bill to sacrifice himself? That he should be stricken with guilt for it? Look at him! He feels so bad about what he did that he can hardly even function any more! It destroyed him!"

"It really has, Bob," the Mechanist agreed miserably. "You have no idea—"

"Shut up!" Leonidas spat at the Mechanist. "Everythin' that Bob said to you just now was one hundred per cent true! If your idea of repaying Bill's sacrifice is to constantly mope over the fact that Bill had to sacrifice himself for you, then it probably would've been better if he'd just let you die and saved himself!"

"I know that!" the Mechanist sobbed, having broken down as Leonidas spoke. "I was . . . I was just so distraught by what happened. . . ."

"And there's the problem in all this," Leonidas replied conclusively, looking back and forth between Bob and the Mechanist. "Both of y'all are so obsessed with Bill's death that it's causin' ya to make stupid decisions! I'm sorry for your loss, but it's in the past now! Ya can't let your entire life be dictated by it. Trust me, I know."

"How dare you!" growled Bob. "You have the nerve to talk about my brother like that . . . you didn't even *know* him! You were too busy leading the Noctem Troops to victory over *our* city! What makes you think that you have *any* right to talk about how I should feel?"

"Because every night that I was a member of the Noctem Alliance, I went to sleep feelin' horrible about what I was doin'!" cried Leonidas, tears welling in his eyes now. "I've never had anythin' against lower-level players, or villagers, or anybody that the Noctem Alliance hates! I only joined King Kev's army to save my family, and he made me do terrible things. I joined the Noctem Alliance because I felt like those terrible things had become a part of who I was, and that killin' and destroyin' were the only things that I could do any more.

"I let the past define me . . . and it took the death of the family that I had sworn to protect to make me finally realize that I had a choice. I could either live in the shadow of what I had done or let my past go, and do all I could to make up for my mistakes. *That* is the reason I'm here today, and not over in Element City with the Noctem Alliance plottin' to kill y'all."

There was a moment of silence as Leonidas finished his speech. Bob was staring at Leonidas, no longer totally angry, but feeling a mix of anger, confusion, fascination and sympathy. The Mechanist was staring at Leonidas as well, tears still in his eyes, and looking totally lost for words. Leonidas rubbed his eyes, took a deep breath, and continued to speak.

"I'm not sayin' that ya need to forgive the Mechanist for what he's done right now, Bob. And I'm also not sayin' that ya shouldn't be sorry for what you did, Mechanist. But both of you need to stop lettin' Bill's death cloud your judgment. We're in a war, and we need all the clear minds that we can get, 'specially when they're as brilliant as the ones y'all have.

"Bob," Leonidas said, turning to face the police chief. "You've got the greatest redstone expert in the history of Minecraft at your disposal. Do somethin' with him, will ya?"

Bob sighed, looked up at Leonidas, and gave a begrudging nod.

"And you, Mechanist," continued Leonidas, looking down at the frail old inventory sitting on the floor. "Ya want Bob and Ben to forgive ya, right?"

"More than anything," the Mechanist replied earnestly.

"Then earn it," Leonidas replied simply. With that, he turned to face the wooden door, walked over to it, opened it and walked out, closing it behind him, leaving Bob and the Mechanist sitting pensively in his wake.

Leonidas gave a deep sigh as he walked out of the room. He had entered to get his assignment for the invasion from the police chiefs, but he realized that it wasn't the right time. And besides, he could worry about that later. There was something else that he had to do before he left for battle, perhaps never to return. It was time to take his own advice.

He exited the front door of the building and walked down the street. As he went, he passed several Elementia soldiers, all of whom gave him a smile or a friendly nod hello, which Leonidas happily returned. All these players . . . they had accepted him, despite all the horrible things that he had done in the past. However, before he could fully accept his past himself, there were three more people he had to speak with. Finally, after walking across the village, Leonidas came across the building – a small structure, constructed just in the past few days, made of cobblestone, wood planks and glass.

Leonidas took a deep breath and pushed the door open.

All three members of the villager family were locked in a hug, but broke apart when the door opened. As they saw who had come, all three looked slightly confused.

"What are you doing here, Leonidas?" Mella asked.

"I had to see y'all one more time," Leonidas replied, trying to keep his composure despite the feelings of guilt welling within him. "I'm going to war tomorrow, and I might not come back."

"Ah," Mella replied.

"I heard that you three villagers weren't gonna be there at the battle," Leonidas continued awkwardly. "I heard that you were gonna be staying here at the village, along with like thirty other players who weren't goin' into battle."

"This is true."

"And before I leave . . . I just need you to know . . ." There was a catch in his throat, but Leonidas continued.

"I am so, *so* sorry," Leonidas continued, tears beginning to stream down his face. "I am *so* sorry for everything that I did to you. I know that it's my fault that the rest of your village is dead, includin' Blerge. But I promise ya, I never wanted anythin' but the best for ya. You villagers are my family, and when I saw those soldiers takin' advantage of ya, I got so mad that I wasn't thinkin' straight. I don' expect ya to forgive me, but—"

"Leonidas, we know that the players who were in our village to protect us were not treating us kindly."

Leonidas, who was doing all that he could to keep from breaking down, looked up in surprise. "What?"

"At first, we did not realize that we were not being treated kindly," Mella continued. "We knew that the players were sent there by Stan, who was very kind to us, and so we believed that those players that Stan had sent to us were being kind to us, but in a different way. We did not think that Stan would send bad players to us."

"I'm sure he didn't mean to," Leonidas replied quickly, jumping to Stan's defence.

"I know that he did not," Mella said solemnly. "Stan is a good player, and he made a mistake. You are also a good player, Leonidas. But I am not sure what you did was a mistake."

"It was," Leonidas replied glumly. "Even if those guys were terrible to you, they still would have fought off the Noctems when they attacked the village. They would've wanted to save their own butts."

"Maybe they would, maybe they would not have," Mella continued. "What is important is that you were not trying to hurt us, Leonidas. You were only doing what was best for us . . . or at least, what you thought was best for us. And now my family and me are no longer surrounded by bad players.

We are surrounded by players who are good, and nice to us . . . and you are one of them, Leonidas."

Leonidas's heart lifted as Mella gave him a warm smile. Then, Oob stepped forwards. He looked Leonidas directly in the eye and spoke.

"When I was a little villager," he spoke slowly, his face screwed up in concentration as if he were trying to meticulously pick every word he said, "I was told by my family about a player named Leonidas, who we called the Sacred One. I learned about how, when bad players came to our village, the Sacred One gave himself to them for the sake of protecting us. I always wanted to meet this player, who was so kind, so brave and so selfless. Now that I am finally meeting you, Leonidas, I would just like to say . . . thank you for everything, o Sacred One."

Tears of joy ran like rivers down Leonidas's face. He rushed forwards and scooped up the three villagers into a tight embrace, his spirit lifting as the memory of the villagers, the guilt that had been weighing him down for all these weeks finally evaporated. He was with his family once again, and they forgave him. If he died in battle tomorrow, it would now be with no regrets.

Stan opened his eyes and surveyed the area around the spawn point, which had once been a featureless expanse of grass blocks. Now, however, it wasn't anything close to flat; the terrain bore evidence of countless hours of training. The surface of the ground was pockmarked with craters, and half-destroyed structures stood proud and tall, looming against the brilliant pastel colours of the setting sun.

"Sally?" Stan cried out quizzically. He knew that she wanted him here. In the midst of the greetings upon his return to the Adorian Village, Stan had definitely heard her voice ring out from beyond the server. It was different this time, though, very staticky and fragmented, causing Stan to wonder if everything was still OK.

"Coming!" Sally's voice echoed from somewhere Stan couldn't see. He waited for a moment before Sally emerged from behind a tall tower of bedrock blocks with a few holes punched through the centre. She levitated towards him until she finally reached him and set her feet firmly on the ground. Stan smiled; it was always nice to see her.

"Thanks for coming, noob."

"No problem, always happy to visit," Stan replied. "Is something wrong? You haven't contacted me for nearly a week now." Even though his training was complete, Stan had found it odd that, after contacting him almost daily since their lessons began, she had been silent since their last meeting before the invasion of the Adorian Village.

"Well . . . there is a bit of news," Sally replied slowly,

causing Stan's heart to sink, "but we'll get to that in a minute. First, tell me how the invasion of the Adorian Village went. Did you manage to take it back?"

Stan nodded, and spent the next ten minutes detailing all that had happened since their last meeting. Through the recounting of the battle, Stan momentarily forgot his worry about Sally, but instead a new uncomfortable feeling took rise within him. When Stan told Sally about the attack on Nocturia, her eyes widened.

"Whoa whoa, back up," she exclaimed, trying to process what he had just told her. "Are you saying that . . . you managed to take out over a hundred Noctem Alliance soldiers, including one of their generals, in one fell swoop?"

"Yes," Stan replied, feeling slightly queasy. "And I've been feeling sick to my stomach ever since."

"Why? That's amazing, noob!" cried Sally, her face totally lit up. "Do you have any idea how much easier it's gonna be for you to take down the Alliance when you have one less general and a hundred less troops to deal with?"

"Yeah, I know, but . . . those troops weren't even in combat. Lord Tenebris . . . ugh . . . *Herobrine*," Stan corrected himself under Sally's glare, "ordered that all troops return to Element City except for them. That means that those troops probably weren't meant for fighting at all."

"You don't know that," scoffed Sally. "He was probably

just keeping them there so that they could sweep through Element City and mop up whatever was left of you after the big battle was over."

"Yeah, I guess . . ." Stan murmured before another thought occurred to him. "But what if some of those players were actually just upper-level players who didn't want to live under the republic anymore? I mean, Nocturia wasn't a military base. It was the capital of the Noctem Alliance's country. They stopped launching attacks from there as soon as the battles on the Cold Front ended, so doesn't that mean that I technically killed over a hundred citizens? I mean—"

"Stop it, Stan," Sally ordered in such a voice that he immediately ceased talking. "You can't worry about it now, the deed is done. Maybe it was right, maybe it wasn't. All that matters now is that you're going into an even fight, and you have that much better a chance of defeating Herobrine and his army."

"Yeah . . ." Stan said after a minute. "I guess you're right. . . ." But as hard as he tried, he still couldn't get the image of the crater where Nocturia used to be out of his mind.

"Anyway," he said, eager to change the subject, "you said you had news?"

"Yeah, I do," Sally replied. Stan's stomach clenched; he recognized that tone of voice, and he knew that it was seldom followed by good news.

"What happened?" Stan asked.

"Well . . ." Sally replied. "Have you wondered why it's taken me so long to get back to you after last time?"

"Well . . . yeah . . . but I just assumed it was because the training was over."

"Oh, come on, Stan," Sally laughed bitterly. "You're my only means of finding out what's going on in Elementia. I'm not just gonna stop contacting you!"

"Your friendship means a lot to me, too," Stan said sarcastically. "So why didn't you contact me?"

Sally sighed. "Security became even tighter somehow. I was really close to figuring out how to hack into the player files and give you operating powers, but then, out of nowhere, new software showed up. My computer didn't even recognize it. It just said that it wasn't possible to even look at the internal mechanisms of the server any more."

Stan cursed under his breath. "So all the work you've done so far has been for nothing?"

"Pretty much," Sally said sourly. "I'm gonna have to totally restart my efforts to get you operating powers, Stan . . . and that's actually what I want to talk to you about."

"Wait . . . what do you mean?"

"Well, you're planning to invade Element City soon, right?"

"Yes. We were planning on suiting up tonight, and marching out tomorrow."

"Yeah, well . . . I think it might be best if you held off until I got you operating powers."

"Wait . . . what?" Stan demanded, incredulous. "You want us to call off the attack?"

"I think you have to," Sally replied sadly. "I think that you'd have a much, *much* better chance of beating the Alliance if you had them, so I think that it's worth holding off."

"But . . . we have so many advantages right now!" Stan cried. "The Noctem Alliance is still reeling from the attack on Nocturia. They've never been more vulnerable than they are now! And we've just trained a hundred new soldiers that the Noctem Alliance doesn't even know about! It's only a matter of time before they discover that we have them. If we want the element of surprise, then we have to attack tomorrow!"

"But Stan," Sally said fearfully, "they've got Herobrine."

"So?" Stan demanded. "They've got one of him. We've got a hundred soldiers! Are you saying that Herobrine alone is going to be powerful enough to make up for a hundred unexpected fighters, *especially* when the Noctem Alliance is so disorganized right now?"

"That's the thing, Stan . . . *we don't know*," Sally replied darkly. "Nobody has any idea how powerful Herobrine is, and you won't find out until you fight him. You only have one shot at this, Stan, and I think that when you take it, you should be as ready as you possibly can be. From what you've told me, the Noctem Alliance seems to be willing to hold out in a stalemate a little while longer. Why don't you use that to buy time for me to get around this blockage?"

"And how do you know that you're gonna get past it, huh?" Stan demanded, staring at Sally accusingly. "You've been trying nonstop for months now, and every time that it seems like you're close to cracking it, something else pops up out of left field and makes you start back at square one. You're telling me that I shouldn't strike now while we've got a tiny window of opportunity just so that you *might* be able to get me operating powers, when you've been trying and failing to do it for weeks?"

Sally raised a blocky finger again and opened her mouth, then closed it. She stared at the ground for a moment, in deep thought, then looked back up at Stan.

"Stan, I told you what I think you should do," Sally said calmly. "You're going to return to Elementia, and I'm not going to be there. You're the president, and so it's your choice. Whatever you say, your people are going to go with. So choose wisely, noob."

Stan looked at Sally for a moment, unsure of what to say. Then he nodded and turned his back to the setting sun, away from Sally. He knew that their conversation was over. He took a deep breath, and the words appeared in his head.

DISCONNECT FROM SERVER?

"Stan!"

Just as he was about to leave, Stan turned around to face Sally one more time. As the sun disappeared under the horizon behind her, Stan saw the earnest meaning in her face.

"Please do the right thing," she said.

Stan held her gaze for a moment, nodded again, then turned away. The words reappeared in his head, and as Stan prepared to say the words, the crater in the midst of the tundra where Nocturia had once been flashed in his mind. As the image of the troops being engulfed in a wave of fire resurfaced, Stan knew that he would rather die than have the deaths of those hundred players be for nothing.

"Yes."

Ben, Bob and Charlie heard a whooshing sound behind them, and they looked up from their schematics, spinning around. Stan had appeared in the other end of the hotel's planning room, right beside the window that showed the sun setting behind the skyline of the trees of the Great Wood over the village wall.

"Hey man," said Charlie, giving Stan a polite nod of the head. "How'd the talk go?"

"Fine," Stan said purposefully. "Guys, I've made my decision about the invasion."

The three players stared at Stan, their eyes wide and their ears perked. They had been waiting for Stan's decision for hours now.

"Go on," Ben said in anticipation.

Stan took a deep breath, and then replied.

"Prepare the troops. We invade Element City tomorrow at the stroke of noon."

Although he was trying to focus on the battle plans that he had propped up on his pig's head, Charlie couldn't help but notice that the further that they marched down the road toward Element City, the darker the midday sky was becoming. He glanced up and there, not too far away, he could see the dark grey shroud that the Withers were casting over Element City. The march didn't slow down, however. Charlie still walked on, with the sounds of four hundred heavily armed soldiers marching in unison behind him on their way to take back their home.

The preparations for the invasion had been largely silent. There had been no big speech delivered, no final pep talk, no announcements of any kind. All the soldiers now marching down the road knew exactly what they were heading into. Words were not necessary.

At a glance, anybody would find it impossible to believe that many of these players had only been training in combat for the past week. Besides marching perfectly in unison, each and every player was suited in a glistening helmet and chestplate of diamond armour. The same held true for the weapons. Each player was fully equipped with a diamond weapon of their choice, as well as iron backups. To equip every player with such high-tier equipment, however, came at a cost. The storehouses back in the Adorian Village had been totally cleared out. If this invasion were to fail, there were no remaining materials to fall back on.

Charlie returned the plans to his inventory. He didn't need them. He knew them like the back of his hand by now, and looking at them further would only heighten his already overwrought nerves. Charlie had been aware for a while that he would be commanding the assault on Element City, but now that they were on their way, the full realization of what he was about to do struck him like a bolt of lightning. Charlie took a deep breath. He couldn't think too hard about it. He knew what he was doing, and his only job at the moment was to keep his fear at bay. Only with discipline could he lead his people to victory.

Charlie's thoughts drifted to his commanders, and he turned around, glancing over his shoulder into the massive wave of soldiers that were marching behind him. Jayden, Commander Crunch and Sirus all walked ahead of the troops. All three of them bore the same expression: grim and determined, with no hint of joy in their eyes as they imagined what they would find in Element City. Charlie knew that, somewhere deep within the hundreds of players, Stan, Kat and all the other commanders marched. They had special missions to do while the other soldiers were fighting, so they took to the centre of the assembly to stay inconspicuous.

Charlie imagined that, at this moment, their expressions mirrored those of the commanders out front, including himself.

A crash of thunder sounded from overhead, causing several soldiers in line to raise their heads in alarm. A moment later, a light drizzle of rain began to fall from the sky. Charlie gave an offhand glance at the sky, wondering how much of the discolouration above was from the thunderclouds and how much was from the Withers.

Charlie squinted through the rain, and there, slowly but surely, the Element City wall came into view. As he approached, the silhouette of the newly repaired structure loomed into sight, rising out of the mist. They didn't check their speed as they advanced closer and closer to the main gate of the city. The forest that they had been marching through started to thin out; more and more trees had chunks ripped out of them, or else were just lowly woodblock stumps.

Finally the forest ended altogether, giving way to the badlands that had been torn into the ground by the weeks of warfare around the outer wall. The giant ditch around the entirety of the outer wall sunk far below ground level; to approach the ditch from within it would be an uphill battle. Charlie raised his hand, ordering a stop. When they reached the edge of the trench, he could finally see the wall clearly. He did a double take. As prepared as he was for the attack, he had not expected what he was now seeing.

A bridge had been built across the open expanse of the badlands. Constructed of wood-plank blocks, it was five blocks wide, and extended from the edge of the forest to the base of the wall. Wood-plank blocks also extended from the top of the bridge all the way down into the base of the trench, concealing the underside of the structure. The other end of the bridge sat at the exact centre of a giant rip that had, alarmingly, been left in the centre of the wall surrounding the sprawling city, with the Withers hovering far off over the castle. The entire open portion of the wall was totally filled, from end to end, with Noctem soldiers, clad in black leather armour, all of whom had some sort of weapon drawn and ready. And standing directly at the centre of this massive wall of Noctem Troops, at the exact centre of the bridge's far end, was Drake, his cape billowing in the wind and a leering smile on his face.

The players behind Charlie were dead silent as they stared across the bridge at the soldiers clad in black who would be attempting to kill them within the minute. Charlie heard movement behind him, and he turned around to see Jayden, Crunch and Sirus glance at each other, the same thoughts in each of their heads.

Charlie was on the same page. He had been anticipating a hard fight through the trench to enter Element City. It didn't make sense that the Noctems would not only leave a giant gaping hole in their wall, but also build a bridge to make their entrance into the city easier. Clearly, something wasn't right here.

There was movement on the Noctem side of the bridge, and Charlie's eyes immediately locked on to Drake. The Noctem general had taken a step forwards and was now walking at a strolling pace down the centre of the wooden bridge towards Charlie. Immediately there was a bustle in the front lines of the Elementia soldiers as all of them drew their bows and trained them on Drake. The moment they did so, the Noctem archers at the other end of the bridge did the same, aiming at Charlie, who raised his hand to indicate his men hold fire. *Something is very odd about this situation,* he thought to himself. As he did so, Drake continued to walk, finally coming to a stop at the centre of the bridge. He gave Charlie a look, as if to indicate that he should walk out to meet Drake halfway.

"Wha' do ye want us t' do, General?" Commander Crunch whispered up to Charlie.

Charlie looked out at Drake. He knew that this must be some kind of ploy. There was no way that Drake would do this with no ill intent. And yet, as Charlie made eye contact with Drake, he immediately got a feeling in his gut that Drake wasn't going to attack him . . . and that, despite all his better judgment, he should go out to meet the Noctem general.

"I'm going out to meet Drake," Charlie whispered back. "Keep on holding. Don't fire unless they do first."

Before anybody could respond to him or Charlie could talk himself out of it, he gave a tug on Dr Pigglesworth's saddle, and the pig began to trot slowly forward, onto the wooden bridge and towards Drake. As he travelled across the open expanse of the trench, Charlie could feel all eight hundred of the warriors on both sides training their eyes on him. Charlie took a deep breath and shook off the incredible tension that was hampering his breathing as he continued forwards. Finally, after several agonizing seconds of walking with bated breath, Charlie stood face to face with General Drake.

"That's a fine-looking pig, Charlie," Drake said with a smirk, looking downwards slightly to meet the eye level of the seated Charlie. "It's good to see that you've managed to continue to be useful to your people. Very few have even survived our Silverfish Torture, let alone returned to the battlefield after it."

"Well, I've been a thorn in your side for this long," Charlie replied wittily. "It would be a shame to stop now that we're so close to taking our city back."

"Oh, you think that the city is yours," Drake said, with a

note of pity in his voice, as he shook his head and gave a sad smile. "Oh dear . . . You know, it's going to be a shame to kill you and all your men, Charlie. You're all so clueless that it's nearly pitiful."

Something snapped in Charlie's head as Drake said this, and he growled back, "Don't insult me, Drake. Just tell me why you wanted me to come out and meet you."

"Oh, I just had a few questions for you about the setup you've got going over there," Drake replied conversationally, looking at the wall of Elementia troops, many of whom were still aiming at him with their bows.

"Funny," Charlie said, glancing down at the bridge they were standing on, "I could say the same thing to you."

"So where's your president, anyway?" Drake asked, scanning the rows of soldiers, looking for Stan. "I'd have expected him to be out front."

"That's none of your concern," Charlie replied quicker than he had intended.

"Ah, I see," Drake chuckled. "I suppose that he'll pop up during the battle at some point. I suppose that I'll just have to cross that bridge when I come to it. That ought to be fun."

"Speaking of crossing bridges," Charlie asked suspiciously, "what's the deal with the one we're standing on?"

"Well, it's a manner of courtesy, of course," Drake replied, as if it should be the most obvious thing in the world. "You took all the time to evade us, raise an army, and march all the way to our doorsteps. Lord Tenebris has great respect for you for doing that, Charlie, and as such, he ordered that you should at least have a fighting chance at getting *into* our city before we kill you all. Therefore, the bridge is here for your convenience. You can use it to avoid traversing the trench. I assure you, it's totally safe."

"And why should I believe that?" Charlie demanded.

"Oh, Charlie, would I lie to you?" Drake laughed with a smirk. "I'm a member of the Noctem Alliance, my friend. Although we may not follow your rules, when we set rules for ourselves, we'll play by them to the death. You can trust our word. We're going to destroy you, and don't expect us to play fair for a moment while we're within the city. But I give you my word that the bridge is safe to cross. It's not booby trapped or anything like that. Now, why don't you go back and lead your men across, while I do all in my power to stop you?"

And with that, Drake turned his back to Charlie, and proceeded to march back towards his soldiers. Charlie stood in the light rain in total shock, trying to comprehend what Drake had just said. After a moment, though, he just gave up. Drake was clearly trying to play some sort of mind game with him . . . or else he was just a lunatic. Charlie shook his head; although he knew that the time had finally come to put these psychopaths out of commission, he still felt like this moment hadn't come nearly soon enough. He ordered Dr Pigglesworth to turn around and make his way back to the Elementia soldiers at the far end of the bridge.

Charlie had a gut feeling that Drake was telling the truth about the bridge. As despicable as the Noctem Alliance had proven themselves, the one honourable thing that they did seem to exemplify was sticking to their word. Charlie remembered the first time he had met Drake in the Nether months before, where Drake had sworn during the interrogation that he would not lie to them. Indeed, in time, everything that Drake had revealed had turned out to be true.

Charlie still had no idea *why* Drake had told them those things. The second that the general had tried to escape, he had done so with ease, but Charlie had better things to do than to try to work it out. He had been trying to decipher the warped, maniacal mindset of the Noctem Alliance for far too long now. The days of fighting with trickery and deceit had finally come to a close. It was time to do the fighting in a language they could both understand perfectly.

"What's the deal with the bridge?" Jayden asked, as Charlie reached the front of his men and turned around to face the wall again.

"It's safe," Charlie replied unemotionally, not taking his eyes off Drake. "Charge when I give the word. Have your archers stay back and cover us from the rear."

"What?" Jayden asked incredulously. "How can you be sure that it's safe?"

"I'm your commanding officer. Don't question me," Charlie replied, a bit more harshly this time, causing Jayden to back down. "I'll stay back with the archers and follow you in a bit. Ready your weapons."

"Ready your weapons!" Jayden, Crunch and Sirus replied in unison. Instantly, hundreds of bows and diamond tools emerged into the hands in the army, and readied themselves for an attack.

"Ready!" cried Charlie. "And . . . *charge!*"

Charlie waved his hand forwards and watched as hundreds of diamond-clad warriors rushed ahead, parting around him like a rock in a raging river as they ran towards the bridge. Charlie heard a cry ring out from the Noctem end, and a shower of hundreds of arrows flew into the sky, soaring through the air and crashing down like a meteor storm into the tide of players now surging across the bridge and into the city.

"Cut to the sides!" Charlie bellowed as his soldiers started to fall to the rain of projectiles.

Jayden, Crunch and Sirus at the head of the charge exchanged a quick glance and nodded to each other. Just as the mass of troops barrelling across the bridge was about to hit the wall of Noctem soldiers, now drawing their closer-quarters weapons, Jayden and Sirus leaped off the bridge on both sides, landing firmly in the trench below. The streams of troops followed their three leaders like a diamond snake dividing in three, pouring off the bridge and swarming through the trench, leaving only Commander Crunch's troops to fight the soldiers blocking the main entrance to the city.

As Crunch and his men collided with the black wall of Noctem troops and engaged them in swordplay, the Noctem troops appeared to be disoriented as they tried to branch into sections to break off the three-pronged assault of Crunch, Jayden and Sirus. It was too late, though. By the time the Noctem troops had made their way into the trench to combat Jayden and Sirus's soldiers, the republic soldiers had already drawn Ender Pearls from their inventories and were teleporting to the top of the Element City wall in an ever-growing cloud of purple smoke.

Charlie looked on with a smile at the battle going on before them. He still had no idea why Drake had let them into the city so easily, but whatever the reason was, it had given Charlie's invasion force an upper hand in the first phase of their invasion plan. The Noctem Alliance was now falling back from the city wall as Commander Crunch pushed his soldiers through the gates and into the city. Meanwhile, Jayden and Sirus had both managed to get nearly all their troops over the Element City wall using their Ender Pearls, and Charlie could see that some of them had even stayed on top and were now firing arrows down into the city.

Charlie glanced down at the bridge and saw the bodies of about five Elementia soldiers vanish into nothing, leaving a floating pool of items in their place. His heart clenched as he saw this, but loosened slightly as he saw hundreds of items spilled at the gateway where the Noctem Alliance had been standing guard. He took a deep breath and reminded himself that many of his people were about to die, and he would just have to accept this. With a heavy heart and a mindset that was trying as hard as it could to be optimistic, Charlie dug his heels into his pig and made his way down the bridge and into the city.

As he sprinted through the streets of his city, Stan couldn't believe the scale of the war breaking out all around him as the rain continued to fall. All throughout the streets, hundreds of soldiers were engaged in armed combat, fighting as hard as they could to destroy each other as sparks flew from their connecting blades. Arrows flew across the sky like deadly sparrows, some flying a bit too close to him for comfort. The scents and hues of dozens of noxious potion gases clouded the air, only getting stronger by the second. The bangs and whizzes of the fire charge dispensers and

TNT cannons rang through the air, creating a deafening din that almost drowned out the battle cries of the eight hundred combatants spread across Element City. Every so often, the side of a building would explode as a TNT cannon missed its mark, sending dust, blocks and various debris flying.

Stan felt extremely vulnerable as he sprinted through this metropolitan battlefield, completely devoid of armour and without his diamond axe in hand. He knew that it would render the Invisibility Potion moot if he were carrying anything visible, but the fact that he was so defenceless made him feel jittery and panicked as he ran. And he couldn't have those feelings now . . . not with what he was about to do.

Finally, after running across hundreds of blocks of streets and buildings within the battle zone, the rendezvous point came into sight. Stan hastily made his way into the dilapidated remains of the old Spleef Arena, and wasted no time in ducking into the base of a fountain that still stood in the central plaza. Though the building itself hadn't been used in years, and it had been picked apart by vandals, the remaining structure of the arena still maintained the regal splendour it had in its heyday. The old arena and the flat expanse of overgrown grass surrounding it was calm, but Stan could still hear the sounds of warfare as they spread further and further across Element City. Stan's heart raced; there was nothing to do but wait for his friends and hope that they made it without incident.

As soon as he thought this, Stan heard footsteps above him and, without thinking, crouched to the ground, ready to draw his axe at a moment's notice. The footsteps halted, and after a few seconds of silence, the visible form of Kat leaped up over the side of the fountain and dropped down beside Stan, landing in the stone basin.

"Hello? Is anyone here?" Kat whispered tentatively, her sword drawn and tightly clutched in her hand.

"Yeah, I'm here," Stan replied, and as soon as he said it, he realized that his hand was starting to fade back into visibility. Kat looked at him and gave a sigh of relief, the tension in her body lessening slightly.

"Glad to see you made it here OK," Kat said as she sat with her back to the fountain wall. "You have any trouble?"

"No, it was pretty smooth," Stan replied as he sat down next to her. "How about you?"

"Same," she replied, looking at the ground as she absentmindedly chiselled into the stone with the tip of her diamond sword. "I wish that I didn't have to leave Rex back in the village, though . . . I feel so exposed without him."

"Well, you know it was for the best," Stan replied solemnly. "He won't be any help to us on the mission, and the last thing we want is for something to happen to him."

Kat said nothing in response. Stan hadn't expected her

to. There was nothing to say. They were about to charge into Element Castle to try to take down Lord Tenebris once and for all. To talk about it would only rekindle the fear that the two of them were barely suppressing.

"I wonder where the others are," Stan said after a little while.

"Oh man . . . I hope they're OK," Kat said nervously. She glanced up out of the fountain and towards the grey sky above, from which rain was still falling, occasionally accented by a clap of thunder. Stan looked at her in concern, his heart feeling as if it were being wrung out like a sponge. As he stared at Kat, the rain drizzling down over her and a light mist hanging above them, it truly hit him for the first time that there was a high possibility that some of them – or all of them – would not live to see the end of the day.

"Kat?" he whispered.

"Yeah?" she replied, in equally hushed tones.

"Well . . . it's just that . . . I want you to know that . . . if we don't make it back . . ."

"Don't say that!" Kat hissed, her eyes flaring with anger as she glared at Stan; he immediately backed off. "We're going to kill Lord Tenebris and all walk out of here alive!"

Stan stared downwards at the basin as Kat continued to glare at him. He didn't dare question her. And yet, from the corner of his eye, Stan saw that Kat, too, was looking forwards. She stared intently at the cobblestone-block wall across from her, as if trying to extract some hidden message from it.

"We're all going to be just fine . . ." she murmured to herself, still staring, as if entranced, at the wall.

There were footsteps above, and without thinking, Stan and Kat immediately drew their bows and aimed them up, lest they be discovered by Noctem Agents. But they soon returned their weapons to their inventories. Leonidas's head came into the well, saw both of them, and smiled.

"Excellent, y'all are here!" he exclaimed. "Warp up outta there. We've gotta get a move on. Yo, Cassandrix, they're both down there!"

Stan and Kat both drew Ender Pearls from their inventories and pitched them up out of the well. Stan closed his eyes as he warped onto the solid brick ground above. Brushing off the slight sting in his knees, Stan saw Leonidas and Cassandrix, both clad in full armour glowing with enchantments.

"You're late." Stan sniggered as Kat appeared beside him in a puff of smoke that was instantly dissipated by the strengthening rainfall.

"Be that as it may," Cassandrix replied with an arrogant snigger, "at least the two of us are fully armoured and ready for the assault."

Stan looked down at himself and realized, to his

embarrassment, that Cassandrix was right. Both he and Kat hadn't put on their diamond armour after the Invisibility Potion had worn off. Hastily, Stan tossed the armour out of his inventory to the ground and began to put it on, Kat doing the same as Cassandrix and Leonidas chuckled to themselves.

Finally, Stan secured the diamond helmet on his head. His entire body was covered in glowing diamond, from his head to his feet to the axe clutched in his right hand. Kat looked equally menacing. The radiant lustre of the armour shone through the rain, particularly from the three-pronged enchantment on Kat's sword.

Stan took a deep breath and looked at his three friends, who were no longer laughing, but clutching their weapons in their hands and looking deadly serious. It was time to end the war once and for all.

"Are you ready?" Stan asked.

"Yes, sir!" all three players replied in unison, shouting to be heard over the now raging storm.

"All right," replied Stan, his eyes glinting with fury as a flash of lightning illuminated the sky behind him, accompanied by a crash of thunder.

"Let's do this."

Charlie's eyes widened as he realized that a block of TNT was soaring out of the raging rain and right for him. He yanked the reins of his pig to the right as hard as he could, swerving away just before the flying projectile would have made contact. The TNT hit the ground in a massive burst behind Charlie, leaving a sizable hole in the centre of the street. As Charlie felt the shockwave from the explosion crash over him, he scratched Dr Pigglesworth behind the ears in thanks.

Although the war between the eight hundred players was now spreading throughout the city, the majority of the combat was still confined to the Merchant's District, which bordered the outer wall near the entrance. Charlie had been on his way to the front lines to command the troops, but he could now see that the combat along the main roads was too thick. He instead fell back behind a half-destroyed building, where he found Ben looking at the battle plans laid out on a crafting table, his eyes skimming the pages so fast they nearly appeared as blurs.

"How're we looking back here?" Charlie asked, parking his pig next to Ben's table as the police chief looked up at him.

"Pretty good so far," Ben replied quickly. "We've broken their first line of defence and they're being driven back into the city. At this rate we should make it to the castle within a couple hours."

Charlie sighed at the idea of fighting an uphill battle for the next two hours, especially considering that the longer the combat raged, the more casualties there would be. This thought reminded him to ask Ben about the deaths on both sides so far.

"Well, it's kind of hard to get a certain read," Ben said matter-of-factly, "but based on what I've seen, I'd estimate about fifty dead on each side so far."

Charlie's stomach contracted as if all the air had been sucked out. In the short time that they'd been fighting, both sides had already lost an eighth of their soldiers! Would there be anybody left to fight on either side by the time they got to the castle?

"Calm down," Ben said sternly, sensing Charlie's panic. "It's not surprising that we lost so many during the initial strike. I'm sure the rate of casualties will only go down from here . . . at least, until they make their last stand at the castle, that is."

"Great," replied Charlie miserably.

"Don't mope, Charlie!" Ben ordered, the drill sergeant in him showing itself in full now. "The invasion so far has been a fantastic success, you have nothing to complain about! Now go out there and lead your people."

"Yes, sir," Charlie replied unwaveringly, and he commanded the pig back out into the open. The street was nearly deserted now, as the fighting had moved up the street and deeper into the merchant's district. Charlie knew that he couldn't just march up the street. He'd be taken out by snipers or TNT cannons if he rode up the street alone. Charlie glanced around and noticed an alleyway branching out from the main plaza. It looked like it went in the general direction of the combat, and it appeared totally unoccupied. Drawing his pickaxe, Charlie urged Dr Pigglesworth forwards across the clearing, ducking into the narrow side street.

The two-block-wide path was paved with dirt, unlike the rest of the city, and walls of solid brick rose skywards on either side of Charlie. In fact, the alleyway bore a striking resemblance to the one in which Charlie, Stan and Kat had stayed upon their first-ever entrance into Element City. Another clap of thunder burst from overhead as the rain continued to crash down from the sky in sheets. Charlie edged slowly onward pickaxe drawn, and eyes and ears on the ready to detect the slightest hint that somebody might . . .

It all happened at once. Charlie heard the sound of tele portation behind him, and at the same instant felt the tip of a sword wedged into a chink in his diamond armour, one thrust away from killing him. He froze like a deer in the headlights, pulling back on the saddle to bring Dr Pigglesworth to a halt along with him.

"Move a single block further and you're dead," the voice of Arachnia hissed from behind him.

Charlie was unable to move. He was unable to breathe. He

was unable to process anything other than the shock that ELM had not yet given up their hunt . . . and they now had him.

"It's good to see you, Charlie," Arachnia said with a sly smile as she walked around to face him. Charlie heard the stretch of a bowstring behind him and knew that Lord Marrow had an arrow aimed at his head. "Although I know that the same isn't true for you. You probably thought that we had given up on capturing the president after the episode at the Adorian Village."

Charlie said nothing.

"No matter," Arachnia continued with a faint chuckle. "You will be very useful to us. Enderchick, bring him back to the hideout."

"Should I bring the guh-*ross* pig, too?"

There was a pause before Arachnia replied. "Yes, I think so. I'm sure we'll find a use for it . . . around dinnertime, that is."

Charlie's stomach flipped, and he felt a blocky hand on his shoulder. Before he knew what was happening, everyone in the alleyway vanished in a puff of purple smoke, leaving the ominous corridor deserted once more.

As Charlie reappeared, he couldn't see an inch in front of his face. Although the city outside certainly hadn't been bright in the midst of the rainfall and haze of potions in the air, Charlie's eyes were not ready to instantaneously adjust to the darkness of wherever Enderchick had warped them. He was just beginning to make out the light of a row of windows when a fist slammed into the side of his head. The last thing Charlie heard was the squeal of Dr Pigglesworth as Charlie saw stars and was knocked out cold.

The eeriest thing about Element Castle was . . . how quiet it was. As Stan walked down the stone brick–block corridors of his castle, tailed by his three friends, the sounds of their footsteps echoed, casting the sharp tapping sounds upwards to bounce through the arched ceilings of the main hall. Their Potions of Swiftness had cut the travel time to Element Castle from the old Spleef Arena in half, and they had still encountered no soldiers of either allegiance, even as they had crossed the castle grounds.

Although Stan's friends may have been surprised, he wasn't. He had had a gut feeling that Lord Tenebris would want to enter this duel unaided – the best of the Noctem Alliance versus the best of the republic.

In utter silence, the four players began to ascend the stone-brick staircase. They hadn't spoken a word to each other since they had left the Spleef Arena, and they knew it was no time for conversation. They were now inside the castle, the point of no return left in the dust far behind them. Five players would enter the council room, but without question, at least one of the five would not come out. But if any member of Stan's team was going to go down today, it wouldn't be without a fight.

Cassandrix carried two diamond swords, one at

each hip, both glowing with Sharpness. She was the only one of the four players not to wear diamond armour, instead opting for her white-leather Spleef armour. Much like DZ, she preferred the increased mobility of the lighter, thinner armour. She also opted not to use a bow and arrow, and instead carried numerous Splash potions tucked safely into her inventory.

Leonidas was fully armoured in a diamond helmet and chestplate, as were Kat and Stan. He had two bows, glowing with Power and Fire enchantments respectively, slung across his back. However, his prized bow, which he had named Hornet, was clutched in his hand, radiant with enchantments of Fire, Power, and Infinity. A single arrow was notched in this bow, with dozens of others at one hip and an unenhanced diamond sword on the other.

Kat clutched her fully enchanted diamond sword (Gas-Powered Stick) in her right hand. One sword with a Fire enchantment hung at one hip, and a blade with Knockback was on the other. Slung across her back was Ol' Reliable, a bow with a simple Infinity enchantment. This was widely believed to be the oldest surviving weapon in the entire army. It was the very same bow that Kat had enchanted in the Apothecary's cabin, which she had continuously repaired on an anvil over time.

Stan was equipped exactly the same as he had been the

day that he had fought against King Kev. A diamond axe with Sharpness was held firmly in both hands, with two iron axes swung over his back. A Power bow hung at one hip, and the arrows at the other. Stan had worn this same set of armour the last time that he had dispatched a tyrant; he figured that if it wasn't broken, it wasn't worth fixing.

Finally, after what seemed like a full hour of walking, they were there. Stan, Kat, Leonidas and Cassandrix stood at the iron door to the council chamber. All four players stared at the door. They knew what was on the other side, and they knew that there would never be a better time to face it.

Stan reached out a trembling hand and pressed the stone button on the wall. The redstone mechanism roared to life and the entire team watched with bated breath as the iron door slowly swung open.

Charlie's eyes fluttered, struggling against what felt like some sort of invisible energy that was forcing them shut. Finally, he wrenched his eyes open, and after a moment, they adjusted to the dark. He was lying on a stone brick–block floor, and a very uncomfortable one at that. Not moving his head at all, fearing what might happen, Charlie looked around.

He was lying in a circular room that he recognized as the inside of one of Element Castle's towers, specifically, the one that had to be rebuilt after King Kev had blown it up. Battlements were opened all around the circular room, allowing a segmented aerial view of Element City. Although he could see the city, it was still dark as night within the tower. Charlie was shocked that no monsters were spawning. Leaning against the far wall were Arachnia and Lord Marrow, each holding their weapons, eyes trained on the floor with impatient looks on their faces.

Charlie's stomach filled with acid as he pondered what to do. Every moment that he lay in the middle of this floor, the republic troops were out on the battlefield without a commander. He had to get back down to the battle as quickly as possible. But he had no idea how he was going to do that without Dr Pigglesworth's help and, as he performed an immobile search of his inventory, he realized with a jolt that his pickaxe had been taken from him. He was totally defenceless.

"Hey!" Arachnia bellowed.

This is it, Charlie thought, his heart racing. *She knows I'm awake. What are they gonna do?*

"How much longer until you can warp again?"

"Omigosh, Arachnia, just give me, like, two seconds . . ."

"Do I really have to spell this out for you?" Arachnia said, clearly agitated with Enderchick, whose voice Charlie could hear from directly behind him. "You've got to get out there and find Stan as soon as possible! We can't hold Charlie in this tower forever, and he's probably the only person who Stan will turn himself in for!"

"But I'm, like, still kinda confused. Will Stan know that we have, ya know, the real Charlie?"

"You've got his pickaxe, don't you?"

"Yeah," Enderchick replied lazily, and Charlie's heart leaped as he heard the sound of something clattering to the ground. His pickaxe was now on the floor directly behind him.

"That's all you need. Stan will recognize it, and he'll turn himself in. Then we turn Stan in to Drake and finally call this mission a success."

"But still, like, how will Stan recognize Charlie's pickaxe?"

Enderchick and Arachnia continued to argue as Lord Marrow stared at the ground in stoic silence, but the gears in Charlie's head were whirring. They were planning on trading him for Stan. Arachnia was right, even if she was probably just guessing. Stan definitely would turn himself into them in exchange for Charlie's safety, and Charlie knew that, for the sake of the republic, he couldn't let that happen.

"It's all your fault. If I hadn't brought you, I'd have enough energy to warp again right now!"

A smacking sound echoed throughout the chamber, followed immediately by a squeal of pain. Charlie's stomach clenched. Dr Pigglesworth's sound of anguish had echoed from behind him, and he could hear his pig breathing heavily.

Charlie's mind kicked into overdrive. For whatever reason, the members of ELM hadn't killed his pig yet, and Enderchick had been careless enough to toss his pickaxe to the ground directly behind him. He had everything that he needed to facilitate an escape and return to the battlefield.

There was only one problem. Charlie knew that he had no chance of taking on the three remaining members of ELM by himself. It would take him a few seconds to even mount Dr Pigglesworth from the ground. In the time that took him, Lord Marrow would have already shot a tranquilizing arrow into his forearm. It was only a matter of time before Enderchick felt up to warping again. Charlie had no idea how he was going to escape, but he knew that he would have to act soon.

The light of the council room's torches flickered over Stan and his friends as they stood in a row of four inside the council-room door, weapons drawn. From the windows in the stone brick–block walls, Stan could see the sprawling metropolis of Element City beneath the grey skies. This was the first time that Stan had returned to his council room in weeks, and though it was nearly unchanged, there was one difference that struck a chord of deep discontent within Stan.

The council table had been removed. The block-high platform of stone bricks where Stan and his friends had drawn up the constitution of Elementia and made every law since then was gone. A flat expanse of stone-brick blocks now lay between Stan and the elevated throne on which a single player now sat. Stan found himself unable to move as, for the first time in his life, he laid his eyes on Lord Tenebris.

The leader of the Noctem Alliance was sitting cross-legged on the throne, his blocky hands pressed together and a devious leer on his face. Stan had heard that Lord Tenebris, or Herobrine, had nearly the same skin as him, but he was still surprised to see that, in fact, their skins were exactly identical in every way except one. And like the missing council table, this one subtle difference made Stan's skin crawl with uncanny anxiety as he stared into Lord Tenebris's empty, white eyes.

And, yet, as Stan looked his greatest adversary in the face for the first time, he couldn't help but feel something odd. The emptiness of his eyes bore into Stan's own, forcing him to devote all his willpower to maintaining the bond of contact, but Stan still could have sworn that, deep within the empty sockets, something was familiar.

The sensation lasted only for a few seconds, however, before Stan couldn't help but look away. It had been like trying to stare into the sun. Stan's entire face felt like it was burning up. And after all, it didn't matter what Stan might have sensed in those eyes. All that mattered was that it was finally time to kill the leader of the Noctem Alliance. Stan clutched his axe tightly and looked back up at Lord Tenebris.

"Ah, if it isn't the leaders of the Republic of Elementia," Lord Tenebris said with a chuckle. His voice was deep and calm, yet also menacing beyond compare. Just hearing him speak gave Stan the impression that Lord Tenebris could tell exactly what he was thinking.

"Stand down," Stan announced, sounding much braver then he felt as he stared at Lord Tenebris. "There are four of us and only one of you. There's no use in fighting."

"Oh, Stan, Stan, Stan," Lord Tenebris chuckled, closing his eyes as he shook his head and clicked his tongue. "Let's not be hasty. We're going to have a lot of fun, so why rush? Let me at least greet you before we begin. Let's start with you, Cassandrix."

Cassandrix, who was standing at the opposite end of the line to Stan with her diamond sword drawn, gasped, clearly shocked. "How do you know my name?" she demanded.

"Why, everybody knows your name, Cassandrix," Lord Tenebris replied, almost conversationally. "After all, you are one of the greatest Spleef players in the history of Element City . . . or, at least, you were, until you started to become overshadowed by the new players."

"What?" Cassandrix gasped, blindsided. "What are you talking about? How do you know that?"

"I know all that has ever happened on this server." Lord Tenebris chuckled. "And I know what you've been through, Cassandrix. It *is* a tragic tale . . . always the best player in the Spleef League, but never appreciated, always held back by your mediocre teammates. Then finally, after years of obscurity, Spleef returns to Elementia, and you see your chance to gain the glory you always deserved . . . only to realize that you're outdated and useless in comparison to the new players on the scene."

"Shut up!" Cassandrix growled, but Lord Tenebris continued.

"Why, then, Cassandrix, have you joined their side? You of all people must realize that lower-level players are nothing but verminous scum, infesting our server and taking opportunities from hard-working players like you, who have lived in Elementia since before they even knew what Minecraft was. So why do you defy me, when I, for all intents and purposes, am working for your benefit?"

"I'd rather die than join you!" Cassandrix screamed in rage, glaring at Lord Tenebris with tears in her eyes. "Regardless of whatever you might think of the lower-level players, they're still players, and no player deserves the things that you've been doing to them!"

Lord Tenebris chuckled again. "Very well, Cassandrix," he replied, still keeping his voice very casual. "If you would like to try to fight me, to fight to create a world where the lower-level players have everything gift-wrapped for them at the expense of older players like you, so be it."

"What beef do ya have against lower-levels, anyway?" Leonidas shouted, as Cassandrix stared at the ground, her eyes wide and a horrified expression on her face. "What did they ever do to you?"

Lord Tenebris slowly turned his head and fixed his gaze on Leonidas, who abruptly glanced sideways to avoid eye contact.

"Well, well, well, if it isn't General Leonidas," Lord Tenebris said, the level tone of his voice more unnerving than if he had been shouting at them. "It's so . . . interesting to see you here. I must admit that your treachery surprised me. I pride myself on my foresight, but I did not anticipate that you would ever stand alongside the president of Elementia, with an arrow notched in your bow and trained on me."

"Answer my question," Leonidas hissed, pulling the string of his bow even more taut.

Lord Tenebris laughed. "Leonidas, my friend, you misunderstand. I'm far more than a simple player who was wronged by the new players. Surely, by now, you must have worked it out!"

And with that, Lord Tenebris stood up from his chair, and stretched out his hand. Stan tried to raise his axe to block whatever was about to happen but, to his horror, he found that he was totally unable to move. He felt the horribly familiar sensation of being held in place by Sally's operating powers as he stood, totally immobile, in the psychic grip of Lord Tenebris. Stan's eyes flicked to the side as he realized with an awful jolt that all his friends were frozen as well, as if they were living statues. His heart beating out of his chest with panic, Stan turned to face Lord Tenebris, and his heart-beat stopped.

Lord Tenebris's eyes were open wide, and a gust of wind had started to blow through the open windows of the council room. The rush of air grew stronger and stronger by the second, and within a few moments a hurricane-force gale was ripping through the council room. The air seemed to spiral around Lord Tenebris as he slowly began to levitate into the air, his hand outstretched. His face was no longer jovial and conversational, but intense and twisted, radiating power. A primal rush of fear shot through Stan's body as Lord Tenebris opened his mouth and began to speak.

"I HAVE EXISTED SINCE THE BEGINNING, AND I AM THE GREAT-EST BEING IN ALL OF MINECRAFT!" Lord Tenebris's voice sounded over the raging storm, amplified now to sound as if thousands of voices were speaking from directly within Stan's head. His ears felt like they were about to burst. "MY POWER IS SECOND TO NONE, AND I AM FAR GREATER THAN ANY PLAYER, THAN ANY

OPERATOR COULD EVER DREAM! AFTER THE DEATH OF KING KEV, ELEMENTIA, THE GREATEST MINECRAFT SERVER IN ALL OF HISTORY, HAD FALLEN INTO THE HANDS OF PARASITES, AND I KNEW THAT, AFTER YEARS OF SLUMBER, IT WAS TIME TO RISE AGAIN! I CAME TO ELEMENTIA OUT OF NECESSITY, TO LEAD THE DISGRACED SOLDIERS OF BIRTHRIGHT TO VICTORY OVER THE ROACHES THAT HAD INFESTED THE LAND! AND TODAY . . . TODAY IS THE DAY THAT I WILL FINISH WHAT THE GREAT MARTYR HAS STARTED! I AM THE UNIVERSAL EMBODIMENT OF THE SPIRIT OF THE TRUE KING OF ELEMENTIA! I . . . AM . . . HEROBRINE!"

Lord Tenebris's mouth gaped open, and his eyes seemed to pop out of their sockets, as he let out an animal roar that pierced even the slicing winds of the storm. Outside the council-room windows, Stan could see dozens of lightning strikes, illuminating the now-blackened sky and filling the vortex of space around Element Castle with an awful amalgamation of light and dark. The scene was too much for Stan's senses to comprehend. It was far beyond anything that his worst nightmares could have possibly fabricated for themselves. Stan was now positive where all the power being diverted from Elementia's core was going – more raw power was radiating from Lord Tenebris than Stan had ever sensed before in his life.

Then, all at once, the lightning stopped. The pitch-black sky outside the windows brightened, returning to the murky grey cloud of the Withers. The cyclone of wind spiralling around the levitating Lord Tenebris quickly died down, and he himself took a deep breath, letting it out as he sunk downwards, touching down on the stone-brick floor. He was no longer on the elevated platform on which the throne sat, but instead stood with his back to the stone brick–block wall, on the same level as Stan and his friends. With a start, Stan realized that he could move again, and instantly raised his axe into a block, the weapon shaking uncontrollably in his now trembling hands.

Lord Tenebris's face was tranquil once again, no longer smiling, but not showing any other emotion either. He raised his hand again, and before Stan could even realize what had happened, he felt an intense heat well up behind him. He jumped forwards as fast as his legs could carry him, desperate to avoid the fire that had sprung up behind him. As he landed on the floor, next to his equally disoriented cohorts, Stan glanced around the room. The entire council room perimeter had been ignited into a blaze, fire ringing the room and blocking the door. Within the ring of fire was the flat expanse of stone-brick blocks where Lord Tenebris and the four players stood.

"I, like the Alliance that I lead, hold the principle of honour very close to my heart," Lord Tenebris said, as if presenting a business proposal. "Therefore, I am going to give you a choice as to your fate."

Stan was too terrified to respond. Never in a thousand years could he have possibly prepared for what Lord Tenebris was capable of. He had just displayed a show of power far greater than any player, even one with operating powers, could ever achieve.

"Your first option," Lord Tenebris continued, "is to come with me to the battlefield. There, in front of all the citizens of Elementia, you will surrender to me, and declare the war over. I will then proceed to execute each of you, as well as the rest of your commanders. It will be swift, it will be painless, and all the rest of your citizens will be allowed to live in peace under the rule of the Noctem Alliance.

"Your other option," Lord Tenebris said, after a brief pause to let his offer sink in, "would be to remain here, and fight me, four on one. I will not hold back on you, I will show no mercy, and I shall draw it out for as long as I possibly can. Once I am finished, I will go to the battlefield and assist my soldiers in wiping out all who serve you.

"This is not something that I wish to do. The war is over, and I do not wish to kill civilians unless absolutely necessary. However, the choice is yours."

There was a moment of silence, with only the sound of the light breeze blowing through the council room and the crackling fire all around them. Stan was too stunned even to think properly. Only one single thought permeated all his thoughts: *I am about to die.*

He had no choice but to obey Lord Tenebris. There was no way that any of them could possibly escape from the council room with their lives, and even if they did, Lord Tenebris would find them. To fight Lord Tenebris would be torture. Stan remembered during the fight with King Kev, when his opponent had set him on fire and repeatedly tossed him into the air. Stan had never felt any greater agony in his life, but he knew that it would surely be child's play in comparison to what Lord Tenebris would put them through if they refused to submit to him. And that was only what he would do to *them*. If they tried to fight Lord Tenebris, their fate would be shared with all who had ever followed Stan.

But on the other hand, if they did choose to be executed and end the war . . . then what? The citizens of Elementia would live on under the rule of the Noctem Alliance. Was that fate really so much better than a torturous death? Most of Stan's followers were lower-level players. They would be banished from Element City and sent to fend for themselves in the wild. Even with the skills that they had learned in training under Commander Crunch, it would be difficult to survive. The Noctem Alliance probably wouldn't leave them alone, either. Wherever the new players started their civilization, Stan was sure that upper-level players would go out of their way to harass and abuse them. If Stan surrendered, then his people might live on, but so would the hatred.

"I'm waiting," Lord Tenebris said, sounding slightly irritated now. "I don't know about you, but I'd prefer to stop this fighting as soon as possible to preserve as many of my followers as I can. If a decision is not made soon, then perhaps I briefly forget about my honour and go through with the option that I would find most fun."

Stan's throat felt as though it were being squeezed shut as his mind raced, trying to decide the lesser of the two evils. Somehow, the fact that he was going to die no matter what he chose barely even registered to him. All he could think about was which choice would result in less despair for his subjects, who had given their all to fight the Noctem Alliance and deserved as little pain as possible when the chips fell where they may.

Suddenly, Stan became aware of a new sound in the voiceless room – the sound of footsteps. Stan looked up and saw Kat stepping forwards. Her hands were empty, and from where he was standing, Stan couldn't see her face, only the back of her diamond armour. He watched, transfixed, as Kat walked directly in front of Lord Tenebris, knelt down, and sunk into a deep bow.

Lord Tenebris smiled as Stan found himself unable to even process what he was seeing. "So, Kat . . . you're willing to speak for your president and your country, and surrender to me?"

Kat said nothing. Instead, in one motion, she let out a ferocious war cry as she sprung upright, her enchanted diamond sword in her hand, and headed directly for Lord Tenebris's unprotected stomach.

Lord Tenebris acted just as quickly as Kat. He knocked the point of the sword away with his left hand, and instantly stretched his right hand out towards Kat.

Kat froze. She was still frozen in the midst of recovering from her attack. At the same moment, Stan felt the telepathic grip of Lord Tenebris lock him in place, and once again he felt the utter helplessness of having no control over his own body. Lord Tenebris no longer looked smug or arrogant. Instead, his face showed nothing but shock, which slowly morphed into rage, a burning hatred that contorted his features into an ugly ball of resentment.

"Wrong choice," he hissed dangerously.

A blast of thunder rang from directly outside the battlements, and Charlie had to use all his willpower to keep from moving. With no warning, a hurricane-force gale had begun to rip through the tower, and Charlie could see an electric storm outside, sending slashes of light and energy across the black sky. Charlie knew that this couldn't be a natural storm, and with a start he realized that Stan and the others had probably started to battle Lord Tenebris. They were probably right below him in the council room.

Charlie didn't allow himself to think about his friends, though. Right now, he had to focus on saving himself, for the sake of his troops. His mind raced, trying to conceive a way in which he could hop on his pig and ride out of the tower before ELM cut him down. Try as he might, though, he couldn't think of any way to make it work.

"I'm almost ready to go, Arachnia!" Enderchick chortled from behind him.

"Well, get a move on, then," Arachnia replied darkly, speaking at a normal volume as the winds died down just as suddenly as they had started. "I don't know what caused that storm, but I do know that I want to get off this tower as soon as possible. I don't like being so close to Lord Tenebris."

Charlie's heart skipped a beat. They were getting ready to put their plan into motion! The instant that Enderchick disappeared with his pickaxe, Charlie knew that there was no way he could possibly escape – the tool was the only thing that he had to fight off Arachnia and Lord Marrow. Charlie desperately tried to picture his surroundings. He had lived in this castle for months, and he knew it like the back of his hand. There had to be something around him that he could use to facilitate an escape. . .

Then, suddenly, Charlie heard it. It was faint, and he could barely make it out over the light breeze, the drizzling rain and the sound of distant warfare . . . but he could still unmistakably hear it. A breathing – deeply pained, horrifically raspy, almost metallic – a sound that vacuumed all hope and warmth from the air.

Without really thinking, Charlie turned his head to peer outside the battlements. It didn't matter if he was seen; he had to know if he was hearing correctly. Sure enough, there it was, flying not too far outside the walls of the tower, pure darkness seeping out of its body and floating into the sky, its three skeletal heads looking out over the city. Charlie had no idea what the Wither was doing there, but he wondered if perhaps he could use it to his advantage.

In the space of a second, an insane plan flooded Charlie's head. He knew that there was next to no chance that it could possibly work. He had never before come up with a plan where so many things could go wrong. In the next second, Charlie heard the sound of Enderchick, right behind him, standing up, and giving a yawn. Charlie imagined she was probably stretching out, feeling refreshed after her long rest. It was do-or-die time.

OK, Charlie, you got this, he said to himself, trying not to think too hard. *Just act. One . . . two . . . THREE!*

Charlie leaped onto his knees and grabbed the handle of

his pickaxe on the ground, right as Enderchick grabbed the diamond pick. Before she had even realized what happened, Charlie wrenched the weapon from her hand, took aim, and threw the weapon as hard as he could. As all three members of ELM leaped to their feet and trained their weapons on Charlie, the diamond pickaxe spiralled out one of the open battlements, through the rainy sky, and directly into the back of the Wither's centre head.

The effect was immediate; the boss mob let out a horrifying roar. Before they could attack him, the three members of ELM spun around, glaring out the window to see what had made the noise. What they saw made their eyes widen, and they dived out of the way to avoid the massive explosions as the blasts from the Wither tore the wall of the tower to shreds. In the midst of the recoil from the blast and the flying rubble, Charlie reached to the floor and, with two hands and his good leg, propelled himself upright, hopping to the side and landing on top of Dr Pigglesworth. He gave the pig a sharp kick with his heels, and the two of them sprinted across the floor of the tower towards the door that led to the castle bridge.

"Get him! He's escaping!" Arachnia's strangled cry erupted from the tumult within the tower. "Enderchick!"

Charlie glanced behind him and saw Enderchick standing in the centre of the tower, her eyes trained directly on him. So focussed was she on Charlie and his pig riding away from her at a breakneck pace that she didn't even notice the Wither, which had floated into the room and was now aiming all three of its heads directly at her. Before she could even make a move, all three of the black skulls struck her, sending her flying through the air, a trail of dropped items leaving her body as she went.

Charlie couldn't help himself. He ordered Dr Pigglesworth to stop in the middle of the castle bridge, and he turned back around to watch the tower. Through the lingering smoke from the explosions, Charlie could see the two silhouettes of Arachnia and Lord Marrow. Though they initially tried to dodge the blasts of the undead demon, the explosions engulfed the room, tearing through the walls and eventually obscuring them from view.

Charlie stared, transfixed, as the entire tower ruptured from the inside out, in a constant barrage of blasts that continued for a full minute until, finally, the Wither flew over an expanse of stone-brick blocks, pockmarked by the dents from the explosions. In the midst of the dust and still-falling rubble, Charlie could make out three bodies lying on the still-intact floor, items levitating on the blocks around them.

There was no time for Charlie to react. He couldn't think about the three players that he had just killed. He couldn't even be relieved that the bounty hunters who had been hired to capture his best friend were now eradicated. All Charlie saw was the Wither, levitating above the bombed-out tower, its six eyes trained on him.

Charlie turned his pig around and kicked it into high gear just as the first black skull left the Wither's mouth. It exploded behind him, and Charlie immediately regretted stopping to watch the destruction of the tower. He raced forwards on Dr Pigglesworth's back as countless black skulls rained down right on his heels, destroying the flat expanse of stone brick on which King Kev and Stan had fought many months ago.

The other tower, Charlie thought desperately to himself, fixing his eyes on the tower at the other end of the bridge. *There's a staircase into the castle in there . . . if I can just get into the other tower . . .*

A massive blast erupted right in front of Charlie. He grabbed Dr Pigglesworth's reins and yanked backwards on them, causing the pig to squeal and screech to a stop less than a block away from plummeting into the abyss below. He glanced around wildly, looking for an escape route, but there was none. The hole in front of him blocked his route into the castle, and the entire castle bridge behind him had been completely blown apart, leaving nothing but a sheer drop to the rotunda floor hundreds of blocks below.

The Wither was levitating directly above the hole it had just blasted into the ground. The beast took in a raspy breath, and in a burst of light, a skull shot out of its mouth. This projectile wasn't black like the others. It was light blue and travelled much more slowly – heading for Charlie.

He had nowhere to run. All he could do was steer Dr Pigglesworth out of the direct path of the slow-moving blue Wither Skull before it struck the single, tiny remaining piece of ground he was standing on and exploded.

Stan devoted all his willpower to moving the arm that was holding his diamond axe, but it was no use. Lord Tenebris's supernatural grip on him was too powerful. He glanced over at Cassandrix and Leonidas, and saw that they had given up fighting, recognizing the futility. They were only focussed on Kat.

Kat stood in front of Lord Tenebris, her diamond armour shimmering in the glowing orange light of the fire. Although her arm was still in position from her deflected attack on the Noctem leader and she, too, was totally immobile, she glared at Lord Tenebris with a defiant look on her face.

"So," Lord Tenebris whispered, his white eyes staring deeply into hers. "You thought you could trick me."

Kat said nothing. She just continued to stare unwaveringly into the empty white sockets of Lord Tenebris's eyes, almost radiating her hatred of him and the Alliance he commanded.

"Perhaps you didn't understand me, Kat," Lord Tenebris continued in a soft voice that sent chills down Stan's spine. "If you care for your people in the slightest, I believe that it would be in your best interest to bow down to me."

"Never," Kat growled, speaking for the first time since entering the council-room chamber. Her face was contorted with grit and determination, and no fear showed in her eyes as she stared down her opponent, her resolve blazing as brightly as the fire that surrounded her.

Lord Tenebris's eyes widened. Within an instant, all sense of restraint and subtlety went right out the window. His face twisted, his features accentuated by the fire, and he seemed to be the embodiment of a demon as he stared back at this player who defied him.

"I said . . . **BOW!**"

Kat sank to her knees. Her hands were forced down onto her thighs, and slowly, she began to lean forwards, her head moving closer and closer to the floor. She was shaking like mad, streams of sweat trailed down her face, veins popped in her head, and her teeth gnashed together as she did all she could to battle Lord Tenebris's telekinetic grip. Despite all her efforts, her head continued to sink. Right as her forehead was about to press into the stone-block ground, she spoke.

"No . . . you . . . *don't!*"

It was as if Stan was watching in slow motion. Kat's head

snapped upwards, her body flying up out of the kneeling position, arching backwards as she broke free of Lord Tenebris's hold. As the force of her motion carried Kat upwards and back onto her feet, she let the arrow notched in the bow in her hand fly forwards, directly into Lord Tenebris's unguarded chest.

Lord Tenebris glanced down at the projectile protruding from his heart. He didn't look pained, or angry, or even surprised. He merely looked confused, as if he had no idea where it had come from. Stan could only see the expression for a split second, however, before Kat's sword struck Lord Tenebris across the forehead.

Lord Tenebris stumbled backwards, dazed and unprepared as Kat let loose another blow, this time across his stomach. The Knockback and Fire enchantments on the sword took effect as the supreme leader of the Noctem Alliance burst into flames. Kat didn't stop. She was like a machine, rushing forwards and delivering strike after strike after strike to Lord Tenebris, sending him flying further and further backwards across the council-room floor.

Stan felt himself released from Lord Tenebris's psychic grasp, but he was still unable to move. He could only watch as Kat dominated Lord Tenebris, the foe that they had been fighting against for months.

Within seconds, Lord Tenebris had been pushed all the

way across the floor. He slammed into the elevated platform on which his throne was perched with a dull smack. He slumped down, his back against the wall, and his arms, legs and head limp as he sat in the midst of the ring of fire, flames engulfing his entire body.

Despite her rush of adrenaline, Kat took a moment to catch her breath, never taking her eyes off Lord Tenebris. As she stood in the centre of the chamber, the eyes of her three friends locked on her with awe and utter disbelief, Kat came to an alarming realization. Lord Tenebris was still alive! If he had died, she would have seen the telltale burst of items around him – even in the fire they would linger for an instant before being burned into oblivion.

She had delivered sword blows to all of Lord Tenebris's vital points, and he was sitting in a vortex of fire. Kat knew that if he was still alive, he wouldn't last much longer. She could very easily just stand by and let the fire finish him off. But . . . no. Kat knew that she couldn't do that. After all that this demon had put her and her friends through in the past months, she wouldn't be satisfied with anything less than delivering the killing blow herself.

Kat grasped the hilt of the diamond sword firmly in her hand. She glared at the unconscious form of Lord Tenebris. Her eyes flashed, and she let out a savage cry as she rushed forwards, her sword trailing behind her, and when she was just a few blocks away from Lord Tenebris, she leaped into the air, soaring through the flames and bringing the blade down with all her might.

The diamond sword halted in place when it was just pixels away from the crown of Lord Tenebris's head. Kat had frozen in midair.

Lord Tenebris was still lying in a slouch against the throne platform, limp and unconscious . . . limp, that is, except for his hand. His blocky right hand was raised, clenched into a fist, and suspended directly in front of Kat's face. All at once, Stan felt Lord Tenebris's grip tighten again. He was totally unable to move, leaving him, Leonidas, Cassandrix and Kat to watch as Lord Tenebris opened his eyes.

The Noctem ruler stood up straight. Detestation was ripe in every line of his still-burning face as he inhaled deeply, then let it out. In an instant, all the wounds that Kat's sword had inflicted upon him vanished. The arrow popped out of his chest and fell into the fire, to be consumed by the inferno. The fire erupting from his body extinguished, and he was totally unaffected by the flames all around him as he began to fly upwards, his hand still outstretched toward Kat, who levitated slowly upwards with him.

The two players, one standing upright, the other still in the final stage of a killing blow, continued to float upwards, until finally, they were level with the platform on which the throne sat. Lord Tenebris looked up at Kat. He was looking at her differently now, as if he was just realizing what she was, and that something was horrifying and detestable.

"Why, Kat?" Lord Tenebris asked, sounding disgusted. "Why do you fight me? Why do you continue to fight when you know you cannot win?"

"Because I used to be like you."

Kat was no longer angry or shocked. She spoke with a passion, a drive that outshone anything that her anger could ever produce.

"I was violent, I was arrogant, I wasn't afraid to step all over others for my own good. I thought that others were lower than me, even when they were kind to me and showed me mercy. I realize now that kindness and mercy made them higher than I could ever hope to be.

"Lord Tenebris, I will never stop fighting you. As long as you're still brainwashing the misguided players of Elementia, manipulating their hatred instead of curing it, I will *always* be there to stop you. You can do whatever you want to me. You can torture me. You can terrorize me. You can kill me. But no matter what you do, I will never break!"

Lord Tenebris said nothing. There was a long silence, during which he just stared at Kat, an inquisitive look on his face. Then, without warning, he jerked his right hand hard to the left.

Kat was flung through the air across the room and hit the left wall of the council room with a smack. Lord Tenebris then quickly moved his hand to the right, fist still clenched, as Kat followed, hurtling through the air at breakneck speed as she hit the opposite wall with a smack. Over and over, Lord Tenebris jerked his hand in every which way, sending Kat bouncing from wall to wall, accented by a pronounced smack, and an occasional crunch.

Finally, Lord Tenebris slowly lowered his hand, and Kat hovered near the ground. She was unconscious, her limbs sprawled out around her and various wounds covering her entire body, but her sword still tightly gripped in her hand. Lord Tenebris took a deep breath, flipped his hand upwards, and then unclenched his fist.

Kat was launched into the air. No longer held rigid in place by Lord Tenebris's mind, she spiralled through the air, spinning ungracefully like a top about to fall over. She continued to fly upwards, losing momentum until finally she peaked, and she began to fall back to the floor, rapidly gaining speed.

She never reached it.

Lord Tenebris glared at the falling girl with empty, unfeeling white eyes. Closing one eye, he took aim, drew back his fist and, when he had a clear shot, pushed his hand forwards, an invisible pulse of energy leaving him and heading directly for Kat.

The explosion rocked the council room.

Ordinarily, Stan would have panicked at being unable to raise his diamond axe to block the attack. Ordinarily, he would have had to grit his teeth as the shockwave from the explosion crashed over him, sending ripples through his body as if it were made of gelatin. Ordinarily, he would still be in shock, trying wildly to figure out how Lord Tenebris had survived the assault he had just endured.

But Stan didn't think any of that.

Instead, all he could do was stare, seeing but not believing, not feeling, not comprehending, at the body of Kat, lying in the centre of the council-room floor. She was sprawled out face-down on the ground, her limbs crooked, as the perfect ring of items sat on the floor around her. A slight distance from her hand, her diamond sword lay on the ground, having left her hand for the last time, still glowing with many marvellous hues from its various enchantments.

11: HEROBRINE'S MESSAGE

Stan had been in Elementia for over half a year now. In that time, he had made many friends, a good number of whom had been struck down in the battles against King Kev, and then the Noctem Alliance. He had seen terrible things, but after he had gotten through the death of DZ, more than a month ago, he thought that he could handle anything.

And yet, as Stan found himself unable to remove his eyes from the centre of the council-room floor, where Kat's body had vanished, leaving only her sword and other items in her inventory remaining, Stan found himself completely and utterly floored with disbelief. This wasn't just another one of his friends, this was Kat . . . *Kat*, who had been with him through thick and thin since he had first joined Elementia, who was his closest friend other than Charlie, who had come so far, changing from a girl who leaped out of the woods to ambush unarmed players into a brave warrior who would give her all to defend those she cared about.

Was that player . . . was Kat . . . one of his closest friends . . . really gone?

A shriek of anguish sounded to Stan's right, and he whipped his head to the side to look at Cassandrix. She had completely lost it; her eyes were wild, her face was twisted with insane fury, and although her teeth were gritted, a wild cry of hatred still radiated from her mouth as she rushed towards Lord Tenebris. Stan found this the most odd – he was still unable to move.

Lord Tenebris stared at her in surprise before levelling his right hand directly at her. She froze in place for a moment, bending forwards from the weight of Lord Tenebris's invisible grip, but with an animal cry she snapped back upright again. Stan watched, thoughts and emotions exploding within him like fireworks, as Cassandrix slowly struggled forwards. Somehow, she was managing to fight through Lord Tenebris's psychic hold, her eyes nearly dripping contempt as she advanced on the flabbergasted demon. He seemed nearly unable to move as he watched in incredulity as Cassandrix stood in front of him and drew her sword, raising it over her head.

"ENOUGH!" Lord Tenebris bellowed. In two rapid motions, Lord Tenebris stretched out his arms to either side of him, fists clenched, before sending them slamming together directly in front of Cassandrix's face.

The white-clad Spleef player found herself flying backwards across the council room, unable to resist the sheer power of this blast. At the same time, Leonidas, who had been standing beside Stan with his mouth hanging open, totally nonplussed by what he was seeing, shot forwards, as if he had been hit by an equally powerful energy blast from behind. The two players flew across the room at nearly the speed of sound. In the exact centre they collided, their heads bashing together and bouncing off each other with a loud crack. Stan watched, his heart plummeting, as Cassandrix and Leonidas fell lifeless to the floor in a crumpled heap.

Stan glared at them intently, refusing to accept what he had just seen, refusing to imagine what Lord Tenebris had possibly just done to his friends. Stan's heart gave a tiny jump as both of the players let out tiny moans of pain. They weren't dead. They were just unconscious.

Suddenly, Stan became aware that somebody was standing directly in front of him. He allowed his gaze to move away from his two comrades, and slowly looked forwards to stare into the blank, callous eyes of Lord Tenebris.

"Ah, President Stan," Lord Tenebris said with an evil smile, no trace of sympathy or regret on his face. "You have no idea how long I've waited to be in this position. Just you and I . . . face to face."

As much as he wanted to look away, Stan didn't let himself. He had no idea what Lord Tenebris was about to do to him. All that mattered was that he did all he could to spite this demon. Stan refused to give Lord Tenebris the satisfaction of seeing him back down and submit to him. And so, he forced himself to look Lord Tenebris directly in the eyes as he spoke.

"You know, Stan, I could have destroyed you a long time ago if I had wanted to," Lord Tenebris continued. "It would have been so easy for me to just teleport into Element Castle and kill you in your sleep from the start. However, I didn't. You are the player who killed King Kev, and went on to create the most disgusting regime in the history of Elementia. I figured that it would be best to let you think that you had a sporting chance before I crushed you. After all, it's like they say . . . the higher you are, the harder you fall."

Stan still didn't break his gaze. Staring into the eyes of Lord Tenebris was one of the most difficult things that Stan had ever done – the two empty voids of whiteness seemed to project some sort of dark sorcery that made Stan feel as if his soul were being withered away the longer he stared. It was only Stan's desperation to deny Lord Tenebris his satisfaction, and the knowledge that he was about to die anyway, that empowered Stan to keep looking.

"But oh, Stan," Lord Tenebris replied, sounding wild and manic as he licked his lips. "Your fall has scarcely begun."

Lord Tenebris drew back his right hand, and Stan tried to brace himself for the blast, forgetting that he was still bound rigidly in place. Instead of firing at Stan, however, Lord Tenebris punched upwards, and a second later, the roof of the council room exploded. Lord Tenebris bent his legs and leaped into the air, rocketing into the sky. Stan felt his insides squish into the lower half of his body as he accelerated to match Lord Tenebris's pace in the space of a split second. He could only close his eyes as he flew upwards towards the open sky above, falling debris and rain battering his face like a barrage of bullets.

Within seconds, Stan had burst through the hole in the council-room roof. He looked down and realized with a start that he was flying nearly fifty blocks over the castle. His stomach clenched as he stared down at the castle and the city far below him, terrified to think of what Lord Tenebris was planning to do to him up here. Refusing to look down any longer, Stan turned his gaze out over the sprawling metropolis and saw the smoke rising from the distant battle zones.

"Don't worry, Stan, I'm not going to drop you," Lord Tenebris said smoothly. Stan looked above him and saw Lord Tenebris staring down, wearing a sadistic leer. "I just figured that up here would be the best place to enjoy the show."

Stan barely had time to question what he meant by that before he felt a light-speed rushing sensation, not unlike when he used an Ender Pearl, which lasted for the blink of an eye before he felt normal again. Jolted by the unexpected teleportation, Stan opened his eyes, and repositioned himself. He glanced up at Lord Tenebris, who was looking down with an ecstatic expression. Stan followed his gaze to the ground. What he saw made his heart nearly stop.

Below him was the Avery Memorial Courthouse, in front of which the entirety of both armies, close to seven hundred total players, had congregated. However, they weren't fighting, and as Stan focussed, he realized with a horrified jolt that all his men had been totally surrounded. Less than half the troops wore diamond armour, and they were all huddled together in a cluster, unarmed with their hands above their heads, looking nervously at the ring of armed black-armoured troops that surrounded them.

Lord Tenebris cackled above him. "Honestly, Stan . . . did you really think your army stood a chance? The Noctem Freedom Fighters are the highest-level players on the server, fighting with the highest tier of weaponry, fuelled by the blazing convictions of their belief in their superiority. Did you think for even a second that you could train your pathetic, spoiled lower-level subjects enough to match them . . . and in just *one week*, no less?"

Stan didn't care how Lord Tenebris knew that they had been training for only a week. He barely even heard him at all. All he could do was look down into the diamond mass that, based on the cloud of grey smoke rising from the ground, had just been sprayed with a cloud of knockout gas. His fear for his friends' safety coursed through his veins as he thought of Charlie, Jayden, Ben, Bob, the Mechanist, Commander Crunch and so many others who were down there, and now totally at the mercy of Drake and Spyro.

"Don't worry, Stan, my generals aren't going to hurt them now that they've stopped fighting," Lord Tenebris said, as if he could read Stan's mind. "They won't do anything without the go-ahead from me, and we still have some business to attend to before we can address those traitors."

Stan barely had time to ponder what he was talking about before they were again hurtling through space at the speed of light, then coming to rest in midair. Stan opened his eyes, still dazed from the teleportation but wondering where they were, and what Lord Tenebris was going to unleash on him next.

Stan looked up, and immediately, something felt wrong. The sky above him was dark, and he could see countless stars, and the white rectangle that was the moon. And if he could see the sky, that meant that there were no more Withers around, which meant . . . they weren't over Element City any more. Stan looked down, and his racing heart stopped dead.

Below them sat the Adorian Village, surrounded by forests and illuminated with torchlight. The wall still stood strong, but there were no guards in sight.

"I have to say, Stan, there was one thing in particular you did that impressed me. I was very surprised that you managed to take this village from me," Lord Tenebris said slowly.

His face was stagnant, and Stan couldn't read his emotions. "Of course, from what I've heard, the assassins whom Drake hired ended up helping you indirectly, so perhaps I shouldn't give you too much credit. Nonetheless, you did manage to catch me off guard, which is not something that is easily done.

"And what a perfect place for you to set up your base of operations! I mean, the Adorian Village was founded out of the belief that new players ought to be treated like toddlers who need their pathetic little hands held as long as they're playing the game. I suppose that you could call the Adorian Village a symbol of all that you stand for, Stan."

Lord Tenebris's lips curled upwards into a wily smile. Suddenly, Stan realized with a horrible lurch of his stomach what Lord Tenebris was implying.

"No, please don't," Stan stammered.

"Do you know what I need to do, Stan?" Lord Tenebris asked in a mockingly playful voice. "I need to do something big, something grandiose. It must be something that will last, and serve as a reminder to the posterity of the power I possess, and what happens to those who are foolish enough to fight back against the most righteous ideals of the Noctem Alliance—"

"Lord Tenebris, I'm begging you!" Stan pleaded, and before he could stop himself, he blurted out, "There are civilians down there! Dozens of players who are too weak or too wounded to fight are in that village right now! And there are NPC villagers, too!" Tears were gushing from Stan's eyes, as he desperately tried to appeal to the heartless monster who possessed him, willing to do anything to save Oob, Mella, Stull and the rest of his players.

Lord Tenebris's eyebrows raised for a moment, but then, without warning, he looked enraged. "Do you mean to tell me," he growled, "that you have more soldiers down there? And they abandoned you because they were too terrified to face my men?"

"No!" Stan bellowed. "They're just civilians. They couldn't fight even if they wanted to! You said that you wouldn't attack civilians! Please, at the very least, bring them back to Element City, with the rest of my people! Your soldiers are there, too!" Stan cried, suddenly remembering. "The troops we captured in battle are imprisoned in the village! Are you really going to kill your own men?"

But Lord Tenebris paid no attention. The gale-force winds from the council room had returned, kicking up from nowhere and swirling around Lord Tenebris like a cyclone. The clear night sky above them was rapidly being overrun by looming grey storm clouds. Far below, Stan could see players swarming out of the houses, gazing up at the sky and trying to figure out what was going on.

Lord Tenebris took a deep breath and closed his eyes. Then slowly, he stretched his right hand out over the city, and opened his eyes.

Instantly, every single house in the village burst into flames. Even if Stan wasn't being held still by Lord Tenebris, he still would have been frozen, in body and mind. The people below screamed in horror as their dwellings were engulfed in the blaze. Stan saw several players pointing up to the sky at them. He, too, looked up at Lord Tenebris, waiting to see what else this fiend could possibly do, and saw that his hand was glowing with a radiant light. Without warning, the light intensified, shining so brightly that Stan was forced to look away. Back down in the village, the winds were blowing even harder now, and Stan could see his people struggling just to stand upright.

There was a crack of thunder, and a bolt of lightning struck the roof of the Town Hall, causing a chunk of it to be blown away in the static discharge. In the split second after the strike, everything was silent, and Stan felt as if the air were alive, as if all the energy around him was evaporating. Then, in an instant, the dark night sky was filled with light, sound and power as thousands of thunderbolts rained from the heavens, covering the Adorian Village in blinding light. Stan closed his eyes, but the radiance was so bright that it scorched Stan's retinas even through his eyelids, sending his senses into overdrive with the cyclone winds and sounds of explosions below.

Slowly but surely, Stan's eyes adjusted, and he even found himself able to open his eyes a little. Looking down at the Adorian Village was still like looking into the sun, but Stan managed to glance up at Lord Tenebris, whose glowing hand seemed nearly dull in comparison to the flashes below them. As he looked up at the face of his captor, Stan's already crippled heart felt like it took another ice-cold stab as he saw the twisted features, illuminated and shadowed to look infernally cruel and evil in the light.

Then, as suddenly as it had started, all of it stopped. The winds stopped blowing, Lord Tenebris's hand stopped shining, and the lightning strikes stopped. Such a drastic shift in light left Stan blinded, and it was about half a minute before his eyes had fully adjusted. As Stan saw more and more of what was below him, he felt the air drain from his lungs. Eventually, when his sight had completely returned, Stan felt as if he were about to pass out from the sheer magnitude of horror that lay below him.

The Adorian Village, which had just this morning stood proud and strong in the midst of the Great Wood, had been totally razed. Not one single building was still standing. The site where the wooden motel had been was now as featureless as if players had never been there before. The tiny wooden hut where Oob and his family were staying was nowhere to be seen. The brick Town Hall had been torn to shreds, and despite that it was the most complete remaining building in the village. Only two brick-block wall segments, connected at a right angle, remained upright.

There was not a single player in sight.

Stan barely had time to take in what he was seeing when, in a blink of teleportation, he suddenly found himself in the midst of it. The psychic grip released him, and he fell to the ground on top of one of the only sections of gravel road that had not been torn apart by the lightning. Stan raised his head, and though his body was shaking, he managed to look around.

The village was far worse from this level. The ground had been torn into an uneven, cratered landscape, not unlike the war-torn trench outside Element City. The fires seemed far more numerous, and the smoke and heat spiralling around him threatened to choke Stan, but not nearly as much as the items. Now that he was at ground level, he could see the dropped inventories of countless fallen players, scattered across the barren landscape.

As Stan's mind attempted to make sense of all that was around him, he felt as though his brain was full of fuzz, and not able to totally process what he was seeing. Stan realized that somebody was watching him. Slowly, he turned his head to look directly ahead of him, where Lord Tenebris stood at the other end of the patch of gravel. He was looking down at Stan, totally emotionless. Stan stared back. He felt nothing towards Lord Tenebris. No anger, no hatred, not even fear. Stan's mind was too overwhelmed to feel anything, and so he just stared blankly up at Lord Tenebris, like a child processing the world around himself for the first time.

"You knew that this would happen, Stan," Lord Tenebris said in a deadpan. "Perhaps you tried to convince yourself otherwise, perhaps you lied to yourself and believed that you somehow had the upper hand in this war, but you never did. In fact, even calling this a war is giving you far too much credit. After all, in a war, there must be at least two sides."

Stan said nothing.

"Why, Stan? If your fight was so futile, then why did you bother to put up one at all? Did you really think that you could overthrow the Noctem Alliance through tactful and honest methods, the same way you did to King Kev and his kingdom? I refuse to believe that you didn't know who I was before you challenged me today, Stan. And the moment you found that out, you should have given up the fight, right then and there. You must have known that, regardless of what you did against the Alliance I command, you could never beat me."

Stan remained silent.

"And now look at you. Your pitiful resistance has been crushed, your troops have been captured and your leaders are being lined up for the firing squad as we speak, awaiting my command to finish the job. You have no backup, you have no contingency plan and your best friend is dead. You're pathetic and weak, totally at my mercy. If I wanted to kill you now, I could do it without raising a finger. But . . . I won't."

Stan, who had been staring up vacantly at Lord Tenebris, now looked down to the gravel below him, failing to imagine what Lord Tenebris could possibly do to bring him lower.

Lord Tenebris took no notice of Stan's movement. Instead, he focussed intently on both his hands. In his right hand appeared a golden apple, shimmering with a brilliant lustre, brighter in the darkness than any golden apple that had ever been seen in Elementia. In the other hand, a glass bottle appeared, filled to the brim with blood-red potion.

"I will say this, Stan. As pathetic as you are, I still find that I have a great deal of respect for you. Your ideals may be self-ish and misguided, and your arrogance and pride may well be admired by your followers. However, I cannot deny that your devotion to your people is admirable, and that, while it may have been pointless in the long run, you did manage to evade my grasp for far longer than I had anticipated. Therefore, out of respect for you as an adversary, I only see fit to give you one final choice."

Lord Tenebris reached down and placed the golden apple and the potion side by side on the block in front of Stan. He looked up from the ground, and stared at the two items.

"These two items are very special, Stan," Lord Tenebris explained. "The apple is not just any golden apple. This is an enchanted golden apple. It is the best healing item in all of Minecraft. If you eat it, you will find yourself totally reinvigorated, and more ready to fight than you have ever been in your life. The potion, on the other hand, is one that you should recognize – the Potion of Harming. This particular potion is from my personal collection. It is brewed to Level Three, which is much more potent than any potion regularly available. It is strong enough to kill you the moment it touches your lips."

Stan felt as though a black hole were opening in his chest as he realized where Lord Tenebris was going with this.

"Here is your choice, Stan. You may choose to eat the golden apple, and return to Element City to challenge me. There, we will have an honourable duel to the death in front of all our people, and the winner shall be crowned the new ruler of Elementia.

"Alternatively, you may choose to drink the Potion of Harming and save yourself the humiliation. It will be quick, painless, and instantaneous."

Lord Tenebris was quiet for a moment to let his offer sink

in. Stan continued to stare at the two items, still with almost no comprehension, for a full minute before Lord Tenebris spoke again.

"You have until sunrise to make your choice. I will be waiting back at Element City for you to challenge me. If you choose the second option, I will know. If you adhere to my deadline, then regardless of your decision, none of your people will be punished for their actions under your command, with the exception of your leaders and closest friends. I would tell you not to run away, but I know that you aren't going to."

And with that, Lord Tenebris turned his back on Stan, walking slowly into the cloud of smoke that was descending over the blazing ruins of the city until he had totally faded from view.

For the longest time, Stan remained still. Within the past ten minutes, so much had happened. Stan needed ample time to process it all. It was only after the last bit of information had been realized that the depression came crashing over him.

Stan had failed himself, and he had failed his people. He should have known that Lord Tenebris would be far too powerful for him and his friends to handle. And that fiend was right about him – how could he have possibly expected an army of anything less than the most talented, skillful and experienced players to take down a force of four hundred

Noctem fighters? They should have trained longer, and with that thought, Stan remembered with a horrible jolt what Sally had said. If they had waited just a little bit longer . . . Stan might have had operating powers, and all this could have been avoided. . . .

Stan realized, though, that this thought was moronic. Even if he had somehow managed to get operating powers, there was no way that he ever could have taken down Lord Tenebris. Summoning gale-force winds on a whim, sending down a storm of thousands of lightning strikes – these were things that he had never seen before, far greater than anything a normal operator could achieve. Whatever Lord Tenebris had done to himself, Stan knew that he was far beyond anything that he could ever . . .

Suddenly, something else that Sally had said struck Stan like a rock thrown at his head. Stan teetered over and fell to the ground, his heart stopping dead as he remembered. Lord Tenebris was siphoning energy from the server itself. He was drawing in more and more power from Elementia to make himself stronger. Eventually, the lack of power would corrupt Elementia, creating a game-breaking glitch that would throw the server into chaos. And that glitch could travel across the internet as a virus, infecting countless other servers until multiplayer Minecraft ceased to exist.

That meant that . . . by failing to defeat Lord Tenebris . . .

Stan had condemned all of Minecraft to be destroyed. This game, which had meant so much to him, his friends, and so many others across the world, this game that had enabled people to play in their own world, to do what they wanted, and to have the freedom to build, explore and fight at the pace they wanted – it was all going to be gone.

Stan glanced down at the two items on the ground in front of him. The golden apple was truly a thing of beauty, shimmering in marvellous hues of gold even in the darkness of the smoldering city. The Potion of Harming looked innocuous, sitting on the gravel with its deep red contents, but Stan knew better.

Stan wondered if there was any point in returning to Element City and challenging Lord Tenebris. What would it accomplish? He would show up, and Lord Tenebris would wipe the floor with him, putting him through excruciating pain and humiliation before finally ending his life. In terms of his people, it didn't matter. Stan believed that Lord Tenebris would allow most of his people to live on, but Stan could do nothing to stop the execution of his friends. If he went back, his friends' last memories in Elementia would be of their leader being mutilated and destroyed. What's more, Stan found that he hardly even cared that he and his friends were on the verge of death. He was already too dead inside to feel anything.

Stan reached down to the ground and clasped the bottle of blood-red potion. Slowly, he raised the potion bottle and looked at it intently. In his reflection, slightly warped in the reddened globe of glass, Stan saw a player who looked damaged, pathetic and utterly defeated. A sigh of apathy escaped his mouth. There was no hope any more.

Stan put the glass of the bottle to his mouth, and slowly began to tilt it backwards.

"Arf!"

Right as the potion was about to enter his mouth, the noise startled Stan. He looked around wildly, trying to see what made the noise, and when he looked behind him, he saw it. There, standing in the middle of the torn-up road, panting slightly with his blocky tongue hanging out of his mouth, sat a wolf. Miraculously, despite being in the centre of the razed city, this wolf was totally unharmed, and hadn't even gotten dirty.

"Hey, Rex," Stan breathed.

At the sound of his name, Rex's tail began to wag, and he bounded over to Stan, leaping up on his hind legs and beginning to lick Stan's face. Somewhere within his deadened soul, Stan felt a slight warmth begin to ignite within him as he returned Rex's affection, scratching him behind the ears and beneath the collar as the wolf tapped his foot in pleasure. For a while, Stan just sat there, playing with the wolf, and he began to feel a little bit of joy.

"How did you manage to survive, boy?" Stan asked, still baffled.

Rex lowered himself down onto all fours again, and he tilted his head to the side in confusion. Stan wondered just how much the wolf could understand. He had never owned a dog himself, and he had never talked to Kat about . . .

At that moment, for the first time since Lord Tenebris had blasted him out of the council room, the realization of what had happened washed over Stan yet again, threatening to crush him like a steamroller. Stan had endured so much since the battle had begun, so much had been destroyed and so much lost, that he had barely had time to comprehend any of it fully. But now, in the midst of the ruined Adorian Village, for the first time, the realization truly hit Stan that one of his best friends was gone from Elementia forever.

"You're looking for Kat, aren't you," Stan said quietly, as tears started to well in his eyes.

At the sound of his master's name, Rex's ears perked up, and his eyes widened with joy. The wolf looked around, as if expecting to see Kat appear at any moment. Stan struggled to choke back sobs as the wolf began to pace the ground around Stan, sniffing everywhere, and looking so hopeful. When nothing was found, Rex looked inquisitively up at Stan, his head curiously cocked to one side.

"Well, you can forget about it," Stan managed to get out. "Kat's dead."

Rex was silent and immobile for a moment. Then, he tilted his head to the other side and let out an inquiring yip, as if he didn't understand what Stan was trying to tell him.

"Didn't you hear me?" Stan moaned, his voice shaky and uneven. "Kat is dead, Rex. She's not coming back for you."

Rex looked extremely confused, staring at Stan intently, as if trying to read him. The wolf realized that Stan was on the verge of breaking down in tears, and he began to mirror Stan, his eyes widening in sorrow as he began to let out soft whimpers. Suddenly, without warning, Stan felt an intense surge of anger at Rex for being so empty-minded, so uncomprehending.

"Don't you get it, you stupid animal!" Stan bellowed, his face contorted with agony and tears gushing down his face like rapids now. *"Your master is* dead*! She's* never *coming back for you! You will never . . . see . . . her . . . ever . . ."*

And with that, Stan broke down. He let out a wailing cry of *"aga-aain*!" as he burst out into unapologetic sobs, collapsing onto the ground and burying his face into Rex's neck. He hugged the wolf tightly around the neck, desperate for anybody to share in his grief and heartache. Stan felt as though a giant piece of himself was being torn out and digested in acid. Rex sat tall and strong, letting out his own whimpers of grief, but not moving in the slightest as he let Stan, one of the first players that he had ever trusted, cry into him as Stan's body shook with spasms of unquenchable pain.

For the longest time, the player and the wolf sat in the middle of the bombed-out graveyard that was the Adorian Village. Stan's sadness showed no signs of slowing as he remembered everything that he and Kat had been through together – their first meeting in the woods, their training with Sally and her friends, their quest to take down King Kev, their time on the council, rebuilding Elementia, their war against the Noctem Alliance, their journey to return home to their city and the last stand, which felt as though it had happened a thousand lifetimes ago.

Suddenly, time stopped. Everything around Stan ground to a halt. His world seemed to pause, as he was hit by a massive realization. He remembered when he had stared into the eyes of Lord Tenebris . . . those empty, white eyes, which pained him to even look at. He had had a feeling that he had seen those eyes somewhere before, although, for the life of him, he couldn't remember where . . .

Not any more. Stan remembered who the eyes belonged to.

He remembered what seemed like an eternity ago. Adrenaline coursing through his veins and with his entire world on the line, Stan had pitched an Ender Pearl up onto the wall of Element Castle, and landed on the bridge. He had turned to look at his adversary, and there stood King Kev, leering at him, his sword drawn and pointed at Stan in a clear challenge. Stan had only had a split second to look into his eyes – eyes, of course, that were unique, different from all other players in Minecraft – before the fight had commenced.

Earlier that night, as Stan had challenged Lord Tenebris, he had been forced to look away. The eyes of Lord Tenebris possessed some sort of demonic power, radiating from deep within them, and making it impossible to hold contact with them. And yet, through all the evil and all the power, Stan had recognized something in those eyes – the same indescribable, unique quality that he had seen in the brief seconds before he had charged King Kev, intent on wiping the dictator off the face of the server. Stan felt as though everything that he knew to be true in the world now hung in the balance as he realized what this meant.

Lord Tenebris . . . and King Kev . . . could they possibly be . . .

Questions erupted in Stan's head like fireworks, as he thought of all the reasons that this couldn't possibly be true. And . . . yet . . . he was so sure. Despite everything that Stan knew to be true that contradicted it, he knew what he had seen. The eyes were the only true way to tell one Minecraft player apart from another, for although skins could be changed, eyes stayed the same regardless of what a player looked like, even remaining the same across different accounts. But . . . how? Even as Stan's mind kicked into overdrive at the thought that Lord Tenebris and King Kev could possibly be one and the same, he knew that this couldn't be possible. King Kev was dead. Stan had fought him, and he had watched the king die. Furthermore, King Kev had given up his operating powers long before Stan joined the server. If he had them, he surely would have used them when Stan and the Apothecary had threatened his life. And even if, by some crazy stretch of the imagination, King Kev had returned to Elementia with his operating powers intact, Lord Tenebris – or rather, Herobrine – clearly was not a player. He had demonstrated skills and abilities far more than an operator was capable of. Last but not least, there was no way that he possibly could have hacked his way back in because of the Modelock Mod. If what Sally had told him about the mod was true, there was no way that King Kev could have tampered with the code of his own server. Clearly, only Herobrine, a glitch, would be able to bypass the code of Elementia and attain such unbelievable power.

Stan tried to convince himself that it couldn't be true. He had no idea what Herobrine was capable of. It was more than possible that he had somehow changed his own eyes to mirror King Kev's just for the sake of unnerving Stan. Or maybe what Stan recognized in both of them was their equally sinister nature. Or maybe . . .

Stan was snapped out of his thoughts by the faint crunching of four-legged footsteps on gravel, growing softer and softer. Stan looked up and saw Rex dashing across the uneven street.

"Hey!" Stan called out. "Rex! Where are you going?"

At the sound of Stan's voice, the wolf stopped in his tracks. Slowly, he turned his head to the side and looked up at Stan, his eyes showing an almost humanlike level of importance and determination. Rex raised his front right leg, still looking at Stan, and gave two upward swipes, a clear gesture for Stan to follow him, before turning back around and continuing on.

Stan was floored. His head felt like it was about to explode as he tried to process everything. So many different thoughts, feelings, and emotions were welling in Stan that he felt as if he were about to blow a gasket and pass out in the street. Then, all of a sudden, he decided to stop. Everything that was running through Stan's head stopped. He took a deep breath and stored the thoughts in the back of his mind for later. He stood up from the ground and pocketed the Potion of Harming and the enchanted golden apple. His mind was clear, and he began to follow Rex.

As the wolf led him through the streets of the Adorian Village, Stan pondered what he was doing. He was following

Rex through the bombed-out village . . . but why? Where was he going? He realized that he might be going crazy, but it wasn't his lunatic thoughts that were driving him to follow Kat's pet – it was his instincts. A feeling of anticipation washed over him and he felt as though there was something mysterious somewhere in this village, which he would find if he just kept following Rex.

After leading Stan down countless ruined streets, past destroyed houses, Rex finally arrived at the outer wall of the Adorian Village. Although the village had been blown sky high, the wall remained largely intact, except for a crater that had been blasted into the wall, leaving a hole in the base just wide enough to walk through. Rex made his way into the crater and up the other side, walking through the hole with Stan right on his tail.

Now, they were in the Great Wood, which stretched right up to the wall of the Adorian Village. Stan made his way through the trees, having to jog so that he didn't lose sight of Rex. As he made his way through the floor of the forest, weaving through blocky tree trunks as the moonlight cast ominous shadows onto the forest floor, Stan looked around nervously. He clutched his axe, prepared for hostile mobs to sneak out from around the corner of a tree at any moment. And yet, the farther they went, Stan didn't even *see* any mobs as he glanced through the darkness. He had seen monsters lurking in the shadows of the Great Wood even in broad day-light . . . why weren't there any now?

Rex continued to walk forwards, and as Stan followed, he realized that the wolf wasn't just ambling around randomly. He had determination, and he knew where he was going. The longer they walked, and the further that they travelled from the Adorian Village, the more Stan felt a curious sensation that they were approaching something. He had no idea what, but Stan knew that they were getting closer and closer to something.

Finally, after walking for many minutes, Rex emerged from the trees and into a clearing. The clearing was a totally flat circle of grass blocks, not large enough to hold an NPC villager's house. A light fog swirled around the ground as Stan stepped into the clearing, something that he had never seen before in Minecraft. Rex's ears perked up, and his tail wagged as he bounded across the clearing, plopping down loyally at the feet of the player who was standing on the other side.

Stan's heart began to race as he stared at the player. He knew this player. While the stories and rumours had circu-lated among Stan's friends since their reunion, Stan himself had only seen the player once before. Just days ago, Stan had stood outside the Nocturia complex, debating whether to pull the lever that would detonate the entire city, when the player had appeared in a gust of snow and ice. His black cape and hood that covered the upper half of his face, his deep blue trousers and brown shoes . . . Stan had seen them all before.

"Please," Stan whispered to the Black Hood. "I'm in my most desperate hour. My army has been captured, the Adorian Village is gone, the Noctem Alliance has taken Element City and one of my best friends is dead. Can you help me?"

For a moment, the Black Hood said nothing, standing perfectly still as the fog danced quietly around his feet. The faint moonlight still came down from the sky, radiantly illuminating the Black Hood. A half-frown was plastered onto his face as he looked back at Stan.

"Please," Stan repeated, his voice ripe with desperation. "You must have brought me here for a reason."

"That I did, Stan2012."

Stan gaped at the Black Hood, his eyes wide and his jaw hanging half open. The Black Hood had just spoken to him – something that had never happened to him, or any of his friends. He had what sounded like a Swedish accent. Stan was about to ask him what the reason was when something happened that made the question die in his mouth.

The Black Hood raised his right hand and grabbed the top of his hood. In one single motion, he pulled the head covering backwards, revealing his whole face. As he put his hand back by his side, Stan could see that his hair was brown, and that the Black Hood looked nearly identical to himself. Except, that was, for the eyes.

The eyes of the Black Hood were as white as snow, and shined as radiantly as the moonlight above. For a split second, Stan panicked, fearing that Lord Tenebris had materialized in front of him, before he realized that this was clearly not the case. Where Lord Tenebris's eyes were unnatural and sinister, and caused physical pain when looked into, the eyes of the Black Hood were the polar opposite. They were warm, inviting, and Stan found himself drawn into them like a moth to a light. As he stared into the eyes of the Black Hood, he felt that all was right in the world, despite his bitter knowledge that this was as far from true as possible.

"Who . . . who . . . who are you?" Stan managed to get out.

The Black Hood stared directly back at Stan, and, for the first time since he'd shared a glance with Leonidas all those weeks ago, he smiled.

"They call me Herobrine," he replied.

The Black Hood watched, slightly amused, as Stan stood at the far end of the clearing, clearly flabbergasted. He had expected such a reaction when he finally revealed himself to Stan. He chuckled inwardly. This was the first time that he had fully revealed himself to a player in many years, and the reaction was just as priceless as he remembered. The brief moment of humour was bittersweet, though. The Black Hood knew that by revealing himself to Stan, he had driven the nail firmly into his own coffin – he undoubtedly had only hours to live now.

Although the Black Hood let out a sigh of resignation at this thought, he knew it was worth it. Stan needed him. Elementia needed him. Minecraft needed him.

"But . . . what . . . how the . . . who . . . I thought . . ." Stan sputtered, his eyes darting around wildly as he tried to comprehend the impossible.

"I realize what you must be thinking, Stan2012," the Black Hood said wryly. "Just minutes ago, your life was completely uprooted by a player bearing my name and likeness."

"So . . . you're really . . . Herobrine?" Stan replied weakly.

"Yes," the Black Hood replied plainly.

"But . . . I thought . . . I thought Herobrine was

evil!" Stan cried. "So you . . . you can't be Herobrine! You've been helping my friends and me for weeks now!"

The Black Hood looked at him sadly. "Stan2012, the popular belief that I am a violent, demonic glitch is no longer true. To be frank, the majority of the atrocities committed in my name since the days of Minecraft Alpha, including everything that Lord Tenebris has done, were in fact not my doing. I still fully blame myself for them, but I was not the culprit . . . not directly, anyway."

Stan stared at the Black Hood, as if trying to detect any hint that he was lying. When Stan saw none, he closed his eyes and pressed his hand to his head.

"OK . . . let's say I give you the benefit of the doubt, and believe that you really are Herobrine. If so, then . . . what . . . are you?"

The Black Hood was silent for a moment before responding.

"To tell you the truth, Stan2012, I'm not sure. I don't know where I come from, how long I have existed, or anything regarding my nature or what I am. However, Stan2012, you needn't tell me that this is your most desperate hour . . . although I have the power to see all that has ever happened in Elementia, I don't need to use this power to see that you need me."

"Oh, I see," Stan spat bitterly. "So you're like, I don't

know, my omnipresent spirit mentor who knows *all that once was, and all that will be*, and is now coming to show me what my future will be like if—"

"Do not ridicule me, Stan2012," the Black Hood cut in, a frown returning to his face. "I have information that you desperately need if you are to save yourself and your country, but if you want it, then I demand that you take me seriously."

Stan's eyes widened. As sceptical as he was about all the Black Hood was saying, for some reason, Stan felt compelled to believe the Black Hood, although he had no idea why. Perhaps it was because of the truth that seemed to shine from his eyes, perhaps it was because this being had clearly defended his friends in the past. Whatever the reason, Stan trusted him.

"Our time here is short," the Black Hood continued, as if he could sense that Stan had opened up and was ready to listen to him. "Lord Tenebris intends to hold his deadline for you, and will begin to execute your friends if you do not return by sunrise."

"Hold up . . . back up," Stan said slowly, as he realized what the Black Hood being Herobrine meant. "If . . . *you're* Herobrine . . . then what is Lord Tenebris? How did he manage to get powers even stronger than an operator if he isn't Herobrine?"

The Black Hood sighed again. "Because, Stan2012, Lord

Tenebris *is* an operator. He's been an operator of Elementia since the day the server was first created, and since then, he's only grown stronger and stronger through his own twisted experiments."

"But . . . how is that possible? In the history of this server, there have only been two operators, Avery007 and King Kev, who're both dead!"

"It's possible because Lord Tenebris and King Kev are the same player, Stan."

The Black Hood allowed Stan a moment to process this. The Black Hood knew that Stan had guessed at this while he was grieving in the Adorian Village, but it didn't make the information any less difficult to comprehend. He watched as Stan struggled to process the claim. The Black Hood could almost see Stan making a mental list of every single reason why that couldn't be possible, before turning to face him.

"I don't believe you," Stan said bluntly, though he still sounded is if he were trying to convince himself more than anything. "That's not possible."

"Well, Stan2012, why don't you tell me why you think that, so that I can explain to you why it is," the Black Hood replied kindly.

"Ha!" Stan scoffed. "How would you know anything about Lord Tenebris or King Kev? How do you know anything about this server?"

"You're forgetting who you're talking to, Stan2012," replied the Black Hood with a smile. He pointed his hand down at Rex, who was still curled up at his feet. The wolf began to levitate into the air and looked around wildly before his tail began to wag. Rex started to fly through the air on his own, paddling his legs as if swimming, as Lord Tenebris continued to talk, absent-mindedly keeping his hand pointed at Rex.

"I am the one true Herobrine, Stan2012. I have access to the history of every Minecraft server in the world, including this one. In fact, I first came here because I sensed a great disturbance in the balance of this particular world. I have since familiarized myself with all that has happened in Elementia since its creation, and I will be more than happy to answer any questions that you have."

The Black Hood guided Rex downwards, and the wolf touched down on the ground, returning to his sitting position, as Stan stared in wonder. After a moment of stunned silence, Stan finally gathered his thoughts and replied.

"OK, fine. First of all, King Kev is dead! I watched him stab himself in the chest with his own sword, and then get blown to bits as the tower exploded. Can you explain to me *how* he survived that?"

"King Kev didn't survive the Battle for Elementia, Stan2012. He died in the tower, just like you thought that he did."

Stan did a double take. "But . . . then . . . how . . ."

"Tell me something," the Black Hood said. "What did King Kev look like right before he died?"

As wildly as his head was spinning, Stan tried to think back to that day all those months ago. "Well . . . I knocked him into the tower against the wall . . . and I hesitated to stab him for a few seconds . . ."

"And what did he look like during those last seconds of his life?" the Black Hood pressed on.

Stan stared at the Black Hood incredulously. "What does that have to do with anything?"

"Answer the question, Stan2012," the Black Hood replied, a bit more sternly this time.

Baffled as to why the Black Hood was so focussed on this minute detail, Stan pictured the fight in his head once again. "Well, King Kev got knocked to the ground, he was really weak from our attacks . . . he got slammed into the wall, and accidentally opened all the windows . . . and then I wasn't sure if I could bring myself to kill him, he looked so pathetic . . . his face was screwed up in anticipation, just waiting for me to finish him off . . ."

"That wasn't anticipation, Stan2012," the Black Hood replied. "While you were debating whether or not to kill King Kev, he was quickly setting himself up for the greatest escape in the history of Minecraft."

"What does that mean?" Stan demanded.

"As King Kev lay with his back to the wall, he knew that he couldn't win the fight," the Black Hood explained. "Between fighting Avery007, Apothecary1 and you, Stan2012, King Kev had been weakened to the point where fighting was futile. He knew that he had failed, and that his only chance to maintain power in Elementia was to start over again and build a new empire from the ground up: The Noctem Alliance."

"But that still doesn't explain how he escaped!"

"He escaped by changing the game mode of Elementia," the Black Hood replied. "As he sat against the wall, he changed the difficulty setting of Elementia from Hardcore PVP to Normal PVP as quickly as he could. This meant that players who died could respawn. As soon as he did so, he killed himself, respawning at Spawnpoint Hill and immediately proceeding to change the difficulty setting back to Hardcore PVP, so that, once again, any players who died would be banned from Elementia."

Again, the Black Hood stood quietly for a moment, as Stan tried to digest what was being explained to him. Moments later, Stan replied. "There's no way that that happened."

"And why not, Stan2012?" the Black Hood replied patiently, as he prepared to rebut each of the arguments that Stan was about to throw at him.

"Well, first off, you need operating powers to change the

game mode of the server!" Stan said. "And King Kev gave up his operating powers a long time ago."

The Black Hood chuckled. "King Kev *said* that he gave up his operating powers a long time ago, you mean. Think about it, Stan2012 . . . did you ever once see or hear of any evidence that King Kev truly gave up his operating powers, beyond the fact that he never used them?"

Stan opened his mouth to respond, but the retort died in his mouth when he realized that the Black Hood was right. Throughout his time in Elementia, Stan had been told that King Kev was once an operator but had given up his powers in order to keep his people happy. However, he had never once heard of *how* King Kev had given up his operating powers, or, in fact, seen any proof that he had, beyond the fact that he had never used them.

"But . . . then . . . OK," Stan continued, collecting his thoughts. "If King Kev had operating powers this entire time, then why didn't he use them when he was fighting me on the bridge? I mean, I understand why he didn't go using them all the time if he was pretending that he had given them up, but I think he probably would have been OK with using them if his life was in danger!"

"And therein lies King Kev's fatal flaw," the Black Hood replied sadly. "He is arrogant, and he thinks very highly of himself. He was too overconfident to use his operating powers to finish you off quickly. He wanted to toy with you first before destroying you. This trait, and also this fatal flaw, have carried over into King Kev's new identity as Lord Tenebris. Even when Avery007 challenged him, King Kev was far too proud to use his operating powers. If he didn't beat Avery007 fairly, in equal combat, his pride would have been hurt.

"And besides," the Black Hood continued before Stan could respond, "even if King Kev hadn't been too full of himself to use his powers, he wouldn't have anyway, on the off chance that somebody might find out. If the upper-level players discovered that King Kev was deceiving them, their faith in him as a ruler would have vanished."

The Black Hood paused yet again to let Stan absorb what he had just said. Stan looked desperate, grasping at straws to try to find another reason why King Kev's return was impossible. Finally, he spoke.

"OK, let's say by some crazy stretch of the imagination, what you're saying is true. King Kev kept his operating powers this entire time; he changed the difficulty setting of the server, which allowed him to respawn; then he immediately changed it back. Well, if the server was changed off Hardcore PVP mode, even for a few seconds, then shouldn't at least one other player have respawned? I mean, we were in the middle of a huge battle. Players were dying all over the place.

Shouldn't somebody have died and then respawned in those few seconds that King Kev changed the difficulty setting of the server back to Normal PVP?"

The Black Hood smiled. "Can you think of nobody who somehow managed to respawn in Elementia without explanation, Stan2012?"

As soon as he said this, the memory returned to Stan in a flash. He remembered when he and his friends were tunneling back into Element City and had been ambushed by ELM underground. They were about to be overwhelmed when a giant mass of prisoners barrelled through the tunnel, driving the bounty hunters away. Leading the charge was a player with a wild glint in his eyes . . . a player that Stan knew to be dead . . .

"Sirus," Stan breathed.

"Yes," the Black Hood replied. "Sirus666 was killed during the battle of Elementia at the exact moment that King Kev changed the difficulty setting of the server to Normal, and thus, he was able to respawn along with King Kev. They both returned to Spawnpoint Hill at nearly the same time. Of course, King Kev hid, terrified of being seen, but Sirus666 had been hit by a hallucinogenic potion at the time, so even though he saw King Kev duck into the woods, he didn't recognize him."

Stan's head was spinning as all the information came

together. He had been expecting to be able to punch dozens of holes in the Black Hood's argument, but yet . . . somehow . . . Stan found that it all made sense.

"So . . . ," Stan whispered weakly, "it's . . . true? Lord Tenebris and King Kev . . . really are the same player?"

"Yes," the Black Hood replied.

Stan sank to his knees and put his head into his hands. The Black Hood gave a sad sigh as he watched Stan try to comprehend this horrible truth. For the longest time, Stan had believed that King Kev and Lord Tenebris were two different entities, one of whom had built off the back of the other, and had fought independently of each other to take him down. But only now did Stan see that it was all the work of a single player, who had defied death itself to return to Elementia and do all that he could to destroy Stan and his friends.

"I . . . have another question," Stan managed to get out, even though he felt as if all the air had been vacuumed from his lungs.

"I will do my best to answer it," the Black Hood replied.

"Well . . . it's just . . . *why*? Why did King Kev go through all this trouble to return to Elementia? I mean, why didn't he just cut his losses and start another server after he died?"

The Black Hood took a deep breath. The answer to this question was long and complex, yet it held great truths that

Stan must learn if he were to have any chance of vanquishing King Kev for good. The Black Hood knew that he had to express himself correctly.

"The answer to that is quite simple, Stan2012. King Kev still had unfinished business in Elementia."

"Do you mean the lower-level players?" Stan asked, outraged. "Did he really care about getting rid of them *that much*?"

"Getting rid of the lower-level players never really mattered to King Kev, Stan2012."

"*What?*" Stan shouted, causing Rex to bark in surprise. "Are you crazy? I've lost everything trying to take down two different dictatorships created by this guy, and the main reason that both of them existed was that he hated lower-level players!"

"I'm sorry, Stan2012," the Black Hood replied. "I didn't mean that. Of course getting rid of lower-level players mattered to King Kev. However, it did not matter to him nearly as much as it mattered to the other members of the Noctem Alliance. Do you know the reason why, all those months ago, King Kev made the proclamation that started your journey?"

"Well, I assume it was because he hated the lower-level players," Stan said slowly. He thought that this was obvious.

"King Kev did take issue with the lower-level players, but that's not why he passed that law. He passed the law because

Caesar and Charlemagne asked him to. The only purpose of the law was to keep the upper-level players, the ones with the most power, happy and on his side. This is because all that King Kev has ever wanted in Elementia is power, complete dominance over the server. This is the driving force behind everything that he has done to you, both as the head of the Kingdom of Elementia and as the head of the Noctem Alliance."

"But . . . that makes no sense!" Stan exclaimed. "If he had operating powers the entire time, then why would it matter that he keep the upper-level players happy? He could just force them to do whatever he wanted!"

"Indeed, in the early days of King Kev's rule, that is exactly what he did. After Avery007 was defeated, and King Kev stood as the only remaining operator in Elementia, the server lived in an era of fear. All who stood up against the King were silenced, and many high-level officials were killed for suspected treason. Mecha11, Apothecary1, Bill33, Ben33, and Bob33 were all banished into the wilds. Nobody was happy, not even the upper-level players. Fear spread through the countryside like a pack of wolves, and it soon manifested itself in revolt.

"Many players determined that freedom was worth dying for, and they attempted to take down King Kev, much like what you did, Stan2012. With his operating powers, King

Kev crushed rebellion after rebellion, most of which were led by upper-level players. However, King Kev also realized that Elementia had become a hateful, ugly place. This was not the type of server that he wanted to rule. Therefore, he vowed to turn over a new leaf, and make Elementia a better place. Not many believed that he was capable of it, but when he claimed to give up his operating powers, turning him into a normal player, just as powerful and mortal as any other player, people rallied around him, believing that he truly had changed, and Elementia entered a new age of prosperity."

"But he didn't give up his operating powers. He lied to everybody!" Stan retorted.

"Yes he did, but he was also careful never to use his operating powers again. The only reason he kept them was as an absolute last resort . . . such as when you were moments away from killing him."

"But . . . I still don't understand," Stan replied, perplexed. "If everybody in Elementia was happy after the King said he gave up his operating powers, then how did stuff get so bad for the lower-level players?"

"That, Stan2012, is because King Kev was very clever and manipulative. He knew that if he was going to be benevolent and kind towards his people, he needed the most powerful players to become loyal to him. That way, if a rebellion ever did occur again, he would have a strong group to stand by him through thick and thin. Because of this, while he tried to be kind to everybody, King Kev gave special privileges to the upper-level players who had been in Elementia the longest, and acquired the most resources for themselves. He established a governing council, the Council of Operators, which he filled with upper-level players. Because of this special treatment, the upper-level players loved King Kev, and were willing to do anything to keep him in power.

"At first, the lower-level players weren't oppressed at all. Although they missed out on the special privileges of the upper-level players, they were still able to live in peace. Then, as the prestige of Elementia grew, more and more new players joined Elementia. The upper-level players became scared of the growing majority of new players. They asked King Kev to pass the Law of One Death, which would change the mode of the server to Hardcore PVP, and stop the new players from respawning if they died. Desperate to keep the new players happy, King Kev agreed.

"However, the upper-level players were still scared. The new players outnumbered them. The upper-level players realized that the Law of One Death didn't just apply to the new players – it applied to them, too. Therefore, the upper-level players asked King Kev to banish all new players from Element City. I believe, Stan2012, that you are well aware of what happened from there."

"But after King Kev died, he didn't have any power any more!" Stan pointed out. "His whole plan to use the upper-level players to stay in power fell apart when the kingdom fell, so why did he come back to Elementia as Lord Tenebris?"

"You're right, Stan2012, that after the kingdom had fallen, King Kev couldn't use the upper-level players in the same way. However, when you took over Elementia, he saw an opportunity to use the upper-level players in a new way.

"King Kev knew that many upper-class players had lost their leader and their special privileges when you won the Battle for Elementia. He saw that most upper-level players hated you and the lower-level players that you protected. Therefore, he took on the new identity of Lord Tenebris, and told the upper-level players that their hatred of the lower-level players was justified. He rallied the upper-level players around him, uniting them under the banner of their hatred and spite toward the lower-level players.

"At first, the upper-level players only joined the Noctem Alliance to take revenge on lower-level players, and take back what was lost in the revolution. Now, however, they have become unwaveringly loyal to Lord Tenebris, eternally grateful that he has restored them to their former glory, and they will follow him no matter what he says . . . the same way that they became loyal to King Kev.

"Back in the old days of the server, it took King Kev years

to unite his people under him, under the banner of trust and camaraderie. It only took *Lord Tenebris* four months to unite his people under fear and hatred. By founding the Noctem Alliance, Lord Tenebris gave the upper-level players what they were looking for: a new leader to rally around, a chance to win back their dominance over the server and a group that they could blame for everything that had happened to them. That group, of course, was you and your followers.

"This is how the worst tyrants of history form their empires, Stan2012. Desperate people unite under ruthless leaders, often under the banner of hatred of another group. It is a swift and effective way to gain control, but that amount of power given to such a hateful cause will inevitably lead to a permanent scar on the face of the world."

As he finished his speech, the Black Hood watched as Stan pondered what he had just told him. The Black Hood was quite impressed by Stan. He had been through so much in the past day, and yet somehow he was still able to process the information that he was being provided.

"OK," Stan said when he finally stopped looking as if he were about to pass out from sheer exhaustion. "I have one more question for you."

"Yes?"

"Well . . . it's just . . . ," Stan said awkwardly. The Black Hood could tell that, whatever he was about to ask, Stan was trying not to offend him. "Well . . . if you've known all this the entire time . . . then why didn't you say anything to me or my friends before now? I mean, all my friends have told me how you've protected them a bunch of different times . . . and you appeared to me outside Nocturia. . . so why didn't you tell me this before?"

The Black Hood gave a sad sigh. He knew that Stan was bound to ask this question sooner or later, and he didn't want to answer. Even as he stood here now, the Black Hood felt himself getting weaker and weaker, and the more information he gave to Stan, the faster his demise would be. However, the Black Hood knew that his own death was inevitable. Hopefully, he would be able to provide Stan with all that he needed before then.

"Stan2012, how much do you know about the history of Herobrine . . . about *my* history?"

The realization washed over Stan yet again that he was talking to Herobrine, the mythical Minecraft being who so many had called a demon, yet who had been working tirelessly to keep Stan and his friends safe for weeks. It only lasted for a moment, though. Stan knew that his time was running out, and Lord Tenebris's deadline would be on him before long. He couldn't shake the innate sense that, if he continued to talk to the Black Hood, the answer to his problems would somehow find him. "Um . . . I know that everybody thinks that you're some sort of glitchy demon that lives in Minecraft and haunts people . . . and that's about it."

The Black Hood chuckled again. "Indeed, Stan2012, that is true, and there is a reason that so many think of me that way. It's because . . . for the longest time . . . I *was* a force of destruction and chaos in Minecraft."

"What?" Stan asked, surprised. "But . . . you've been so helpful to me and my friends! You've done nothing but good in Elementia."

"This is also true," the Black Hood replied. "But that is not how it started. As I have told you before, I honestly do not recall where I came from, and my earliest memories are jumbled and foggy. All I remember for sure is that I came into being during the Alpha days of Minecraft, and soon found that I had access to all the powers that were possible for a player to have in vanilla Minecraft.

"At first, I saw no need to destroy or corrupt worlds. I saw Minecraft as a beautiful place, a place of wonder and splendour. I was particularly fascinated by the players, these beings from a realm outside of Minecraft, who could manipulate the natural world in much the same way that I could, and used this ability to create fantastic structures in a way that I could never hope to. I made a habit of watching the players work from a distance, enchanted by the various things that they built. I never let myself be seen, fearing that if they noticed me, they would stop the work that I found so fascinating.

"However, one day, a player did see me, captured me in a screenshot, and posted it online. I didn't think much of it at the time. . . People posted fake pictures of player-like glitches all the time. I assumed that nothing would come of it. However, before long, I was shocked to find that the Mojang team released a patch of the game that banished me from entering any Minecraft world ever again.

"I was confused and angry. I hadn't been harming anybody, I had just been watching the other players! Why would Mojang want me to be removed from the game? In any case, I found that it hardly mattered . . . after all, I am a glitch who is capable of adapting, and I soon found that the banishment was not too hard to get around. Before long, I was back in Minecraft, determined to never be spotted, lest Mojang try to kick me out again.

"Alas, my attempts to be inconspicuous were in vain. Mojang soon released another patch, which banished me yet again, this time making it even harder for me to re-enter. Now I was beyond angry; I was furious. Why was I being kicked out of the game? Because of my odd appearance? Whatever the reason was, I didn't care. I was more determined to re-enter the game than ever, but now I no longer wished to watch the players. Rather, I wanted to attack, haunt and frighten the players, to get back at the game that had arbitrarily decided that I had no place in it.

"I learned that the one who had captured me in a screenshot had fabricated a story about me, saying that I interfered with the world by creating pyramids and tunnels, that I was the spirit of Notch's deceased brother, and that my name was Herobrine. I adopted the persona and the name, and terrorized players all throughout Alpha and into the early stages of Beta. Although Mojang constantly tried to remove me, I found ways around their defences, always re-entering Minecraft to terrorize more players, growing stronger and stronger as more new abilities were added into the game for me to mimic.

"As the official release of Minecraft approached, I knew that the Mojang team was trying to iron out as many glitches as possible in preparation for the new game engine of the Adventure Update. However, I never could have predicted what they put into the game to counter me."

"What did they put in?" Stan asked with bated breath.

The Black Hood closed his eyes. "To this day, I'm not sure exactly what it is. All I know is, whatever they coded into the game, it's not just a patch meant to keep me out. Whatever it is, it's alive, sentient and capable of adapting, just like I am. I don't know what it is, but I've named it . . . The Voice in the Sky."

As soon as the Black Hood said the name, a crash of thunder sounded from overhead. Stan whipped his head skywards. The rainstorm had stopped a while ago, and the sky above them was clear.

"That was him, Stan2012," the Black Hood replied quietly. "He lives in the sky, watching me."

"Wha . . . what does he do?" Stan asked meekly.

"I'm . . . not sure," the Black Hood replied frankly. "I don't know who he is, what he is, or what he does. All I know is that, whenever I enter a Minecraft server and interact with the blocks, the mobs, the players, or anything else, the Voice in the Sky tells me to stop. Then . . . if I do not stop . . . my energy begins to rapidly drain."

The Black Hood paused for a moment to catch his breath. As he spoke about the energy draining from his body, it was happening to him. Revealing his face to Stan had given the Black Hood an adrenaline boost, as he was excited to finally be talking to a player again. However, now, the fatigue caught up to him, and he felt his life force draining the longer that he engaged in this forbidden activity.

"To avoid withering out of existence," the Black Hood continued after a moment, "I stayed out of Minecraft servers, forever condemned to hang in the void of cyberspace between thousands of Minecraft worlds. I could watch the worlds from a distance, but I could never enter them, interact with them, or wreak havoc in them again without the Voice in the Sky catching me.

"And . . . yet . . . as I watched these hundreds of thousands of Minecraft worlds from afar, I no longer felt the need to destroy them. I watched the players working together, building together and creating amazing structures and worlds together. The amazement with Minecraft that I had felt upon first entering the game returned to me, and I realized how wrong I had been. Minecraft is a beautiful game . . . more than a game, really – it's a beautiful world. It allows people to have a place where they can do anything they want, where the only limit is their imagination. I realized that I had been foolish for wanting to corrupt such a marvellous universe.

"However, the damage was done. The Voice in the Sky was still watching me, and every time that I entered a Minecraft world, I could feel my life force fading more and more by the second. The only time I was ever safe was when I floated in limbo between the Minecraft worlds, watching longingly from far away.

"What I saw shocked me. Even though the players in the worlds had nothing holding them back, nothing trying to keep them out, many still found the need to antagonize others. While I saw many players building together in harmony, I also saw countless Griefers, going out of their way to make the Minecraft experience miserable for others. As I watched these players fight, I couldn't help but feel responsible. I was the original Griefer, the one who introduced the concept to Minecraft. Because of me, Minecraft was no longer a world solely of creativity and wonder, but a world where you had to constantly watch your back, lest you be destroyed.

"Stricken with guilt, I knew that I had to make up for it somehow. I swore to myself, right then and there, that if anything were to ever threaten Minecraft on a large scale, I would do everything in my power to stop it. My opportunity came fairly recently, when my attention was drawn to your Minecraft server, Stan2012."

"Let me guess," Stan said with a dark grimace. "You sensed King Kev pulling energy out of other servers to make himself stronger, and realized that it might create a glitch that could destroy Minecraft."

"Precisely," the Black Hood replied darkly. "I realized that, if King Kev was not stopped, then his unquenchable lust for power may lead him to unwittingly create a glitch that would destroy his beloved server, and countless others along with it. I knew that, regardless of what happened, I had to stop it.

"And yet, I knew that I couldn't. I was well aware that, if I were to try to tell King Kev what he was doing, the Voice in the Sky would intervene. He would destroy me before I could even reach the head of the Noctem Alliance.

"Therefore, I looked into the history of the server of Elementia, to try to see if there was some other way that I could possibly prevent this ghastly fate. And that, Stan2012, is where I first learned of your story – the most remarkable story in the history of Minecraft."

"What?" Stan exclaimed. "How is my story so remarkable? I've hardly done anything!" He thought glumly about how true his words were as he spoke on. "I led a rebellion against King Kev but didn't even have the guts to finish him off, letting him cheat his way back onto the server. If I had stabbed him the second I had a chance, he wouldn't have been able to change the difficulty setting! Then, when I tried to take him down again, he totally wiped the floor with me!"

"You're right, Stan2012," the Black Hood replied. Stan stared at him in surprise. He had expected the Black Hood to contradict something that he had said, and tell him just how spectacular he really was.

"Hardly anything that you've done matters in the long run," the Black Hood continued. "You were held back by your own mercy in the tower of Element Castle that day, and that did allow King Kev to escape and found the Noctem Alliance. And the moment King Kev turned into Lord Tenebris, and was no longer afraid to use his operating powers, you never stood a chance against him. However, Stan2012, there is one thing that you aren't giving yourself enough credit for."

"And what's that?" Stan spat bitterly.

"You never stopped fighting," the Black Hood replied. Stan was floored to hear the incredible passion in his voice. "So deeply did you believe that the lower-level players of this server did not deserve to be oppressed that you never gave up, and you never surrendered, even when you had impossible odds stacked against you."

"But none of it worked!" Stan cried. "So what does it matter that I tried if I didn't succeed?"

"Stan2012, you must realize what you managed to do," the Black Hood continued, his voice still enriched with passion. "You managed to rally an entire country around you during your fight to take down King Kev, and even if you failed to destroy the King himself, you succeeded in taking down his kingdom. For the first time in years, Elementia was a place where people of all levels could live together in harmony.

"Do you think that your people are ever going to forget what it feels like to live in a country of happiness and equality? Do you think that, now that they've experienced what true freedom is, they will ever stop fighting to get it back? Of course not! And all because *you*, Stan2012, were brave enough to take a stand against the injustice you saw around you. It takes a special kind of person to take a stand when injustice is the law, and you, Stan2012, are one special person."

Stan hesitated for a moment before responding.

"OK, let's say you're right. Let's say that I'm so special and that long after I'm gone, people keep fighting back against King Kev. It's not like they're going to win! King Kev is the only operator on the server. He's never going to be taken down! My people will just keep on fighting back until they're all dead!"

"And then King Kev will be right back to square one," the Black Hood replied triumphantly. "He'll be in charge of an empire of misery and despair, just like he was when he first defeated Avery007. Remember that all King Kev really wants is power. He doesn't care who he has to step on to get it. And through your example, Stan2012, your people will let King Kev know that they won't be stepped on without a fight."

For a while, neither Stan nor the Black Hood said anything. They simply stood in the clearing as the fog swirled around their feet, becoming lighter and lighter as the sun began to rise.

"Stan2012, I would like to thank you," the Black Hood said, and Stan was shocked to see a tear streaming out of his radiant white eye and down his face. "For the longest time, I believed that I had ruined Minecraft. I thought that, through my chaos and destruction, I had set an example for Griefers and tyrants all across the countless servers of the game. Your story showed me, though, that however bad things may get, there will always be those who are willing to stand up for what's right.

"I guess what I'm trying to say is . . . thank you, Stan2012, for doing the right thing, no matter how hard it was," the Black Hood replied, as he gave Stan a gracious smile.

Stan took a deep breath and let it out. He knew that the Black Hood was right. He had never failed to do what he thought was best for Elementia, and he couldn't stop now. Stan clutched his axe tightly in his sweaty palms and looked at the sky. The celestial lights of the sky were beginning to fade, and a light pink glow was starting to illuminate the eastern sky.

"I've got to go back there, don't I?" Stan said gravely, as he turned to look northwards, toward Element City.

"Yes," the Black Hood replied. "Element City needs their president now more than ever."

Stan reached into his inventory and pulled out the enchanted golden apple and the Potion of Harming. It seemed like eons ago that Lord Tenebris had stood before him in the wreckage of the Adorian Village, offering both of the items to him. Stan looked down at the two items in his hand, and in both the shiny gold curve of the apple and the red-tinted face of the potion bottle, he saw his reflection. He saw the face of a brave, proud player who had never once turned his back on his country, and would fight to the death to defend it and the ones he loved.

He raised the golden apple to his mouth and swallowed it in three bites. Instantly, a surge of energy shot through Stan's body, coursing from his head through his core and spreading to his limbs. He felt as though he were under the effect of ten Potions of Swiftness at the same time. Stan glared hatefully at the Potion of Harming in his other hand and, in one motion, he pitched the toxic potion as hard as he could into the woods. Seconds later, in the far distance, he heard the shattering of glass.

Stan clutched his axe as the rising sun illuminated the right side of his face. He took yet another breath and let it out in a determined grunt. Stan knew that, within the hour, he was going to be dead. Lord Tenebris was going to do horrible, horrible things to him before destroying him in front of his people, along with the rest of his closest friends. However, Stan knew that none of the people who had followed him would ever forget their sacrifice, and although he might die, his spirit of rebellion never would.

Stan turned back to face the Black Hood one last time. The glitch player's eyes still shone brightly in the rising daylight as he looked proudly on Stan, the player who had given so much to Elementia, and was prepared to give more than could ever be repaid. The Black Hood sighed and looked Stan in the eye.

"Stan2012, I have tried to do all that I could to help your

cause without jeopardizing my own existence," the Black Hood said carefully. "I have helped each of your friends in numerous ways, but I have still failed to do anything to help you."

"That's not true," Stan replied with a bittersweet smile. "You helped me realize what I can do to save my people, and you risked your life to do so. I can never thank you enough."

"Still . . ." the Black Hood continued slowly. "I feel that I owe it to you to do something for you that might help you . . . in a different way."

"That's OK," Stan said darkly. "Where I'm going, I won't need any help."

"It wasn't a recommendation," the Black Hood said simply, and with that he reached out his hand towards Stan.

Instantly, Stan felt himself being pulled forwards towards the Black Hood and being forced to his knees. Stan recognized the horribly familiar sensation of being held in Lord Tenebris's psychic grip. Stan was just about to let out a shout of terror when the Black Hood reached out with his free hand and put it to Stan's head.

Suddenly, Stan wasn't terrified any more. The power from the golden apple coursing through his veins seemed to amplify, expanding further and further until finally, Stan felt as though he were exuding energy from every pore of his body. The power continued to grow and grow, until finally, the energy reached its peak. Stan fell to the ground in a crumpled heap, shaking as he tried to contain the sheer power that he now felt inside himself.

"What . . . what did you do to me?" Stan managed to get out as his entire body twitched with spasms.

"You'll see in a moment," the Black Hood replied as Rex began to wag his tail beside him.

"Stan! Stan, answer me right now!"

Stan looked up with a jolt. Of all the things that he might have anticipated at that moment, Sally's voice, ringing out of the ether with no static, clear as crystal, was not one of them.

"I'm here, Sal," Stan replied, looking at the ground as he tried to focus on her voice. "Can you hear me?"

"Yes, I can hear you!" Sally replied. Stan was amazed at how clearly she was coming in. "Stan, did you just do something to Elementia's code?"

"What? No!" Stan exclaimed. "Why? What's happening, Sally?"

"I'm not sure," she replied. She sounded excited. "All I know is that somehow, I have no idea how, a hole opened up in the defences of Elementia's coding."

Stan's heart skipped a beat. "Wait . . . really?"

"Yes," Sally replied. She paused for a moment. Then . . .

"Stan . . . I think that I might have just given you operating powers."

Stan said nothing in reply. His heart was racing as he dropped his diamond axe to the ground and held out his right hand. He took a deep breath and, not believing that it was possible, he focussed as hard as he could on the hand, imagining a diamond helmet.

There was a faint pop, and a diamond helmet appeared in his hand.

Stan's mouth hung open, and widened further and further into a smile as he spawned in more items – bowls of mushroom soup, flint and steel, jungle-wood blocks, gravel, end stone – the pile of random items on the ground below him grew larger and larger. Stan drew back his fist and, taking aim at a nearby tree, he fired off a punch. Instantly, the tree exploded as the invisible burst of energy hit it. Laughing wildly now, Stan took a deep breath, jumped into the air . . . and floated in place, held aloft by his newly acquired operating powers.

"Did it work?" Sally's voice called out of nowhere.

"Yes!" Stan exclaimed, pumping his fist as he soared into the air, doing a loop before touching back down on the ground.

"Fantastic!" Sally cried. Stan could almost see the smirk on her face. "Now go on, noob, don't waste any more time . . . go kick Herobrine's butt! Tell me how it went when it's over."

And before Stan could respond, Sally's voice vanished with a slight static crackle.

Stan was beside himself with glee. He had operating powers now! He wasn't going to have to just hand himself over to Lord Tenebris to die. He had a fighting chance. There was a possibility that he might actually be able to destroy Lord Tenebris and the Noctem Alliance.

All at once, Stan realized what must have happened. He realized why the hole in the defences had opened up. He realized that he now had the powers of an operator. Slowly Stan turned around to face the Black Hood . . . only to find that he had vanished. Stan looked around the clearing, perplexed, but there was no sign of the glitchy, white-eyed player – or Rex, for that matter.

Stan remembered what the Black Hood had said – the more that he interacted with the players, the weaker he would become. Stan realized that was the reason the Black Hood had only appeared to his friends when they were in very real danger. He also imagined that, just by talking to Stan, the Black Hood had taken a huge risk, jeopardizing his very existence. Was it possible that, by enabling Sally to access the code of Elementia, the Black Hood had . . .

Stan heard an explosion from somewhere far in the distance, and he snapped out of his train of thought. There was no time to ponder what had happened to the Black Hood now. There would be plenty of time for that later. For now, Stan knew what he had to do.

As Stan stood in the clearing, his face illuminated by the light of the rising sun, Lord Tenebris was surely lining up his friends for the firing squad. If Stan didn't show himself soon, they would all be killed. Stan knew that Lord Tenebris's operating powers had been boosted by the power he had stolen from the server, but there was one thing that Stan had that he didn't: the element of surprise. Lord Tenebris had no idea that Stan now had operating powers, and if he played his cards right, then he just might be able to overpower the leader of the Noctem Alliance and finally end this war.

Regardless of what his odds were, though, Stan knew that he at least had to try. As long as there was even the tiniest glimmer of hope left, Stan knew that he always had to try.

And so with a deep breath, Stan picked up his diamond axe, focussed as hard as he could on the Avery Memorial Courthouse, and in an instant, he vanished into thin air, leaving the clearing full of swirling mist totally vacant.

Leonidas winced as a bright light shone over his eyes. He grunted as he forced his eyes open to find that he was staring directly into the rising sun. He glanced down at the ground to avoid looking into the rays, and shook the cobwebs out of his head. He was standing on wood-plank blocks, and he could see a gravel street a few blocks below his feet. Leonidas realized that he was standing upright, his back was to a wall of wood-plank blocks, and his arms were propped up on levers that had been attached to the wall.

Leonidas's temple was throbbing at the place where he and Cassandrix had cracked heads. He soon became aware that the air around him was filled with noise, and his head began to pulse with even more pain. Slowly, Leonidas opened his eyes. The sun was indeed shining directly into his eyes, but it was darker than he had expected, as it was shining through the thick veil of clouds cast over the city by the Withers hovering in the air above him.

As his ears and eyes slid back into full focus, Leonidas could see a crowd of soldiers surrounding the platform he was standing on, their heads nearly level with the two-block-high wood-plank platform. The Noctem Army was still wearing their black armour, and were erupting with jeers and taunts at those on the platform. Leonidas realized that he wasn't alone. He looked to his right and left, and saw that all the leaders of Stan's army were propped up on the wall. They were all standing upright, their arms raised up on levers, as still as statues.

Leonidas's heart skipped a beat as he realized what this was – a firing squad.

Leonidas did a quick check and realized to his dismay that his inventory had been totally emptied. He had lost his best bow, Hornet, back at Element Castle, and his other two bows and his sword were now gone as well. Not that it mattered. He knew that if he even tried to lift a finger, let alone arm himself, he would be killed in a matter of seconds.

Out of morbid curiosity, Leonidas looked down the line to see who was there. They were all about to die anyway. He might as well get a good idea of who was about to bite the dust with him.

There was only one player to the left of him before the row stopped, and that was Jayden. His eye was black and he had a sizable gash on his forehead, but he looked more exhausted than pained. Glancing to his right, Leonidas recognized Ben, who looked utterly defeated, and Bob, who was sitting on Ivanhoe, a sick look on his face. Leonidas wondered with a horrible lurch of his stomach if the pig would be executed as well.

Beyond those two were the Mechanist, who appeared to be in deep thought; Sirus, who was glancing around in a twitchy and nervous manner; and Cassandrix, whose face was contorted into a furious, twisted rage. And at the end of the line stood Commander Crunch, who was yelling something that Leonidas couldn't make out into the sea of heckling Noctem soldiers, occasionally interspersed with a hearty seaman's laugh.

Leonidas did a quick headcount: There were eight of them, including him. He went through a mental checklist to see who was missing, and came up with only three.

He wasn't surprised at all that Stan was missing. As the leader of the republic, Leonidas imagined that Lord Tenebris probably had special plans to deal with him. He most likely was still alive and would make an appearance at some point, during which Lord Tenebris would surely make an example out of him.

As for Kat . . . Leonidas didn't think that the image of Kat begin flung around that council room like a rag doll would leave him. Leonidas and Kat hadn't talked much since he had joined their army, but he still knew that she was a tough player with a keen eye for justice who wouldn't take crap from anybody. The image of such a strong-willed and powerful player rendered totally helpless was haunting. Although he knew that the others in the army would be grief-stricken when they found out that Kat had been killed, Leonidas, who had hardly gotten to know her, found her death far more terrifying and unsettling than anything else.

And that left the last missing player. While he hadn't gotten to know Kat all that well, Leonidas had gotten to know Charlie. Charlie had gone from hating Leonidas to accepting him as an ally and friend. The thought that now, after they had finally became friends, Charlie might be gone made Leonidas's stomach clench with dread. He tried to convince himself that there was a possibility otherwise. That maybe, somehow, he had escaped, and he wasn't actually dead. After all, Leonidas had nothing to go on. There was no evidence that Charlie was gone.

But then, all at once, Leonidas stopped thinking about it. It was as if somebody had turned off his ability to care. After all, what was the point? They were in front of a Noctem Alliance firing squad. They were all about to die anyway.

Almost immediately after he thought this, a figure appeared on the wood plank–block platform in front of the lined-up players with a loud crack. This player was skinned identically to Stan, but although Leonidas could only see him from the back, he knew better. He was a little bit surprised that Lord Tenebris was revealing himself to his people. From what he understood, nobody, besides him, had ever seen Lord Tenebris's face and lived. Then again, this was a special occasion.

All at once, the taunts and boos emanating from the rowdy crowd of Noctem Soldiers ceased. For the first time ever, they were beholding the face of their leader. Leonidas watched as the entire crowd stood transfixed and speechless for a moment before turning away uncomfortably, as they found it impossible to hold Lord Tenebris's gaze for more than a second.

"Greetings, my loyal subjects," Lord Tenebris said, his voice deep and booming, carrying across the silent plaza of the Avery Memorial Courthouse without effort. "Today is a historic day in Elementia. Not only is this the day that I first reveal my face to you, but it is also the day that we celebrate our victory over the forces of Stan2012's Republic of Elementia! Viva la Noctem!"

"VIVA LA NOCTEM!" the crowd rang out. It was the most passionate chant that Leonidas had ever heard the people of the Noctem Alliance let out.

"Standing here before you, totally at my mercy, are the leaders of the Republic of Elementia," Lord Tenebris said, turning around to face them and gesturing with his hand. As the crowd proceeded to continue their booing and heckling, Leonidas heard several of his friends pinned to the wall give gasps of horror as they viewed Lord Tenebris's face for the first time and found themselves unable to look into his eyes.

"These players marched into our city yesterday at high noon," Lord Tenebris continued, his followers instantly going silent as he turned to look over the crowd yet again, "with the intention of taking it away from us. They believe that Element City should welcome all players with open arms, regardless of whether or not they've earned their place here. In fact, a good percentage of their invasion force was composed of lower-level players. That's right. Such is the arrogance of these players standing before you that they believed that, after a single week of training, their lower-level friends were equal in skill to you, the Noctem Freedom Fighters, who have lived in Elementia for years."

Shouts of outrage erupted from the crowd, followed by a fresh round of heckling. Lord Tenebris did nothing to stop this, and Leonidas could almost picture the sadistic grin on his face.

"I would like to thank you, my citizens," Lord Tenebris continued, quelling the ruckus yet again. "I would like to thank you for tolerating the feeble attempts of the republic to fight back for so long now. For months, the Noctem Alliance has gained strength, preparing for the day that we would take back what is rightfully ours. And yet, wherever we went, the forces of the Republic of Elementia were there to make our jobs ever so slightly more annoying, like a fly buzzing around our heads that was nearly impossible to swat.

"But today," Lord Tenebris continued, "today, the fly has finally been squashed. On this day, I claim the Minecraft server Elementia in the name of the Noctem Alliance! Viva la Noctem!"

"VIVA LA NOCTEM!" the crowd echoed back to him.

"And now, we shall all witness the death of the republic, and we shall witness it the same way that we started – together. May I draw your attention to the remaining fighting forces of the Republic of Elementia."

Leonidas's head snapped upright, and he followed the gaze of the hundreds of players around him in the centre of the crowd, where there was a large, fenced-off area devoid of players that Leonidas hadn't noticed before. There, with a great roaring of redstone mechanisms, the ground rose until it was several blocks off the ground. Standing on top of this massive elevated platform were close to a hundred and fifty players, all the survivors of the attack. They had been stripped of their diamond armour, and they were huddled together like cattle, looking absolutely petrified.

"I suggest that you step back from the platform," Lord Tenebris said over the insults and verbal abuse being thrown at the players. "The platform is rigged with TNT blocks, and it will be detonated immediately if any of them try anything funny."

The mass of three hundred soldiers in black leather

armour expanded away from the platform, but the foul language and name calling didn't slow down until Lord Tenebris spoke again.

"The players on the platform will be spared, provided that they cooperate with me," Lord Tenebris continued. Leonidas's eyebrows shot up, as did many in the crowd.

"These players have had their minds poisoned by their leaders, standing on the platform before you. They will serve time in Brimstone Prison for their crimes. As soon as they are transferred to the prison, the remainder of the citizens of this city, who are presently locked in the prison, will be released. These terms are in accordance with an agreement that I made with President Stan."

The crowd had been waiting since the speech began to hear the name of the most wanted player in the Noctem Alliance, and now they were so quiet that a pin drop could be heard. Lord Tenebris paused for a moment and glanced at the square sun, which had now risen in full above the horizon.

"President Stan was supposed to be here by now. The agreement was that if he had not come here to duel me by sunrise, I would begin to execute his friends. Tell me, does anybody here see President Stan2012 around?"

Several shouts of "NO!" erupted from the crowd as the Noctem soldiers laughed. Leonidas just looked at the ground bitterly. He knew that Lord Tenebris couldn't possibly be telling the truth. Stan definitely would have turned up if he had agreed to it. More likely, Lord Tenebris had killed or crippled Stan, and was just trying to make Stan look bad for entertainment. Leonidas shook his head. He didn't even care any more. He was just ready for it all to be over.

"However, before the show begins," Lord Tenebris said as the laughter died down, "I must ask if any players who are about to die would wish to say any final words."

There was a pause as Leonidas tried to think of something to say. However, he couldn't think of anything. And even if he could, he really didn't want to say it. The Noctem Alliance had won.

Lord Tenebris looked back at them and gave a snide little smirk. "Well then, if that's the case . . ." But then, Lord Tenebris's remark was cut off by a lone pair of footsteps. Leonidas glanced up and saw the Mechanist, not looking beaten but rather determined, as he made his way to the edge of the platform.

"Well, well, well," Lord Tenebris chortled as the Mechanist walked up beside him. "If it isn't the great Mechall, redstone architect of most of this city and the inventor of the TNT cannon. I must admit, it's a shame to kill such a brilliant player . . . almost. Come now, share one last bit of wisdom with us from that radiant mind of yours."

Despite the mean laughs erupting from the crowd, the Mechanist looked unfazed. Rather, he took a deep breath and began to speak.

"I have a few things that I would like to say both to my fellow commanders and also to the brave warriors standing out on the platform in the crowd. First of all, I . . ."

Leonidas was surprised to hear that the Mechanist's voice sounded rather shaky, almost as if he were on the verge of tears. The redstone genius then took a deep breath, composed himself, and continued.

"First of all, I want to apologize to all of you. During my time as your leader, I did not serve my country well. I let the pressures of leading go to my head, and I tried to escape it in ways that" – the Mechanist halted with a catch in his throat before he continued on – "that resulted in the loss of a friend. I then let my grief and guilt overtake me, and I ignored the needs of my people because of it. I take full responsibility for all the misery that you had to go through while you were down in the mine.

"But none of that matters now."

Leonidas, who had been cringing as he anticipated a long, self-deprecating speech about how everything that had gone wrong was the Mechanist's fault, raised his head, his ears perked up.

"I'll tell you what does matter . . . *you*." He pointed out at the players who were standing on the platform and staring at him, intently absorbing every word he said.

"My friends and I are going to die today. There is nothing that we can do to stop that. But you are all going to live on to see another day. It will be difficult for you during your imprisonment in Brimstone, but you'll all survive. And even though we weren't able to overcome those who put us where we are now, I implore you to never forget what it felt like to be a citizen of the Republic of Elementia.

"Remember your freedom. Remember how it felt to walk down the streets and feel safe. Remember how it felt to know that your families and your friends were just a monorail ride away. There may be nothing more that I, or any of my friends, can do to help you. But if you cling tightly to those memories, then one day, I guarantee that you'll be able to help yourselves, and turn Elementia back into the place that you remember so fondly – a place of justice and equality for all."

The Mechanist finished talking. He took a deep breath, let it out, and began to walk backwards. As he did, the crowd of Noctem soldiers let out sniggers and snide remarks. Leonidas, on the other hand, stared at the Mechanist in amazement as he reached the wall and put his hands back up over the levers that held them up.

Leonidas looked from the Mechanist to the soldiers

elevated on a platform above the crowds. All of them wore a nearly identical expression: pensive and determined. Leonidas knew that the Mechanist's speech had connected with them. They would never forget it – and the Mechanist was right. One day, however far in the future it may be, those players would return to Elementia. And maybe they'd be able to turn it back into the place that Stan and his friends had worked so hard to create and defend.

Leonidas's heart leaped as he realized that the Mechanist had redeemed himself. He very well may have just inspired the future of Elementia for the better.

"That was very touching, Mecha11," Lord Tenebris replied nonchalantly. He turned to look down the line. "Would anybody else like to say something?"

"I have something to say."

Leonidas's ears perked up. He recognized that voice. His head turned to the right, along with all the other heads in the congregation, to where the voice had come from. There, entering the plaza from the side street, his clothes tattered and worn, was Stan2012, his hands empty and his face knit into a leer as he stared down Lord Tenebris.

Immediately, the crowd erupted. The Noctem soldiers let loose their loudest, harshest round of jeers yet, which just barely drowned out the cheers and applause that burst out from Stan's allies spread across the two elevated platforms.

As Stan made his way up the stairs of the firing-squad platform, standing directly opposite Lord Tenebris, the noise had gotten so loud that Leonidas could barely hear himself think.

"SILENCE!" Lord Tenebris boomed. Leonidas recognized the awful sensation of Lord Tenebris seemingly yelling from directly within his head, making his ears ache. Immediately, all noise stopped.

Slowly but surely, all players from both sides looked up to see Stan2012 and Lord Tenebris staring each other down from both ends of the platform. The two rulers held each other's gaze in the dim sunlight that shone from under the grey veil of the Withers. Leonidas stared at Stan in amazement. How was he holding Lord Tenebris's gaze for so long without breaking it?

"You're late," Lord Tenebris said.

"I apologize," Stan said with a smirk. "I met an old friend, and we had some catching up to do."

Lord Tenebris returned the smirk. "Well, I sure hope that your meeting was worth it. I was seconds away from executing your friends, you know."

"Trust me," Stan said. "It was well worth my time."

Suddenly, Leonidas felt something strange wash over him. It was a sensation that he hadn't felt before. It lasted for only a few seconds.

"I assume that you remember the terms of our deal," Stan said evenly.

"Indeed I do," Lord Tenebris replied. "The winner of this duel is the rightful ruler of Elementia."

As the crowd of Noctem soldiers sniggered, Leonidas suddenly became aware that his inventory was no longer empty. He checked the contents as inconspicuously as he could and found, to his utter bafflement, that his inventory now contained an unenhanced bow and two stacks of arrows.

Leonidas heard a soft gasp beside him, and as he looked down the line, he saw that all his friends were wearing equal expressions of amazement. Was it possible that *all of them* had mysteriously gotten weapons?

"Well then," Stan said after the sarcastic laughter died down. "How about we stop wasting time and begin?"

"With pleasure," Lord Tenebris replied. He took a deep breath, and a diamond sword materialized in his left hand, glimmering with various enchantments.

Stan didn't move. He merely stood there unarmed, as he smiled at Lord Tenebris. "Go ahead," he taunted. "Make the first move."

Leonidas stared at Stan with confusion. Why didn't he have a weapon drawn? What was he playing at?

Lord Tenebris stretched out his empty right hand at Stan, took a deep breath and then grunted. As he did, an arrow materialized from his fingertips, flying directly at Stan. Stan stood totally still, not even bothering to defend himself. Leonidas's eyes widened, and he flinched right as the arrow was about to enter Stan's chest. . .

But it didn't. Right as the arrow was upon Stan, it changed trajectory, curving left and flying past Stan's left arm.

A collective gasp rose from the crowd on both sides as Lord Tenebris raised an eyebrow. He lifted his hand again, and sent three more arrows flying directly at Stan. All three times, the same thing happened – right as the arrows were about to hit Stan, they suddenly changed course, flying in three different directions.

The crowd was now totally silent, and Leonidas's jaw dropped. What was he watching?

Lord Tenebris's mouth opened slightly, and his eyes grew wider as he tried to comprehend what was going on. He raised his right hand again, throwing a punch that produced a fireball. The fireball flew just as fast as the arrows had, directly at Stan.

Without even batting an eye, Stan raised his right hand. As the fireball made contact with his hand, he caught it, stopping it dead in its tracks. Lord Tenebris watched in bewilderment as Stan held the fireball up, then proceeded to clench his fist, crushing it. When he opened his hand again, nothing was left but a few light grey wisps of smoke, which were quickly carried away by the wind.

Lord Tenebris didn't look confused any more – he looked angry. He drew back his fist, took a deep breath and launched it as hard as he could at Stan. It appeared that nothing had left Lord Tenebris's hand, but Stan knew better, as he sensed the pulse of explosive energy heading towards him. Stan reached out his right hand and caught the pulse of energy, using the force to spin around and release it, sending it flying right back at Lord Tenebris.

The Noctem leader let out a faint shout of surprise as he sensed the blast coming, and he crossed his arms over his face as the blast hit. The explosion knocked Lord Tenebris backwards toward the edge of the platform. He lowered his arms, still smoking from the explosion, and stared at Stan, who was standing perfectly still. Disbelief was etched on every pixel of the Noctem ruler's face.

"What did you . . . how did you . . . ," Lord Tenebris managed to get out. "What are you doing?"

Stan stared at him for a moment, total confidence on his face, and taking in every moment of Lord Tenebris's shock before responding.

"Taking back my country," he said with a determined grin, before shouting, "Armies of Elementia! *Charge!*"

Immediately, Leonidas raced forward and attacked the Noctem soldiers on the ground. He allowed his instincts to carry him forwards, rushing past Stan, off the platform and into the crowd, drawing his bow as he did so. He looked at the other commanders of Stan's army in amazement. On one side of him Jayden was pulling out a diamond axe, while on the other side Bob drew out a bow and charged on Ivanhoe over the side of the platform and into the crowd of stupefied Noctem soldiers.

Lord Tenebris looked around wildly, trying to figure out what was happening. His eyes landed on the platform where the imprisoned republic fighters were stationed. To his utter surprise and dismay, these players, too, were pouring over the sides of the platforms, diamond weapons drawn. *How is this possible?* he thought to himself. *Their inventories were empty! Well, I suppose it doesn't matter . . . they're all about to die anyway!*

"DETONATE THE PLATFORM!" Lord Tenebris cried out, desperately hoping that his soldier manning the lever that detonated the platform would pull it. And yet the soldiers still continued to pour over the edges, into the crowd of baffled troops.

Lord Tenebris repeated his shout two more times, but to no avail. The platform remained solid and intact. By now, nearly half the players on the platform had jumped off and were engaging the Noctem Forces, who were totally caught off guard, in battle. Lord Tenebris was beside himself with fury. *Why isn't anyone pulling that lever?*

"Looking for this?"

Slowly, Lord Tenebris turned around to face Stan. He was still standing calmly at the far end of the platform, and in his outstretched hand was a lever, the redstone dust falling to the ground indicating that it had been freshly yanked off a circuit. Stan released the lever, and it dropped to the ground with a clang.

For a moment, Lord Tenebris just stared at Stan. He was totally unable to process what had happened. *How had Stan suddenly gained these miraculous abilities?* Stan didn't let him ponder it for long, though. He jumped into the air and began to float just above the ground as a glowing diamond axe materialized in his hand. Lord Tenebris's mouth opened slightly, but then he closed it as a savage sneer crossed his face.

Fine, he thought to himself, *have it your way, Stan.*

He switched his enchanted diamond sword to his right hand, held it in front of him, and leaped into the air, rocketing at top speed towards Stan, who mirrored him and flew directly at Lord Tenebris. It was only a matter of seconds before the two players, flying directly at each other, met in the centre of the wood plank–block platform. Their blades clashed together, sending a shower of sparks down to the ground below them as the two operators teleported away.

As Jayden looked around, he realized that most of the Noctem soldiers had managed to get over their shock and were beginning to fight back. Indeed, Jayden still had absolutely no idea how a diamond axe had appeared in his inventory, nor how the same thing had happened to all his friends and allies.

All he knew was that, whatever was happening, it was because of Stan, whom Jayden had seen fly towards Lord Tenebris and warp into the sky. Stan had clearly gotten operating powers somehow, and was now using them to fight Lord Tenebris. As soon as that fight finished, Jayden was sure that Stan would help them subdue the Noctem armies. Until then, though, Jayden knew that they had to buy Stan as much time as they could.

"Well, well, well . . . look who we have here," a voice with a Welsh accent spoke from behind him.

Jayden spun around and saw three players staring at him with contempt. He realized with a jolt that one of them was Zingster, the harsh corporal who had overseen Jayden's training in Nocturia. The other was LemonKipper, who had the skin of a mermaid and was a stuck-up member of Jayden's class. He didn't recognize the third player, who had no face. His or her skin (Jayden couldn't tell) was totally black, except for a giant number 4 that stretched from the player's head to their toes.

"Hey guys," Jayden said, raising his axe and dropping

into a fighting stance, "long time no see." He had seen Zingster and Kipper fight, and he knew that he could take both of them.

"Don't sound so chipper," Kipper snarled at him. "We're gonna make you pay for what you did to Nocturia, Councilman Jayden."

"Wait . . . that's right," Jayden said, realizing that Kipper and Zingster should probably be dead. "How did you three escape Nocturia?"

"I got caught swiping some QPo," Kipper said, no hint of guilt in his voice, "and Zingster decided to take me out into the tundra to teach me a lesson. When the bomb went off, we decided to head over here."

"I let him get away with the theft," Zingster grunted. "Because we've got bigger fish to fry!"

Zingster drew out his pickaxe and rushed into Jayden as Kipper did the same with his sword. Jayden knocked the pickaxe out of the way and locked the blade of his axe into the sword. The two players struggled to overpower each other for a moment before Zingster recovered and attacked again, forcing Jayden to feint away from Kipper and dodge.

Well, they've both gotten better, Jayden thought to himself as he swung his axe at Zingster's hand. The Noctem corporal dodged and used the opening to body check Jayden, sending him to the ground with a thud. Immediately, he rolled to the side to avoid a stab of Kipper's sword, and rolled several more times to avoid the sword that repeatedly plunged into the gravel. All of a sudden, Jayden felt his axe fly out of his hand, and looked up in time to see Zingster raising his pick-axe for another strike, just as Kipper did the same.

Jayden rolled to the side while swinging his feet around, dodging the sword strike while sweeping his legs behind Zingster's knees, sending him tumbling down, his pickaxe flying into the air. Jayden used the momentum to leap to his feet, catching Zingster's pickaxe while using it to counter Kipper's sword strike. Once again, the two players pressed into each other's blades, sending sparks flying, until Jayden finally started to win. He came closer and closer to overpowering Kipper, and was about to overtake him when he sensed something flying at him from the corner of his eye.

Instinctively, Jayden ducked, and the flying potion hit Kipper squarely in the face. The impact knocked him to the ground, right on top of the recovering Zingster. The cloud of grey smoke from the bottle wafted to the ground, surrounding the two players and knocking them unconscious.

Jayden had gotten slightly sprayed by the gas, too, and he felt a little woozy. He turned to face the thrower, and found the player skinned with the 4. Without another word, the player produced another potion bottle from nowhere, and tossed it at Jayden with a grunt.

The good news was that, from the grunt, Jayden could tell that this player was female. The bad news was the barrage of Potions of Slowness flying from her hands directly at him. Still armed with Zingster's pickaxe, Jayden didn't have enough reach to block the potions without getting hit, so he was forced to dodge, duck and weave between the bottles. The fumes of the potions began to rise, and Jayden felt himself becoming more and more affected by the vapours.

Before long, Jayden decided to call it quits and sprint away from the player. As fast as he tried to run, though, the potion weighed down on him, making him feel as if his legs were just blocks of lead. He knew it was futile as he heard the player approaching him from behind, but he kept running until the player body checked him, sending him careening forwards. He landed at the base of the Avery Memorial Courthouse, slamming his head on the bottom step and sprawling out on the ground, knocked out cold.

The player with the 4 on her body smiled and drew a Potion of Harming out of her inventory. She walked over to Jayden and held the Potion of Harming over Jayden's face. She was about to let it go when—

"Hey!"

The player looked up, and there, at the top of the steps of the courthouse, stood another player. He was wearing a light tan leather tunic and trousers. His clothes were covered in burn marks, but he still sat tall and strong atop the pig he was riding. The player was aiming a bow at the girl.

"Get away from him," Charlie growled as he let the arrow fly.

His aim was dead on, and the potion bottle shattered in her hand. The cloud of red toxins enveloped her arm and she gave a screech of agony before looking up at Charlie contemptuously, drawing two more Potions of Harming as she set her sights on him.

Charlie stood still, and gave a smile. He knew that he wasn't good enough with a bow to repeat that shot, so instead, he raised his hand and gestured forwards.

The player with the 4 looked slightly confused, but then her eyes widened in horror as a massive wave of players began to pour out of the courthouse directly towards her. She turned and sprinted as fast as she could onto the battlefield, desperate to avoid the massive wall of thousands of players who were dashing down the stairs. All of them were unarmoured but were holding up various weapons of different materials, chanting, "Down with the Alliance!" and "Long live President Stan!" as they charged into the plaza to fight the Noctem forces.

After a few minutes, all the thousands of players had left the courthouse and were joining the battlefield. Looking out at the plaza, Charlie gave a satisfied grin as the players he had just led from the courthouse joined the fight. He glanced down the stairs and noticed that Jayden was still lying there, and he was starting to stir.

Charlie ordered Dr Pigglesworth down the stairs and pulled up next to Jayden. He extracted a bucket of milk from his inventory and poured it into Jayden's mouth. Instantly, the effects of the potion vanished, and Jayden sat up straight, rubbing his head where he had fallen on the stairs. He looked around in a daze, and when his eyes landed on Charlie, they widened.

"Charlie?" he asked in awe.

"Yeah, it's me," he replied with a smile.

"But . . . how did you get here?" Jayden asked as Charlie helped him to his feet. "And . . . *where* did you get that many players to help us?"

"Well, it's kind of a long story," Charlie said as Jayden extracted a Potion of Healing from his inventory.

"Give me the short version," Jayden requested as he started to drink the potion.

"Well, basically, ELM captured me and warped me up to the tower, and I got the attention of one of the Withers to help me escape," Charlie said. "It did manage to kill them, but it also blasted me off the tower."

"Yikes!" Jayden exclaimed. "How'd you get out of that one?"

"The same way that Stan did," Charlie replied. "I had a Potion of Fire Resistance on hand. Well, it wasn't totally the same," he said as he scratched his pig between the ears. "I gave mine to Dr Pigglesworth as we were falling, and he kind of acted like a fireproof life raft and swam me out of the lava moat after we landed. I got a little burned," he said, gesturing to the scorch marks all over his clothes, "but I shook it off."

"OK," Jayden said with a nod, "but that still doesn't explain where you got thousands of players to come and fight for us!"

"Well, being in all that lava got me thinking," Charlie replied, "and I realized that with all the fighting going on in Element City, there was probably nobody guarding Brimstone besides the Wither Skeletons. I had been away from the battlefield for so long that it probably wouldn't have made a huge difference if I went back or not, and I realized what we could probably use most were reinforcements. So after we got out of the lava, I snuck back into the castle and went to the Nether."

"And you freed everyone who was locked up in Brimstone?" Jayden asked, amazed.

"Yep. Actually, to be honest, I have this little guy here to thank," said Charlie, smiling as he pet his pig on the head again. "I was able to use the bridge to get from the castle's Nether Portal to the prison, but I still had the Wither Skeletons to deal with, and I didn't have a weapon. Dr Pigglesworth was able to dodge all the Skeletons' attacks, and I was able to free all the soldiers and citizens who the Noctem Alliance locked up in there . . . which, I had forgotten, was the entire population of the city."

"And they all joined the battle?"

"Yep," Charlie said. "I told everybody that our final battle against the Noctem Alliance was going on, and everybody said that they wanted to help out. They looted the storehouse at the prison, scraped together any weapons they could, and followed me to the portal in the courthouse. So that means that, as of right now, the entire population of Element City, citizens and soldiers alike, is out there fighting the Noctems."

The two players turned to look out on the battlefield again. Indeed, now that the citizens from Brimstone were out on the battlefield, the Noctem forces were outnumbered ten to one. Jayden and Charlie both knew that, despite the massive advantage in quantity, the Noctem soldiers were still skilled fighters, and the two Withers were still raining their skulls of death down into the battlefield. They still had a long way to go before the battle was won.

Bob!"

Ben looked up from the map he'd pulled off a dead Noctem soldier and saw his brother riding Ivanhoe towards the abandoned store that he was concealed within. As Bob rode through the doorless frame, Ben was relieved. The map had showed him some very odd things that he needed to ask about.

"Hey, bro," Ben replied as Bob reached him. "What's going on out there? Because either this map is malfunctioning or about a thousand new players just entered the battlefield."

"That's no malfunction," Bob replied, and Ben was shocked to see that his face was lit up with joy. "Charlie just came back, and he brought everybody who was locked away in Brimstone with him."

"Really?" Ben said. "That's fantastic! And all of them are fighting?"

"Yes, but that's not entirely a good thing," Bob replied solemnly. "On the one hand, we now outnumber the Noctems by a ton. But on the other hand, we still have to worry about *that*."

Bob pointed out the window, and Ben followed his finger until his gaze locked on one of the Withers. The giant skeletal mob, which had been harmlessly floating in the sky, was now firing indiscriminately into the crowd. A rapid-fire barrage of black skulls flew from the three mouths of the monster, creating a blitz of explosions that was spreading through the crowd.

"Now that there are so many republic fighters in the crowd, the Wither isn't afraid to hold back any more," Bob explained, an urgent note in his voice. "It realizes that, regardless of who it fires at, it will probably hit more of our soldiers than theirs. We've got to take that thing down, and fast."

Ben was blown away by the notion that any mob in the game would have the reasoning skills to think like that. Then again, Lord Tenebris's psychic grip on this particular Wither had probably bent its mind in odd and unexplainable ways. Anyway, it didn't matter. Ben knew that his brother was right, and their top priority had to be taking down the Withers.

"All right," Ben replied. "Let's go."

Ben yanked a Potion of Swiftness out of his inventory, guzzled it down, and immediately felt a surge of energy course through his veins. He took a deep breath and ran out of the building and onto the battlefield, Bob right behind him. Ivanhoe was fast enough to keep up with the potion-enhanced Ben, so it was side by side that the two brothers raced across the outskirts of the plaza and towards the Wither.

As they ran, Ben looked at the fighting players and saw, to his delight, that the Noctem forces were starting to be overwhelmed. He saw various throngs of black-clad players all fighting back to back as they were swarmed by the sheer number of republic players who were now on the battlefield. His stomach lurched with disgust when he saw a republic fighter fall to the ground, items flying about him in a falling halo, and it only encouraged him to sprint faster.

After dashing as fast as they could, the two police chiefs were finally close enough to the Wither that they could hear the screams of its victims as it continued to fire its life-draining projectiles into the crowd. Ben looked at his brother, who pointed to a brick-block building at the corner of the plaza, the bottom floor of which had been partially torn apart by TNT blasts. Ben nodded, and the two of them sprinted into the building. He hardly noticed the dilapidated remains of a store on the ground floor. His eyes immediately locked onto a staircase. He didn't break his pace as he raced up the stairs, his brother on piggyback right behind him.

They burst onto the roof and looked out over the Avery Memorial Courthouse plaza, where thousands of players were now fighting. Not too far away from them, the Wither was hovering high over the battlefield, still bombarding the field with skulls. Although the explosions were tearing rifts in the groups of Noctem and republic players alike, nobody made any attempts to stop the monster; they were all too busy fighting one another.

"How are we gonna take that thing down?" Bob asked,

desperation in his voice. He looked at his brother, who appeared to be in deep thought. "Do you have any ideas, bro?"

"Well . . . I do have one. . ."

"Spit it out!" Bob cried.

"Well . . ." Ben said, pausing for a moment, as if unsure that he wanted to suggest it, then finally replying, "We could try Operation Hook, Line and Sinker."

Bob stared at his brother for a moment, mulling over this insane idea.

"But . . . that operation was designed to take down Ghasts! That thing probably has twenty times the firepower of a Ghast!" Bob said, sounding overwhelmed. "And also, in order for that to work, we'd need Bill."

"Well, I'm sorry, do you have a better idea?" Ben demanded as a particularly large blast sounded in the middle of the battlefield, accompanied by another morbid chorus of screams. "At the very least, we'll be able to distract it for a little while, and hopefully we can hold it at bay until Stan's ready to come down here and finish it off!"

"Might we be able t' help ye?" a voice came from behind them, cutting off Bob's reply. The two brothers looked behind them and saw Sirus and Commander Crunch walking across the top of the roof, bows and arrows in their hands and enthusiastic smiles on their faces.

"Yeah, you can!" Ben shouted with glee, happy with any backup they could possibly get.

"How did you guys know we were up here?" Bob asked.

"Oh, we were just over on the roof of that building over there" – Sirus pointed over to the building next door – "and it was pretty funny 'cause, at first, we ran in there to avoid the Wither, but then we saw it was an anvil store, so we've been dropping anvils off the roof onto the heads of the bad guys ever since then!"

"Uh . . . guys?" Ben said slowly. He looked back and forth between the two players as if they were insane. "You . . . both have bows and arrows in your hand. Why didn't you just use those?"

"Oh, I be sorry, Mister Reason 'n' Practicality," Commander Crunch spat sarcastically. "Pardon me if, in th' midst o' all o' this ghastly warfare, we felt th' need t' inject a wee bit o' classic cartoon-style comedy into the mix."

Ben and Bob stared at him for a moment, now absolutely positive he was insane, before realizing that it didn't matter. Sirus and Crunch were here, and they were both competent with a bow and arrow – that was all that really mattered.

"OK, here's the plan," Ben explained, as Sirus and Commander Crunch listened intently. "You three shoot at it from behind me. I'll have my sword out, and I'll block all its attacks."

The three other players nodded and, wasting no time, they stood side by side behind Ben, notching arrows in their bows and training them on the Wither. Ben dropped into a fighting stance, his sword raised and ready to deflect.

"Ready . . . aim . . . FIRE!"

On Ben's command, three arrows flew over his head, over the crowd of warring players, and directly into the backs of each of the Wither's three heads. The giant boss mob shrieked in agony before spinning around and setting its sights on the rooftop where the four players stood. Bob, Commander Crunch and Sirus didn't stop, continuing to send arrows flying into the Wither's body as the monster let loose its first flurry of attacks.

Ben leaped into action, swinging his sword through the air and cutting all the Wither Skulls in two, creating small grey explosions that just barely grazed his skin. The Wither and the players continued to fire at each other. As more and more arrows sunk into the scattered pieces of black flesh hanging from the beast's skeletal rib cage, Ben spun his sword around, deflecting countless explosions, the Knock-back Enchantment on the sword keeping the blasts far enough away that he hardly took any damage from them.

Before long, the Wither started to tire. It was clearly taking heavy damage from the barrage of arrows, and its rate of fire was beginning to drop.

"Come on guys, keep going!" Ben shouted as he knocked two more skulls out of midair in a double explosion. "It's almost dead!"

As the three players continued to send arrows into the giant mob, the Wither stopped firing for a moment. Ben was confused and a little disturbed. Why would the Wither cease its barrage? He watched the boss mob open its mouth and, as if in slow motion, it fired a single projectile out of its centre mouth.

As Ben raised his sword to deflect the blast, he realized that it wasn't in slow motion. A single skull had shot out of the Wither's mouth and was moving towards him at a crawl. Unlike the other projectiles, which were black and charred like the heads of the monster, this one was a cerulean shade of blue. Ben hardly had time to question what this was before the slow-moving blue skull was upon him. He raised his sword to block the attack, cutting through the air in front of the skull and sending a Knockback shockwave slicing into the skull.

As soon as the wave of energy made contact with a skull, it ruptured into a massive black explosion, which knocked Ben off his feet and sent him flying backwards. Bob, Commander Crunch and Sirus had no time to react as Ben slammed into them, sending them all falling to the ground in a crumpled heap.

Ben felt as though he was covered in some sort of corrosive sludge as he lay there on top of his friends. He had taken the full brunt of the blast from the blue skull, and he felt his energy draining as he tried to force himself to get up. It was futile, though. He felt as though he suddenly weighed several tons, and was unable to move. He watched in dismay as black smoke began to rise out of his body and drift towards the Wither floating above them. Upon reaching the Wither's body, the dozens of arrows sticking out of its rib cage began to pop out, falling to the rooftop with a clatter.

Ben was stupefied, and found himself unable to move as his brother, his friends and Ivanhoe struggled to push him off them. The Wither was floating closer and closer to them. It was all he could do to watch, his heart stopped in place, as the monster's three mouths opened and began to glow. Ben heard three collective gasps from behind him as he closed his eyes, his face screwed in anticipation of what was to come. . . .

"Hey!"

The shout came from Ben's left, and he opened his eyes just in time to see a diamond pickaxe flying through the air and lodging itself into the right head of the Wither. As the head let out a ghastly wail and rolled limply to the side, the tool still sticking out of its skull, the Wither turned to face the noise, letting out a wail of outrage. Ben turned as well, as did his three fellow fighters, and he had to do a double take to ensure that he was seeing correctly.

There, on top of the house immediately to their left, standing next to a loaded TNT cannon made out of cobblestone, was the Mechanist. Another diamond pickaxe was clutched in his right hand, and his left hand held a lever on the side of the cannon. He was staring at the Wither with daggers in his eyes and a glower on his face.

"Try this on for size," he said as he yanked down on the lever.

There was a hissing sound from within the mechanism next to him, and a second later, a muted explosion rang out as a lit block of TNT came soaring through the air on a collision course with the Wither. The ignited explosive struck the Wither in a massive burst of light and sound, and the skeletal demon proceeded to let out a ghastly wail of agony as it slowly sank down to the ground.

Ben watched, awestruck, as the Mechanist sprinted as fast as he could towards the edge of the building. He leaped over the gap between the two buildings, touching down as the Wither reached the ground, still dazed from the blast as an odd white force field seemed to envelop it. What the energy field surrounding the Wither did, Ben never found out, as the Mechanist jumped into the air, delivering a flying kick that knocked the monster to the ground. Without missing a beat, the Mechanist raised his pickaxe and drove it as hard as he could into the skeletal chest of the monster.

All at once, a horrible, high-pitched screech rang out from within the Wither, causing all in the vicinity to cover their ears. The Wither's eyes and mouths flew open in agony, glowing with a radiant white light as the skulls began to crumble, turning into a fine black dust that was immediately blown away by the soft wind. The Wither began to shake, and the ear-piercing screech continued as all the bones and flesh that composed the monster began to vanish, turning into dust on the wind.

Then, without warning, a white light flashed from within the Wither. The daze was so bright, and so unexpected, that Ben, the Mechanist and all the others on the rooftop were momentarily blinded. It only lasted for a few seconds, though, and by the time their vision returned, all that remained of the Wither was a stain of black dust on the roof of the building.

The Mechanist took no time to reflect over his kill. Instead, his eyes were immediately drawn to the limp body of Ben, still lying sprawled out on the ground as the others attempted to untangle themselves. The Mechanist pulled out a red potion that he had gotten from a dead soldier, just as Bob realized what had happened to his brother.

"No," he said, his voice uneven as he awkwardly pulled himself over to Ben. He shook his head back and forth as he clutched Ben by the shoulders. "No . . . you're OK, bro . . . you've *gotta* be OK. . ."

"He's fine," the Mechanist replied, gently pushing Bob out of the way before he could object. He poured the potion down Ben's throat.

"What . . . what happened to him?" Bob asked, still staring at his brother as Sirus and Commander Crunch pulled him up and helped him remount Ivanhoe.

"The blast range of the blue skulls is bigger than that of the black ones, and more powerful, too. The blue ones can blast through anything except bedrock," the Mechanist said almost robotically as he put his hand to Ben's head. "He got hit by the blast and inflicted with the Wither effect. It's a worse kind of poisoning that can be fatal if left untreated."

"So . . . is he gonna . . . ," Bob stammered, his face as white as a ghost.

The Mechanist turned to face him and smiled. "Your brother will be fine, Bob. The potion I just gave him will give him enough strength to survive until the Wither effect wears off."

"Mechanist . . ."

The Mechanist looked down at the source of the feeble voice and saw Ben looking up at him, his eyes fluttering open. Bob's face broke out in relief, but Ben only looked up to the old redstone mechanic with the wild white hair. He looked exhausted, yet still a smile crept to the corner of his mouth as he spoke.

"Thank you. And . . . I'm sorry."

"You don't have to be," the Mechanist replied, returning Ben's slight yet earnest smile.

Ben opened his mouth as if he were about to reply, but then shut it and gave a sigh of contentedness as his eyes closed, his head rolled to the side, and he passed out.

Leonidas emerged from the rabble of brawling players, and he took a deep breath. The fighting that had now spread across the entire plaza was intense, and he had just sprinted right through the thick of it. Everywhere he looked, the glut of republic soldiers and citizens were teaming up to bear down on the Noctem soldiers with full force, and the black-clad forces were fighting back just as hard. Twice, Leonidas had halted his run through the crowds, taken aim and sent an arrow into a Noctem soldier, thus preserving the life of a citizen the soldier was about to overpower.

He might have stopped more than twice, but he had a job to do.

As he was fighting, he had seen Bob run with his brother into an old run-down store, above which one of the Withers floated, firing its deadly blasts down into the crowds. Leonidas knew that, with the only archer as good as he was occupied fighting the boss mob, there was a very important task he had to do.

Even if it wasn't his job, he still would have sought the task out anyway. This was personal.

Leonidas walked slowly around the outer ring of the battle-field, and the further away from the courthouse he went, the higher the number of Noctem soldiers in the crowd. The soldiers of Lord Tenebris were truly giving it their all, charging into the battle with weapons blazing and fire in their eyes, but Leonidas could also see another trait present, written all over their faces: fear. For the first time, as the Noctem soldiers gave it their all against the thousands of republic players, a pit opened in their stomachs as they considered the possibility that they might not win this battle.

Leonidas was nearly back at the execution platform, and he saw that this was the only place on the entire battlefield where the majority of the players wore the black colours of the Noctem Alliance. This was where the Noctem Alliance was digging in their heels and fighting most ferociously. Even as he watched for just the space of a few seconds, Leonidas saw nearly ten Elementia players try to fight their way into the mass of black leather and get cut down in the process.

Leonidas's heart gave an unpleasant jolt as he saw these players die, but it confirmed what he had guessed. The execution platform was where the Noctem Alliance was fighting their hardest, and this would be by far the most difficult area for the republic forces to take. If his target was going to be anywhere, it was here.

Trying to avoid attracting attention from the Noctem forces, Leonidas covered his face as he stealthily slipped into the decrepit house closest to the execution platform. Judging by the weathered sign Leonidas saw above the door, it used to be part of the Apothecary's chain of potioneers. Indeed, as he made his way through the ground floor, he saw empty cauldrons and brewing stands strewn haphazardly about, shattered glass bottles covering the floor and making it appear to shimmer. Leonidas was careful to avoid making a sound as he scaled the stairs to the second floor.

This floor was totally barren; Leonidas assumed it used to be someone's living space, but not a single item remained on the flat wood-plank floor. He made his way across the floor to the window. From there, he could see all the way across the sprawling plaza in front of the Avery Memorial Courthouse, filled to the bursting point with players that Leonidas was sure, for better or for worse, were fighting the final battle of the war.

Leonidas knew that the biggest thing he could do to ensure the republic's victory in the war was to eliminate the opposing leaders, so he drew his bow. Notching an arrow in it and pulling the string taut, he looked out the window, scanning the cluster of black forms right below him. He scanned every single face that he could see, desperate to find one of the two players that he was looking for. His heart started to race as he searched. Leonidas knew that the longer he stood looking out this window, the better the chance that . . .

"Looking for me?" a voice called out from behind Leonidas.

Slowly, Leonidas turned around, his bow still raised, until he was facing Spyro. The Noctem general stood at the top of the stairs, his glowing diamond sword shining an eerie light on his black leather armour as he dropped into a fighting stance, a wicked grin on his face.

For a moment, the two players stared at each other. Leonidas remembered, long ago, when Spyro had been a mere private, helping him to construct Nocturia. Back then, he had been so innocent, so curious and so open-minded, even going so far as to question if the Alliance he had joined was doing the right thing. Now, though, Leonidas stood across from a savage killer, twisted by months of leading an organization of hate and intolerance. He knew that he had no choice but to destroy the Noctem general . . . but he also knew he had to at least try to avoid the conflict.

"Stand down," Leonidas said in a monotone, his bow still trained on Spyro's forehead. "I don't want to hurt ya, Spyro.

You're not a bad person . . . you're just lost. The Noctem Alliance is gonna fall today. Please, don't fall with it."

"That's funny," Spyro replied, raising an eyebrow. "The great General Leonidas who trained me would never try to negotiate a surrender. He would just start the fight as fast as possible, and end it even faster."

"The General Leonidas *you* know is dead," Leonidas replied proudly. "I ain't never pickin' a fight again unless I have to, and I don't want to do it today. Please, Spyro . . . I'm beggin' ya . . . stand down. Stop this."

For a moment, Spyro's mouth hung open, and his eyes were wide, as if he were in deep thought. Then, all of a sudden, his eyebrows creased, his eyes grew bloodshot, and his face contorted into an ugly mess of rage as he gave out a battle cry, sending a Splash Potion of Harming directly towards his former master.

Leonidas didn't even flinch. He may have promised himself to never start a fight again, but he would never hesitate to finish one. Within an instant, an arrow had shot the potion out of the air in midflight, and Leonidas had sent a flurry of arrows flying from his bow, directly at Spyro. Despite Spyro's best effort to deflect the attacks with his sword, the arrows came too many, and too fast. It was only a matter of seconds before one of the arrows found a chink in Spyro's armour, and he slouched down to the ground as five more arrows sunk into the weak points.

As Spyro lay on the ground, six arrows sticking out of him, struggling to stay alive, Leonidas advanced on him, one final arrow in his bow. He stood over the Noctem general, staring down at him with pity, while Spyro returned a glare of utter loathing.

"Do ya have any last words?" Leonidas asked sadly as he pulled the arrow back, aiming directly for Spyro's temple.

Spyro said nothing. Instead, in a surprisingly swift motion for somebody who was teetering on the verge of death, he raised his hand to his mouth and let out a long, high-pitched whistle.

Leonidas had no time to comprehend what he was doing. Seconds after he started to whistle, the wall behind Leonidas exploded, showering him with dust and debris and knocking him to the ground, sending his bow and the arrow notched within it flying out of his grasp. Leonidas squinted his eyes through the dust, and as he looked out the massive hole where the wall used to be, his heart stopped dead. There it was, floating directly above him, its raspy, metallic breath wheezing through its charred black rib cage as the six eyes of the Wither trained on Leonidas.

"There!" Spyro coughed, and Leonidas tore his horrified eyes off the giant skeletal mob to see Spyro pointing over at Leonidas's bow, which was still sitting in the corner of the room. As he saw his weapon lying on the wood-plank block floor, for the first time, it hit him like a stack of bricks that he was unarmed, and totally defenceless. No sooner had he begun to move towards the corner of the room, desperate to retrieve his bow, than he heard the sound of the Wither firing another attack from behind him. Leonidas barely had time to raise his arms over his face before the skull connected with the bow lying on the floor. The force of the explosion slammed into Leonidas, sending him tumbling back to the ground, now with black wisps of smoke rising from his arms.

In horror, Leonidas looked over at where the patch of floor had been, only to see that the entire corner of the house had been totally blown to bits. His weapon was gone.

Leonidas's heart rate, already racing from the Wither's attack, now skyrocketed to dangerous levels as he realized that he was totally defenceless. He still had a glut of arrows in his inventory, but nothing to fire them with. He had no way of fighting back against the Wither, which was now aiming for him again.

It was all Leonidas could do to dive-roll to the side, desperately trying to avoid the onslaught of explosions tearing the ground around him to shreds. Leonidas's head whipped around wildly and saw that nearly the entire floor had been blasted apart by the Wither's attacks. Only a few wood-plank blocks remained levitating over the ground floor of the shop below. Leonidas looked above him and saw a window. Without thinking, acting on pure survival instinct, Leonidas launched himself off the floor, flying out the window before the Wither could blow him to bits.

Leonidas felt himself falling through the air for a moment before landing with a crunch on the dirt blocks below him. He let out a shout as pain seared in his legs, and he allowed himself a second to lay still to let the pain die down. In that second, he looked around him. He had landed in a narrow alleyway, about four blocks wide. The building on one side of the alley Leonidas recognized as the seafood restaurant next to the Avery Memorial Courthouse. The other side of the alley was the Apothecary store, or rather, what was left of the store. The Wither's explosive attacks had blasted off huge chunks of the second floor, so the only things remaining that Leonidas could see were a few fragments of brick-block wall.

A raspy breathing registered in Leonidas's ears, and he knew that his brief respite from the fight was over. Although his legs still felt as though they were blazing with flames, he forced himself to stand, just as the Wither floated out from around the side of the house. All six of its beady white eyes trained on Leonidas, who was trembling as he imagined how he was going to fight this thing with no bow.

All of a sudden, an Ender Pearl flew down from the

second floor of the Apothecary store, and landed just below the Wither. Leonidas's jaw dropped in disbelief as out of the cloud of purple smoke walked General Spyro. He was no longer full of arrows and clinging to life by the skin of his teeth, but he looked totally happy, healthy and sadistic. As Leonidas stared at him, he noticed that the Noctem general was smoking with the red fumes of a Potion of Healing as he looked up at the Wither and pointed toward Leonidas.

"Finish him off," Spyro ordered with a cruel smile.

The Wither took another breath in and fired three skulls directly at Leonidas. Despite the colossal strain on his legs, Leonidas still found the strength to hop backwards, dodging the explosions that blasted giant holes in the ground.

As Leonidas caught his breath, trying to keep his will to continue fighting alive, he realized with a start that the holes the Wither had blasted in the dirt-block ground of the alleyway had not made a crater. Instead, they had opened up a hole that revealed a drop of more than ten blocks down into a cave. It dawned on Leonidas that they must be over one of the abandoned mines underneath the city. He saw a bright light shining up from the cave, but he hardly cared what it was. All he knew was that he had already sustained a lot of damage, and he didn't have enough health to survive a more than ten-block fall. If the Wither's blasts knocked him down there, he would be killed on impact with the ground.

The Wither fired a steady stream of projectiles at Leonidas, not giving him a moment of rest as he dodged the stream of explosions by mere inches. It wasn't long before Leonidas realized that it was futile to dodge the blasts that were ripping the alley apart, revealing more and more of the old mine below them. Desperately hoping that he could outrun the Wither's attacks before one managed to connect, Leonidas turned around and began to sprint down the alley as quickly as he could.

What he didn't expect was to run headfirst into a brick wall.

Leonidas fell to the ground in a daze, looking up and realizing, with a horrified lurch of the stomach, that the alley was a dead end. Instantly, the adrenaline kicked in as Leonidas leaped to his feet, desperately looking for a way out. But there was none. And there, hovering over the torn-up dirt floor of the alleyway, floating closer and closer to him, was the Wither.

Leonidas was just about to break down, losing all self-control in the midst of this horrific turn of events, but instead he let out a sigh. He took a deep breath, and realized that there was nothing that he could do about it. His time had simply come. He had defied death one too many times, and now, it was all over for him. He closed his eyes, reflecting on how content he was to have made up for all the mistakes in his past, as he readied himself to be blown to smithereens by the Wither.

"Arraaaughh!"

Leonidas winced as a grating, high-pitched wail rang out from the other end of the alleyway. He opened his eyes and followed the gazes of Spyro and the three heads of the Wither to see what had made such an ear-splitting noise. What he saw made him question whether or not the Wither effect that was poisoning his body had affected his brain in any way. He couldn't possibly be seeing correctly.

There, at the other end of the alley, standing in the opening between the two brick buildings, stood Oob, Mella and Stull. The three villagers were shrieking and wailing while looking up at the Wither, as if they were giving some sort of ghastly singing performance. The Wither, meanwhile, turned and surveyed the three villagers quizzically.

While Spyro just looked stunned, Leonidas's heart had dropped into his stomach. *What're the villagers doing here?* he thought to himself desperately. *Why aren't they in the Adorian Village? It's way too dangerous for them here!*

Spyro finally seemed to snap back to his senses, and he glanced up at the Wither, who was now staring intently at the villagers, as if it were absorbing every single wail that they let out.

"What are you doing, you stupid monster?" Spyro

demanded, glaring up at the Wither indignantly. "Destroy those impudent villagers, and then destroy Leonidas!"

The Wither didn't shoot the villagers. Instead, it turned around and glared down at Spyro, rage ripe in all six of its eyes. Spyro's jaw dropped, and he cowered as the Wither let out a deadly, hollow roar. Its three mouths aimed at Spyro, and he cringed in preparation for the blast that never came. The three heads just kept pointing, white mouths glowing menacingly.

"It is OK, Leo-nidas!" Mella called across the ravaged alleyway to Leonidas, who was still staring at the renegade Wither, refusing to believe his eyes. "The big black boss skeleton monster thingy is on our side now. It will not attack you any more than it has already attacked you."

"But . . . but . . . what did ya do?" Leonidas sputtered, trying to comprehend what had just happened. "And what're y'all doin' here?"

"We told the big black boss skeleton monster thingy to stop attacking you!" Oob said, sounding as though this should be obvious. "And we are here because we were bored of staying in the Adorian Village and wanted to come help you. It is a good thing, too, because we heard a large boom right after we—"

"But . . . then . . . why did it listen to ya and stop attackin' me?" Leonidas cut in.

"The big black boss skeleton monster thingy listened to us because we spoke to it in its native language. We remember how to speak in that language because we learned how to speak it by getting turned into Zombies. Getting turned into Zombies was bad, because we wanted to eat players, but it was good because we learned how to talk to the big black boss skeleton monster thingy!"

"Wait, hold up . . . you guys still remember how to talk in the language of the Wither? And ya just told it to stop attackin' me?"

"Is that not what we just said to you, Leo-nidas?" Mella said in exasperation. "The . . . um, how do you say it . . . Wither . . . will always listen to something that talks in its own language before it will listen to something that talks in the language of players and villagers."

"But . . . if ya could stop the Withers all along . . . then how come y'all waited till now to do it?" Leonidas sputtered.

"The reason that we waited until now to talk to the Wither is because we did not think of talking to the Wither until now. Um . . ." Oob looked to the ground and blushed before he continued talking to Leonidas. "Well . . . please do not tell this to the other players, Leo-nidas . . . but I have realized that when compared to players, we villagers are not very smart."

Leonidas rolled his eyes and chuckled. He was about to

thank them for saving him when something caught his eye. A figure emerging behind the villagers, sword in his hand. . . .

"Look out behind you!" Leonidas bellowed, but it was too late; Drake had already plunged his sword into Mella's back and pulled it out, sending her falling face-down to the ground. Before her sons could react, Drake grabbed Stull by the scruff of his brown collar with one hand and raised his glowing diamond sword to the front of the baby villager's neck with the other.

Leonidas gave a holler of fury, and was about to yell out at Drake when he felt a horrible lurch in his stomach. He looked down at his skin and saw black smoke rising from it. He realized with a jolt that, in his elation over being saved by the villagers, he hadn't even noticed the deadly poison from the Wither's attack getting stronger and stronger. He attempted to get out one final word, but the toxins overwhelmed him, and he slumped to the ground, unconscious.

Oob looked wildly back and forth between his mother, his brother and the Noctem General. Mella lay on the ground, totally immobile, and making no sounds. Oob couldn't tell if she were dead or alive. Stull looked petrified, afraid to make even the slightest movement as he stood still as a statue, a horrified expression on his face and a sword held to his throat. Drake looked absolutely sinister, holding the sword totally still and calmly glancing over to see Spyro still cowering under the threefold glare of the Wither. He looked back at Oob.

"If you don't want this little one to end up like her," he said slowly, jerking his head toward Mella, still lying on the ground, "you'll tell that Wither that from now on, it is no longer allowed to take commands from villagers. Only from members of the Noctem Alliance."

Oob's mind was racing. His concern for the limp form of his mother barely registered as he looked at his brother. Oob was torn. On the one hand, he knew that if he gave the Wither back to the Noctem Alliance, they would use it to do bad things . . . *very* bad things. But on the other hand . . . if he didn't . . . they would kill Stull.

Drake chuckled as his lips curled upwards into a smile, amused by Oob's inner conflict that showed on his face. "Don't feel bad, little guy," Drake growled maliciously as he raised his sword closer to the baby villager's neck. "This would be a hard choice for a *player* to make, and you . . . you are far, *far* less than a player. You're nothing but a simple-minded, ignorant, useless little—*Aaaauggh*!"

Drake let out a cry as the arrow sunk into his right hand. The sword fell to the ground with a clang as his left hand flew out wildly to the side. He involuntarily released Stull, sending him flying through the air and crashing into his older brother. Cringing, Drake ripped the arrow out of his hand, and spun around to see another player standing at the end of the alley-way, lowering her bow. Her leather armour was pure white, stained with the marks of warfare, and he hardly noticed her giant, red lips next to the outraged scowl on her face.

"Don't you *dare* touch them," Cassandrix hissed.

Desperately, Drake snatched his sword off the ground and raised it over the two villagers, who were still lying in a heap on the ground next to their mother. *Fine,* he sneered to himself. *If I can't have the Wither . . . no one can.* Drake plunged his sword downwards, and it was about to enter Oob's back when a massive force collided with Drake. Cassandrix slammed shoulder-first into Drake, sending him tumbling across the ground, coming to a stop at the very edge of a hole the Wither had blasted into the ground.

Within seconds, Cassandrix was upon him. Before Drake had a chance to even regain his footing, her diamond sword had sliced through his black leather armour, sending him tumbling backwards. Down he plummeted into the old mine, but not before reaching up and grabbing Cassandrix's foot, pulling her down with him.

The two players fell for a few seconds, tumbling through space, before hitting the dirt-block ground below them with a thud. They rolled in opposite directions from the impact for a few blocks before coming to a stop. Cassandrix opened her eyes and winced. The fall had dealt quite a lot of damage to her, and it felt as though a few of her insides had been displaced. From behind her, she heard a moan, and instantly she felt wide awake. Drake was damaged, too – this was her opportunity to finish him off. Cassandrix forced herself to a standing position and, as fast as her damaged legs could carry her, she made her way over to Drake, who was still struggling to get to his feet.

As she walked, she noticed something peculiar. The sound on the dirt blocks below her feet seemed different than usual, yet somehow familiar. Cassandrix looked around the cave and saw several holes in the ground, through which a bright light was shining. One of them was right next to her. Cassandrix peered down into the hole, and her heart skipped a beat as she saw a massive lake of lava nearly twenty blocks below them. As she examined the hole further, she realized with a jolt that the entire expanse of dirt that she and Drake had landed on was only one block thick.

All at once, she was hit by a rush of comprehension as she realized what this was – an expanse of dirt blocks, forming a one-block-thick platform over a lake of liquid. As she stood across from her opponent, who was just tossing an empty potion bottle to the side, fumes of red smoke started to rise off him.

All right, Cassandrix, she thought to herself. *Time to earn the title of Elementia's greatest Spleef player.*

Cassandrix raised her sword as Drake raised his, but stood still as he began to charge at her. *I'll have to play defensively,* she thought. *I've taken a lot of damage, and he's all healed up from his potion, so I'll have to let him tire himself out.*

Drake was nearly upon her now, and he raised his sword to strike. Just as the blow was about to fall, Cassandrix sidestepped the slash, spinning around and sweeping her feet underneath Drake. As he toppled to the ground, Cassandrix raised her own sword, and she knew that Drake would expect her to stab him and roll out of the way, and that's exactly what she let him do. As he rolled backwards, Cassandrix drove her sword into the dirt block, gripped it tightly, and twisted. Instantly, the frail dirt block was destroyed, falling down into the lava below and disappearing into a puff of smoke.

Drake was back on his feet, and he reared up to deliver another strike. Cassandrix felt the pain of the fall searing through her legs and knew what she had to do. As Drake charged in, she sidestepped yet again, lessening the impact as Drake brought his blade down on her, only to be countered by her own diamond weapon. For a moment, the two players pressed their weapons into each other, sending sparks onto the dirt-block ground every time they slid across each other. Bolstered by the potion, Drake began to overpower Cassandrix, and she took a deep breath and drove her sword downwards, still locked onto Drake's. The two swords tore through the dirt-block ground, cutting a crescent-shaped hole into the ground, revealing the lava below.

Drake hardly noticed the molten liquid below. He was more interested in Cassandrix, who proceeded, with a calm and calculated air around her, to sidestep every attack that Drake threw at her. More often than not, Drake's sword stabbed deep into the dirt, and once the sword was free, the block broke with a crunch, falling into the lava pit below.

After a minute of fighting like this and not landing a hit, Cassandrix could tell that Drake was starting to get frustrated. His eyes were wild and manic, and his sword strikes were getting more powerful and less precise, now destroying a bit of the floor with every single strike. Cassandrix kept a level head, continuing to move around Drake in a circle, dodging blow after blow as he stood in place, wrecking the floor around him. The floor was now so thin that she had to hop between single blocks that were floating over the now-exposed lava moat, but Drake's attacks were so wild in his aggravation that she was able to dodge them effortlessly.

After a few minutes had passed, Cassandrix stepped away from Drake after a particularly fierce sword strike and looked at him with a smile on her face.

"It's over, Drake," she said.

"What are you talking about?" Drake demanded, spit flying from his mouth in rage. "Neither of us have landed one single attack!"

"Yes," Cassandrix replied smugly, gesturing to the floor around Drake, "*you* have."

Drake looked down at the floor, and his mouth dropped open in shock. He was standing on a tiny island of blocks that was floating in the middle of a ring of emptiness that stretched all the way down to the lava. Drake looked around in desperation, hoping to find some way to escape this island, but then he saw, to his horror, that Cassandrix was reaching her sword out into the pitfall, destroying all the remaining blocks that Drake might have had any hope of jumping onto.

When she finished, she looked up at Drake. His eyes widened, and his pupils shrank down to tiny dots as he watched Cassandrix draw out her bow.

"No! No, please!" Drake begged, dropping to his knees. "I beg of you . . . have mercy!"

"I might, Drake," Cassandrix replied as she pulled back the string, hatred etched into her face. "If *anybody* else had stabbed an innocent villager and threatened to murder a child, then perhaps, if he pleaded insanity, I might've let him live. But you forget, Drake . . . you're nothing but a simple-minded, ignorant, useless little Noctem."

And with that, Cassandrix let the arrow fly.

Drake whipped out his sword as fast as possible, deflecting the arrow, but two more were already on their way. Drake tried to block the stream of arrows flying from Cassandrix's bow, and at first, he was successful. However, it only took one misstep for an arrow to sink into Drake's hand yet again, causing him to howl in pain and drop his sword into the pit of molten lava below him.

From there, it was all over. One more arrow to the chest was all that it took to send Drake tumbling off his little island, down into the molten pit below.

Cassandrix raced over to the hole and trained her bow on Drake's falling body, lest he have a Potion of Fire Resistance and survive the impact. But she didn't have anything to worry about. The second that Drake made contact with the lava, his items burst out around him in a ring and were instantly burned to a crisp as his body slowly descended into the lava and ceased to exist.

Cassandrix took a deep breath and let it out. She still hurt badly from the fall down into the cave, and there was nothing she wanted more than to sit for a moment, allowing herself to heal before returning to the battlefield. But Cassandrix knew that she couldn't do that. Despite eliminating one of the three remaining leaders of the Noctem Alliance, she knew that she hadn't earned the luxury of a break. She needed to get Mella and Leonidas some medical attention before it was too late, and then she had to figure out what to do with Spyro.

Cassandrix reached into her inventory and pulled out an Ender Pearl that she had looted from a dead soldier on the battlefield. Not looking forward to the additional pain in her legs the pearl would cause, Cassandrix took a deep breath and pitched the turquoise sphere towards the fractured street floating above. The pearl flew through one of the craters and landed on the street, causing Cassandrix to disappear in a puff of purple smoke, leaving the oozing pit of lava that had just consumed one of the generals of the Noctem Alliance bubbling beneath her.

As soon as he felt the rush of teleportation ending, Stan pushed off Lord Tenebris's sword, as his adversary did the same. The two players tumbled through the air away from each other, and came to a stop about ten blocks apart. They were surrounded by the grey, cloudlike mist that the Withers had cast into the sky; it wasn't thick enough to obscure their vision, but it did give both players a dark tint to their skins. Not too far away, Stan saw the peaks of the tallest skyscrapers in the city rising to about their same height. In the distance, Stan could see Element Castle, which rose even further into the sky. Hundreds of blocks below them, Stan saw the two warring factions spread throughout the plaza of the Avery Memorial Courthouse, which would surely be the last battlefield of this war.

He had no time to focus on these details, however, as he dedicated all of his focus to the white-eyed doppelganger floating across from him.

Lord Tenebris didn't look shocked by the fact that Stan now had operating powers. Rather, he appeared to be in deep thought as he stared at Stan. It was as if he were trying to gaze through Stan, as though if he focussed hard enough, he would be able to read Stan like a book and determine where he had gotten his new abilities.

"I must admit, Stan, that you managed to catch me off guard," Lord Tenebris said after a moment of silence. "This is something that no player has ever been able to do before."

"I'll take that as a compliment," Stan replied snarkily.

"However, it doesn't matter to me how you attained these powers, Stan," Lord Tenebris said, his eyes looking more sinister by the moment as a rumble of thunder sounded in the distance. "Your strength still pales in comparison to the might of I, the great and powerful Lord—"

"You can drop the act now that we're up here," Stan cut in bitterly. "I know who you really are, Kev."

Lord Tenebris opened his mouth for a moment, looking outraged, and Stan was sure that he was about to burst into some sort of tirade. But then, as quickly as his anger had risen, it ceased. He had heard something in Stan's voice that he had, again, not been expecting: certainty. Stan was not simply making an unfounded claim to get under his skin — Lord Tenebris was floating across from a player who unquestionably knew the truth about him.

"So . . . you finally figured it out," Lord Tenebris said, looking at Stan in a calculating manner.

"Yep," Stan replied, looking at Lord Tenebris and shaking his head. "I always had trouble believing that two egomaniacal dictators would be able to gain total control on the same Minecraft server in the span of just six months. At least it makes a bit more sense now that I know it was you all along."

"I must ask, Stan," Lord Tenebris said evenly, his eye twitching at Stan's comment as he tried not to show any cracks in his self-assured persona, "what tipped you off? I thought that I hid my trail quite well."

"Well, let's just say that I had a run-in with a friend who was able to help me put together the pieces of the puzzle," Stan said audaciously. "As a matter of fact, it was the same friend who helped me get the powers that are letting me float up here and talk to you now."

Lord Tenebris's eyes widened, and then his face contorted into an ugly sneer.

"It was that mongrel Sally, wasn't it?" Lord Tenebris snarled at Stan. "She's been a thorn in my side for months now, never ceasing her attempts to break through my defences, to peel back the layers of protection that I installed to protect my beloved server. . . She finally succeeded in getting in. . ."

"Well, Sally did help me quite a bit," Stan replied, his cheery, conversational tone of voice making Lord Tenebris's rage build. The Noctem leader was used to every player whom he spoke to cowering in fear, not treating him like a joke. "But she wasn't the one I was referring to."

"And I suppose that you're not going to tell me who did," Lord Tenebris scoffed.

"Well, I might," Stan replied, his steely gaze equalling Lord Tenebris's as he clutched his axe tightly in both hands, "if we didn't have more important business to attend to."

"Indeed we do, Stan, indeed we do," Lord Tenebris said softly, raising his sword in front of his hollow, white eyes as his face twisted into a sick smile. "The time has come to end this once and for all. It's time for the showdown that was always meant to be. You and I, Stan, one on one, with no armies, no traps and no tricks.

"Oh, and don't forget, Stan . . . I'm a man of my word," Lord Tenebris simpered, bowing his head. "The terms of our duel remain unchanged. Whoever wins this fight shall be proclaimed the rightful ruler of the Minecraft server Elementia."

"I wouldn't look so cocky if I were you, Kev," Stan shot back, as he returned his axe to his inventory and raised both of his hands in front of him. "I beat you once before. . . and I'll do it again."

"Oh, that's cute. You're right, Stan, you did beat me once." Lord Tenebris laughed as he, too, pocketed his sword and mirrored the position of Stan's hands. "But you forget – up here in the sky, you don't have Avery or the Apothecary to die for you. The only one that you have to rely on is yourself."

"And that's exactly who I'm counting on," Stan replied as he took a deep breath, drew back his fist and sent a pulse of explosive energy flying through the air at Lord Tenebris.

Dropping into a fighting stance, Lord Tenebris teleported out of the way of the blast, reappearing a few blocks away, where Stan immediately aimed another blast at him. The two of them repeated this six more times, each time Lord Tenebris reappearing closer and closer to Stan. After the sixth blast, Lord Tenebris was within close range of Stan, and a sword appeared in his hand as he stabbed it at Stan's stomach. In turn, Stan conjured an axe in his own hand, knocking the sword to one side and, in one motion, summoning a globe of dozens of Blazes around himself and Lord Tenebris while warping away.

Stan reappeared ten blocks overhead and looked down to see countless flashes of fire as all the Blazes in the globe opened fire on Lord Tenebris. Then, without warning, all the tiny flashes were totally overpowered by a massive blast of light and sound as Lord Tenebris created an explosion around himself, destroying all the mobs in one fell swoop and sending a shower of Blaze rods falling to the ground far below. Lord Tenebris skyrocketed up to Stan's level and, from ten blocks away, raised his hand and fired a salvo of hundreds of arrows at Stan.

Stan knew that he couldn't redirect all those arrows with his mind at once, and so he raised his hand, summoning a cow to appear in front of him in a puff of smoke. As the arrows all pierced the hide of the animal, killing it instantly as it plummeted down to earth alongside two raw pieces of meat and a leather skin, Stan focussed with all his might on the air above Lord Tenebris. Instantly, in a series of pops, dozens of blocks of gravel appeared in midair over his head and began to fall down around Lord Tenebris's head.

The Noctem leader was preparing another attack as he got clobbered in the head with the first block, knocking him out of his focus and sending him tumbling down, directly into the path of the next falling block. Lord Tenebris looked up and realized that he was in a storm of falling gravel and, with a deep breath, he aimed a skyward punch. The invisible pulse of energy connected with one of the blocks, creating an explosion that wiped all the other gravel from existence. Lord Tenebris then aimed a punch directly at Stan, who was still recovering from the effort of creating blocks in midair.

By the time he sensed it coming, it was too late for Stan to block the explosive pulse of energy. It was all he could do to catch the invisible sphere of deadly energy in his outstretched hands. The invisible force powered towards Stan's core, but he found to his utter amazement that, with all his focus, he was actually able to keep it from reaching him and blowing up. Also, the more that Stan focussed on keeping the pulse away from him, the stronger it became, and the harder it fought to come towards him. The pulse grew and grew as

Stan tried to keep it at bay, holding the energy pulse between his hands. When he felt as though he couldn't hold it any longer, he pushed both of his hands forwards, sending the powered-up blast back at Lord Tenebris.

He felt the enhanced blast long before it reached him, and Lord Tenebris knew that, whatever Stan had done to the invisible shot of energy, it was far more powerful than anything that he had ever created. He doubted that he would be able to survive this explosive blast, or even deflect it if he tried. Lord Tenebris raised his arms in front of him and devoted all of his focus to creating a three-by-three-block barrier of obsidian in front of himself. As the explosion hit the three blocks and ruptured with massive force while Lord Tenebris remained completely safe behind it, he knew that he had just made a huge mistake.

Indeed, at almost the exact moment that the three blocks appeared in midair in front of Lord Tenebris, Stan stretched his hand out towards the shield of obsidian. Before Lord Tenebris could even muster the will to teleport away, the blocks of obsidian expanded off the shield, occupying the same space as Lord Tenebris and continuing to grow until he was totally smothered by the black rock.

Stan looked at the five-by-five cube of obsidian with satisfaction. Lord Tenebris had been totally encased. He would be unable to move, and would soon die from suffocation.

Stan didn't want to take any chances, though. He didn't trust anything or anyone besides his own hand to finish off Lord Tenebris. Stan willed a diamond sword to appear in his right hand, and he stretched it out in front of him as he rocketed directly towards the obsidian prison.

As Stan flew at the giant cube of black rock, he could hear a faint rumbling inside and picked up his pace, desperate to spear Lord Tenebris with his sword before he could try anything funny.

Just as Stan's sword was about to puncture the tip of the obsidian prison, it exploded into a million tiny pieces. Stan screeched to a halt in midair, and even then, he had to warp backwards to avoid the hundreds of diamond pickaxes that were whirling in the air around Lord Tenebris. The pickaxes were rotating around him as if in orbit, spinning at a dangerous velocity as Lord Tenebris floated in the centre, a devious smile on his face and his white eyes locked on to Stan.

Man, thought Stan to himself as his heart crawled to a stop. *I don't know what he did to give himself so much power, but I sure wish that I . . .*

Suddenly, Stan realized with a jolt that he had made a horrible mistake. He had been so intent on showing off his new powers, on leaving Lord Tenebris completely and totally stunned, that he had nearly forgotten the peril that this server and all of Minecraft was in. And if Lord Tenebris was using new abilities like this by drawing power from the server . . . then that meant . . .

"Kev! Stop!" Stan desperately shouted into the tornado of spiralling pickaxes. "You have to stop using . . ."

But it was too late. Lord Tenebris had already stretched his hand out towards Stan, willing the globe of pickaxes to break from their orbit and come spiralling directly at him. Stan was afraid to teleport for fear of appearing in the path of a flying pickaxe, so he dropped his diamond sword and willed an axe to appear in its place. The pickaxes came flying full force at Stan, and he spun and twirled his axe around. Each time a flying pickaxe struck the blade of his axe, it bounced off in a shower of sparks with a clang and began to fall to the ground far below.

As the globe of spinning diamond pickaxes started to thin out, Lord Tenebris took a deep breath and stretched both of his hands out towards Stan. In one motion, all the pickaxes flew directly at Stan. There were too many of them for him to block all at once. Although he spun his axe as fast as he could, desperate to deflect all of them, one pickaxe slipped through a crack in Stan's defences and struck him cleanly between the eyes.

Luckily, Stan was hit by the blunt part of the blade and not the point or he would have been impaled through the head. Still, the force of the blow was enough to send him tumbling down, and he dropped his axe as he clutched his face in agony. After falling for dozens of blocks, Stan righted himself and opened his eyes, only to realize that he couldn't see a thing. Taking a deep breath, he focussed all his energy on healing, and restoring the health that he had lost. Instantly, Stan felt better, and his eyesight returned to normal – just in time to see Lord Tenebris flying at him at maximum speed, sword outstretched and pointed directly at him.

Stan didn't have time to conjure a new axe and block the attack. All he had time to do was will an enchanted diamond chestplate onto his body before the point of the sword drove into Stan's stomach. He felt a massive crack shatter through the centre of the armor, but it didn't go through. However, in the split second after the sword made contact, Stan saw the sword glowing with all three kinds of enchantments. The effects of the Knockback and Fire took effect, as Stan burst into flames and was hit with the blunt shockwave of the sword.

Stan plummeted through the air, far faster than he was aware an entity could travel in Minecraft. He was totally dazed, and barely able to think properly. When his thoughts returned to him, the first thing he noticed were the flames erupting from his body, leaving a trail of grey smoke behind him as he rocketed through space. He willed himself to be protected, and he felt the tickling sensation of Fire Resistance.

As hard as it was to do while shooting forwards at such a high speed, Stan forced himself to look where he was going, and saw to his dismay that he was about fifty blocks away from crashing into a skyscraper. It was all he could do to shed his chestplate and encase himself in a new set of head-to-toe enchanted diamond armour right before he made impact with the side of the building.

Stan's body had the same effect as a wrecking ball as he barrelled straight through the core of the skyscraper, tearing countless blocks away as he did. As hundreds of blocks were ripped from their place by Stan's body-turned-projectile, he went into a sort of trance, where his senses nearly shut off. He simply turned into a living meteor as he ripped through the core of the building, burst out the other side, and slammed into the stone-block street below. Stan felt himself propelled deep into the ground with a sickly crunch before finally slowing to a halt.

For quite a long time, Stan lay there in his crater on one of the many roads that crisscrossed through the buildings of Element City's Skyscraper District. Slowly but surely, Stan's senses returned, and he came to the realization that he was still alive. He wasn't entirely sure how – even with full enchanted diamond armour and his enhanced level of dura-bility as an operator, he was sure that he should have died from such a huge impact.

Stan opened his eye just the tiniest crack, and his heart jumped as he saw the form of Lord Tenebris, descending from the grey sky to where he now lay. Stan knew that he had to get out of there. As much as he wanted to lie there forever, there was far too much on the line to risk anything now. With a single deep breath, Stan once again felt a wave of healing wash over him, just as Lord Tenebris touched down beside him. He raised his diamond sword over Stan, preparing to finish the job.

Just as the sword fell, Stan vanished, reappearing in the middle of the street directly behind Lord Tenebris. The sword plunged into the stone at the bottom of the crater with a clang, and Lord Tenebris cursed loudly before whipping around, realizing that Stan was there, and meeting his eye.

"I need to talk to you, Kev," Stan said authoritatively. "If you don't stop using—"

He was cut off as a bombardment of dozens of fireballs shot out of Lord Tenebris's hands, directly at Stan. He warped out of the way just in time, and the fireballs flew behind him and collided with the nearest skyscraper in a wave of heat. Instantly, the base of the colossal building burst into flames, and even as Stan watched, the flames began to climb higher and higher up the walls, threatening to engulf the entire tower within minutes.

Stan barely had time to register this, though. He was

too busy dodging the mixed flurry of fireballs and explosive blasts that Lord Tenebris was firing at him like a machine gun, punching back and forth between his hands. Each new burst was accompanied by a grunt from Lord Tenebris, whose face bore a look of insanity.

Stan warped side to side, each time just barely missing the attacks, and each time condemning another building to burst into flames, or be torn apart by an explosion as the missed attacks flew off into the city. Stan tried to speak to Lord Tenebris for just a moment, to beg him to stop for his own sake at least, but every time he reappeared, a new blast of fire and volatile energy was upon him.

Before long, Stan began to tire; having to constantly warp around was really wearing him out. Thus, after one particularly close call, Stan didn't warp again, but instead took off, leaping into the air and flying through the city like a rocket. Behind him, he heard the sound of another player taking flight, and he glanced back to see that Lord Tenebris had taken chase, gaining on him while continuing his barrage of fire from his outstretched hand.

Stan felt the heat as the fireballs gained on him, and rolled to the side, leaving the fireballs to crash into the side of a cobblestone building. Stan cut a sharp turn to dodge another flurry of fireballs, and then began to fly straight up before swerving around the edge of a skyscraper. Behind him, he saw the top of the skyscraper he had just turned around explode with massive force as Lord Tenebris's missed attack connected with it.

Stan continued to fly, weaving in between the mile-high buildings as fast as he could, desperate to come up with some sort of plan to stop Lord Tenebris and speak to him before it was too late. Stan felt a series of explosive bursts coming up on him fast, and he did a barrel roll to dodge them. On and on Stan flew through the city, just barely managing to evade the rapid-fire string of explosions that were shooting from Lord Tenebris's hand. Stan glanced behind him and saw that the buildings in the city were being torn to shreds by what seemed like a straight line of explosions, slashing the buildings like a machete that drew closer and closer to Stan.

Then, all at once, the blasts just stopped. Stan continued to rocket forwards through the city, but the line of explosions slashing across the facades of the buildings had totally ceased. His heart skipped a beat as he realized what had happened, and he looked forwards again and there, sure enough was Lord Tenebris, floating directly in front of him and aiming his fist directly at Stan.

Finally, Stan thought to himself.

In one motion, Stan summoned an axe in his hand and cut in front of himself, hitting the explosion midflight as it went off in his face. Barely noticing as the blast tore off his remaining diamond armour, leaving him unscathed, Stan let go of his axe, allowing it to fly down to the ground below, as he stretched both of his hands out towards Lord Tenebris, just as the Noctem leader did the same to him.

Instantly, Stan's entire body went rigid, and he found himself nearly unable to move as he was locked into Lord Tenebris's psychic grip. He looked up in shock and saw that Lord Tenebris, too, had gone as stiff as a board, unable to move as he held his hands out towards Stan. The two operators floated, still locked into each other's telekinetic grips and totally immobile. When Stan realized he could talk, he knew that his chance had come.

"Kev, for your own good," Stan implored to Lord Tenebris. "Please listen to . . . *aaugh!*"

All of a sudden, Stan felt the invisible grip that was holding him intensify tenfold. As hard as he tried to fight it, Stan felt his arm moving backwards. He glanced up in desperation and saw Lord Tenebris radiating some sort of blue energy from his body, rising off his skin like flames as he stared intently at Stan.

As it moved of its own volition, Stan felt his arm twist awkwardly behind his back. He let out a scream of agony. The more he tried to fight it, the harder Lord Tenebris's power bent his body, twisting it in odd and unnatural ways. Stan's back arched inwardly, far further than it would normally go, and he felt his legs splay apart and begin to travel towards his head. He felt as though his entire body were being compressed in a trash compactor, and he was about to suffocate under the sheer unnaturalness of how he was being contorted by Lord Tenebris.

A ringing cackle filled Stan's ears, and he looked up to see Lord Tenebris laughing. Even as he was trapped in Stan's psychic hold, Lord Tenebris was laughing maniacally as he used his mind to torture Stan.

The more he listened to this evil, sadistic monster laugh, the more it occurred to Stan just who was doing this to him. He was being tortured by King Kev – and by Lord Tenebris. This was the player who had attempted to force all lower-level players to leave his city. This was the player who had destroyed the Adorian Village – twice. This was the player who had ordered the abuse, attack and murder of the NPC villagers just for his own personal gain. This was the player who had tortured Charlie to the brink of insanity. This was the player who had killed so many of Stan's friends – Adoria, the Apothecary, Sally, DZ . . . and Kat . . .

Suddenly, Stan looked at Lord Tenebris and saw the player that he hated most in all of Elementia, who had done so many cruel and heinous acts, both directly and through his followers, that he was far beyond redemption or remorse. Stan knew that there was no way he could allow himself to be humiliated and tormented by this monster. Stan felt a great power building up inside of him, fuelled by his rage and hatred of the one who floated across from him, contorting Stan's body into unnatural shapes as he laughed with pleasure. The power built and built, and when it finally reached its breaking point, Stan released it.

"ENOUGH!" Stan bellowed, his voice booming from directly inside Lord Tenebris's head with the volume of a thousand TNT blasts. Lord Tenebris's hands flew to his ears in shock as Stan uncurled himself into a standing position and thrust his arms and legs, creating a massive explosion around himself. The shock wave crashed over Lord Tenebris, pushing him away from Stan as he continued to speak.

"KING KEV, YOUR TAMPERINGS WITH THE INNER MECHANISMS OF ELEMENTIA HAVE PUT YOUR SERVER AND ALL OF MINECRAFT IN GREAT DANGER!" Stan shouted, a bolt of lightning striking behind him as he continued to bellow as loud as he could at his arch nemesis. "STOP WITH YOUR UNNATURAL AND SORCERER'S WAYS RIGHT NOW, OR YOU RISK DESTROYING ELEMENTIA AND EVERYTHING THAT YOU HAVE WORKED SO HARD TO CREATE!"

Stan felt his fury building up inside him, threatening to erupt out of him as Lord Tenebris stood watching him break down, totally stunned. Then, as suddenly as his outburst had started, Stan stopped. The thunder clouds that had begun to gather over his head parted, and Stan took a deep breath, opening his eyes and looking at Lord Tenebris. He knew that he had to stay calm if he were to win this fight.

"What . . . what are you talking about?" Lord Tenebris asked incredulously.

"While Sally was digging through the code of Elementia, trying to give me operating powers, she found evidence that you were drawing power from the server itself to try to bolster your own strength."

"And so what if I was?" scoffed Lord Tenebris. "This is warfare, Stan. Nothing is off limits."

"What she found," Stan continued calmly as if he hadn't been interrupted, "is that by drawing power from the server, you were weakening it. The more that you used abilities that were beyond the scope of your normal operating powers, the closer you came to creating a glitch that could corrupt Elementia, causing this world that you have worked for so many years to create to be lost forever. And from there, the glitch could travel over the internet, corrupting every other Minecraft server it comes into contact with."

Lord Tenebris stared at Stan. As much as he hated to believe it, he knew that Stan was telling the truth. He had guessed that there might be some side effects to strengthening himself in such a way, but he never imagined that the consequences could be so severe.

"You and I are very different people, Kev," Stan continued evenly. "We have very different philosophies, and very different methods of leadership. I will not deny that I despise you, and will never rest until you're dead. However, there is one thing that I believe the two of us have in common, and that's our love of this server, Elementia."

Lord Tenebris stared at Stan for a moment. Then he looked down for a moment before looking up at Stan again, and giving a begrudging nod.

"Both of us have fought long and hard for this server, each trying to impress our own vision of justice and liberty on it. And yet, look at what we've done to the place we both love so much!" Stan exclaimed.

Lord Tenebris followed Stan's finger, and his gaze landed on the Skyscraper District. Several buildings had been torn to shreds by their explosive battle, and some skyscrapers, including a few of the tallest ones, had been totally engulfed in flames. Black smoke rose thick and pungent from within the district, and in the distance both players could see more black smoke rising from other districts in which the fighting, both between them and their people, had taken place.

"We've been so set on destroying each other that we've nearly destroyed the very thing we've been fighting for," Stan said earnestly. "We have to stop this madness now. If we don't, then there isn't going to be anything worth fighting for any more."

"Ha, what are you suggesting?" Lord Tenebris scoffed. "That we broker some sort of peace treaty, and live side by side from now until you realize just how ignorant you've been, and come crawling back to me?"

"I never said that," Stan said slowly, although a fascinating idea sprung up in his head as Lord Tenebris said this. He pocketed the idea in the back of his mind, sure that he would have use for it later.

"I said it before, and I'll say it again: I despise you, Kev, and I won't rest until you're dead. I'm just as ready for this war to be over as you are, and I would never want to live in a server that had you in it. I'm sure that you feel the same way about me. However, I think that there are ways to settle our differences without so much collateral damage and risk to our server."

Lord Tenebris looked at Stan pensively. "What are you suggesting, Stan?" he said slowly.

Stan took a deep breath and responded confidently.

"Kev, I challenge you to a duel. A *traditional* duel, just like the one we had on the bridge of Element Castle all those months ago. No operating powers. No flight. No drawing any energy from the server. No healing or enhancements of any kind. Just you and me, armed with only our weapons and our wits, fighting to the death as if we were just normal players.

The terms of the duel remain unchanged from before – whoever walks away is the true and rightful ruler of Elementia."

Lord Tenebris raised an eyebrow, chuckled for a moment, and then replied, "Stan, I accept your challenge."

Stan smiled. He knew exactly what Lord Tenebris was thinking. The last time they had fought, he had outclassed Stan by such a large margin that Stan was foolish to ask that they replicate it now. But Stan knew better. He had only gotten stronger and stronger by the day since the Battle for Elementia, while Lord Tenebris had sat up in Fungarus ordering troops around, doing no fighting of any kind. The Noctem leader was out of practice, while Stan was at the top of his game.

Stan looked below him and focussed as hard as he could. With a pop, a single block of bedrock appeared in midair, floating high above the burning Skyscraper District. With a deep breath, Stan willed more blocks to appear, and in the space of a second, a twenty-by-twenty-block square of bedrock materialized. Stan and Lord Tenebris both floated down to opposite ends of the bedrock, totally empty-handed. They kept their eyes locked, glaring at each other until their feet simultaneously touched down on the platform.

The two players took a deep breath, and instantly, enchanted diamond chestplates and helmets appeared on their bodies. Two enchanted diamond axes latched themselves onto Stan's back, while a diamond sword enchanted with Knockback appeared at Lord Tenebris's hip. A bow and a quiver of arrows appeared on Lord Tenebris's other hip, while the same appeared on Stan's. Last but not least, each player's weapon appeared in his hand. Stan's axe had been enchanted with Sharpness, and the purple lustre shimmered under the dark cloud cover. Lord Tenebris's sword glowed red and purple, and he grasped the hilt firmly in his hand.

For a moment, the two rulers of their two governments looked at each other. No words were spoken. They both saw the great irony in the situation. After months of fighting, of power struggles, of attempting to get the upper hand on each other, here they were, back at square one. So much had changed since then, and yet, so much had remained the same. As the two players looked at each other, they knew that the time had come to end their conflict once and for all.

With no verbal cue, the two players took off at the exact same time. Stan trailed his axe behind him the same as he had the first day that he had ever picked up an axe in the Adorian Village, while Lord Tenebris had his sword pointed directly towards Stan, the same as he had on the bridge of Element Castle when they had first crossed weapons. In the exact centre of the platform, the two operators collided and began to duel.

As the weapons spun and collided with loud clangs, sending sparks falling to the bedrock beneath their feet, Lord Tenebris was immediately struck by how much Stan had improved since their last fight. No longer was he a budding axe fighter who was vastly outclassed by the master swordsman with whom he was in combat. Stan's axe moved fluidly up and down across Lord Tenebris's body, finding countless openings that were just barely blocked by Lord Tenebris's sword, and in turn deflecting his counterstrikes almost effortlessly. He was fighting at the level of a true axe master.

As the duel continued on, the weapons nearly invisible for how fast they were moving, Stan slowly started to press his offensive. He drew back his axe and started to spin it around himself, the blade slashing back and forth in front of him in a spiralling X pattern. Lord Tenebris stepped away from him, further and further towards the edge of the floating platform, but he wasn't worried. Rather, he grinned. Stan had made his first mistake.

Right as Stan's axe was about to cut across him again, Lord Tenebris stepped in close and brought his sword up against the handle of Stan's axe, shoving it down until it met his hand. Stan let go just in time, sending the axe clattering backwards across the bedrock platform as Lord Tenebris brought his sword back down and slashed across the front of Stan's diamond chestplate, leaving a trail of fire blazing across it as Stan tumbled backwards.

Lord Tenebris rushed forwards, hoping to capitalize on Stan's vulnerability while on the ground. However, just as the sword plunged, Stan rolled backwards and, reaching behind him, sent one of the diamond axes on his back flying through the air, right at Lord Tenebris. The flying diamond axe struck Lord Tenebris right across the top of the head, sending him to the ground and causing his enchanted diamond helmet to fly off, hurtling through space and off the edge of the bedrock platform into the city below.

Stan picked up the axe that Lord Tenebris had knocked from his hands and charged back towards the Noctem ruler as he got back to his feet, shaking his head out of the daze caused by the impact of the axe. Lord Tenebris's immediate thought was to generate a new diamond helmet for himself, but he caught himself at the last moment. He had sworn that he wouldn't use his operating powers, and he wasn't going to start now. Instead, he raised his diamond sword to counter the axe that Stan had swung at him.

The two weapons collided in a shower of sparks, and the two masters continued to duel. They were very close to the edge of the platform now, the fighting angled parallel to the edge. Stan tried to force Lord Tenebris to feint to the side, take a misstep, and go over – after all, if either of them went over, they were honour-bound not to fly and would fall to their death. Lord Tenebris realized what Stan was trying to do and in one motion he lowered his sword.

The momentum that Stan had been pushing with carried him forwards, and he careened precariously close to the edge. As Stan kept himself from falling over the side, he sensed something coming fast from behind him, and knew that Lord Tenebris was about to knock him over. As quickly as he could, Stan ducked under the attack, feeling the rush of the diamond blade travel over his head as he rolled backwards. Lord Tenebris recovered from the powerful frenzied sword slash and looked at Stan, just in time to see Stan's other spare axe flying directly out towards him.

It was by a few pixels that Lord Tenebris managed to dodge the axe, and by an equally narrow margin that he managed to dodge the follow-up swing of Stan's single remaining axe that would have knocked him over the edge.

Lord Tenebris started to panic. He was being pushed back quickly now, overwhelmed by the sheer speed, strength and ferocity of Stan's axe swipes. In his desperation, Lord Tenebris's blocks and counterstrikes were becoming more and more wild and frenzied, while Stan's attacks, though still powerful, were much more controlled and deliberate. Lord Tenebris didn't manage to land a single hit on Stan, but every few strokes of the axe, Stan made contact with Lord Tenebris's chestplate, sending him staggering back and struggling to block the next strike.

Lord Tenebris found that he was being pushed back faster and faster. In one moment, Lord Tenebris looked below him and realized with a start that he had been driven all the way across the bedrock platform and was now standing at one of the corners, just a few blocks away from the edge. Then, without warning, Lord Tenebris felt a sharp pain in his hand, and he cried out. Stan's axe had cut into the Noctem leader's hand, sending his sword flying into the air and off the platform.

Lord Tenebris fell to the ground with a thud, clutching his hand in agony as he slid across the bedrock platform, coming to a stop right where the two sides of the square platform met. His hand was in agony as his head dangled off the platform, the rest of his body sprawled out over the corner. He forced himself to look up and saw Stan advancing on him. Stan raised the axe high over his head and swung it down as hard as he could at Lord Tenebris's head.

The attack never connected. Lord Tenebris's fist shot forwards, sending an invisible pulse of energy squarely into Stan's chest.

Stan's axe flew out of his hand and over the edge as he caught the energy pulse with two hands, once again giving all his energy to keep the pulse from touching him. As he winced with focus, Stan looked up, trying to comprehend what happened, only to see Lord Tenebris levitating back up on to the platform, taking a deep breath as red smoke started to seep from his pores.

A shot of rage coursed through Stan as he struggled to hold back the explosive blast in his hands. Lord Tenebris had cheated and used his operating powers.

As he filled with rage, Stan felt the pulse of energy in his hands growing stronger and stronger, until he could barely contain it. Finally, when Stan could hold it no longer, he forced his hands forwards, sending the explosive energy blast right back to where it came from.

Lord Tenebris sensed the energy coming and gave Stan a look of undiluted hatred as he took a deep breath and, once again, erupted into some sort of blue aura. Stan's heart skipped a beat as Lord Tenebris stretched out his hands to catch the energy pulse. He was drawing power from the server again.

The invisible pulse hit Lord Tenebris like a truck, and he slid back towards the edge that he had just been hanging over, his face screwed up with the effort of containing such a massive power. For a second that seemed like an eternity, Lord Tenebris held the pulse in his hands and, even from a distance, Stan could feel it growing stronger and stronger. Then, with a mighty roar, Lord Tenebris pushed the pulse of energy forwards, sending it back toward Stan.

Stan could feel the energy coming. He could even see a slight shimmering in the air now, like heat rising off pavement, as the pulse travelled towards him. Stan nearly began to panic as he wondered if this super-powered explosive blast was going to overwhelm him the moment he touched it. He was already drained from the last time he sent it back to Lord Tenebris. Then, all of a sudden, Stan's brow knitted, he dug in his heels, and he stretched out his hands in determination. It didn't matter if he would be able to send it back or not – he was too tired to warp. He had to try.

Never before had Stan even imagined the sheer intensity of the energy pulse that he caught in his hands now, sending him sliding ten blocks backwards across the bedrock. Although the pulse was now little more than a block in size, it felt as though Stan were struggling to keep a planet from crushing him as he held the ball of undiluted power in his hands. Stan tried to push the pulse off him, but it was as if he were trying to stop earth itself from moving. Slowly but surely, despite all his best efforts, the pulse of energy pushed into him . . . crushing him . . . threatening to overwhelm him . . . until finally . . .

Stan, an eerie, familiar voice called from inside his head. *Don't let the power dominate you . . . fight back, Stan, you must . . .*

"I . . . can't . . ." Stan got out as his breathing became

shallow in the midst of his monumental struggle. "It's . . . too . . . much. . ."

Remember why you fight, Stan, the voice echoed into his head yet again. *You fight in the name of justice. . . You fight for those who cannot help themselves. . . You fight in the name of those who have fallen. . . You fight for the protection of the game of Minecraft and the server that you love. . .*

Stan's eyes flew open. He had to overcome this. If he didn't, then not only would Elementia be destroyed, but Minecraft, the world that he and so many others had come to love nearly as much as their own, would be destroyed. He couldn't let that happen. And if he gave up a part of himself to save it . . . then so be it.

Stan let out a savage cry as he straightened his back, standing upright for the first time as he held the ball of energy tightly to his stomach. As the shout continued, Stan poured all his energy into the blast that he was holding before him – all his love for his people, his server and his game – and, slowly but surely, it grew larger and larger. Before long, Stan knew that he could give no more. Despite his newfound resolve, the intensity of the energy was beginning to force him to the ground yet again. With one great motion, Stan dug in his heels and forced the ball of energy out of his hands and back at Lord Tenebris.

Stan collapsed to the ground. He couldn't stand, and he

could hardly move. He had given all of himself to this one final attack. If it didn't destroy Lord Tenebris, even with all his extra stolen power, nothing would. And there was no way that it wouldn't . . . there was no way that even an operator could return an explosive blast of that magnitude. Stan imagined that he would be lucky if he himself were not wiped out by the sheer force of the blast when it hit. Slowly, he forced himself to look up, to see the impact.

What he saw, he couldn't believe.

Lord Tenebris stood in place, still radiating with a cerulean aura. His eyes were closed, and he hadn't even bothered to hold up his hands to catch the pulse. Instead, he had only one hand outstretched, clutching a diamond sword that was pointed directly at the enormous energy blast. Stan watched as the explosive pulse made contact with the sword and seemed to travel down the blade and into Lord Tenebris, as if the diamond weapon were some sort of lightning rod absorbing the sheer power behind the attack. The energy engulfed Lord Tenebris, causing the aura around him to glow brighter and brighter until it was nearly pure white, and a split second later, a flash emitted from the Noctem leader, so intense that Stan felt as though his eyes were being fried.

For a moment, everything was white. Stan's head fell to the ground, and he could not see a thing. He was totally blinded in the aftermath of the burst of light, and too exhausted from his final effort to kill Lord Tenebris to move even a single muscle in his body. All he could do was lie on the bedrock surface like a rag doll, praying that his plan had worked, desperately hoping that whatever Lord Tenebris was doing had backfired, and that he had disintegrated in the dazzling light.

But as Stan's vision finally started to return, and he found himself looking upwards at the grey sky, his heart stopped with dread as he realized that a dark figure was standing directly above him. As his eyes shifted back into focus, Stan could see that Lord Tenebris actually wasn't dark at all; the light blue aura that had engulfed his body before absorbing the blast had now changed colour to a royal gold, and tiny little sparks of electricity danced around his body.

Despite feeling as though he were made from rubber, Stan forced himself to raise his head. He was acting purely on instinct. His mind was too deadened from energy loss to form any cohesive plan. As Lord Tenebris looked down at him like a hawk eyeing a wounded mouse, Stan took aim and shot a punch at Lord Tenebris. Not even a tiny explosive attack flew from Stan's hand, and he flopped to the ground yet again, too exhausted to hear Lord Tenebris chuckling at the feeble attempt.

"Thank you, Stan," Lord Tenebris simpered, as he looked down at the pathetic shell of a player that was Stan, lying on the ground. "Thank you for so generously handing me everything that you had. I now have the strength of two fully-fledged operators infused into my body. And now that I know not to draw power from this server, I will draw from all the other servers instead, and destroy them. Elementia will reign supreme as the sole remaining Minecraft server, and I shall be its undisputed and unstoppable ruler."

Stan said nothing. He could hardly comprehend what Lord Tenebris was saying. He had no energy left for thought.

"But for you, Stan . . ." Lord Tenebris said, holding up the sword that had conducted all of Stan's energy into its owner's body and running his finger across its length lovingly as if it were the most precious object in the world.

" . . . it is over."

Lord Tenebris raised the sword high above his head. Stan didn't realize what was going on. He was lying unconscious on the ground, not a care in the world, and finally happy that, after everything that he had been through since he had first joined Elementia, he was finally resting.

The sword plunged down.

At the exact moment that the sword shattered the back of Stan's diamond chestplate, there was a rush of light and sound, followed by a metallic clang. Lord Tenebris was knocked back with fantastic force, tumbling along the ground as his golden aura trailed behind him like the flame of an Olympic torch, his sword spiralling high into the air and landing with a clatter right next to Stan's unconscious form.

Lord Tenebris skidded to a stop yet again at the edge of the bedrock platform. Grunting with shock, he looked up and saw a figure standing in front of Stan. His vision was a little hazy due to the shock, but as he squinted, he could make out a blue-greenish body with a black cape billowing behind him in the wind.

Lord Tenebris rubbed his eyes as he pulled himself to his feet, sure that he wasn't seeing correctly. Once he was standing upright, he opened his eyes to take another look . . . only to find himself staring into a pair of white eyes, glowing as radiantly as the moon, standing a single block away from him.

His mouth dropped open, and his own white eyes widened as he stared into this mirror image of himself with a black cape, hood and shawl wrapped around his upper body. Lord Tenebris began to shudder with pure, undiluted fear as he stared into the face with the glowing eyes, the face that was looking more and more furious and disgusted by the second. This being that he was looking at . . . he didn't exist . . . Lord Tenebris *knew* that he didn't exist . . . he was dressed up as this demon to elicit fear in the eyes of the gullible idiots who believed that it was real. . .

Panic overtaking all else within Lord Tenebris's mind, he

willed himself to vanish and reappear on his throne, only to find that he was locked in place by an unseen force, totally unable to warp, or even move. He was forced to stare straight ahead, into the white eyes of the demon, which seemed to be staring directly into his soul with contempt and hatred. Lord Tenebris began to hyperventilate, totally scared witless over his possession by this demon that was staring him down.

Lord Tenebris struggled, trying to use all his willpower to move, to attack, to do anything to get out of this situation. However, what happened instead elevated his panic to incredible heights. The golden aura, which had been radiating out of his body the entire time, suddenly turned cerulean blue once again, and then faded into nothingness entirely. At the same moment, Lord Tenebris felt a huge amount of energy drain out of his body.

"What . . . are you . . . doing . . . to me?" he stammered weakly as he began to shake violently.

The demon didn't respond. He simply continued to stare through Lord Tenebris, who was forced to stand immobile in front of the white-eyed monster as he started to unhinge.

More than a dozen blocks away, Stan's eyes flew open. He had no recollection of what had happened after he had let his explosive blast, imbued with all his energy, fly at Lord Tenebris. Suddenly, though, he felt wide awake, and as he looked down at his arm he saw, to his utter amazement, that a dazzling blue aura was radiating around him, identical to that which had blazed around Lord Tenebris when he had drawn energy from the server. Stan barely had time to comprehend what this meant before another surge of energy coursed through his body, and the blaze around him changed from cerulean to a brilliant gold.

As Stan pulled himself to his feet, quivering at the sheer amount of power that had somehow been injected into his body, he looked down to the other end of the bedrock platform. There, right at the edge, he could see Lord Tenebris, looking weak, drained and totally petrified as he stared into the face of another figure, whose back was to Stan, and whose head was obscured by a black hood. As soon as he realized who it was, a blue glint caught the corner of Stan's eye. He turned to look, and there, sitting on the ground, was Lord Tenebris's sword, which he had used to absorb Stan's dying attack.

All at once, Stan was struck by a thought. Actually, it wasn't really a thought as much as it was a fact. Stan knew what he had to do, and as he reached down to pick up the sword of the Noctem ruler, Stan felt as though it had been his purpose to carry out this plan since the very beginning.

Stan took a deep breath and, clutching the diamond sword glowing with the lustre of enchantments, he began to run towards the two figures at the far end of the bedrock platform. As he reached his top speed, he found himself able to run even faster, as if he were under the influence of QPO. Before long, Stan found that he was moving too fast for his legs to keep up with, and so he leaped into the air, accelerating even faster as he flew forwards, skimming over the surface of the bedrock, directly at the two players.

Right as he was about to make contact with the Black Hood, Stan's instincts kicked in, and he stabbed the sword out in front of him. To his amazement, the Black Hood stretched his right hand out, too, mirroring Stan's position perfectly. He kept rocketing forwards, not checking his speed in the slightest as the diamond sword pierced through the back of the Black Hood. In an instant, the Black Hood vanished into thin air in a cloud of purple smoke, leaving Stan to look directly into the face of Lord Tenebris, who stared back at Stan with a total lack of comprehension.

Stan couldn't have stopped if he wanted to. He was moving far too fast. Although Lord Tenebris had been released from the psychic grip of the Black Hood, he had no time to react before his own diamond sword, held outstretched, struck the centre of his chestplate. The diamond armour shattered into a thousand tiny fragments, reflecting the brilliant dazzling of the enchanted sword as it entered Lord Tenebris's heart.

Stan's eyes locked onto the eyes of his greatest adversary,

and time seemed to stop as they shared their final gaze. Defeat was ripe in every single inch of Lord Tenebris's face, as he exchanged one final, sad look with Stan. Then, right as the ring of items began to burst out from his stomach, Lord Tenebris took one final breath, closed his eyes and faded out of existence.

For a brief moment, as Stan plowed through the ring of items, scattering them wildly through the air, he was struck with a note of panic. *What if he changed the game mode again?* Stan thought to himself. *What if he finds some other way back in?*

Then, all at once, Stan found himself struck by an overwhelming, calming sense of peace. A voice sounded out, clear as day in Stan's head, as a bright light appeared at the exact location where Lord Tenebris had disappeared.

Do not fret, Stan, the Black Hood's voice said calmly, as the light expanded, soon engulfing Stan in a giant supernova of light and sound. *He will not come back. It is over.*

nstantly, all fighting stopped. The hundred or so remaining members of the Noctem Alliance, who had been pushed back onto the execution platform, and the leaders of Stan's army, who made up the border between the two factions, all looked up, along with every other player in the plaza. The explosion was massive, illuminating the sky and sending a blast of sound crashing down over all the players whose faces were lit by the white light shining down from the sky. Every single player knew in their gut that, for better or for worse, the clash of the two leaders was over.

As the sky returned to its previous dull, washed-out grey colour, the players all continued to look up. It was as if they had forgotten that their opponents existed, that they were even fighting at all. Slowly, each and every soldier, citizen and villager in the plaza could see a square of blocks floating high in the sky, as if it were some sort of platform. And next to this platform, a single, almost imperceptible dot could be seen, slowly growing larger and larger as it sunk downwards, and taking on the form of a player.

Slowly, this player descended from the sky, glowing sword clutched in his hand. His eyes were closed, so there was no way of telling which of the two great leaders it was. However, all the Noctem fighters felt their hearts lift, as all the citizens of Element City and republic fighters felt theirs plummet. After all, the figure was holding an enchanted sword . . . and when was the last time that Stan had ever used a sword in battle?

Charlie, Jayden, Leonidas, Ben, Bob, the Mechanist, Sirus, Cassandrix, Commander Crunch and the villagers all stared intently at the figure as they stepped back, creating an empty space in the midst of the crowd for the descending player to land. Even at such a close distance, they couldn't tell if this player was their best friend or their greatest enemy, who was skinned identically, save the eyes, which were still closed.

For a moment, the player just stood there, a solemn expression on his face. He took a deep breath. Then, he opened his eyes, revealing the blue pupils of Stan2012, looking victorious, yet also exhausted and, somehow, wiser than he had been.

Immediately, the entire plaza burst out into uproarious applause, with hoots and hollers abounding, ringing through the sky. Elation shone like sunlight out of the faces of every citizen of Element City who was packed into the courtyard, as they realized that their long nightmare was finally over, and that their beloved president had vanquished the harbinger of darkness and pain for good.

Charlie leaped off Dr Pigglesworth, limping as fast as he could toward Stan, tears streaming down his face as he threw himself at his friend, wrapping his arms around him in a tight hug. Leonidas nearly knocked the two of them over as he joined in, embracing his friend closely as he realized that Stan had destroyed the leader of the organization that had almost claimed his own life. Next to come was Cassandrix, whooping with joyous laughter. Oob and Mella followed, red smoke still spewing from the wound in her stomach, latching on to the group hug as Stull sat on his mother's shoulders shouting out "Victory! We have attained victory!"

Then Jayden, the Mechanist, Commander Crunch, Ben, Bob, Sirus and all the others joined together in a massive group hug, as the group of players, who had been through so much together, who had given everything to their fight for justice and peace, had finally succeeded in their valiant struggle.

In the midst of the massive group hug, as he heard the joyous sobs and shouts of thankfulness for his safety and his victory, Stan allowed himself a small smile, as he realized that they were right to celebrate. After so long – after so much hatred, violence, and bloodshed – they had accomplished their goals. Elementia was free, and they had now, for the first time since Stan had been in the server, reached the true dawning of a new age.

It was only as Stan realized just what ushering in a new era would entail that his smile vanished, to be replaced again by a look of sad solemnity.

Slowly but surely, the celebrations died down. Although the people of Element City still looked almost joyous enough to brighten the sky that was still dark and grey, they all noticed something. The citizens of Elementia all looked at the cluster of leaders that held their adored president in the center and realized that, since he had landed, he hadn't said a word. Within a minute, the entire plaza had returned to being as silent as moments before, as they had watched Stan descend from the sky.

In due time, Stan's friends also realized that they were expecting him to say something. They all began to shrink away from him, giving him some space. As Charlie hopped back to Dr Pigglesworth on one foot, Stan took a deep breath and let it out. Little did his friends know that he was thinking long and hard about what he was about to say; without a doubt, what he said here, on this day, would shape the future of the server of Elementia for years to come.

"Stan?" Leonidas asked, looking concerned as Stan looked more and more downcast the deeper into thought he went. "Are ya OK?"

Stan looked at Leonidas, his eyes wide and meaningful. He said nothing. There would be time to talk to his friends later, time to thank his followers for their selflessness and devotion to their cause. But now was not that time. Stan had a more important matter to attend to, a matter of historical importance.

Stan took a deep breath, closed his eyes, and began to float into the sky. He heard countless audible gasps from the crowd at this display of his operating powers, but as Stan looked down, he heard a commotion. The higher up he floated, the more black-adorned players within the crowd dashed away from the mass of other players. Stan was satisfied – this was the reaction that he was hoping for.

As he watched from above, it looked as though ink were trickling out of clear water as the few remaining Noctem soldiers scattered among the thousands of republic soldiers in diamond armour. As if drawn by magnetism, the Noctems made their way onto the execution platform. There, Stan looked to see General Spyro, standing as still as if he were a statue, his gaze skywards. Stan turned his head, following the stare of the petrified Noctem general. Floating in the sky next to him, pointing all three of its heads at Spyro, was the Wither.

Stan floated up to the Wither and hovered directly in front of its middle head. The skeletal boss mob looked confused, as if perplexed as to why a player was flying in the same way that it could. Stan turned round so that his back was facing the Wither, and stretched out his hand, concentrating hard on the air in front of him.

In an instant, a ring of obsidian blocks appeared hovering in front of Stan, and a split second later, the centre of the ring erupted into a vibrant purple flash, which receded into the glowing purple haze of the Nether Portal. There were more gasps and even a few shouts of surprise from below at the sudden appearance of these blocks, but Stan was only focused on the Wither. Its white eyes widened as it felt the presence of the portal, almost as if some unseen force were calling it to enter the Nether.

Slowly, the Wither floated forwards through the air, as if entranced, and into the purple mist. There was a flash of purple light as the Wither disappeared, having returned to the dimension that it knew as home. Stan then proceeded to raise both hands towards the portal, and at once, it vanished, disappearing into thin air as black particles rained to the ground two dozen blocks below him. Stan lowered his hands in front of him and closed his eyes.

"Go in peace," he whispered, as the dark clouds evaporated from the sky, allowing the square block of the sun to shine down freely once more.

After a moment of silence, Stan opened his eyes and started to sink down yet again. Below him, the faces of all his friends lit up, as they assumed that he was finally going to address them. However, to their bewilderment, Stan didn't float towards them. Rather, he sunk down lower and lower, and floated forwards, towards the execution platform.

The platform was tightly packed. Every single remaining member of the Noctem Alliance had managed to fit onto the elevated wood-plank stage, which by no means was designed to fit a hundred players. As Stan approached them, still airborne, the ripple of fear that had been bubbling among them since Stan had first appeared now escalated into all-out panic. Although Stan's face still looked grave, with no hint of aggression in it, the fighting forces of the Noctem Alliance let out shouts and cries of alarm as this all-powerful player came closer and closer to them. They were afraid to move, afraid to address Stan. Even now, though, in the face of complete and utter defeat and disgrace, they still stood united as a team, a giant mass of black ready to stand together to the end.

As Stan finally landed on the edge of the platform, there was a shuffling in the crowd. Somebody was pushing their way forwards. After a moment, Spyro burst out of the crowd. He had a diamond sword held in his hand and wasted no time in pointing it at Stan, although he had a hard time keeping it pointed that way, his hands were shaking so hard. His face showed a mixture of loathing, grief and terror. For a few moments, the two highest-ranking members of the two warring factions stood still, staring at each other. Then . . .

"You came down here to force us to join your side, didn't you?" Spyro said in a rasp, his voice as shaky as his hands.

Stan said nothing. He simply looked back at the Noctem general sadly.

"Well let me tell you right now, Stan . . . it will *never* happen!" Spyro bellowed at the top of his lungs, his sobs of grief and fear threatening to overpower his voice as he shouted at the operator standing before him. "Not one single member of the Noctem Alliance will ever join your despicable republic! We will never stop fighting for justice in the land of Elementia for as long as we're alive! No matter how many times you beat us down, no matter how low you drag us, we will never stop coming back to fight you! You killed Lord Tenebris . . . the greatest being in all of Minecraft . . ." Spyro's sobs nearly overcame him by this point, and he was echoed by the hundred members of the Alliance behind him, before his anguish morphed into rage a moment later.

" . . . and, Stan, for this, we will *never* forgive you! Long live the Noctem Alliance! VIVA LA NOCTEM!"

"VIVA LA NOCTEM!" the crowd of Noctem soldiers echoed from behind him, and from the tone of their voice, Stan knew that they believed in every single word that Spyro had said. That they truly would rather die before they cooperated with the republic.

Therefore, once again, Stan offered no response. Instead, he reached into his inventory and extracted an enchanted diamond sword, levelling it at Spyro.

Although several Noctem soldiers totally lost it at the sight of the weapon, breaking down into sobs or screams, Spyro stood firm, his body shaking as much as ever, but his eyes showed determination as he prepared to become the next in a never-ending line of martyrs for the radical upper-level players of Element City. Closer and closer, Stan walked towards Spyro until he was standing within striking distance of the Noctem general. Not backing down, Spyro closed his eyes, preparing for the blow to fall. . . .

"Take it."

Spyro opened his eyes and stared at the diamond sword that Stan was holding in his outstretched hand. He wasn't holding it out in an attack stance; rather, he was holding it out in a gesture, as if he were offering it to Spyro.

"What . . . what are you talking about?" Spyro demanded.

"Take the sword," Stan said softly to him, speaking so that only those on the platform could hear them. "This sword belongs to your leader. He used it in the last battle that he ever fought. I want you to have it. Do whatever you want with it. Build a memorial to him and incorporate the sword into it somehow, if you'd like. Just do whatever you have to and commemorate Lord Tenebris as you see fit."

Spyro stared at Stan, uncomprehendingly. Slowly, he reached out, grabbed the handle of the sword, glowing with enchantments of Fire, Sharpness and Knockback, and took it from Stan. For a moment, he looked at the diamond weapon in reverence, as if it were the most priceless treasure conceivable. Then, in a swift, sneaky motion, he pocketed the sword, and looked up to Stan contentiously.

"What are you playing at?" Spyro hissed.

Stan took a deep breath and looked directly at Spyro, causing him to recoil slightly in intimidation. This effect was accidental and, not wanting to send the wrong message, Stan smiled a tiny smile. When he spoke again, it was loud enough so that even those on the ground could hear him.

"General Spyro of the Noctem Alliance, I hereby declare that you, and every member of the organization that you now command, will be allowed to live, and will not be imprisoned for your crimes against Elementia."

A collective gasp washed through the crowd before it exploded into pandemonium. The citizens of the republic erupted into shouts of outrage and accusations of conspiracy, while the hundred Noctem troopers standing on the execution platform looked dazed and confused. All of Stan's friends looked at him as if he had lost his mind, as did Spyro. Out of the corner of his eye, Stan saw a white form burst out of the crowd, and he turned to see Cassandrix standing at the base of the platform, looking totally flabbergasted.

"Stan, what are you doing?" she demanded as Stan looked down at her. "Do you not remember what the people of this organization have done? Do you not remember the last three months of war and suffering? Do you not remember that these are the people who . . . who killed Kat?"

At the sound of the name, a wave of anguish rippled up Stan's spine, affecting his heart, stomach and finally his head as they all contracted in pain and he realized, once again, that one of his best friends was gone for all time. He turned round to look again at the stunned Spyro, who had done so much evil, who had caused so much pain. For a moment, as his stomach blazed with the fires of revenge, he considered retracting his statement and blasting Spyro to dust, along with every other member of the Noctem Alliance that stood behind him.

Then, once again, as suddenly as the fury had flared up, it vanished. Stan took a deep breath as he realized that he was an operator now. He was by far the most powerful player in Elementia, and he could kill anybody that he wanted to effortlessly. The citizens, who were still jeering at him from the crowd from his announcement, believed that, as their leader, Stan would help them to enforce their will on all who disagreed with them. But Stan knew that if he were to fulfill his promise to himself, and truly turn Elementia into the place that King Kev had intended for it in the server's founding, he must not make the same mistakes that King Kev had made. History was one step away from repeating itself, and

Stan knew that now was the time for branching off to create his own path.

"Quiet, please," Stan spoke, willing all who stood in the plaza to hear him. While he had not shouted like Lord Tenebris had, the voice still projected itself into the heads of each and every player in the plaza. Instantly, the riots ceased, as Stan turned round and, catching Cassandrix's eye, began to speak yet again.

"I stand by my judgement that General Spyro and the Noctem Alliance will not be punished for their crimes. I would like to emphasize, quite clearly, that this does not mean I believe that their crimes are any less heinous. They still robbed, tortured and murdered countless players, and committed acts of terrorism that turned our beloved Elementia into a cesspool of darkness and hatred. However . . . I believe that we have far more important things to focus on than dealing retribution."

Stan paused for a moment as the citizens of Elementia murmured among themselves, while the Noctem soldiers continued to look at Stan, trying to figure out what he was trying to do.

Stan had a decision that he had to make. If he wanted to, now would be the most opportune time to reveal the identity of Lord Tenebris to the public. Now that he was dead, there was nothing to stop Stan from spreading the truth. However, as he thought about it, he decided against it. Not only would it weaken the argument that he was about to make, but it would also lead to more outrage and hatred towards the Noctem Alliance, who would surely deny his claims. Stan decided that he would continue to refer to Lord Tenebris and King Kev as separate entities. For now, at least.

"Nobody knew exactly what Lord Tenebris was," Stan said simply. "Some believe that he was a glitch, others believe him to be the reincarnation of King Kev's spirit. But regardless of what he was, he had powers nearly equivalent to those of an operator. He attempted to use those powers to enforce his own will, and his own beliefs, over the people of Elementia. What resulted was three months of the worst war that has ever plagued our server, which has resulted in scores of dead players and an atmosphere of hatred and animosity that has lingered over the countryside.

"Now . . ." Stan continued, carefully thinking, picking and choosing his words before speaking, "Lord Tenebris is dead. I am the sole remaining operator of Elementia. As such, it would be extremely easy for me to argue that, since the Noctem Alliance has lost this war, their ideals were wrong. Therefore, I could argue that because their ideals were wrong, *my* ideals are one hundred percent correct, and then I could go on to use my powers to enforce my own beliefs over the people of Elementia. However . . . I'm not going to do that."

Stan allowed a moment of silence for this message to sink in. His friends were staring at him, no longer thinking that he was crazy, but instead wondering where he was going with this. Stan continued.

"It is true that I believe that all players, regardless of their level, should have a chance to live in Elementia, even if that means that the upper-level players occasionally must lose out on some of their hard-earned possessions for the sake of the lower-level players. However, if you do not agree with me, I won't hold it against you. I might disagree with you, and at one point I might explain my point of view to you in the hopes that you might change your mind, but I will still be able to coexist with you, provided that you respect my opinions and beliefs as much as I respect yours.

"The reason that I went to war with the Noctem Alliance," Stan said, turning back to face the black-clad soldiers, "is because they did not respect my opinions. Rather than attempting to peacefully coexist, they declared war on my ideals, which are shared by many other players on this server. I was forced to fight back, for the sake of protecting my people.

"But it doesn't matter now," Stan said quickly, as the Noctem troops leered at him aggressively, and boos and shouts towards the Noctem Alliance started to slowly rise from the crowd. "I'm not here to point the finger of blame.

The war is in the past now. The time has come to look to the future. While we must never forget the past, we can't let it define us either. Now is the time to let the past go and see the world around us for how it is, not how we want it to be. Because, if you take the time to look, you'll find that this world contains plenty of fantastic opportunities for all players – young and old alike."

Stan took a deep breath. He knew that, in a few moments, he would be announcing something that would shock every single player in Elementia. Regardless of how unpopular this announcement might be, Stan knew that he had no choice but to go through with it if he was going to create his own path.

"For the past three months," Stan continued, "the players of this server have been divided and warring with each other over their beliefs. Due to our fighting, the server of Elementia lies in ruins."

Stan raised his hand out over the skyline of Element City. The eyes of all players in the vicinity looked around, scanning the countless clouds of black smoke rising from the various districts of the city, the blazing fires and the skyscrapers with massive chunks torn from them.

"Despite having different ideas of what was best for Elementia," Stan went on, "both factions only wanted just that: the best for Elementia. And yet, through our ignorant stubbornness and refusal to coexist, and work to seek out a compromise, we have torn Elementia apart, ravaging it, and creating a giant mess that will only be repaired with the combined efforts of all of us. As we all stand here in this plaza today, the war finally over, we're presented with a new opportunity."

Stan's heart was racing so fast that it felt like it were about to burst. Here it was: the proclamation that would change Elementia forever. Stan took a deep breath and let it out.

"As the operator of this server," Stan said confidently, "I, Stan2012, hereby announce that both the Grand Republic of Elementia and the Nation of the Noctem Alliance are both disbanded. As of today, neither exist any more."

It was as if everybody in the crowd had been slapped in the face as they stared up at Stan, trying to comprehend that he had just announced that he was getting rid of both of their countries, which they had worked so long and hard to raise and defend.

"Both of these countries were founded out of warfare with each other, and if they stay intact, I doubt that the wounds will ever fully heal. Now especially, the wounds are still fresh. Therefore, I don't believe that the people of the former republic, or of the former Nation of the Noctem Alliance, will be able to live together peacefully. From now on, there shall be two cities in Elementia," Stan said, a small smile on his face as he revealed the plan that he had formulated for the future of his server. "In one of these cities, the law of the Noctem Alliance shall remain supreme. Only older players will be allowed in, and they will have full control over what they have earned, not being forced to share with anybody. In the other city, players of all levels will be allowed in. The older players will help the new players learn and thrive, and the newer players will pay it forward by helping the new players when they themselves become upper-level players.

"But before you get too anxious, my friends, don't think for a moment that I would ever leave you to build a new city from the ground up!" Stan exclaimed. "With my operating powers, I will help both groups build their cities. I shall favour neither over the other, and before long, every player shall have a city of their own to call home.

"I honestly hope that, in the future, the people of Elementia will be able to live as one," Stan said, a slight element of sadness returning to his voice. "I hope that, as time goes by, the people of Elementia will be able to put their differences aside and coexist. However, in the wake of this war, now is not the time. That work will be done in the future. For now, I invite members of Elementia to clap if they are in favour of the idea of the creation of the two cities."

For a moment, the plaza remained silent. Stan wasn't surprised. After all, he was suggesting a radical idea that would change Elementia forever and require work and cooperation on everyone's part. Stan only hoped that they could see what he saw: two groups divided not only by ideals but by hatred, who needed time to heal before they could ever be united. And besides, Stan would be surprised if both sides didn't find the idea of their own city, without the other side, appealing.

Before long, Stan heard a single pair of hands clapping. He looked down into the crowd and saw Leonidas in the front row, clapping slowly. No sooner had Stan noticed him than Charlie, sitting next to Leonidas on the back of Dr Pigglesworth, began to clap as well. The clapping soon spread through all of Stan's friends, and then over the rest of the crowd, evolving from cheers into hoots, whistles and full-blown applause at Stan's proposition. He smiled as he looked out over the crowd, before turning round to face the members of the Noctem Alliance on the platform behind him.

All the members were standing still as statues, not clapping, staring forwards at their leader, alone at the front of the group. Spyro was looking at the ground as he mulled over Stan's proposition. As he sensed Stan's gaze on him, Spyro looked up and met his eye. The two leaders exchanged glances.

"I promise you, Spyro," Stan whispered so that only he could hear, "I'm not trying to take advantage of you. I just want what's best for *all* members of this server."

CHAPTER 15: THE TWO CITIES

Spyro continued to stare at Stan, who couldn't read his face as he tried to determine whether or not to trust him. Then, slowly, he raised his hands in front of him and began to clap. As soon as their leader began to clap, the other members of the Noctem Alliance clapped without hesitation.

Stan was overjoyed that the citizens of Elementia were willing to follow his plans. Now that the entire plaza was cheering, thrilled at the idea of living in a brand-new city free of conflict, Stan knew that there was one more matter that had to be resolved before the rebuilding could begin.

"Thank you, everybody, for your support," Stan said with a smile as the applause died down. "I'm sure that, with my help, you will be able to build the greatest cities in the history of Minecraft. However, there is one more matter that must be settled: If we are going to live as two people, in two cities, we still have to decide what will become of the city we already have."

A tense murmuring erupted throughout the crowd as they realized what Stan was talking about. Both sides had given countless lives, and endured awful hardships throughout this war, for the prize of Element City. Now that the war was over and they were dividing . . . what would become of this place?

"I think," Stan continued, "that it would be foolish to create two totally new cities, when we already have one. True,

Element City may have sustained heavy damages throughout the fighting, which may take months to fully repair, but it's easier to repair it than to build a completely new city from the ground up. And, in the great spirit of democracy, I believe that the only way that we can truly decide who takes Element City is through a vote."

As the murmurs in the crowd intensified, Stan glanced over at Spyro, who, like the other members of the Noctem Alliance, was eyeing Stan with contemptuous disbelief. After all, there were thousands of members of Element City and only a hundred members of the Noctem Alliance. If a vote was taken, they were sure to lose.

Indeed, Stan knew that it would probably be the easiest, and the most fair, to simply give Element City to the citizens of the former republic without question. After all, they did outnumber the Noctem soldiers fifteen to one, and it would be far easier to just keep the majority of them happy (especially considering that Stan agreed with their ideals). However, Stan knew that he couldn't do that. If he was going to lead the server of Elementia to a brighter future as an operator, he had to be impartial. He had to give both sides a fair chance, and he knew how to do it.

"However," Stan said slowly, causing the whispering in the crowd to cease, "not every citizen in the server is going to have a vote on this matter. This is because, although I do not believe that they are superior by default, I do believe that the older players have accumulated more wisdom than the younger players. They have lived in Elementia the longest, and they will decide what is best for the server that they have called their home for so long. Therefore, only those players who have played in Elementia for a year or longer may vote."

Spyro's eyes widened as shouts of outrage erupted from the crowd. The sea of thousands of players looked angry and betrayed, as they realized that their votes wouldn't count in making this monumental decision. Even Stan's friends, who had appeared pensive while they mulled over Stan's idea of the two cities, now looked at him as if he had lost his mind. Charlie came forwards out of the line and glanced up at Stan.

"Stan, what're you doing?" he demanded. "How can you let the older players decide? All the Noctem soldiers are older players!"

"Charlie, I've put a lot of thought into this," Stan replied, his voice calm and patient. "I have a plan that will benefit everybody, and this is part of it."

"But you . . ."

"Charlie, do you trust me?"

Charlie raised his eyebrows, his mouth hanging open from his retort as Stan cut him off. For a moment, the two friends held each other's gaze. For so long now, they had

had each other's backs, fighting off countless dangers and depending on each other to live to see the next day. And now here was Stan, asking Charlie if he trusted him to reform the server that they had worked so hard to win.

Charlie took a deep breath and, his gaze never wavering from Stan's eyes, nodded.

"Thank you," Stan said, and with that, he stood up straight, looked over the furious crowd, and said in his booming, penetrating voice, "Silence, please."

Once again, his voice seemed to have some mysterious influence over the players in the plaza, and their voices faded to silence.

"I would like to assure you all that I have put a lot of thought into what I'm asking you to do right now," Stan said, a slight authoritative note to his voice. "I only want what is best for Elementia, and all who reside here. And to those of you who think that I might give you the short end of the stick because I disagree with your beliefs, you are mistaken. From this day on, I am loyal to no faction, but rather to the entire server and all its players. I will do what I must to restore balance and order, and I will only take action against a group if they threaten that balance.

"And so I repeat, once again: Only those who have been playing in Elementia for a year or longer will be permitted to vote to see which group gains control over Element City."

CHAPTER 15: THE TWO CITIES

Stan raised his hand towards the execution platform and took a deep breath. A few Noctem soldiers cringed, imagining that he was about to attack them. Instead, the platform of wood blocks that they were standing on expanded, tripling in size instantaneously. One side of the platform extension was made entirely out of lapis lazuli blocks, while the other was made entirely out of iron blocks. Both expansions were the same size as the wood-plank block platform that they branched off from.

"Members of the Noctem Alliance, we'll start with you," Stan said, looking at Spyro. "If you would like Element City to become a city of upper-level players alone, walk onto the platform of iron. If you would like it to become a city of players of all levels, walk onto the platform of lapis lazuli."

Even before Stan had finished speaking, Spyro had begun to walk across the wooden platform, and by the time Stan had finished, he was already standing on the iron platform. Immediately, the entire group of Noctem soldiers trickled off the wooden stage to join Spyro on the platform of iron. As the players walked, Stan counted them and, with his operating powers, checked to see if they had in fact been in Elementia for a year or longer. Indeed, Stan saw that they all had, and by the time the last Noctem soldier had walked over onto the platform, Stan had counted one hundred and four of them.

"All right," Stan said, not surprised by this number. "Now,

I invite all players dispersed among this crowd who have been in Elementia for a year or longer to please step forward and take your side."

The crowd churned a bit as the older players snaked their way through the throng of newer players, finally reaching the front of the crowd and ascending the stairs onto the execution platform.

As Stan watched them pick sides, his heart lifted as a nearly unbroken stream of players banked a sharp right toward the lapis lazuli platform. They spread throughout the blue square of blocks like gas expanding into a container, almost faster than Stan could count. And yet, not all of them went to the right side. Stan counted an additional ten players who broke off from the stream and joined the iron platform that held the Noctem Alliance.

Stan was shocked. If those upper-level players hadn't been in his army, that meant that the Noctem Alliance had imprisoned them in Brimstone. Why would they possibly want to join their city? Then Stan reminded himself that this wasn't a city for just the Noctem Alliance – it was for anybody who agreed with the ideals of the Alliance as well. Stan supposed that there were indeed some players who agreed with the Alliance who still hadn't joined them.

After a minute or so, the stream of older players from the crowd waned into a trickle and then stopped altogether.

Stan had counted one hundred and fourteen on the iron side and one hundred and nine on the lapis lazuli side. The platform that held all the Noctem soldiers was larger. Stan's heart sank. He was about to announce this to the people when he noticed movement in the front row.

Stan looked down and he saw Leonidas, Ben, Bob, the Mechanist, Cassandrix and Commander Crunch step onto the stairs. Stan imagined that they must have stayed behind to count how many players were on each side, and as he did the maths for himself, his heart lifted. If all six of his friends went to the lapis lazuli side, they would outnumber the iron side by one, and they would get to keep Element City.

Stan watched, with a huge smile on his face, as Commander Crunch, Ben, Bob, Leonidas and the Mechanist all walked proudly to the right and joined the lapis lazuli platform. Stan opened his mouth, and was about to declare that Element City would be open to players of all levels, when he suddenly realized that, according to his count, the two sides were tied. Stan was confused. Had he counted wrong?

Then, Stan looked back at the wooden platform. There, standing directly in the centre of the two platforms, was Cassandrix. Rather than following the others directly to the blue platform, she looked back and forth between them, debating which one to join.

Stan's heart skipped a beat. He knew that he had promised

himself to be impartial but he couldn't detach himself from all he had done against the Noctem Alliance and he knew in his heart that he wanted the players on the lapis lazuli platform to win. And while he had expected all his commanders to join that side, he had totally forgotten about Cassandrix. Looking at her now, in deep thought, Stan legitimately had no idea which side she was going to join.

For a long time the two sides stood there, staring at the big-lipped, white-cloth-wearing player. As far as Stan knew, none of the other players knew how close the vote was, besides his friends, who were looking at Cassandrix with their breath caught in their throats.

Finally, after looking at the ground for several minutes, Cassandrix looked up and opened her eyes. She took a deep breath, looking once more towards the iron side and once more towards the lapis lazuli side before turning towards her friends and walking over to join them on the blue platform.

"The results are in," Stan announced loudly, struggling to keep a neutral face while his friends broke out into huge smiles. "By a margin of a single player, Element City will be open to all players, regardless of their level!"

An explosion of cheers erupted from the lapis lazuli side and the crowd below, so loud that it could probably be heard from Spawnpoint Hill. Stan's friends lunged forwards and threw themselves onto Cassandrix in a group hug, which she accepted with a warm smile. Stan looked over at the lapis lazuli platform and, making sure that nobody on the other side could see, he allowed himself a small smile in celebration that after all his effort and hard work, Element City was finally a place of true equality and justice for all players.

This moment of happiness lasted only for a few seconds, however, before Stan turned round to face the platform of iron. Spyro's face matched that of every other player who stood behind him. They had a look of absolute and total shock, in contrast to the smug assurance that the Noctem soldiers had been wearing since Stan had announced that only the older players would be voting. Stan walked across the wooden platform until, yet again, he was face to face with Spyro.

"Don't worry," Stan said, as he stared into the hateful eyes of the Noctem leader with no fear. "I'm going to help you build a new city, and reclaim what you've lost. Also, you should know that you, and anybody on this platform, will always be welcome in Element City."

"As long as there are lower-level players in our city, we will *never* live amongst them," Spyro spat, trying to jam as much scorn and disgust as possible into the sentence.

"Just remember, Spyro," Stan said, struggling to keep his voice steady as his hatred for the Noctem Alliance welled up yet again, "I'm giving you a second chance, and that's a privilege, not a right. I could very easily have killed all of you for what you've done."

Stan moved even closer to Spyro until their faces were inches apart and, for the first time, he allowed his face to mirror the loathing on Spyro's.

"Don't you even think," Stan hissed, "that for as long as I'm alive, Spyro, I'm going to forget what you did to the NPC village . . . or to the Mushroom Islands. I don't want to fight you any more, and I'm still going to help you to construct a new city. But never forget, Spyro, I'm going to do what I have to do to keep all citizens of this server safe. If you, or any of your people, try to hurt or threaten new players, or anyone else, my generosity will end very quickly."

As Stan took a step back, Spyro continued to look at him. A wide variety of emotions seemed to be running across his face as he processed what Stan was telling him. Finally, he let out a beaten sigh and he looked up at Stan.

"Fine," he said softly. "Where do you want us to go?"

"Go back to the bridge at the entrance of the city for now," Stan said. "Bring your people with you, and wait there for me. When I'm done here, I'll set you up with some temporary shelters that you can use until we can find a good plot of land out in the wilds for you to build your city on."

Spyro gave a begrudging nod and shouted back at those clustered on the iron platform to follow him. Immediately, the 114 members followed him across the wooden platform and down the stairs. Stan watched them walk by and caught several dirty looks. He continued to look on as the entire horde of black-clad players, with a few other colours interspersed, stepped off the platform and followed their one remaining general down one of the side roads.

On and on the mass of players went, tramping through the city streets amid countless buildings that had large chunks torn away by TNT or burned away by fire charges. They continued through the streets, their black uniforms blending into the black billowing smoke rising from over half the buildings. Stan continued to watch, keeping his eyes on them until, finally, the last remaining members of the Noctem Alliance vanished from sight, en route to a new home.

Stan took a deep breath. Again, despite his pledge, he couldn't help but feel a sense of pure satisfaction as he watched the enemies he had been battling for so long vanish into the horizon.

Stan turned round and looked over the citizens who had chosen to remain in the city. Up on the wooden platform, Stan's friends were still revelling in their victory. Hugs were exchanged like gifts as everybody tried to adequately express their joy at the departure of the Noctem Alliance.

Stan saw Charlie and Leonidas hugging it out, while Ben, Bob and Ivanhoe all danced in celebration (no matter how much he did it, Ivanhoe's moonwalking never got old). The Mechanist appeared to be graciously thanking Cassandrix, who in turn complimented the Mechanist on the speech he had given to rally the citizens for the battle. Commander Crunch, Sirus and Oob seemed to be partaking in a strange celebration of tossing Stull through the air, playing keep-away from Mella, who was desperately trying to catch her son. From the looks of it, Stull was having the time of his life as he sailed through the air like a football.

Stan smiled. At some point, he would surely join in the celebrations. But now, as he looked out over the sea of thousands of players who were partaking in festivities much like those of his friends, Stan didn't feel like it quite yet.

Stan knew that he may have just made a huge mistake. Not only had he allowed the Noctem Alliance to live on, but he had also given them their own city. He may now have operating powers, but there was still only one of him. Not only that, but he had kept the two factions divided instead of trying to force them together. He knew that there was a very real possibility that, from this division, new hatred would spawn to poison Elementia in the future.

Regardless though, Stan's fears were just those: fears. He had done what he believed was right for Elementia. The road ahead of him would be long, hard and taxing, as he sent his server down a new path. Whether it would be a good path or a bad path, Stan didn't know. But he knew that he would always be there to watch over the server, and as long as that remained true, it was bound to be, at the very least, a better path.

With that, Stan took a deep breath and let it out, allowing all his anxieties to float away like a balloon into the sky above Element City, which, for the first time in weeks, was blue. With one final look towards the place where Spyro and the rest of the Noctem soldiers had disappeared to, Stan turned round and walked across the wooden platform, ready for whatever the future would hold . . . for better or for worse.

A faint breeze swept across the sun-cooked dunes of the Ender Desert. Despite the long day of baking in the heat, the blocks of sand that made up this vast biome were cooling down now that the sun had sunk behind the western horizon. A rectangular sliver of moon sat in the black dome of sky, alongside the thousands of tiny shimmering dots that spoke of distant cosmos. The cacti stood proud and tall against the endless sea of tan blocks, and the mobs were just beginning to spawn, ambling aimlessly about without a care in the world.

The night was beautiful. It was as if the server itself was aware that a great conflict had been resolved and it could finally be at peace.

As the moon rose higher into the night sky, a figure trekked through the dunes, travelling out of the jungle above which the sun had set. He began his walk through the desert, setting a course for the dead centre of the desolate expanse of sand. A few mobs turned their heads towards him as he passed and were about to attack before an odd feeling swept over them, compelling them to leave this particular player alone.

On and on the player walked over the dunes, weaving through the cacti. The slice of moon shone down on the player, revealing brown hair, a turquoise shirt, blue trousers, and blue eyes. Stan2012's face bore a look of determination and solemnity.

As the night went on, the heavens spinning slowly above him, Stan continued to walk. He wasn't sure exactly where he was going, but he knew that he would have the right feeling when he got there. Stan was well aware that he could fly instead of walk, or even warp directly where he wanted to be. However, he opted against it. He was going to complete this journey, and he was going to do it on foot, without using his operating powers.

As he walked, Stan thought back on all that had happened since yesterday, when Stan had defeated Lord Tenebris and disbanded the two nations of Elementia. The celebrations in Element City had lasted all throughout the day, and would have gone all night had Stan not told them to get some rest for the next day's work. Stan, however, had not attended those celebrations. He had spent the evening at the outside wall of the city, providing temporary shelters and a supply of food and gear to Spyro, who had been unanimously elected to be the leader of the people who had gone to the iron side of the platform.

Following a good night's rest, Stan had bore witness to the birth of two new nations in Elementia. Spyro had organized his people into the Ironside Kingdom, while the Mechanist had been voted the temporary leader of the Lazuli Republic.

Stan found it amusing that both countries had named themselves after the sides of the execution platform that they had been arbitrarily assigned to, but it hardly mattered to Stan; he wouldn't be joining either of them.

Stan had helped the new Lazuli Republic begin repairs on their city, delegating supplies from the storehouses of Element City. At the same time, he had ensured that the Ironside Kingdom had all they needed to survive in their temporary shelters until Stan returned from his journey and could help them find a new place to build their city.

Although Stan knew there was much work to be done, he wasn't going to rush this journey. He had made a promise, and he was going to fulfill it.

Stan reached the top of a particularly tall sand dune and realized that it would provide him with an excellent vantage point from which to scout out what he was looking for. He peered through the darkness, and after scanning the horizon for a few seconds, he saw a strange colour in the endless hills of sand. He looked closer and realized that it was an oasis, a pool of water surrounded by grass blocks. It was the perfect place for what Stan was going to be doing.

As Stan made his way over to the oasis, he remembered his favourite part of the past day. Right before he had left for the desert, a familiar voice had rung out in his head, clear as day. Stan had taken leave from Elementia for a while, returning to SalAcademy.

For the longest time, Stan told Sally everything that had happened in one long, rambling story, while Sally just sat there and took it all in. She hardly reacted to it in the slightest. All that changed was her smile, growing larger and larger the more that she heard. By the time that Stan was finished, he had one question.

"Sally, do you think it was a mistake – disbanding the countries, separating the people, and starting over?"

For a moment, Sally just stood there, thinking. Finally, she looked him in the eye and replied, "I'm not sure, noob."

Stan stared back. He didn't know what to say. Then, slowly, Sally's smile returned, but now it wasn't the huge smile it had been – now, it was Sally's trademark sarcastic smirk. At that moment, it struck Stan that it didn't matter if it was a mistake or not. What was done was done, and he would just have to go with it. The important thing was that, no matter what, his friends would be there by his side . . . including Sally.

Or, at least, most of them would.

Stan was now upon the oasis, and he forced himself to clear his mind. As much as he wanted to dwell on the sweet sensation of victory and the thrill of sharing it with Sally and the rest of his friends, he knew that he couldn't. Not now. It wasn't a time for celebration.

The oasis was small. The pool was a square of three-by-three blocks, which had several odd blocks of water jutting off it. Stan reached into his inventory and pulled out a wooden shovel. He had crafted it with wood from the jungle he had just emerged from not long ago. If he was going to do this, he was going to do it manually.

Stan walked away from the oasis and immediately began to dig through the sand until his shovel struck a hard surface. Switching the shovel for a wooden pickaxe, Stan harvested the sandstone block, and a second one beneath it. He continued to dig around in the hole, expanding it as he harvested more and more sandstone blocks. Sand would periodically fall down to where he was attempting to dig, and he would clear it out with his shovel.

After several minutes of digging, Stan had enough sandstone. He placed a sand block down and then jumped on it, repeating the process until he had climbed his way out of the sinkhole. Stan made his way back over to the oasis and, sandstone in hand, he began construction.

First, he built a sandstone pillar, three blocks high, at each corner of the pool of water. This left a cross of water between the pillars. Stan then built a sandstone staircase on the grass, three blocks high, which extended over the water to be level with the tops of the pillars. He filled in the cross pattern on the top block of the pillar until he had a sandstone platform, elevated above the water by the four pillars.

Stan pulled a chest from his inventory and placed it in the centre of the platform. He opened it, revealing several vacant compartments. Stan took a deep breath, reached into his inventory yet again and pulled out a diamond sword, glowing with an enchantment of Knockback.

His eyes teared up as he remembered the time he had spent wielding this sword and, more poignantly, the time that he had spent with its owner.

Stan had never met anybody like DZ before and he doubted that he ever would again. On the surface, he seemed to be an offbeat, somewhat crazy player who took everything with a grain of salt and never failed to make you smile with his sheer zany charm. While that was still true, upon getting to know DZ better, Stan realized that he was much more than that.

Beyond being a master swordsman, DZ's wild coating was merely a facade, behind which hid a deep, introspective person who was trying to find his place in the world. He was an incredible friend, steadfast and loyal, who had sacrificed his own life so that Stan could escape Mount Fungarus.

Stan had never had a chance to thank DZ. And now he never would.

As a tear rolled down Stan's face and he gave a sniffle, he placed the sword carefully into the chest. It lay still, immobile, yet still alive with the blue enchantment that shimmered and glowed like the stars in the heavens above.

Stan reached into his inventory one more time, his hands shaking now. As he struggled not to break down into sobs, he pulled out another diamond sword. This one was glowing even brighter than DZ's, bearing three different enchantments of Sharpness, Fire, and Knockback.

Gas-Powered Stick. Kat's sword.

Even after all this time, Stan could not pinpoint the reason that he had asked Kat to join him on his journey to the Adorian Village when he was learning to play Minecraft for the first time. It was probably a foolish thing to do. After all, she had just burst out of the woods and tried to kill him and Charlie. Yet, for whatever reason, Stan had asked that Kat join them and she had agreed.

Slowly but surely, throughout the course of their quest to take down the Kingdom of Elementia and the months succeeding it, the girl who had jumped out of the woods demanding that he and Charlie give her all that they had, ceased to exist. She had transformed into one of Stan's best friends in Elementia. She had lost her reckless abandon and disregard for others, gaining wisdom and compassion while not abandoning her willingness to take risks. She always took care to tell people exactly what they needed to hear, even if they wouldn't like it. Perhaps above all else, she was fiercely loyal to those who deserved it, and was unwilling to take crap from anybody.

As Stan travelled across the server in the race to take down King Kev and then navigated the republic through the minefield of the Noctem Alliance, and then struggled to take back their server from Lord Tenebris's forces, he had always been amazed to have such amazing friends. Charlie and Kat were the two best companions that he could have ever hoped to have, and Stan had legitimately felt like the three of them could accomplish anything that they wanted to together.

The fact that one of them was now gone forever tore Stan's heart to shreds.

Stan couldn't stop the shaking, nor the sobs escaping his mouth, nor the tears now rolling down his face in waterfalls. All he could do was place Kat's enchanted sword into the chest next to DZ's, propped up against the corner with dignity. Stan took a deep breath and, before he could look at the weapons of his two deceased friends one more time, he closed the chest with a creak and a bang.

Even with the weapons no longer in front of him, the grief of it all spiralled around him, threatening to consume him as if it were all hitting him again for the first time. DZ . . . and Kat . . . two of his closest friends . . . dead . . . and gone forever . . .

Stan took a deep breath and looked up into the sky. If he looked carefully through the blurry lens of his teary eyes, he could see the cosmos moving above him. This server, Elementia . . . it was such a beautiful place. This game, Minecraft, held so much wonder, so much potential, and so much freedom – and, less than two days ago, it was all on the brink of extinction.

And yet, it would survive. And the owners of the two blades now sitting safely in the chest before him were the reason for it.

Kat and DZ had given their lives to the revolution against King Kev. Images of the dozens of things that his friends had done flashed through Stan's head.

Kat leaping out of the lava sea, surrounded by a red aura, stabbing Becca through the back and flinging her into the molten pool. DZ leaping into a pit of Zombies and taking them all out in seconds with two slices of his sword. Kat in The End, fighting off dozens of Endermen all at once. DZ thrusting his sword into the neck of the Ender Dragon, causing it to burst into radiant light. Dozens of other images rolled through Stan's head.

Stan's sobs ceased, but the tears continued to roll. The more he thought about the fact that he would never see either of his friends again, the more it felt as if some sort of dark void had opened within him that threatened to steal his happiness and never return it. And yet, as Stan realized what they had died for, and that the game of Minecraft had been saved because of them, he knew that he would be able to go on with his life. It would be very difficult, and the pain would never go away fully . . . but he would live.

Stan pulled the blocks of sandstone from his inventory and surrounded the chest with a ring of them. He then proceeded to cover the ring with a three-by-three square, hiding the chest from view. Never would anybody guess that two enchanted diamond swords were hidden inside. They would remain there forever. If someone were to climb the stairs to the top of the monument, they would find two signs that Stan had placed on top, side by side. They read:

KITKAT783 "KAT"
AND
DIEZOMBIE97 "DZ"

HEROES OF
ELEMENTIA
R.I.P.

Stan descended the sandstone stairs and surveyed the monument. It expanded upwards, out of the oasis, and looked striking against the flat expanse of the desert and the short cacti within it. Any players who saw it would climb the sandstone steps and learn the names of these two marvellous players who had sacrificed everything to save the server they loved.

Stan took a deep breath and, tears still flowing from his eyes, turned his back on the shrine and began to walk out into the desert. He extracted a diamond axe from his inventory and clutched it in his hand. Stan knew that the mobs would notice him, and he would have to fight them off. It was what he wanted. Months ago, DZ had asked him on his deathbed to wander the desert for a week after Stan won the war, remembering him and detaching himself from worldly problems.

Stan would do exactly what his friend had asked of him. His stomach rumbled, and it occurred to him that he would also have to hunt his own food while he was out here. It was as if he were a new player, alone and vulnerable in the world for the first time. With a slight chuckle at the thought, Stan wiped the tears from his eyes and set off to hunt.

As he watched Stan leave the shrine and make his way out into the desert to begin his vision quest, the Black Hood smiled as his cape billowed slightly in the wind. The people of Elementia were in good hands. The Black Hood knew that, whatever happened between the players of the server, Stan would always be there to keep them in balanced order.

The Black Hood chuckled ironically at the thought. Here he was, glad that Stan would be able to use his great powers to protect Elementia . . . when he himself could just as easily do the same thing. And yet, the Black Hood knew that this was a foolish thing to think. By speaking to Stan, and helping him attain his own operating powers, the Black Hood had nailed his own coffin firmly shut. In fact, he was absolutely astounded that he had participated in the battle itself and was still alive at all.

The Black Hood knew that he was dying, however. From the moment he had spoken to Stan, he had felt his energy dimming. When Stan had struck him with his sword, the Black Hood had been totally drained of all power, just barely hanging on to enough consciousness to tell Stan that Lord Tenebris had been defeated for good. Since then, the Black Hood had been saving his energy, and not until now had he managed to take physical form.

The Black Hood heard a roll of thunder crash over the desert. He glanced off and saw sheets of rain bombarding the distant jungle. To any players in the vicinity, including Stan, it would appear to be just another thunderstorm. But the Black Hood knew better. He felt a shift in the energy of the server there, a presence that he hadn't felt in months, since the day that he had first entered Elementia and attempted to use his powers.

The Voice in the Sky had returned.

The Black Hood stood perfectly still on the crest of the hill, his eyes closed. He had helped Stan to defeat Lord Tenebris and save Elementia, along with all other Minecraft servers. He had brought Rex into the woods, removed his collar, and returned him to the family of wolves from whom he had been separated months before. And now, as a last order of business, the Black Hood had seen Stan, building and hunting in a way that he still, to this day, found most fascinating. Now that he had seen it for one last time, all was done. There was nothing left for the Black Hood to do in Elementia . . . or in Minecraft.

YOU HAVE INTERFERED WITH THE AFFAIRS OF PLAYERS FOR THE LAST TIME, the Voice rang out in the Black Hood's mind as another thunderclap sounded overhead. **NOW, AS PUNISHMENT FOR YOUR TAMPERING, YOU SHALL DIE.**

"I accept my punishment," the Black Hood replied aloud.

Another roll of thunder and the Black Hood felt himself begin to fade. His very existence started to thin out, like threads being pulled one by one from a tapestry.

I may be leaving this world, the Black Hood thought peacefully to himself, as his ability to think began to fade as well, *but at least Minecraft, a game of such wonder and promise that had never been seen in the world before, lives* on . . . *and will live on forever, as long there are others who are willing to build.*

And with that final thought, the Black Hood ceased to exist, never to return to Minecraft again.

THE END

FROM THE AUTHOR

Thank you for reading *Herobrine's Message*. I hope you enjoyed it. If you did enjoy it, please tell your friends and write an online review so that others can enjoy it too.

—SFW

ACKNOWLEDGMENTS

As the Elementia Chronicles trilogy draws to a close, I find it more bittersweet than anything else. Over the course of writing the series, I truly feel as if Stan, Kat, Charlie, and their friends have become a part of who I am, and it saddens me to see them go. Writing the Elementia Chronicles has been the greatest experience of my life, and there are several people who have helped me to share my story with the world.

I would like to thank the South Kingstown High School Drama Club of 2014–15. It truly was thanks to you guys that high school was not just tolerable, but amazing.

I would like to thank Lindsey Karl, Matt Schweitzer, and Julie Eckstein, my team of promoters at HarperCollins who helped me to get the Elementia Chronicles out into the world.

I would like to thank Pam Bobowicz, my editor, for helping me transform my rough drafts into full-fledged novels.

I would like to thank my brother Eric, who always knows what to say to keep me humble.

I would like to thank my brother Casey, the first megafan of the Elementia Chronicles and the one who convinced me to share my story.

I would like to thank Rick Richter, my agent from Zachary Shuster Harmsworth, for helping me join HarperCollins and for always offering up his expertise and wisdom.

I would like to thank my grandmother, who is not only probably the biggest fan of the Elementia Chronicles, but has also supported me in everything that I do, from writing to beyond.

I would like to thank my dad for being a one-man tech-support team and helping the Elementia Chronicles break into the digital world.

I would like to thank my mom for devoting countless hours to promoting and beta-reading the Elementia Chronicles, and for doing everything in her power and more to help me find success with my work.

And last but not least, I would like to thank all my fans, from those who read *Quest for Justice* when it was first self-published to everybody else. It's your praise, criticism, and support that inspires me to share my stories, and the Elementia Chronicles would not be where it is today without you.

ABOUT THE AUTHOR

Sean Fay Wolfe was sixteen years old when he finished writing *Quest for Justice*, the first book of the Elementia Chronicles trilogy, and seventeen when he finished *The New Order*. He is an avid Minecraft player and loves creating action-adventure tales in its endlessly creative virtual world. Sean is an Eagle Scout in the Boy Scouts of America, a four-time all-state musician, a second-degree black belt in Shidokan karate, and has created many popular online games in the Scratch programming environment. He goes to school in Rhode Island, where he is deeply involved with his school's drama club. Sean lives with his mother, father, grandmother, two brothers, three cats and a little white dog named Lucky.

WHERE IT BEGINS...

THE Elementia CHRONICLES

AN UNOFFICIAL MINECRAFT-FAN ADVENTURE

THE Elementia CHRONICLES

BOOK ONE:
QUEST FOR
JUSTICE

SEAN FAY WOLFE

THE QUEST CONTINUES...

THE ELEMENTIA CHRONICLES

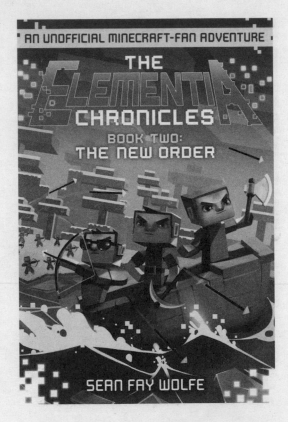

CONNECT WITH SEAN

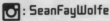: www.sfaywolfe.com

: www.facebook.com/elementiachronicles

: @sfaywolfe, #ElementiaChronicles

: SeanFayWolfe

Links to buy Sean's paperback and ebooks are on his webpage.
Links to Sean's online games can also be found on his webpage.
Go to www.goodreads.com to rate and/or review this novel.